The

Murray Davies was
MA in First World
and spent more than twenty years on Fleet Street as a
news reporter and a feature writer on three national
newspapers. *The Samson Option* is his second novel.

The Drumbeat of Jimmy Sands

MURRAY DAVIES

THE SAMSON OPTION

HarperCollins*Publishers*

HarperCollins*Publishers*
77–85 Fulham Palace Road,
Hammersmith, London W6 8JB

www.**fire**and**water**.com

A Paperback Original 2000
1 3 5 7 9 8 6 4 2

A catalogue record for this book
is available from the British Library

ISBN 0 00 651156 2

Set in Meridien by Palimpsest Book Production Limited,
Polmont, Stirlingshire

Printed and bound in Great Britain by
Caledonian International Book Manufacturing Ltd, Glasgow

For the Boys of the Byline Brigade

ACKNOWLEDGEMENTS

I would like to offer warm thanks to Dr Chris Collins, MBE, Consultant, World Health Organization for his unique knowledge of viruses and laboratory procedures, Dimitri Beliakov in Moscow for his unrivalled insights into Russian crime, old and new, David Ives for explaining the horse racing world and the intricacies of betting, Dick Durham for his sailing expertise, David Ball for talking me patiently through the mysterious miracles of computer science, Andy Graham for his knowledge of dead bodies, and others who cannot be named.

AUTHOR'S NOTE

The Samson Option is a recognized and chilling terrorist scenario. It is a reference to Samson in the temple of the Philistines. It means simply: *If I'm going down, I'll take you all with me*. Western intelligence analysts fear Saddam Hussein will launch the Samson Option to strike out in his death throes.

On 13 April 1988 Soviet scientist Nikolai Ustinov was accidentally infected with the Marburg virus while developing biological weapons. When he died seventeen days later his colleagues used his blood and spleen to culture a virulent strain called Marburg variant U – four hundred times more deadly than anthrax.

Nassir al-Hindawi, the father of the Iraqi germ warfare programme, planned to defect to the West. He was arrested by Iraqi security police days before he was due to flee in spring 1998.

An all-ports warning was issued in Britain on 18 March 1998, alerting customs to the danger of Iraqi agents smuggling biological and chemical weapons into Britain. The government launched a damage-limitation exercise when the news leaked out.

The CIA believes it is inevitable that a terrorist group or even an unhinged individual will launch a biological or chemical attack within the next ten years. It is a question of when, not if, they say.

PRELUDE

13–30 April 1988

He was weeping tears of blood. It could not be long now. The nurse knew. Her face was hidden in her space helmet, but the way her shoulders sagged as she dropped the red tissues into the waste bin to be incinerated told him she too was ready to be defeated by the finality of it all. Propped up in his hospital bed, cotton wool in his nostrils, uncomfortable in the saturated incontinence pad, he reached slowly and painfully for his notebook.

Dr Nikolai Ustinov was a good scientist. It was the duty of a good scientist to observe and record.

And so he charted his own death.

The room swam before his eyes, crimson-filled by the blood proteins and water leaking from the tiny capillaries which flowed like tributaries from his veins.

He will never leave this grim windowless room; this cell locked behind airtight steel doors. When he dies, everything will be burned. The chairs, sheets, linoleum, even the old iron bed frame destroyed.

Spring is on its way. Nikolai wishes he could smell the air, heavy with the scent of pine resin. He would give anything to see again the smoke rising from peasants' huts on calm days, a grey cord binding heaven and earth; to suffer again a Siberian winter with lancing winds and the snowflakes encrusting his eyelashes.

Eyelashes! He'd lost those with most of his hair a week ago.

Two spacemen entered the room in a gentle whoosh of air and began reading his chart. The room is under negative pressure so air leaves only through extractor filters.

Everyone finds it amazing he is still alive, and terrifying

1

that the whole might of the Soviet Union cannot prevent him from dying.

Nikolai will never again touch a human hand – except through two pairs of rubber gloves.

The thought saddens him more than his impending death, and he wished again he'd told Yevgenia he loved her that last morning. Now their words over the internal telephone were stilted and public.

But how were they to know?

Yevgenia had been busy getting the boys off to school and Nikolai had wanted to get to the laboratory early. He grabbed a slice of rye bread and a hard-boiled egg and hurried out of the stuffy sixth-floor apartment into the drab dawn on his way to the Vector Biological Research Institute, one of the most secret sites in the whole Soviet Union. The huge complex, set in silver birch forests outside Kol'tsovo, a dreary industrial suburb of Novosibirsk, specialized in viruses causing haemorrhagic fever and Venezuelan encephalitis.

Nikolai was just forty-four years old, with deep intense eyes and a steely enthusiasm for everything he did. He had previously worked on plague at Obolensk under Vladimir Pesechnik, who had turned the Black Death from a medieval scourge into a modern weapon of war.

Both establishments were among Biopreparat's eighteen research and development institutes, set up in contravention of the 1973 Biological and Toxic Weapons Convention signed by 140 countries including the Soviet Union, Britain and the United States. The Russians believed the West was ignoring the treaty. They decided to do the same.

Nikolai was usually one of the first to arrive at the six-storey concrete cube which housed the Toxic Animals Department. This morning he planned to monitor a potential antidote to Marburg virus batch 244, which had been injected into monkeys four days earlier. And he

2

would begin testing a variant of the new strain on guinea pigs. Marburg killed monkeys in droves, but for guinea pigs it was a complete slate wiper. They died in hours, the males with purple testes the size of golf balls. It was proving difficult to engineer a slate wiper for monkeys.

He locked away his wedding ring, fountain pen and heavy steel wristwatch, undressed and put on his green surgical scrub suit. It was faded and thin at the knee. They had applied for new suits three months ago. He must chase them up. He pulled on the surgical cap and peered in the foxed mirror above the chipped sink to tuck in wayward strands of dark hair. His young assistant Sergei Krotov bustled into the changing room.

'Damn!'

'You'll have to get up earlier, Sergei. You obviously find that new wife of yours more attractive than a cage full of monkeys.'

'Olga's on to me to put my name down for a week's holiday at an Institute dacha on the Black Sea. She says she needs a break from Siberia. Do you think I stand a chance?'

'Couldn't say. I've never tried,' replied Nikolai, not unkindly. 'But Olga's only been out here for six months.'

'She's missing Moscow,' admitted Sergei, hurrying to catch up with his boss.

'Take your time,' advised Nikolai. 'See you in there.'

The door to the research suite stuck slightly, held in place by the difference in air pressure. Nikolai passed through an ultraviolet light shower to an outer room, where he rolled his hands in chalk dust and slipped on a pair of latex gloves. He inspected his yellow all-in-one space suit for holes before stepping into it. He flexed his fingers inside the suit's heavy rubber gloves, testing for movement and cracks before he zipped it together and finally lowered the plastic helmet over his head.

The Americans had lightweight helmets which were clear all round. The Russian ones were claustrophobic and cumbersome. Nikolai hated the first breathless second as the visor misted over. He snatched for an airline and plugged it in. There was a rumble as his suit inflated and the mask cleared. Using the foot pedal, he opened the stainless steel door to the airlock.

In the 1970s the United States had divided pathogenic micro-organisms into four categories and set levels of laboratory standards for dealing with them. The world's scientists followed suit.

Level 1 was no risk.

Level 2, moderate risk.

Level 3, high individual risk. Like TB – dangerous but could be treated.

Level 4 – no vaccine available. No effective treatment.

Level 4 viruses are the world's most deadly agents. Lassa fever, Ebola, Kyasanur Forest fever, Venezuelan equine encephalitis, Hypr, Junin, Machupo, Kumlinge, Russian spring-summer encephalitis and Marburg. In a level 4 laboratory all manipulations should be performed in a gas-tight glovebox or isolator, avoiding direct contact between the infectious agent and the investigator at all times.

The airlock door closed with a hiss behind him before a green light told Nikolai that he could open the door to the level 4 laboratory. The monkeys went berserk at the strange figure entering the room. They leapt around their cages, rattling the bars, screeching 'Kra Kra.' These were healthy vervet monkeys with slim pale human fingers and inquisitive eyes. Their turn was to come.

In the next room the monkeys sat silent and passive, only their eyes following Nikolai as he inspected the banks of cages lining the walls. Many monkeys had green mucus and slime around their nostrils and pools of blood lay in pans under their cages. In the far corner a large male was huddled over, dead.

Nikolai was disappointed. He had hoped more monkeys would have died from strain 244.

Back in the third room in the suite Nikolai selected a

4

guinea pig. Sergei Krotov joined him. Conversation was difficult in the helmets, but each knew the routine. Sergei began filling a small syringe with 0.5ml of pale red liquid.

The safety of a system is determined by its weakest point. Gloves are the most puncture-prone part of the barrier separating virus and researcher. Nikolai wore two pairs of gloves.

He held the guinea pig, stroking it behind the ear to soothe it as Sergei prepared to inject it just above the tail. As he went to insert the needle, the guinea pig kicked out. Nikolai's hand moved. So did Sergei's.

There were those who said later that Sergei was not concentrating. That he was worrying about the morning's tiff with fiery young Olga, that he had applied for a larger apartment and been turned down, that he was thinking about holidays. But really, his hand just slipped. The guinea pig squirmed at the wrong moment and instead of having slow hands, Sergei Krotov committed the ultimate sin. He had fast hands. Instead of waiting until the guinea pig was still, he tried to compensate for the animal's movements and jabbed Nikolai in the thumb.

For a second Nikolai stood absolutely still. He became aware he was still holding the guinea pig. He felt his stomach fill with a funereal weight of lead shot. And over the rumble of air inside his helmet he heard his own heart tolling a death knell.

Suddenly he was moving, holding his left arm stiffly to his side like a repugnant growth. The airlock served as a decontamination shower with nozzles for water and chemicals. The programme took four minutes and he could not open the far door until it was complete. Normally he would have held up his arms, turning slowly so the sprays completely drenched his suit, but now he kept his left arm absolutely still. He felt – in spite of all his medical knowledge – that the more he moved his arm, the quicker the virus would spread.

Part of him was screaming *hurry up, hurry up. Get me out*

of here. But most of him was calmer than he had ever been. Sergei was still in the lab – in shock.

At last Nikolai pushed open the door. He gently removed his left inner glove. No sign of a hole. He squeezed as hard as he could to force out the poison before plunging his hand into a disinfectant tank of hypochlorite solution. He could tell himself that no virus had actually passed into his thumb, the disinfectant was being drawn up into the hole killing the virus. Or that he had imagined the whole thing. Nikolai dabbed his hand dry and examined his thumb through a large magnifying glass. There was no sign of a puncture hole. Perhaps, just perhaps, he had got away with it.

Except he knew he hadn't.

He had been injected with Marburg virus.

Marburg virus lives in the African jungle. Occasionally it ventures out to kill. It is a parasite, carried harmlessly by its host species but always searching for new hosts. Despite thirty years' research by the World Health Organization, no one to this day knows Marburg's true home. It has stayed hidden, a cuckoo in a secret nest, waiting to break out at random.

At first scientists believed Marburg was related to rabies. They were wrong. Rabies is a cuddler compared with Marburg's true relation – Ebola.

The Russians did not know how effective Nikolai had been in engineering Marburg into a weapon. Consequently they took no chances. He was escorted directly to the high security biocontainment medical unit, known in the Institute as *na narakh* – behind bars – where the air was filtered and doctors and nurses wore biohazard space suits.

Samples of his blood were treated as if they were venom. His breath as the plague.

In the first hours they called Yevgenia, who worked as a paediatrician at Vector. Nikolai and Yevgenia could see each other through the protective glass screen. They lied to each other on the internal phone. He told her everything

6

would be fine and she agreed. Krotov was beside himself, blubbering. Striving to be brave, Yevgenia comforted him and told him not to blame himself.

Nikolai began to feel unwell that first night – the way you do when you're about to go down with flu. He began to record his illness. Over the days the headache behind his eyes increased until he thought someone was beating a bass drum in his pupils. His muscles ached and he recorded severe myalgia especially in the lumbo-sacral region. His temperature spiked at 40 degrees Celsius and the fever broke.

The virus liked Nikolai. It took to him. And it was ferocious. Nikolai recognized he was manifesting classic symptoms of acute viraemia – the physical responses to the new virus in his bloodstream. The lymph nodes in his throat turned to sandpaper so he could not eat. His spleen became inflamed.

The red rash appeared on the fourth day, making his skin too sensitive to be touched. Nikolai had never known such pain. The virus was consuming his body. It was copying itself – eating away at him as it did so.

The vomiting began. Nikolai emptied everything in his stomach and still he heaved. The diarrhoea came soon after. He kept notes, weak as he was. His vomit changed colour, becoming a thick black tar speckled with fresh red arterial blood.

The vomit was loaded with viruses. You could see fear in the eyes of the nurses and orderlies who held the basins to catch his puke and the way they involuntarily twitched when drops landed on their space suits. His vomit reeked of the charnel-house. His diarrhoea was dark with blood.

Specialists in tropical diseases, virologists, biochemists, haematologists, microbiologists, physicians and pharmacists were flown in from all over the Soviet Union. They attacked the virus with every known weapon in their scientific and medical arsenal. This was their creation, their Frankenstein's monster. Now they would see if they could control it.

Nikolai's condition worsened. His fever spiked again. The abdominal pains increased.

The doctors tried transfusions, but it was difficult to find a vein. When they gave him plasma the fresh blood poured out of his mouth and rectum. The disease-fighting mechanisms in his body were losing the battle. Some surrendered without a fight, others were being overrun.

Haemoglobin was down to 11.1g/dl from a norm of 14.4. The white cell count plummeted to 1.8($\times 10^9$/1), then 1.6 before rising to 2.0. The normal range is between 4 and 11($\times 10^9$/1). Platelets, which stop bleeding, should have been between 150 and 400 ($\times 10^9$/1). They tumbled to 90.

Doctors tried to stop the bleeding with an intravenous loading dose of 2,000 units of the anticoagulant heparin followed by a constant infusion of 10,000 units over twenty-four hours. They injected 3 million units of human interferon, a crucial chemical in the immune system, into Nikolai every twelve hours. The secondary fungal throat infection was fought with amphotericin B lozenges and they fed him intravenously to balance his diarrhoea-depleted electrolytes.

The Marburg raging inside Nikolai Ustinov came from an Australian backpacker who died in the 1975 South African outbreak. His girlfriend and nurse contracted Marburg but survived. Serum cultured from their blood would help Nikolai, but KGB agents had only stolen serum of the dead man. They could not ask Britain or the United States for help because they would be admitting their biological warfare programme. Instead they turned to an older sample, cultured from a veterinary surgeon and his wife from Belgrade who went down during the original 1967 epidemic. The wife lived. 450 ml of serum from her blood was heated at 60 degrees Celsius for one hour, tested for hepatitis B surface antigens and antibodies, and given by slow infusion for four hours. Three days later Nikolai received a further 330 ml.

Marburg had moved on. Nikolai's blood separated like curds and whey. It thickened but would not coagulate. Even though Nikolai was bleeding to death, small clots began appearing in his bloodstream. The blood flow slowed. The clots silted up together on the linings of the blood vessels. As the mosaic thickened, large clots broke away. Larger particles like platelets blocked up the peripheral capillaries, while the smaller blood-clotting molecules which prevent uncontrolled bleeding disappeared altogether.

Because the capillaries were clogged, the red blood cells backed up, giving Nikolai a crimson glow.

With the red blood cells immobilized, the oxygen normally carried by them was not reaching its destinations. Nerve endings screeched and died.

The heart was having to work harder to pump the sludge blood even though the body was weaker.

The virus was attacking all the tissues in his body. AIDS took ten years to do this. Marburg was doing it in ten days. Nikolai's hair began falling out.

The virus turned its attention towards his brain and he turned sullen and aggressive. It attacked the fluid inside his eyeballs and he wished he was dead – except that some of him already was and every day other nerve endings failed and died, so the pain was less than he had expected. His skin peeled off as cells starved of oxygen and nutrients died by the million. Most painful was the peeling around his testes, now shrunken and rotten.

When Yevgenia came to talk to him through the glass, nurses wrapped him up to his neck in fresh clean sheets so she would not see his mouldering body.

Scientists took biopsies of Ustinov's tissue, a mixture of living and dead cells. What they saw under the electron microscope was chilling. They were looking at a primeval killer. Remorseless, implacable, unstoppable. Nikolai's cells had not merely died, they had been ravaged. The living

9

cells were swollen and pregnant with viruses, sometimes so thick that they looked like knotted rope. Broods were getting ready to hatch, ready to break away to search for other victims. To drift in the bloodstream, taking over more cells.

All the scientists in the Soviet Union could not help Nikolai live – they could only prolong his dying.

The red rash turned into large black-blue bruises tinged with yellow. Nikolai's skin filled with pockets of blood, the skin almost separating from the underlying tissue. This is third spacing. Nikolai had already bled into his lungs, the first space. Into his stomach and intestines, the second space. The third space lies between skin and flesh.

On the seventeenth day he put down his notebook and saw his thumb print in blood. Blood was seeping out of his pores. He was sweating blood. He was bald, shrunken, without dignity and he was about to die. He was glad.

There was the sound of tearing calico. The lining of Nikolai's intestines came away from his body. Normally this happens three days after death. Pieces of the lining were expelled with the blood.

Doctors and nurses were tumbling through the airlock in their cumbersome space suits, hooking up more drips, trying to find a vein for an injection.

Nikolai is bleeding from every orifice. Blood seeping out of his eyes and ears. From his nose and mouth trickles fresh shining blood. Small red spots stand out on his nipples and burgundy dribbles from his penis. He is unconscious.

Through the glass Yevgenia whispered goodbye.

Nikolai Ustinov, good scientist, good fellow and a good husband and father, stopped breathing.

The autopsy was conducted the same day, 30 April, in an ultra-sterile isolation room. The pathologists wore rubber hooded containment suits the colour of grass, knee-high boots and two pairs of gloves. They removed Nikolai's spleen and liver and from a leg vein, using a special nine-inch glass syringe, they sucked his blood, crazed

10

with Marburg. They froze it and turned it into weapons grade dust.

Tests on monkeys showed it was several hundred times more deadly than anthrax. Ironically, they had achieved Nikolai's aim of making Marburg a slate wiper.

They called the new strain Marburg Variant U – in Nikolai's memory – and sent it to Stepnogorsk to be weaponized and loaded on to missiles and bombs.

Nikolai's body was placed inside a triple-lined zinc coffin and buried in the cemetery with its silver birches. It remains there, under the headstone showing a picture of Nikolai, resolute and intense, to this day.

The following year, 1989, Vladimir Pesechnik, who had been Nikolai Ustinov's team leader at Obolensk, defected to British intelligence.

Three years after that, President Boris Yeltsin agreed to halt research on offensive biological weapons. Kol'tsovo was retitled the State Research Centre of Virology and Biotechnology. Despite public undertakings, scientists there still carry out secret research.

Biological weapons stocks were destroyed and production facilities partially opened to the suspicious West. Hundreds of litres of Marburg Variant U were incinerated in top security. Only one small flask remained in perma-freeze, a deadly sleeping beauty waiting to be woken.

23–24 February 1998

The dark mass of Bradwell Magnox power station loomed out of the night like a pair of children's building blocks. Tim Platt's stomach lurched into his mouth as the Gemini inflatable reared up and slapped down heavily on the choppy water. He licked the salt spray off his lips and gave up trying to see through his night vision goggles until it was calmer.

Mickey New touched his arm and indicated the blurred lights of West Mercia on the starboard bow. The drizzle lifted for a moment and he could see the outline of Cobmarsh Island. The coxswain cut back the Yahama to a purr.

'Tango's well starboard of Virley Channel. If he carries on like this, he'll end up on the Nass.'

Tim nodded, feeling his gorge rise and his forehead prickle in cold sweat. It was hard going running up the Blackwater on a full tide into a stiff westerly.

'X-ray Foxtrot. Tango heading two four zero. He's going south of Osea Island. My Sierra five knots.'

'Roger Foxtrot. Estimate four hundred metres astern of you. Negative visual.'

'Bloody hope not.'

Tim grinned at the breach of RT procedure. It was inevitable. Never mind how well trained, when the nerves were jangling and you were hyped up to Mars you had to say it.

Somewhere ahead in the oily blackness four members of S squadron SBS in wetsuits were astride their semi-submersible chariot. This was the first time the chariot, a new addition to the SBS's repertoire, had been used in action. It could act as a surface raider or, by filling ballast tanks, sink just below the waves like a submarine. To follow the MV *Sheila-Na-Gig* the SBS men wore breathing gear with their shoulders and heads above the water. They were getting a rough ride.

The chariot was 200 metres astern of the *Sheila-Na-Gig* as she headed up the Blackwater on the most miserable night she could have wished for. The rain settled like an opaque curtain and Tim found it impossible to tell where the water ended and the coast began. The lonely, low-lying Essex coast with its forlorn creeks, shallow inlets, marshes and mud flats was ideal for bird life and smugglers. And nothing else.

The Blackwater was deep at its mouth but soon became shallow. Their quarry had timed her run for high tide but those on the bridge would be keeping a weather eye on the echo sounder. The *Sheila-Na-Gig* was a floating gin mansion rather than a palace. Built in Bremen in the 1930s for a minor Nazi industrialist, she had the sporty rake of her time with wooden decks and a spacious day cabin. On top she had a formidable cluster of radar scanners and communication aerials. And she was fast. She had made the crossing from Holland surprisingly quickly. The Dutch 7NDR SBS had had their work cut out to keep up with her and finally had handed over to an RAF Nimrod.

They had planned initially to take her on the high seas as they had taken the 280-ton MV *Simon de Danser* off Portugal under the Criminal Justice International Co-operation Act, but the *Danser* had been a mother ship to be met offshore and her drugs cargo cross-decked to smaller craft. The *Sheila-Na-Gig* was going all the way – wherever that was. They were going to find out and see who her contacts were.

Without a visual point of reference Tim's stomach lurched again as the inflatable's nose dipped into a trough. He didn't mind the cold, the fatigue, the discomfort. He was used to that. It was the bloody motion sickness. A life on the ocean waves! You could stick it. He'd rather jump out of an aircraft any time. He sucked in more air and became aware of Mickey New grinning at him, his teeth abnormally white in his blackened face. His sergeant was as happy as Larry back with his SBS mates away from the London office where they worked. Tim concentrated on the denser ribbon of black between the estuary and the sky which must be Tollesbury marshes. His earphone crackled.

'X-ray Foxtrot. Tango's south of Osea Island. Looks like she's going for Lawling Creek.'

'Roger Foxtrot. November, do you copy?' The customs and police team on land was poised to seal off a semi-circular bite out of the coastline around the creek.

'Let's close up,' ordered Mickey.

The *Sheila-Na-Gig* wasn't going to have much time. She drew too much to linger in the creek for more than half an hour after high tide. Any longer and she'd be left literally high and dry. It was going to be a speedy operation. And Mickey wanted to be there at the hit.

The wind freshened and the Gemini juddered and jarred.

'You all right, boss?' asked Mickey.

'Fine,' replied Tim through clenched teeth.

'Only I've never seen anyone so pale when they're wearing cam cream.'

'Fuck off. If I throw up it'll be over you.'

'X-ray Foxtrot. Tango's turning away from Lawling Creek. Heading for Northey Island. Course two seven five. Sierra four knots.'

Shit!

The *Sheila* was running out of options. Tim put his NVGs to his eyes. There she was! A black-hulled ghost ship gliding along leaving no wake. The Gemini was level with Osea Island. Tim made out the Doctor, the single lit buoy, south-west of the island. Ahead of them Maldon was an amber glow, with Heybridge Basin to starboard. If the *Sheila* locked in there, she'd be a rat in a trap.

'X-ray Foxtrot. Tango's turning northwards. She's around the west of Osea Island.'

'Roger Foxtrot. Do you copy, November?'

The hit team was shadowing her along the small country roads, trying to be inconspicuous. It was all a matter of compromise. Too near and you scare off the reception party. Too far back and they could slip away or warn off the yacht.

'X-ray Foxtrot. Tango's heading north, bearing three five zero. Sierra niner knots.'

Maybe the *Sheila* had a rendezvous with a dinghy. But why hadn't she met up directly instead of creeping around the south of the island? A chill crept over Tim.

'X-ray Foxtrot. Tango's round the island. Still turning. Bearing zero four zero. Sierra ten knots.'

Hell. Hell. Hell.

'Turn around,' commanded Tim. 'Turn around. Go about or whatever you bloody well call it but go. He's doing a runner. He's playing games with us. Don't know how or why, but he's playing games. Let's go get him.'

'Aye aye, sir.'

The Gemini banked in a tight circle.

'X-ray November. What the fuck's happening?'

'November X-ray. Tango's heading back to sea. Intend to intercept. Foxtrot X-ray. Any indication that Tango has jettisoned cargo?'

'Negative X-ray.'

'Roger Foxtrot. Prepare to close up.'

The Gemini flew along, wind and rain whipping into Tim's face, his sea-sickness forgotten in the adrenaline rush. He ran his hands over the Heckler & Koch MP5 on a sling over his shoulder, checked the safety catch and touched the condom over the muzzle. Mickey and the other SBS men favoured the M16A2 but Tim had used the 9mm MP5 in the Regiment and he believed in using a weapon he was comfortable with. If he had to use his weapon at all.

They roared around the eastern end of the island and turned to confront the yacht. The drizzle lifted and a sliver of pale moon emerged from behind clouds, blackened and tattered like high explosive shell bursts. The *Sheila-Na-Gig* powered towards them.

'X-ray Foxtrot. Two hundred metres astern of Tango.'

'Roger Foxtrot. Prepare to board.'

Tim extended his arm and aimed over the oncoming vessel. There was a sharp crack. One, two, three. Whoosh. The flare exploded in a brilliant white light, washing out the dim coastline and turning the night a ghostly grey. Mickey switched on the powerful halogen searchlight and Tim nodded to the Customs Officer with the loud hailer.

'Her Majesty's Customs and Excise. Heave to. We are coming aboard. *Sheila-Na-Gig*. Heave to. We are coming aboard.'

The motor vessel swung sharply to port, then veered to starboard in a sudden zigzag. Her bows rose out of the water and she aimed straight at them, a malevolent beast about to run down its prey. The SBS men knocked off their safety catches.

The flare sank behind the vessel and Tim sent up another. The Customs man was calling again. '*Sheila-Na-Gig*. We are Customs and Excise. Heave to and prepare to be boarded. Heave to, *Sheila-Na-Gig*, or we will open fire.'

Tim caught sight of the chariot battling through the churning wake. He raised his gun to fire a burst over the yacht. He had taken up the first pressure on the trigger when the *Sheila*'s bows slowly lowered.

The Gemini performed a tight circle to come alongside the yacht. Mickey threw a grappling hook over her starboard rail and the SBS team sprang on board while Tim was still trying to keep his balance.

The assault was violent and loud. Three of the submersible team in dripping wetsuits crashed through cabins and the galley while the Gemini men, faces blackened, commanded the bridge and forecastle. The speed and intensity stunned the yacht's crew into submission. By the time Tim and the Customs man clambered on board, they were spreadeagled face down guarded by two SBS men while the others searched below.

'Can I help you?'

At first sight Captain de Koch was an imposing figure. Tall and sunburnt, with steely grey hair, he appeared the type to command a luxury yacht, but when Tim looked more closely he saw the grey bristles, the frayed collar on the grubby white shirt and the shiny lapels of his blue uniform jacket.

'I have a warrant to search your vessel.'

Captain de Koch raised his left arm in a languid welcome. 'Help yourselves – but I see you are already doing that.'

He's too calm, thought Tim. Anyone who had just had six armed thugs board their ship should be quaking. Why is he so calm? The answer came with their initial search. They found just a quarter of an ounce of cannabis resin in a crewman's locker. There was no sign of the £50 million worth of cocaine belonging to the Moscow Mafiya. A revenue cutter came alongside with a rummage crew. The last time Tim saw de Koch he was wearing the knowing smile of someone who has been wronged.

'Cheer up, boss. Worse things happen at sea, as my dad used to say.'

Tim looked at him as if he was a bill he had forgotten to pay. He finally broke his silence. 'Mickey, I bet you're the sort who starts the singing in the lifeboat.'

The early rush-hour traffic into London was building up and Mickey swung out to overtake a car with a sticker proclaiming Trust British Beef.

'It's not your fault. The rummage crew might find something. There's lots of hiding places on a ship. Takes a good time to search a ship, it does.'

'That skipper didn't protest enough.'

Mickey glanced at Tim slumped in the passenger seat. Poor bugger. He looked tired with deep shadows around his eyes, but more, he looked disappointed. Defeated. It didn't take a lot of imagination to know how Tim must be feeling. The second cock-up in three weeks. And both operations allegedly based on cast-iron intelligence.

There'd be an inquest and a post mortem, Tim knew. Customs and Excise, police, Five, Six, even the bloody RAF this time. They'd all want their pound of flesh. Whining on about their budgets, waste of limited resources. Whatever the opposite of the Midas touch was, he possessed it. Everything he touched turned to dust.

Now he had to face the swells of the Department. He disliked the bureaucracy of the intelligence world, but most of all he hated the way smooth-faced men with their suits and posh accents looked down their noses at him. Nothing said directly, of course. Too well bred; but a slight here, a snub there. Enough to make him feel the outsider. This run of failures was turning purgatory into sheer bloody Hell.

I'm only in this job because I cocked up. No. Not true. I'm here because I insisted I cocked up.

And this operation has been another cock-up. Yet . . . It didn't hang together.

Sheila-Na-Gig had played a game going round Osea Island. Neither the chariot nor the inflatable gave off a radar signature, but the yacht acted as though she knew they were there. Acted a whole play by herself in the dark in front of an audience she could not see.

'It's pointless you coming in. Drop me at Redbridge tube station and get a few hours' kip. I'll do the initial report.'

'Cheers, boss.' Mickey was already reaching for his mobile phone. 'Tell you what. Why don't you pop in for breakfast? Have a shower.'

'If I stop I'll never start again. I'll go straight through. Hell, what's happening here?'

The A12 dual carriageway was coned into one lane. As the traffic crawled past, police were selecting vehicles and waving them into a layby. Officers in flak jackets and carrying machine pistols stood watching.

The inspector took in the two hard men in the green Land Rover Discovery and waved them down.

'I don't know what these armed cops do for villains but they scare the life out of me,' said Tim as they climbed out.

'It was your lot what trained them,' carped Mickey.

'We trained up an elite firearms squad. We didn't know every other copper and his granny would be carrying an MP5. Oh dear.'

'The holdalls.' Mickey was thinking along the same lines. A young bobby was already reaching into the back.

'Don't touch those,' snapped Tim, striding towards the rear.

The nearest firearms officer stared openly at the two men. Both in their late twenties, early thirties. One squat, with a barrel chest, wearing jeans and a quilted anorak, the other taller and slimmer, in jeans and a Barbour. There was something about them; a little too fit, a little too tasty. Essex villains without a doubt. He began fingering the safety catch.

'Leave those.'

The policeman swung the MP5 towards them.

'Point that somewhere else, sunshine, or I'll take it off you and ram it straight up your arse,' snarled Mickey.

'Christ. It's an arsenal.' The young bobby had opened the holdall.

'Put it down,' yelled Tim. The copper aimed directly at them. Any second Mickey was going to flatten him. 'May I?'

He slipped his hand into his pocket and offered the inspector the first identification card he found. *Captain Tim Platt, Operations Studies Group, Ministry of Defence.*

'There are some nasty little things in that holdall and I wouldn't like one of your men to be maimed or blinded.' The young bobby stepped back sharply.

'Why are you in possession of firearms?'

'We're soldiers.' Mickey was running out of temper.

'We've just finished an operation and we're on our way back to base,' said Tim reasonably. 'If you intend to detain us further then I suggest your duty superintendent contact Security Service police liaison. I'll give you the number.'

'The car is registered to the MoD, sir,' called the policeman running computer checks on vehicle registrations.

'Tough shit,' growled Mickey.

Tim's mobile phone rang. 'I can't talk, sir. Sergeant New and I are being held at a police road block . . . No . . . I don't know why. An inspector.' The inspector coloured. 'Yes, I'll put him on. My guvnor in the Cabinet Office wants a word.'

'Twats,' spat Mickey.

* * *

'Do you realize how long it took to put all the pieces into position? The number of people we had to get on side? It was easier launching the Gulf War.' Haydn Williams wondered what Maurice Plumridge knew about Desert Storm, but the M15 man was in full flow, his pink cheeks glowing with indignation. 'It's not just this country but the Dutch and the French. Don't mind the Dutch so much, but the bloody French will be laughing at us. And for what? That's what I want to know. For what?'

From his office window on the tenth floor Williams looked down at a tug towing barges of London's waste downstream to the Essex marshes. There was nothing interesting on the Thames nowadays. Just rubbish barges and tourist boats.

'The intelligence came from your service,' he reminded Plumridge. Five's tip-off that a massive Russian Mafiya cocaine shipment was heading into Britain had been a major coup in their new lead role against organized crime.

'It was good intelligence,' insisted Plumridge.

'Was it? We shadowed the *Sheila-Na-Gig* from the Baltic, apart from that storm when she was off the Friesians and she's clean as a whistle.' Williams, short and Welsh, peered over half-moon spectacles and did nothing to flatten his lilting accent. 'So, she never had the drugs on her, she transferred them under our noses or she jettisoned them when she found she was being followed. Tim swears she dumped nothing in the Blackwater . . .'

'Humph.' Plumridge produced a large silk handkerchief from the top pocket of his tweed suit. 'That's twice now his operations have come unstuck. It doesn't happen to anyone else.'

'Good Luck, she is never a lady but the cursedest quean alive, Tricksy, wincing and jady – kittle to lead or to drive. Greet her – she's hailing a stranger! Meet her – she busking to leave! Let her alone for a shrew to the bone and the hussy comes plucking your sleeve!'

Plumridge rose from the sofa which curled around two

22

sides of the spacious office and unthinkingly straightened the reproduction Canaletto.

'I don't know how much luck has to do with it,' sniffed Plumridge. 'I do know that life is becoming more complicated. You used to know where you were. F branch dealt with the internal surveillance of subversives, K handled counter-espionage, T was counter-terrorism. Now we direct 39 per cent of our efforts against Irish and domestic terrorism, 33 per cent at international terrorism, 25 per cent at counter-espionage and 3 per cent on counter-subversion. *And we announce we do it!*'

'Oh, come on. Five has to evolve to survive. Snatching the lead role against Irish terrorism from Special Branch was a shrewd move a few years ago but what do you do if peace breaks out?' Williams reminded him. 'That's why Five's fought to get involved in areas like drug trafficking. The Security Services Act allows you to assist law enforcement agencies against organized crime whether they want help or not. Your masters are exceedingly wise in the ways of Whitehall.'

'It takes one to know one,' snorted Plumridge ungraciously. 'But on one hand we're expected to cooperate with the KGB to fight Russian organized crime and on the other we're supposed to stop them lifting our best china.'

'The enemy is he who justifies your budget. The enemy is he who tries to cut your budget.'

Plumridge ignored him. 'Do we really care what Russian mobsters get up to? Do we?'

'You know as well as I do the head of the FBI claimed Russian organized crime was America's biggest security threat.'

'Huh!' Plumridge flicked an imaginary speck of dust off his highly polished brogues.

Typical of the old fogeyism which infested his service. They all wanted to look more like colonial policemen than the real ones ever did. Williams was old enough to remember the originals. Plumridge was doing his squire-up-in-town act today, complete with accent. Except Williams knew he had a lower second from Sheffield and had been brought up in Redditch where his father owned an electrical repair shop.

It crossed Williams's mind that that was why Plumridge treated Tim Platt so dismissively. Perhaps he recognized their similar backgrounds and felt uncomfortable with a man who did not pretend to be someone he wasn't. Plumridge had found it necessary to take elocution lessons. Tim hadn't bothered to lengthen his northern vowels.

Williams's own Welsh accent went with his passing resemblance to Lloyd George. But Williams was a legend in an intelligence world running short of characters. Some pointed out that he was the first grammar-school boy to make director grade, others recalled his double first at Cambridge. Adored by the Americans and shunned as an outsider by the former Tory establishment, he had re-created himself so often that no one knew any more whether Williams was a first-class administrator who dabbled on the periphery of intelligence or a field man currently behind a desk.

'The CIA estimate up to two-thirds of the Russian economy is being criminalized.'

'Stuff Russian crime. I'd rather get to grips with SVR hoods on the streets of London. SVR! I ask you!'

'Doesn't have the same ring as KGB, does it?' agreed Williams. 'Mind you, I bet they said that when OGPU became the KGB. They're all the same hoods, to my mind, so they stay the KGB for my part.'

It was almost time for the morning prayers, the daily meeting of heads of department. First Williams charmed a cup of tea out of his secretary, Alison Peach, and said good morning to the temporary secretary. He used his master key to pop into Tim and Mickey's office, the smallest on the floor, and lit a cigarette. He liked it in here, with its lino and smell of stale sandwiches. They faced away from the river – over the confluence of railway tracks going into Waterloo station's twenty-four platforms. From up here it was like having the biggest model train set in the world. Spellbinding. Williams

24

often invented an excuse to call in to watch the trains come and go. He tore himself away, back to his carpeted office with its boring views over the Thames.

'Going on the countryside demo next week, Plumridge?' Livy Hull was asking.

'No. My wife's planning to come up, though, with friends from the village. Feels it's jolly important to show the flag.'

'But you live in Surrey.' Livy, Secret Intelligence Service's lady-in-waiting, wickedly changed direction. 'That's not the countryside.'

'It is as far as Felicity and I are concerned,' Plumridge said stiffly.

He lived in a dormitory village outside Dorking, a fast fifteen-minute train ride away. Livy Hull, only descendant of landed gentry whose family had once owned large parts of Dorset, still kept on the fading Queen Anne house complete with haha to which she tried to return every weekend to do her duty in the parish. There was a Hull memorial recreation field, a Hewitt village hall named after the other branch, a Hewitt bowling green and cricket pavilion, and nearby a Hull-endowed library.

Commander Andrew Penn of the Defence Intelligence Service nodded his greeting and slid along the sofa. A perfect example of the Silent Service, said Williams. Hardly ever uttered a word.

'It's important that the shires make their voice heard, isn't it?' insisted Livy Hull, mischievously determined to goad Plumridge into being even more pompous than usual.

'Absolutely. We're ruled by townies. It's time the country-side rose up.'

'Ay,' said Williams drily. 'Just remember that when the countryside rises, their first target is the landowner. A few burning ricks and torched farmhouses would set the country alight, literally and metaphorically.'

'You're not winding me up like that,' smiled Livy sweetly.

But Plumridge, who did not have the confidence that comes with generations of ruling, protested. 'Farmer and labourer are united against rule by the ignorant. No one in the shires objects to fox-hunting. It's a way of life. And there's jobs at stake. Five thousand jobs.'

The subject was beginning to irritate Williams. 'Why don't they close the hunts and import any they need from Poland or Australia. That's what they did with coal and that act of political spite cost rather more than five thousand jobs . . .'

'Sorry. Not late, am I?' Bill Jones, GCHQ's representative, was always last. He took off his glasses, smiled myopically and breathed on the lenses. He became aware that the collar of his shirt was sticking up and after failing to get it to stay down, tucked it under the lapel of a sagging sports jacket.

'Tim's not back yet,' began Williams. 'We'll go through the parts of the song sheet which don't affect him. Ireland. Surprise. Surprise. Livy has news on Iraq. Money laundering in Cyprus. Let's take Ireland first. I don't suppose DIS has any input on that? No. Thought not. Right, Livy, let's hear from you . . .'

Alison Peach was extending the hand of friendship to Maisie, the temporary secretary standing in for her pal on maternity leave. She'd shown her where she kept the tin of instant coffee, the tea bags, Mr Plumridge's Earl Grey, the sugar and the powdered milk. She'd explained that although nominally it was a non-smoking floor, because the Coordinator smoked, they could do so if they wished – but don't let that cow from management support services catch you. Oh, and keep an eye on Mr Williams because he has a habit of putting cigarettes on the edge of his desk and forgetting about them. One rolled on to the carpet last week and it was only by luck that she'd spotted it before the smoke alarm went off. Where did she normally work?

'On the second floor,' said Maisie. 'Surveillance liaison.'

What were they like? Alison wanted to know. Bit rough and ready, replied Maisie, but that was their trade, wasn't it? To be expected. Hearts of gold really. But it's a bit more refined up here, I expect.

Alison was pleased to agree. Much more refined here in the United Nations as this floor was called – when people were being charitable. The Tower – short for the Tower of Babel – when they weren't. Here on the tenth floor came together the providers and analysts as each empire sent its ambassadors to the court of the Coordinator to cajole, suggest, expedite and enforce.

The Coordinator – that's Mr Williams. He's so sweet. Shuffles around in his bedroom slippers sometimes. Took me to the Ivy for my birthday last month.

Alison will not hear a word said against the Coordinator. She is one of his most committed helpmeets in the vital task of intelligence gathering inside the building; sweeping up unconsidered trifles and seldom offering a trinket in return.

Then there's Miss Hull. Wednesday Legs. You know. When's dey goin' to snap legs. Olive Oyl in a black silk suit. If I were as thin as that I'd be worried; still, they say she's a one for the men and she's thirty-five if she's a day. Can't possibly see what men see in her. She's supposed to be keeping some painter chap. I heard his name but it didn't mean anything. There's Mr Plumridge. Alison pauses. From Thames House. His wife is . . . Alison hesitates . . . demanding. Moneywise. He has to keep his daughters in ponies and horse boxes. She hurries on. There's Bill Jones from Cheltenham – his office is such a mess the cleaners refuse to go in there.

'. . . Hello Tim.'

Maisie looked up to see a tall man, stubble on a face sparse in flesh. Soft brown eyes hollowed out by exhaustion, bushy eyebrows and a full mouth twisted in a sad smile of greeting. It was the mouth that took Maisie. Either sensitive or weak – in a strong face. Someone else's mouth.

'Captain Platt. This is Maisie.'

27

'Tim. Please call me Tim.'

'They're in conference. The Coordinator said for you to go in as soon as you arrived.' Alison is standing now, reaching out to Tim. 'Let me get you a cuppa first. You look done in. Kettle's just boiled.' This is a lie but she feels the need to comfort Tim. It is this need which tells Alison that she will be a perfect mother – when she gets the opportunity.

'Thanks. Mickey will be in later. He's just nipped home and then he's got some kit to drop off at Group.'

Tim went into his office, wondering whether to check his e-mail before the meeting. Basically do anything to put back the moment when he had to confront his failure. There was a cigarette end in the metal waste paper bin – evidence that Williams had been in to look at the trains. Tim too stared down at the tracks and felt the same sick feeling in his stomach as he'd had before his first parachute jump. He hated the idea of having to go into conference and explain another operational failure. He felt the outsider he was. It wasn't so bad for Mickey in these circumstances. He was still an NCO. He knew his place. But Tim was neither fish nor fowl. He was an NCO who'd become an officer.

His job here was an anachronism, the withered remains of an executive strong arm going back to the Cold War. When Williams had taken over as Coordinator he inherited an unchartered private organization with a pro-active tradition. Williams found it useful – and often deniable.

Tim liked Williams. Friendly, unstuffy and bright, Williams was special, but Tim didn't rate the others. His schoolmasters had urged him to stay on for university but he was in a hurry to leave home. The Army had tried to push him towards the Education Corps, but he had joined the Green Howards and then the SAS. If he'd gone back to the Green Howards for his commission, he could have gone to college courtesy of HMG, but he'd stayed in the Regiment, proud of being commissioned in 22 SAS.

'Here you are, Tim.' Alison stood a fraction too close.

'Thanks.' He couldn't put off the moment any longer.

'He's nice,' said Maisie, fishing. 'Really nice.'

'He's the one who gets his hands dirty,' said Alison, repeating the description she'd heard Williams use.

'He's got a lovely smile but he looks so sad.' Maisie was not going to let go.

'He always does.' Alison gazed down the corridor after Tim. 'Something happened before he came. He put up a black mark. Mr Plumridge says that's why he came here . . .' Alison felt she had said enough about her department. 'But he's awfully sweet.'

'Ah, Tim. A long night. Sorry it was a fruitless one.'

Tim was aware he was still wearing jeans and sweater. Not your smart casual let's-go-to-the-pub-Sunday-lunchtime jeans and sweater, but working ones with stains on the knees and a threadbare elbow. He was different. No one looked at him. No one wanted to be associated with failure. The atmosphere in the room was cold and unsympathetic. Plumridge could not be bothered to look up, studiously reading a yellow flimsy. There was a plate of Marie biscuits in front of him. Tim remembered he had not eaten. Williams must have spotted his glance for he leaned across and with a smile pushed the plate towards Tim.

'Bet you haven't had any breakfast, have you?'

'No.'

'When you're ready,' sighed Plumridge.

Tim ignored the biscuits. 'The captain and crew are protesting their innocence,' he said sharply. 'The submersible team are convinced nothing was jettisoned in the Blackwater.'

'Well, you don't just dump £50 million worth of Charley in the briny – not if you're in your right mind, you don't,' observed Livy.

'But why go through the pantomime of sailing round the island?'

29

'A decoy?' queried Bill Jones. 'To attract our attention while the drop took place elsewhere.'

'No.' Plumridge was insistent. 'Our intelligence was pure.'

'But it wasn't, was it, dear?' mewed Livy Hull, lightly as a kitten.

'It was one hundred per cent.'

'But it wasn't, was it, my chicken?' When Livy Hull wanted to make a seismic point or be really bitchy, she switched into the burr of her native Dorset. Neither she nor any of her family had ever spoken like that, but she could get away with more with an accent.

Williams grew impatient with the bickering. 'What was the source?'

A silence deepened and spread until the whole room held its breath.

'I'm afraid I can't say.' Plumridge would not meet his eye.

'Pshaw.' Livy Hull threw up her hands in a histrionic gesture of exasperation, Bill Jones blinked and even Commander Penn registered hurt.

'There are more clearances in this room than the Highlands saw in fifty years,' exclaimed Livy, milking the moment, smiling with scorn and amusement at Plumridge, who coloured. He realized he had made a bad gaffe and tried to recover.

'We are not all cleared for the source, only the product.' He let his eyes slide towards Tim to suggest that Tim was the fly in the ointment; the sole reason why he could not share his secret.

Livy was not going to let Plumridge off easily. 'Then whisper it to me, dear.'

There had grown a farawayness about Tim, a distance from the shell of his body to himself. He was inert and contained. Sticks and stones can break my bones but words can never hurt me. Never show your feelings, especially to a pig like Plumridge.

Bill Jones opened out a sheet of paper and cleared his throat. 'We have two intercepts to the *Sheila* the night before the storm and the night of the storm itself. They are on one-time pads so unless you want them alpha graded . . .'

He meant that unless Williams tagged them priority the GCHQ computers would not get around to decoding them for some time. And with a one-time pad it wasn't certain they'd crack them. But Williams was thinking in another direction.

'Would that storm prevent them cross-decking their cargo?'

There was another silence until Commander Penn realized he was being addressed. 'Oh, um. Not necessarily. What was it, force nine, locally force ten? If she was in the lee of an island, one of the Friesians, or found a sheltered anchorage, it'd be no problem at all. After all, it wasn't a bulky cargo, was it? Relatively easy in fact. Assuming decent seamanship, of course.'

'Their papers say they're all professional seamen,' said Tim.

All of a sudden Williams was keen to end the meeting. He made a show of looking at his watch. 'I'm afraid I've got to get to the Cabinet Office. I'm sorry, Livy, I know you wanted to bring up our friend Saddam . . .'

'That's all right, Coordinator. I might have been premature anyway.'

As the meeting broke up, Williams followed Tim into his office. He found him standing by the window staring down at the trains a hundred feet below.

'Better than an executive toy, that,' he murmured. Startled, Tim came to a semblance of attention, but Williams put a hand on the younger man's shoulder. 'It wasn't your fault. Don't take it personally.'

Tim shook his head. 'I'm sorry, sir. I seem to be a liability.'

'You're unlucky – or a victim. Don't dwell on it.'

31

Easy to say that. You didn't spend two weeks waiting in Cyprus for a Russian Mafiya courier carrying forged bonds worth $400 million – to find they'd been cashed in Beirut. Right time, wrong place. All in all, the past fifteen months had been the worst of his life and it wasn't getting any better.

Tim and Haydn Williams stood side by side watching the trains. Each in his own thoughts. Williams believed he could divine what Tim was thinking but he was wrong. He was only charting the river of misfortune, Tim was at the source.

Linda. Beautiful, bountiful, bloody Linda. His redeemer and his crucifier. His Judas and his Barabbas. The reason he was here.

'Don't hang around here. Draft your preliminary report and go and get your head down,' said Williams, adding, 'Wouldn't this have been wonderful in the days of steam?'

'You wouldn't have been able to see the trains for the smoke.'

'You're not a romantic, boy, are you?'

But Tim was – and Haydn Williams knew he was.

Williams put on his coat and dithered whether to call a driver or to chance a cab. Their building was in that no man's land between Six's posh new edifice at Vauxhall Cross and Jeffrey Archer's penthouse. Not cab country. It wasn't raining and the walk would do him good. Since he'd announced he was going to the Cabinet Office he'd better go there.

He didn't have a clue what he was going to do when he arrived other than bully Edgar Summerfield into buying him that lunch he owed him.

In his local corner shop Tim bought milk, bread and eggs and inspected the street with its tall Victorian terraces. He knew every neighbour's car, and his eyes, while appearing to scan the shelves, looked for occupied parked cars, unusual trade vehicles or anyone strolling slowly. Better paranoid than paralysed by a bullet from someone you didn't even know you'd upset.

The heavy front door closed behind him with an oiled snick as Tim riffled through the mail on the hall table. Nothing for him. He climbed the stairs, which became narrower and steeper until he reached his flat on the very top floor. It was hard to believe that this house was once occupied by a single family. How did they fill all the rooms? Tim knew how they had filled his – with servants. He still had their furniture. The small living room was cluttered with an ancient dining table and chairs, while two overstuffed armchairs sat either side of the small gas fire. There was no central heating this far up.

Egg shells lay on the floor of the kitchen alcove where they had been knocked off the overflowing rubbish bin, probably by the same mouse which had left its paw prints across the congealed fat in the frying pan. Tim failed to find any matches, ripped up a paper bag and lit a spill off the gas fire which ignited automatically. It was damp and cold and he decided to leave the fire on, putting 50p in the meter below the sink.

He threw the tea bag staining the draining board into the bin. The food cupboard was bare apart from two bottles of brown sauce and a tin of corned beef. He heated the fat in the frying pan and dropped in two slices of bread with their middles torn out. The kettle came to the boil. No tea bags! Which was, he now remembered, why he hadn't thrown away the one on the draining board. Tim fished it out of the rubbish bin and rinsed it under the tap before dropping it in a mug. He turned over the fried bread and broke an egg into the centre of each.

He was still smarting about the failure of last night's operation, the failure of both operations. Did people believe it was too much of a coincidence? Was that why Plumridge wouldn't reveal his source? Were they suspicious of his links with Russia? That would be ironic considering he'd only gone on the language course to get an extra stripe.

Then he'd been sent on exchange to the Russian Special Forces' close protection school in Rostov followed by two months' babysitting a Russian industrialist who was dealing missile technology to the West.

That was the way in the Army. Do a job once and you're an expert, do it twice and you're a recognized authority. He finished the egg banjos and began to feel sleepy and grubby with tiredness.

Tim slipped into the unmade double bed and found himself gazing at two photographs lying face down on the cane bedside table. Why hadn't he put them away? Why hadn't he put them in a drawer, a suitcase, the fire? He knew he had to look at them.

He picked up the top one with the same care a mother holds her first-born. Two rows of grinning young men in jungle fatigues holding an assortment of automatic weapons. He was kneeling in the middle, grinning broader than anyone. They had just completed a happy and successful month's jungle training in Borneo under his command. His first command. No one knew then that the sergeant on his right and the trooper standing directly behind him were both to be dead within a year.

He had killed them.

Whatever anyone said, he knew he had killed them.

Tim placed the photograph face down and slid out the other. Bloody Linda with her wide, laughing mouth and larceny in her eyes. The dark parting in her blonde hair could be shadow or it could be roots. He knew now it was roots, as he knew the larceny in her eyes had been there for everyone to see, except him. Tim drew the memory to him, measuring its pain, pressing the point harder and harder, deeper and deeper.

Thursday 26 February

'Come on, you cow. Over you go.'

'Now.'

'No, the bitch won't. She's a steel umbrella.'

'You are too impatient. Tari. Slowly, slowly. Put the nose down and start again.'

At 3,500 feet they were level with the top of Mount Shabah to the east, a blunt pinnacle outlined against the rising sun. In the clear dawn light he could make out the peak of Refai and the awakening land of Syria behind it to the north. Iraq lay to the east across the empty expanse of the Badiet esh Sham. Soon the air would be hot and thin with thermals rising off the parched Jordan desert, making flying bumpy and uncomfortable. He finished his turn over Jebel esh Shefa and studiously went through his HASEL checks. Height – sufficient. Airframe – clean flaps, brakes off. Security – harness tight and hatches locked. Engine – temperature and pressure normal, fuel pump on, pitch fine, mixture rich. Location – clear of controlled airspace and built-up areas. Clear of anything apart from a few flocks of emaciated sheep. Look out. A 360-degree turn.

The instructor was wrong. He was not impatient. He knew the importance of being thorough. It was simply that he always did things quickly – usually they worked.

The Aerospatial ST 150 was about twenty years old but stable, too stable. To stall, the relative airflow had to come up to meet the wings at an angle of attack greater than 16 degrees. It was difficult in a steel umbrella. Tari pulled out the carburettor heat, saw the revs fall, eased back the throttle and pulled back on the stick. The nose rose up so they faced the deep-blue cloudless sky. The prop caught the

35

sun, shimmering in a silver arc, slower and slower until Tari believed he could make out each revolution. His airspeed was down to 50 knots. Buffeting towards the tail told him he had succeeded in stalling.

He was literally falling out of the sky.

Tari kicked hard on the right rudder and as the ST 150 yawed he jerked back on the control stick. There was a moment when they hung in space, then slowly, reluctantly, the left wing began to come over. Tari slowly rose above the instructor until the plane lay on its side, then it toppled over into a spin. Nose first, they plummeted towards the ground, simultaneously rolling, pitching and yawing. It was more frightening than any fairground ride, but Tari enjoyed counting the revolutions, each one carrying him nearer death.

He counted seven full gyrations. He was getting dangerously low. Now, by the book. Neutral ailerons, throttle closed, full left rudder, pause, ease forward on stick, centralize rudder. Tari gently eased out of the dive and applied power. The nose rose above the horizon.

'Good,' said the instructor. 'But if you get into a spin you'll have to get out of it quicker than that.'

'I'm not going to spin,' said Tari.

They descended to two hundred feet and contour chased as the sun rose and reflected off the engine cowling. The instructor made Tari practise circuits at 1,000 feet around a red sandstone bluff, dropping down to fifty feet for imaginary touch and goes before climbing for the downwind leg.

'Excellent,' said the instructor. 'How many flying hours do you have?'

'Almost two hundred, gathered over the years. For their purposes I am a student.'

'Then behave like one. Stop flying ahead of the aircraft,' the instructor criticized. 'Wander off track, find trouble keeping a steady altitude, keep readjusting your trim. Remember you are a pupil.'

Returning to the airfield they flew over a long caravan of laden camels plodding along the ancient trade route to Al Qusayr. Tari sneered at the timeless quality of the scene and looked forward to seeing his two jewels.

'I don't believe it. It's not a service. It's a bloody tyranny,' exploded Williams. 'I'll see them in hell first.'

Oh dear! Livy Hull feared that Williams was about to launch into one of his interdepartmental tirades. Who had attracted his fury this time? It was usually the DIS, whom he frequently referred to as SBH – Sleepy Bloody Hollow.

'What's happened?' She nodded to the letter he was waving.

'Greenwich Council and their ridiculous residents' parking scheme.'

Livy sighed in relief.

'A couple of weeks ago I put a visitor's permit on a friend's car. I was thinking of something else and I scratched out the wrong month. I had the right day, date and year, just the wrong month. A parking warden slapped a ticket on the car. Damn me if it's not the same jobsworth who did me every day for a week last year when he spotted my parking permit didn't match my numberplate. YFC instead of YCF. Three years I'd had that car and no one ever noticed before. I am not going to pay and that's that.' Williams exhaled deeply. 'So what do you want to discuss?'

Livy paused. It was a delicate one and with Williams in this mood she could expect a rough ride. Plumridge took advantage of her hesitation.

'Six believes that Saddam Hussein is about to smuggle biological weapons into Britain in scent bottles.' Plumridge smirked and crossed his legs. 'It's preposterous. Absolutely preposterous.'

Livy Hull scowled at him through her large round spectacles. 'Source Ceres. We are coding and circulating the intelligence as CX.'

'How are they going to deliver this knockout blow? Over the counter at Harrods' perfume department?' Plumridge guffawed at his own joke.

'A fortnight ago we were about to go to war with Iraq because Saddam refused to allow UN weapons inspectors access to secret presidential sites,' said Livy severely. 'Iraq possesses the ingredients to wipe out the world's population. We hope Ceres can point us at their biological weapons plants and stockpiles.'

'Who is Ceres?' Williams leaned back and steepled his fingers.

Livy took a deep breath. 'His name is Nassir al-Hindawi. He's the father of the Iraqi anthrax programme. He wants to come over and this is his dowry.'

'I'd take the ten goats and three camels, personally,' chortled Plumridge.

'Hindawi's seventy years old, but he was the one who put Iraq on the road to biological and chemical weapons. He wrote a secret paper for the ruling Ba'ath party in 1983 setting out military applications for germ weapons. Saddam leapt at it as a viable deterrent to an Israeli nuclear attack. Within a year Hindawi was given a special facility at Al Muthanna. The project was designated a presidential priority and exempted from normal spending and personnel constraints. He hasn't looked back.'

'And now he wants to come over. Why?'

'No old age pensions in Iraq,' suggested Plumridge. There was a leaden silence.

'Saddam has something he's desperate to keep out of sight from the West,' explained Livy, patiently. 'He knows UN sanctions will be lifted as soon as inspectors verify his weapons of mass destruction have been destroyed. Saddam is crippling his country to keep something hidden. *It has to be something very special*.'

'That's all very well,' insisted Plumridge. 'But why target Britain?'

'Because we're the imperialist Yankees' running dogs.

38

We supported the call to arms against Saddam and we're instrumental in keeping sanctions in place at the UN. Spray anthrax in New York and the Americans would vaporize Baghdad by tea time. We'll still be discussing our options in the context of a moral foreign policy in a month's time.'

'So when's it happening?'

'Ceres is coming out this weekend.'

'That's very little time to mount an operation,' objected Williams.

'It's being led by the Cousins.' Livy saw the pucker of disapproval on Williams's face and heard the theatrical groan from Plumridge. 'It's not our operation. Hindawi wants to settle in Britain but he approached the CIA. They're funding him, paying his pension. Our Timmy's job is to walk three paces behind the Americans and bring Hindawi back to this sceptred isle after the preliminary debriefing. The Yanks have unlimited access to him for the next twelve months, then Hindawi's free to dig his allotment, make yoghurt, whatever.'

'I think he's trying to scare us to up his value,' protested Plumridge.

Williams pursed his lips. He knew that during the Gulf War the Iraqis had hidden Scud missiles armed with biological and chemical warheads in the desert under independent launch command, ready to retaliate if the Allies dropped a nuclear bomb on Baghdad.

'We can't ignore him,' he said grimly. 'A recent US war game ended with Saddam releasing biological weapons over Dahran, causing one million casualties and the US taking out Baghdad in retaliation.'

There was a moment's pause while each digested the prospect.

'I'll go and tell Tim he's off on his travels,' said Williams. It would give him an excuse to look at the trains and think what to do about Greenwich bloody Council.

* * *

The sun beat through the canopy and despite having the cold air blower on maximum Tari's shirt was sticking to his back as the rough airstrip came into sight. He set the QFE on the altimeter and went through his downwind checks, trying to think like a student. A black Cherokee four-wheel drive was parked alongside the open-fronted hangar where a handful of light aircraft sheltered from the sun. The Cherokee hadn't been there when they'd taken off.

He hoped Fatima had brought his daughters Leila, four, and three-year-old Soraya up from the camp. She usually did, knowing how much they enjoyed sharing the passenger seat while he flew a circuit especially for them.

Tari lowered the flaps on the crosswind leg and turned finals at 70 knots, idling nicely down the glide slope towards an imaginary centre line. He flared too high, the plane drifted and plonked down with a bump. He pulled off all power and held her nose down to stop her kangarooing back in the air. Not a landing to be proud of – but he was supposed to be a pupil. He pulled back the hatch and the dry ferocity of the desert heat grabbed at his throat. There was no sign of the girls so he switched off and climbed out, feeling drained and elated at the same time. He stretched his slight frame and brushed the black hair off his forehead.

Two men in suits and white open-necked shirts emerged from the Cherokee. They wore sunglasses. Tari's stomach muscles tightened.

The first man nodded without smiling. 'It is time.'

'If you say so.' Tari continued to look for his daughters.

'Leila and Soraya are with us. They will be well looked after while you are away.'

'What!' Tari's deep-set eyes emptied to become shallow pools reflecting the desert light. Those who knew him said this was how he looked when he killed.

The men sensed the change. They moved apart to present separate targets. The elder spoke rapidly. 'It's better than staying in the camp with its bad water and diseases.

40

Their nurse is with them and they will have the best of everything.'

Tari wanted to kick the stones in frustration at his powerlessness. When he had sold his soul, he had not known he would also be pawning his daughters.

'They are happy.' The Iraqi cast a long shadow. 'They're on holiday with a new doll each. You can write to them, through a cut-out, of course. Here's a Polaroid photograph we took before they left.'

Tari snatched the picture of two little girls holding hands. In their other hand each held a rag doll. Their eyes were black buttons and they were smiling, showing small white teeth. Behind them the nurse Fatima smiled for the children's sake.

'Where have they gone?'

'Baghdad.'

Sunday 1 March

The road crawled over the ridge to the scattered settlement which had grown up around the customs post. The fly-blown café, warehouses, goatherds' mud-brick hovels and a barracks baked in the early afternoon heat. Rusty iron rods poking out of the flat concrete roofs gave the place the appearance of being unfinished. Tim Platt had been staring through binoculars at a similar settlement on the Iraqi side since the sun had risen as a pale egg-yolk almost seven hours ago. Now it was past its zenith, blistering the rounded brown hills where barbed wire fences and faded wooden boards with skull-and-crossbones warnings of minefields stretched away into the shimmering emptiness. An ancient wagon, painted in garish greens and yellows and laden with huge sacks, rumbled towards him, leaving a trail of dust motionless in the still air. Two hundred yards away unshaven Iraqi troops hung around three more trucks waiting to cross the border. The Turkish troops were even less tidy. Among the small garrison, doing their best to be scruffier than anyone, was a detachment of special forces.

Tim shifted his weight, feeling the metal bed frame dig into his hip. A large black beetle scurried along the rotting window pane and launched itself out of the sultry darkness of the first-floor storeroom into the sunlight. The mush and crackle of a high-powered radio transmitter came from the back room.

'Anything?'

'No.' No new faces, no big-time operators in flash cars, no welcome committee. Only a pot-bellied driver hitching his belt over his gut and spitting into the dirt before climbing into his cab.

'Shit! I hate this waiting.' Trent Rickenbacker wiped his face with his sleeve, exposing damp patches under the armpits of his safari shirt. 'D'you reckon the bus'll be on time?'

'Wouldn't have thought so.'

The laconic reply angered the American.

'Christ, don't you do anything but lie there! You ain't moved in hours.' Rickenbacker rocked back and forth, a small ball of nervous energy. 'I'm going to check the radio in the cruiser.' Still Tim didn't respond. 'You're not contributing a lot to this operation, buddy. I expect a little more support, more team play, know what I mean?'

'There's a Land Cruiser with military numberplates arriving at a lick,' announced Tim. 'Two pax, one in civvies, one in uniform. No rank badges. Could mean someone senior.'

'So what! Hell, it's a military base. I don't know what you're hoping to see – Saddam arrive in person to wave Hindawi off!' At the low doorway he swung around. 'No, sir. Langley expects support from you Brits in a CIA operation and what Langley expects Langley gets.'

If there had been a door, Rickenbacker would have slammed it. Tim listened to him clumping down the wooden stairs out to their vehicle tucked away at the back. There was a scrape of a chair and Tim sensed Rickenbacker's number two pad into the room. Fifteen-stone Jedd Fry walked very lightly.

'For a man who don't say much, you've sure got a way of getting under Rickenbacker's skin.'

'Yeh, well . . .'

'Me, I'm a country boy from Bare Rabbit Creek, Oklahoma. There we're used to waiting for something to happen. Trent now, he's from New York. Them Yankees is all go, go, go. End up running so fast they disappear up their own backsides. Yep. Gum?'

'Cheers.'

'Trent's not too bad. Just can't relax, that's all,' Fry said

43

by way of apology. 'He'll buy you a drink and call you his brother when it's all over.'

'If anything's going to go wrong, it's already wrong. It's no good panicking now.'

'Yeh, sure. I know that. The seven Ps, eh? Proper planning and preparation prevents piss-poor performance. Yeh, worked with some of you boys before. The seven Ps kinda stuck in my mind. I reckon it's the sign of the true professional to know when it's too late to panic. Trent, now, he reckons it's half-arsed.'

The Iraqi Land Cruiser was heading away in a cloud of dust. Tim made out a third man sitting behind the driver. The sullen air filled his chest and he was grateful for the other's friendliness. A movement in the distance took his eye and he swept the hillside with binoculars until he focused on a scattered flock of goats picking at sparse scrub.

'Coffee.' Rickenbacker was back with a thermos. 'None of that Turkish muck where you have two sips and you get grounds in your teeth. This is real coffee from the US of A.' He slumped against the pile of rice sacks in the corner only to leap away as a swarm of large beetles with hard carapaces rose angrily and made towards the window. Tim was in their line of flight. The dense black cloud buzzed around his head before settling in his hair in a crawling mass. Tim did not move.

'Christ!' exclaimed Jedd. 'Do something.'

'They'll go,' said Tim. After a moment, the beetles rose as one and disappeared out into the sunlight.

'Disgusting,' spat Rickenbacker.

'The bus,' proclaimed Tim, putting out an arm to prevent Rickenbacker going to the window. 'Stay back.'

A battered blue bus was grinding over the ridge, its roof loaded with sacks, bundles and cages of fowls. There was no glass in the windows and the passengers sat with scarves wrapped around their heads.

'Yessir!' Rickenbacker was already at the RT set, reporting

the bus's arrival to their forward base twenty miles back in Cizre where the chopper was on standby.

The bus halted in a painful squeal of brakes. A brawny man in a vest climbed up the ladder at the back and began throwing down bundles. The thirty or so passengers were herded into the largest building as Turkish special forces drifted casually to their firing positions.

'This is the test of a good Joe,' said Jedd quietly. 'Ceres has got to hold his water over the last ditch by himself. This wasn't my favourite way of bringing him out, no sirree. I wanted to bring him over the mountains with Kurdish shepherds, but Rickenbacker and the others reckoned he was too old. If he can't tough it, he'll have to bluff it, they said. Hope to God they're right.'

Trent returned, chewing the knuckle of his right index finger. 'Not long now. Those guys in UNSCOM just can't wait to have a long chinwag with our boy.'

'You mean they know he's coming out?' demanded Tim.

'Yeh, well.' Rickenbacker looked uncomfortable. 'We wanted to keep up their spirits after the way that United Nations bigwig let Saddam pull a fast one last month.'

He clattered down the stairs where he could be heard shouting for Major Kemal, their Turkish liaison officer.

'Not my idea, boy,' growled Jedd.

The first passenger emerged from the building. A man too young to be Ceres, carrying a brown paper parcel and a cardboard suitcase. He walked up to the green and white pole across the road. The soldiers ignored him, so he ducked under the barrier and kept on coming. His face was so taut Tim thought he could strop a razor on his skin. He knew instinctively that he was connected with Hindawi.

Two hundred yards is a long, long way when your back feels the size of a barn wall with a bull's eye painted on it. The man lengthened his stride. Near the Turkish post he raised his head and began scanning the guards as though searching for someone. One indicated towards the open door with his rifle.

Behind the high counter, a customs officer held out his hand for papers.

'Please, please. I have to see someone important. It is urgent.' The man spoke grammatical English with a thick accent. 'It is about my friend.'

The customs official addressed the man in Turkish but he said again in English, 'My friend is in danger. Please.'

Rickenbacker appeared in the doorway from the back office. 'Let him through.'

The man sat down at the wooden table under the slowly revolving fan, his eyes flicking anxiously around the three faces. 'You are American?'

'It don't matter who we are, pal,' said Rickenbacker. 'What do you want?'

'My friend Nassir al-Hindawi . . .'

Rickenbacker was a greyhound straining at the leash.

'Ceres,' said Tim.

'Yes, yes.' A frown, but the man's smiling again, eager to please, desperate to tell his story. 'He was taken sick. Very sick. In his stomach. He needed toilet. He had to get off the bus, five kilometres back at a rest house. He has papers in his briefcase. The rest house is used by many government people and soldiers. He is scared someone will ask to see them. The next bus is not until tomorrow.'

Light-brown eyes, honest eyes, appealing directly to his interrogators. He'd shaved recently. He licked his lips. Nervous, but who wouldn't be?

'How do you know Hindawi?' drawled Jedd Fry.

'I am Ahmet Moffata. Nassir al-Hindawi is my mother's uncle. It is my family duty to stay with him, but he told me to come here for help.'

'Shit. We're going to go get him.' Rickenbacker had made a decision. 'Five clicks. Nothing in a chopper. Infil, hit, exfil. We'll be in and out before anyone knows we've been there.'

'I don't know.' Jedd Fry was hesitant.

'Shit, man. We can't let him rot. We'll be there and back in three minutes. We'll deny it ever took place.'

Tim rose and left to go into the main hall. No other passengers had left the Iraqi side. Tim ripped open Ahmet's brown paper parcel and inspected the contents.

'I'm making an executive decision, Jedd. Let's get that chopper up here and go go go.'

'I must come with you, sir, or he will not trust you,' said Ahmet.

'Yeh, sure.' Rickenbacker strode out, Jedd at his heels.

'You're a brave man, Ahmet,' said Tim, returning. 'Did you work with Nassir al-Hindawi?'

'A little, sir, a little.' He chain-smokes. A pack of Marlboro left by Rickenbacker.

'Why didn't you change your suit?'

'Sorry, sir.' He is confused by the question. He makes an effort to swallow.

Tim passes him a plastic bottle of water. Ahmed takes it gratefully. His mouth is dry. As he drinks, Tim says pleasantly, 'That will poison you because you are lying.'

Ahmed jerks back, spilling water over his dusty blue suit and open-necked white shirt.

'I know you're lying because I've been watching your barracks since dawn. I've seen you twice at the extreme left-hand window on the first floor. I saw you drive away in the cruiser.'

'Sir?'

'You're not getting on that helicopter.' Tim produced a 9mm Browning from the back of his waistband and cocked it. 'I don't believe Hindawi is at the rest house. I think it's a trap to lure western agents to their death or certainly torture.' Tim perched on the edge of the table above Ahmed. 'It's not a very clever plan or a very sophisticated plan. I think Hindawi only cracked very recently, so you've not had time to put anything more detailed into place. You're making it up as you go along, but the temptation to get

47

your hands on a CIA agent or two was too much. It was a gamble. Nice try but it failed. If I were you I'd get back to your own side pretty quickly. I'll grant you safe conduct.'

Major Kemal nodded woodenly. Great man.

There was the faint *whup whup* of the chopper. Christ! That was quick.

Ahmed held out his hands, palms upwards in a gesture of reasonable denial. 'But I only try to help.'

'The CIA do not like to be fooled. If I were you, I wouldn't be here when those two get back. Next time you borrow some other passenger's luggage, find someone nearer your own age. I can't see you in long johns somehow.'

Crack, you bastard. Crack before that bogdaft Yankee comes back with his boy scout troop.

'The chopper will not take off until we've interrogated the other passengers. It's a stalemate. Nice try, but please go home.'

Suddenly the Iraqi was standing and shaking Tim's hand. 'I have your word?'

'Yes.' The Turkish major opened the back door and called out instructions to the concealed troops. The two spoke rapidly together before the Iraqi nodded and disappeared through the doorway. They did not shake hands.

'Let's go.' Rickenbacker was back, exuding energy like a pulsar. 'Where is he? No time for the john.'

'He's gone,' said Tim.

'What'd you mean gone?'

'It was a trap,' said Major Kemal in slow English. 'You must thank Captain Platt for your life.'

Rickenbacker regarded him in stunned silence. The major began explaining when there was a shout from the road. 'The passengers are coming.'

Jedd took Tim's hand. 'Too good to be true, huh?'

'They were tap dancing on water . . .'

'. . . and you couldn't see their reflection. I'm indebted.'

'We'll sweat the bastard.' Rickenbacker had turned vindictive. 'Swop him for Hindawi.'

48

'He's not here. He's gone.'

'You let him go.'

'I encouraged him. It was the only proof I had that he was lying.'

'Boy. You've just bought yourself a court martial,' snarled Rickenbacker, striding off to the chopper.

Jedd formed the index finger and middle finger of his right hand into a gun, cocked it with his thumb and fired an imaginary bullet into the back of his colleague.

The major, smiling for once, brought in a frail teenage boy with a metal brace on his left leg. 'He has something to tell you. He has a speech ready. It is the only English he speaks.'

The boy fixed his gaze upon the wall above Tim's head and began reciting. 'I am the great grandson of Nassir al-Hindawi. If he cannot be here I must say . . .' The boy hesitated and Tim felt a trickle of sweat run down his back. 'The Samson Option. Saddam will use Samson Option.'

Tuesday 3 March

'Biological weapons are known as the poor man's atomic bomb because they're cheaper and easier to make than nuclear weapons and just as deadly.' Dr Diana Philpotts, of the Protection and Life Sciences Division of the Defence Evaluation Research Agency at Porton Down, gave a toothy grin. 'Deadlier.'

Dotty Di from DERA, as she was known, beamed at the faces around the table. A large, jolly woman, who expected everyone to share her passionate enthusiasm for deadly bugs, she had been seconded to the department to offer expert evaluation once Tim had reported Hindawi's message.

'Iraq can produce more than twenty tons of anthrax – enough to wipe out the world twice over. And it won't be a nice death. Anthrax kills over several days. The victim first experiences fatigue and a mild fever, then makes a temporary recovery before declining precipitously when the toxins assault the kidneys, liver and lungs.' A dramatic pause as Diana subconsciously tweaked at her skirt which had been riding up over her broad hips. 'Victims literally drown from fluids generated by the body's useless attempt to protect itself.'

Plumridge raised his eyes to heaven. 'That's all very well,' he retorted impatiently. 'But they have to deliver it. If I have a ten-inch stainless steel knife, I can kill every human being on the planet . . . if they're brought within range and no one interferes with my delivery.'

'Your point?' Diana scowled.

'That any killing system has to have a method of delivery.'

50

'Commander Penn can tell us about a delivery system and warheads,' said Williams. 'They may have some bearing.'

'Ah, yes.' Andrew Penn gathered himself. 'For the past two years, UNSCOM inspectors have searched Iraq for some twenty-five warheads containing deadly germs – it may be anthrax – designed to fit on top of medium-range Al-Hussein missiles. In the Gulf War the warheads were hidden in railway tunnels and buried on the banks of the Tigris River. The Iraqis claim they were later destroyed at a desert site called Nebai. We don't believe them. Iraqi officers have given conflicting accounts of when the warheads were destroyed, which officials knew about it, and what became of remaining parts. As a result, we suspect the germ warheads could still exist. Launched against a major city in the right conditions they would kill between 100,000 and a million people.'

'Are these missiles the Samson Option?'

Mickey New wriggled uncomfortably in the plastic chair. He had to ask. He was lost and he didn't mind admitting it. 'Excuse me, sir. What actually is the Samson Option?'

'Good question,' acknowledged Williams. 'It means if I'm going down, I'm going to bring the temple down with me.'

'You remember how Samson loses his great strength after his locks are shorn,' explained Penn. 'The Philistines were having a feast and Samson, now blind, is brought in as sport. *"And Samson took hold of the two middle pillars upon which the house stood, and on which it was borne up, of the one with his right hand, and of the other with his left. And Samson said, Let me die with the Philistines. And he bowed himself with all his might; and the house fell upon the lords, and upon all the people that were therein. So the dead which he slew at his death were more than they which he slew in his life."'*

'I didn't know you were a biblical scholar.' Williams beamed approvingly.

'Can we stick to the matter in hand?' sniffed Plumridge.

51

'Saddam can't use the missiles against Britain. They don't have the range.'

'He could launch them against British and American forces in the Gulf. The Americans are taking the threat seriously enough to accelerate their anthrax vaccination programme for US military personnel out there,' Livy Hull pointed out.

'The boy didn't mention anything else, Tim?'

'No, sir. He was an odd job boy around Hindawi's home – part of his extended family. Hindawi had been responsible for getting the boy's twisted leg straightened and the boy worshipped him. Last week Hindawi gave him a passport and bus tickets and made him learn the speech in English with the instruction that if anything happens to him he must make the journey alone. One day Hindawi doesn't come home and the secret police arrive . . .'

'So the boy scoots out the back and doesn't stop running until he reaches the border,' scoffed Plumridge. 'I mean, in a police state like Iraq, is that likely? He'd be stopped at internal checkpoints.'

'He was,' snapped Livy. 'But he had the documents and the legend to get through. Iraq is a police state but it's not an efficient one.'

'Surely a biological attack on Britain is unthinkable?' said Bill Jones.

'Germ warfare always was unthinkable until the Aum Shinrikyo let off sarin nerve gas on the Tokyo underground. Once the unthinkable has been committed it becomes the repeatable,' said Williams sourly. 'Our political masters are expecting guidance. If the Samson Option is genuine and an attack takes place without the Government warning the public, they'll be crucified. At the same time, they can't panic the populace if there's nothing to panic over.'

'Saddam is still refusing to let UNSCOM inspectors into presidential sites despite last month's agreement,' reminded Livy. 'The Americans aren't going to put up with it much longer.'

'Thank you,' said Williams, screwing on his pen top to indicate the meeting was over. 'See you all later at Chancey's farewell, no doubt.'

As they filed out, Plumridge hung back. Williams knew what the MI5 man was going to say and it brought an unpleasant taste to his mouth.

'Yes, I know our Tim's failed again.' Williams tried to clip the fountain pen on to his inside jacket pocket without further ripping the torn lining. 'But it was an American operation.'

'He had time,' insisted Plumridge. 'Hindawi was lifted after Tim was briefed. We know there are links between the Ba'ath party and Russian organized crime. Two years ago Iraqis negotiated with a Moscow chemical company to build a germ factory.'

'You're saying Tim tipped off Russian crime bosses who passed it on to the Iraqis. A little far-fetched, don't you think?'

But when Plumridge had left, Williams pulled a resigned face and dialled a London number on his direct outside line.

The woman known as Sally Beck puckered up her lips in an attempt to hold her pen under her nose.

> *As I was going up the stair,*
> *I met a man who wasn't there.*
> *He wasn't there again today.*
> *I wish, I wish he'd stay away.*

The tautness of the metre and the rhymes were giving her problems. Sally did not know whether to concentrate on the timpanic cadences, so hard to translate convincingly into Russian, or the rhymes. Maybe if she employed the scansion of the Russian nursery rhymes. Translate, not transliterate. She rubbed her left forefinger over the bump on her broken nose and sighed. All for an academic exercise.

Why don't I go rollerblading or join Ladies who Lunch. But no, I sit here translating silly verse by Hughes Mearns. Always a good trivia question. Most people knew the nonsense. Most thought it was Lear. Still it made a pleasant change from the heavyweight subjects she normally translated – and her other job.

Sally uncoiled from the sofa and crossed to the kitchen to make a cup of coffee. While the kettle chortled away to itself, she wandered over to the huge windows and looked out over London. There were three factors which determined the price of a place, the estate agent had said. Location. Location. And Location. She slid open the glass door and stepped out on to the balcony. The view from her sixth-floor flat was stunning. A small patch of washed-out blue hung above the distant thicket of the skyscrapers in the City of London. The sky to the west was full of rain clouds. She fancied the rain would win.

Sally murmured greetings to her plants in their earthenware pots and was automatically picking up the watering can before she stopped herself. They didn't need any more water. She'd watered them yesterday and the day before. It was like the way she fed the neighbours' cat when they went away. No wonder they put it on a diet as soon as they returned.

The phone rang and Sally's heart gave a lurch.

'I was hoping I'd catch you. Are you busy tonight?' Williams caught her intake of breath. 'I want you to meet someone from my office. A really nice bloke.'

'If he's really nice, why do you want me to meet him?' She heard Williams chuckle.

'He's having a spot of misfortune. I want to make sure he's not the author of his own grief, if you understand.'

Sally wasn't sure she did. Williams sensed her hesitation.

'You'll meet him anyway when you start coming into the department.'

'You've remembered then.' There was an edge in Sally's voice.

'Ay. I gave you my word, but there's a lot going on now.'

'There always is, Haydn,' said Sally bitterly.

Tim stopped on the stairs, recoiling from the packed cellar wine bar. You couldn't move. Tim panicked at having to immerse himself in such a social cauldron and turned to leave. No one would miss him.

'Ouch!'

'Sorry, boss.' Mickey caught his arm to stop him falling. 'You shouldn't hold up the traffic. Come on, I'll buy you a beer.'

They squeezed through the press to where Livy Hull, concave face alive in company, was handing out glasses of wine.

'There was a free bar, but those tossers from Five finished it,' she shouted before being swept away. Tim and Mickey stood on the edge of an insufferably pompous crowd from Thames House. Plumridge and an imperious woman Tim recognized as his wife were deep in conversation. Plumridge looked through him before offering the merest nod of recognition. His wife was saying, 'If Tabitha has to take Bilberry to Pony Club camp she'll be a laughing stock . . .'

'Nice,' exclaimed Mickey, glancing towards the stairs. A slim, dark-haired girl in a black trouser suit stood hesitantly, one hand on the rail. She gave a broad smile of relief as Williams emerged to greet her. He steered her through the throng towards the bar.

'I don't think you know each other. Sally, Tim, Mickey.'

No surnames, noted Tim. No rank or position. Typical Williams.

The girl had a broken nose and inside-out lips on a mouth too wide for her small, fine-boned face. The bits didn't fit. It made her very sexy.

'You'll be seeing more of each other,' promised Williams. 'Sally's going to be doing some work for us. Excuse me, I must catch Creighton before he slithers away. Forget JIC, this is when the important work is done.' A second later he popped up alongside the mandarin.

'Are you involved in this lot?' asked Tim. It was difficult in present surroundings to ask people what they did for a living. The favourite reply was on the lines, If I told you, I'd have to kill you.

'I'm a translator. Mainly Russian and Arabic. And you?'

'We work on the coal face,' said Mickey quickly.

'Oh.' Sally appeared dumbfounded by the reply. 'Do you know anyone here? I don't. I hate parties like this.'

'I wouldn't worry,' chirped Mickey. 'By the looks you're getting half the men in this room are already in love with you.'

'What about the other half?' smiled Sally.

'They're gay.'

'Which are you?'

'Oooh. I'm not gay, ducky,' minced Mickey. 'Ask my husband.'

Sally was in her mid-twenties, judged Tim. From her slight accent he couldn't tell whether she was foreign or whether she'd been out of the country a long time.

'You're not saying a lot.' Sally gave Tim a friendly look.

'He's the strong silent type,' said Mickey.

'Are silent men brave men?' demanded Sally. Again the eye contact.

Tim had to say something. Why was his bloody mind a blank? 'No. Wasn't it Nym who had heard men of few words were the best men and therefore he scorned to say his prayers lest he be thought a coward . . .'

'Who's this Nym, then?' demanded Mickey.

'I say, don't I know you? Paris, wasn't it?' A smooth face from the FCO, oozing confidence and aftershave, demanded Sally's attention.

Tim looked around to see Livy Hull standing too close to a graduate trainee in accounting. Cradle snatcher. Mrs Plumridge was gesticulating in the middle of a small circle.

She had high spots on her cheeks and Plumridge was almost squirming.

'Excuse me . . .' Sally turned away from the FCO man and looked expectantly up into Tim's face. She liked his face. It was leaner, more angular than the vast majority in this bar. Less confident. She found that appealing.

Again he didn't know what to say. Mickey stepped in. He waved at the increasing loud, heavy-drinking throng. 'I love that story about George Brown having a few too many at an Austrian embassy reception. The band strikes up and George taps this person in a red dress on the shoulder for a dance. The person turns around and says, "There are three reasons why I will not dance with you, Mr Brown. Firstly, this is not a waltz, it is the Austrian National Anthem. Secondly, you are drunk. Thirdly, I am not a woman, I am the cardinal of Vienna."'

Sally put back her head to laugh. It was a controlled laugh, the muscles of her top lip pulling down the corners of her mouth. 'He sounds quite a character. Is he here?'

'He's dead,' said Tim slowly. 'Lord George Brown. Harold Wilson's number two. Deputy prime minister.'

He saw Sally grapple to fill the blankness in her face. 'Of course. How stupid.'

Williams re-emerged grinning triumphantly to announce that the registry was now going to put their de-activated files into the electronic retrieval system. He began speaking quietly to Sally. Mickey was talking to a Special Branch DI who was in the same shooting club. Tim momentarily stood alone. He finished his beer and slipped towards the exit. The prospect of escaping from the throng cheered him. Shame about leaving Sally but he couldn't handle all those people.

'Get after him,' hissed Williams.

As Tim waited to collect his Barbour from the cloakroom, Sally materialized at his elbow.

'I don't like parties, either,' she murmured.

They walked out into the night air. The rain from the

west had been and gone but the wet pavements still reflected the amber street lights.

'I hope you don't think I'm forward, but I need a drink,' said Sally. 'Just one to get over the madding crowd. There's a nice pub over there. Would you mind?'

No, he didn't mind.

They walked in silence across the road. Inside the pub, he went straight to the bar. 'What'll you have?'

'I don't know.' For someone who'd wanted a drink seconds ago, nothing seemed to appeal. 'What are you having?'

'I enjoy a pint of beer.'

'I'll have a small one, then.' It was the only time he ever saw her drink draught beer, he realized much later.

'Would you like to sit down?'

Sally smiled at his boyish eagerness to do the right thing.

'I'm all right standing at the bar. If you are.'

'Sure. Fine.' He tried to think of something to talk about. 'How do you know Williams, may I ask?'

'We go back a long way. He was a friend of my guardian.'

'Don't you have any relatives?'

'Not really.'

'No sisters or cousins or aunts.'

'No.' She pulled a comically sad face but beneath her play-acting, Sally saw pitfalls ahead, especially as she would be seeing Tim in the office. Double jeopardy. Usually the men she consorted with were interested only in themselves. Tim was different. 'And you? Have you any family?' she asked quickly.

'Sort of, but we don't stay in touch.'

'So you're alone.'

'Suppose so.'

'Cinders.'

They broke out laughing together.

58

'You're from Yorkshire. I can tell by the accent. It's very pretty up there, isn't it?'

'Parts of it are,' conceded Tim, who also did not want to talk about his home. 'The Dales are lovely.'

'Is that where you come from?'

'No. I come from a council estate near Leeds. The sort of place they have chip pan fires on Christmas Day.'

Sally gave a polite smile of incomprehension.

'How come you speak Russian and Arabic?' inquired Tim. 'It's a strange combination.'

'I grew up in the Middle East,' replied Sally, answering only half the question. She had a legend ready, well rehearsed and plausible.

'Really. Where?' He was genuinely interested. She could tell.

She opened her mouth, debating where to begin in the maze of half fact, someone else's facts and out-and-out lies. She was saved by Tim's keenness to do the decent thing.

His face creased in apology. 'Forgive me. I shouldn't ask such questions.'

He had taken her hesitation as a delicate way of telling him he was asking things he did not need to know. Infringing on an operational security of some kind. He could kick himself for his crassness. He kept forgetting: in this strange shadow world you didn't ask questions until you knew the answers.

'Oh, no . . .'

'Really . . .'

Putty in her hands. To show there were no hard feelings she smiled into his eyes. 'Tell me why you joined the Army?'

At ten o'clock they took a taxi to Gerrard Street, largely because Tim couldn't think of anywhere else to go. He didn't dine out in London. Chinatown was full, but the gods were smiling because they found a table and ate, drank and talked until midnight. Sally was easy to talk to, ready to smile and when he ran out of things to say, filled the silences with her own stories and chatter. She teased him for his accent and collapsed into giggles, trying to imitate Tim's deliberately broadened rendition of 'Where there's muck, there's brass.'

They parted with a chaste kiss on the cheek but Sally squeezed his hand so hard it hurt. As he travelled home he thought of the beguiling way she looked directly into his eyes as she listened but dropped her gaze when she spoke about herself.

It was only as he opened the front door that he realized he had never told her he was in the Army.

There were three letters on the hall table. Tim scanned them in the dim light, smelling the hot vinegar which told him the ground-floor flat had brought back chips for supper. The first letter was a bank statement, the second his monthly plastic bill, the third was in Linda's handwriting. He pressed the time switch and set off up the stairs in his nightly bid to get to the fifth floor before the light went out. He failed as always and fumbled in the dark for the keyhole.

Tim hung his damp coat on the back of a chair and stared out through the rain-smeared glass across the rooftops at the blurred street lights. Even though Linda's letter wasn't unexpected, it shattered the warmth and harmony of the evening into fragments sharp enough to draw blood. Finally he opened the envelope and tilted the page towards the tasselled lampshade above the table.

Linda hoped he did not mind her writing to him like this but they'd once meant everything to each other and she still had deep feelings for him. It was a shame things hadn't worked out. She hoped he thought of her sometimes and remembered the good times they'd shared.

Yes, Tim still thought of her. Laughing, funny, drunken, the centre of every party, living life as one long carnival, moving so fast the bill never caught up. She flirted shamelessly but anything that blatant had to be harmless, he'd told himself. And Linda tried so hard to please in so many many ways. He was infatuated, in so deep he couldn't see beyond the walls of the well, couldn't hear the stumbling hints from his mates. He – they – had bought a small, run-down house. In joint names. Linda had doffed in £500. He worked round the clock doing it up. Their love nest. He had never been happier. Then he went on exercise in Borneo. When he returned she had become withdrawn and tetchy.

It was almost two months before Linda announced she was pregnant. He was delighted – but the dates weren't right. That month he had been on exercise – his first command as an officer. She hadn't told him until she returned from the clinic – after the abortion.

Why? I wanted to believe. You could have fooled me. Babies are born premature, born late. I'm a man. What do I know? I wanted to believe.

The hag revealed herself. Not that simple, honey, she'd gloated. For in her pain she needed to bring him pain. Her talons were bloody indeed. You'd have noticed. Wrong colour. Always had a soft spot for a black man, just can't say no to them. Talons.

Tim had walked away from the house that afternoon. Walked away and never went back. She'd filled the house with her friends who paid more rent than the mortgage. He returned to the letter.

Things weren't going smoothly any more. Linda had lost her job and the friends had left. She was finding it hard to make ends meet. Perhaps they should sell the house.

I don't want to worry you but I'm hoping against hope that out of the goodness of your heart you will be able to see your way clear to helping me keep up the house, or in any way you can. I'm sorry if I hurt you. I never meant to.

Tim reached in his pocket and brought out another letter that had arrived in the office mail that morning – forwarded from Stirling Lines in Hereford. It was signed 'a well wisher'. The writer wanted him to know that a drugs dealer had moved into his house. There had been complaints about the loud music. The police had been informed.

Wednesday 4 March

Tim was in early next morning to find Plumridge in shirt-sleeves and braces, talking quietly to Alison. She blushed as though she had a guilty secret, but Plumridge grunted and returned to his lair. Tim glanced down at the trains and picked up an overnight report which had landed on his desk.

Defence Minister Marshal Igor Sergeyev had warned a secret session of the Russian Defence Secretariat that discipline had become so weak that there was a real danger of organized crime penetrating military units. The army was no longer capable of isolating itself from a society which was pervaded by banditry. There was an increasingly common practice among officers of striking commercial relationships with criminal businessmen . . .

His reading was interrupted by Alison bringing him a cup of coffee.

'Where were you last night?' inquired Tim. 'You said you were looking forward to the party.'

'I changed my mind. I didn't feel like it. Just as well, as Maisie's called in sick. I knew she couldn't handle the pressure. Was it any good?'

'I'm not the right one to ask. What did Plumridge say?'

'That his awful wife was loud and argumentative. She insisted in public that they had to buy the elder girl another pony. He's very fond of his daughters, isn't he?'

It was the first Tim had heard of it, but then Plumridge did not confide in him.

'Oh, Alison, I was wondering . . .' Livy Hull put her head around the door.

'Boo!'

Livy gave a strangled shriek and leapt, hand to her throat. A grinning Mickey emerged from behind her.

'That was not funny,' winced Livy. She patted his cheek, part slap, part caress.

'How'd you feel this morning?'

'I think I died in the night.'

'If that's all you did . . .'

'Yes. Thank you, sergeant.' Livy followed Alison in search of painkillers.

Mickey last night, sergeant this morning.

'At least she's been home,' commented Tim, noting Livy's different skirt and blouse.

'She always takes them back to her place. Into the spider's web. That poor young lad from accounting didn't stand a chance. I thought she was going to have him in the wine bar . . .'

Livy gratefully swallowed the two tablets and wondered why Sod's Law meant the Cousins always went hyper when she was feeling fragile. Some bright spark in the CIA had decided to take Saddam's Samson Option seriously and speculated that it was linked not to biological weapons but to missing nuclear suitcase bombs.

'At the height of the Cold War the Soviets made around 140 one-kilogram nuclear bombs disguised as suitcases,' she told Williams. 'They can only lay their hands on half of them.'

'Bloody careless. There could be one in a left-luggage locker at Waterloo as we speak.'

'Or Grand Central Station, which is what the Americans are worried about,' said Livy, taking off her glasses. This morning they were just too heavy to wear. 'The Americans can account for every gram of weapons-grade plutonium they've ever made. Perfectly documented and under the strictest security in the world. The Russians don't know how much they've made or where it is. They keep their records in Dickensian ledgers, and in the Kurchatov Institute in Moscow hundreds of discs of 97 per cent enriched weapons-grade uranium are stored in the sort of lockers schoolkids keep their gym kit in. So help me!'

'And these suitcase bombs can do genuine damage?' Williams could see Livy wanted to finish the session. She looked her age this morning – actually much older than her age.

'One exploding in Piccadilly Circus would kill around 20,000 instantly. Prevailing westerly winds would carry the fallout over the City and the East End. It might even sweep over Greenwich.'

'As long as that bloody traffic warden was caught out in it . . . But would Hindawi know about a nuclear device?'

Livy nodded and wished she hadn't. 'Interlocking Ba'ath party circles in the military, scientific and governing communities.'

Sally phoned Tim at four-thirty. She had been talking to someone else in the building first, for her call came through with an internal ring. Telling internal and external calls apart had been Mickey's first lesson.

'Hi. Remember me? Sally Chopsticks. What are you doing?'

'Um . . . Planning to meet you?'

Across the office, Mickey held up a thumb.

'Fuck off,' whispered Tim.

'What?'

'Nothing.'

'I left an umbrella in the Antelope off Sloane Square last week. I'm at the Royal College of Defence Studies so I thought I'd pick it up.' Sally paused. 'I hate going into pubs by myself. Do you know the Antelope?'

Yes, he knew it. 'Um . . . Okay.'

Maybe she sensed his reluctance. 'You don't have to.'

'No. No, really . . .' They arranged to meet at six and Tim told Mickey to stop smirking.

Striding out of the main door, Tim did not see the two men in black leather jackets sitting in a car in the side street.

65

The roving police patrols which quartered this area missed them, as did the CCTV cameras. The passenger jumped out and darted through the heavy traffic to get close to Tim before he was swallowed up in the rush hour. He stood behind Tim as he bought his ticket at Vauxhall underground station and got into the same northbound carriage. At Victoria he stayed very close, worrying that Tim might board a long-distance train which would pitch him out in a dark and alien countryside. Tim changed on to the District Line for one stop and emerged on to the surface. Leather jacket pressed the recall button on his mobile phone and read out 'Sloane Square' in a heavy accent.

Tim pushed open the narrow door to the bar with its old wooden floorboards and mismatching furniture. A comfortable pub – and a favourite with the guys at Group at the Duke of York's barracks a short march away. He was sipping a pint of beer when Sally appeared and Tim felt a surge of pride as other men eyed her. He bought her a drink and she explained she'd been translating Soviet General Staff papers, *circa* 1970. God! They were tedious. How had his day gone? Slowly, he said. There was a barrier between them. Last night they'd talked of everything and nothing. Today they were sober and starting afresh. Both were conscious they needed to make an effort.

Two men came in. One was built like a pit pony, short and sturdy; the other sleek, long-jawed, with dead eyes. Tim saw them and partly turned away. The SAS majors clocked him.

'They're staring at you,' whispered Sally.

'Looking's for free.' Tim nodded to them and they waved back.

Sally's intuition clicked. 'There's people here you don't want to meet, aren't there? That's why you were hesitant.' She placed a slender hand on his arm. Poor, shy, courteous Tim. 'You should have said. We'll go.'

'Once we've finished our drinks.' The officers had turned

away, probably discussing his presence. Tim and Sally made stilted conversation about last night's meal and their respective days until Sally downed her wine and pointed at Tim's glass.

'Come on.'

Outside they hesitated. Five yards away two large men in leather jackets lounging next to a black BMW pushed themselves upright. They reeked of trouble. Tim felt his nerve endings jangle.

'Go back inside.' Tim had no idea what this was about, but he didn't want Sally involved. These guys had picked the wrong place for a bundle, with the two SAS men the other side of the door. Then again, he should be able to handle them himself. They walked slowly towards him. Tim worked out his moves. Slam reverse into the one on his right, back heel into his left knee, elbow into the throat and a boot into the other's groin while he was still looking on. After that – he'd make it up.

The men were close now. Sally backed behind Tim. The nearer man gestured towards the car.

'*Brodyngi.*'

'Russians,' hissed Sally.

The man again indicated to the car.

'Vagabond?' translated Sally uncertainly. 'I don't understand.'

'Bolt?' demanded Tim.

'*Da. Brodyngi* Bolt,' repeated the Russian eagerly. The rear window of the BMW slid down.

'Teem. Teem. S'okay.' A rasping croak came from the back.

Tim approached the car and crouched down so his face was level with the window. In the darkness he made out the bull neck and cropped head of Dimitri Malenko, known as Bolt from the scar around his neck, the result of a knife to the throat in the gulag scab wars of the fifties.

'The *vor v zakonye* sends his greetings.' Bolt's voice barely carried. 'He wants you to have this.'

As he passed Tim a Sony Walkman, the men scuttled into the car. Tim was still crouching as the car pulled away.

'*Vor v zakonye?*' repeated Sally. 'Thief in law?'

'A thief in law is the head of a traditional Russian crime gang. His lieutenant is called the vagabond,' explained Tim.

'You know some strange people.'

Yuri Andreyevich Kornilov. The thief in law. Serious, grey-haired Yuri who had spent forty of his sixty-two years in prison.

'Not really,' said Tim. 'Let's play the tape.'

They squeezed into a booth in a pub across Sloane Square. He pushed the ashtray to one side and held the tape recorder out to Sally. 'Will you translate?'

'Are you sure?'

Yes, he was sure. He had no idea why the gang leader should send him a tape, but it wouldn't hold any secrets. Anyway, Yuri's vernacular, full of Cossack patois and prison slang, wasn't exactly language laboratory Russian.

Tim and Sally leant across the table towards each other. She pressed the play button.

'Greetings, Tim.' It was a peasant's voice, she noted. Old and harsh and used to being obeyed. 'I have a story to tell you. Make of it what you will. Eight years ago the authorities built what they called a scientific processing plant fifteen miles from my dacha near Aksay on the way to Novocherkassk. It was top secret, with Interior Ministry troops, the KGB and the military involved. High security. Deep bunkers. They said it was to make vaccines against diseases. Bollocks. We did not believe them . . .'

Tim had expected Sally to translate the tape in takes, but she kept up a simultaneous translation.

'. . . Soon we learn they are storing germs there. Germs from all over the country. But nothing happens so we forget about it. Recently a young Arab comes to me. He wanted to know if I could get something out of there. I said yes. That is no problem. I asked him why? For research he said. He lied. He asked if I could arrange to transport a small container to England. I said that it was no problem. He would pay $5 million. To see if he was serious, I asked for $10 million. That night he phoned from his hotel in Rostov to Jordan. The man in Jordan said he had to ask someone else. He called back one hour later and said yes. The next day the Arab tells me he cannot pay higher than $5 million. An . . . acquaintance who speaks Arabic listened to the calls so I know the Arab is a liar. I asked him why he is playing with the Devil's vomit and I threw him out. Tim, my friend, I made a mistake. The Arab went to a *tolkachi mussor*, a hustling piece of garbage called Igor Botkin. He will steal the germs and convey them to England. I fear what will happen. Tim, my friend. This is God's truth.'

Thursday 5 March

There was a rustle of papers as everyone read the transcript over again. Williams, at the head of the table, was holding a mug showing a sheep with the words, 'If Wales was flatter it would be larger than England'. Plumridge had a Sèvres cup and saucer, while Livy drank from a chipped and stained yellow mug she was forever rescuing from Alison's rubbish bin.

'If the Samson Option is genuine and Hindawi is out of the game, then it makes sense for Saddam to switch tracks, so to speak.' Williams put down his tea. 'Who is Yuri Andreyevich Kornilov?'

Tim, uncomfortable with everyone's eyes on him, cleared his throat. 'He's one of the leaders of the traditional *Vorovskoi Mir* – the Thieves' World.'

'A criminal?' sneered Plumridge, pulling the plate of biscuits nearer to him.

'Oh, yes,' replied Tim equably. 'The leader of a guild of thieves, a freemasonry, if you like. He's the Godfather of the Rostov on Don region in southern Russia – about the size of Scotland. Yuri's a robber, but privately incorruptible. His band work the old-fashioned way. They pool their earnings into a communal fund called an *obshchak*, take a salary and distribute the rest among the wives and families of those in prison.'

'He doesn't sound like the Russian Mafiya we deal with,' observed Livy.

'The Mafiya are the new criminals who deal in everything from drugs to prostitution. Yuri believes drugs are wrong. The new mob bosses have wealth beyond the ambitions of the old *vors* – but they lack moral leadership.'

70

'The parvenus of crime,' said Williams. Bloody Plumridge was scoffing the biscuits as if he'd not eaten for a week.

'With a parvenu's propensity to greed, ruthlessness and violence,' said Livy.

'Tell us why this man owes you, Tim?' coaxed Williams.

Yuri had heard of Tim's presence on the bodyguarding course – as he heard of everything. He invited Tim to his dacha. The keen young SAS sergeant and the old thief hit it off. In their different ways they shared similar ideals of loyalty and decency. Tim found himself in the middle of a turf war between Yuri and a band of young mobsters led by a twenty-four-year-old Georgian determined to make a name for himself.

'I was with Yuri and his daughter Petra when we were ambushed. I tried to protect her.'

'You were abetting a criminal?' demanded Plumridge.

'I happened to be there when he was attacked,' replied Tim.

'And . . .'

Gun flashes in the dark forest, the smell of damp grass and pine, the hoarse cries of frightened men and the screams of the wounded. The deafening boom of the grenade and he was lying across the soft body of Petra.

'We beat off the ambush,' he said shortly.

'Casualties?' Livy was leaning forward, eager to hear about spilt blood.

'Three dead, two wounded. They suffered more.'

'I bet he was delighted to have a Special Forces instructor as his right-hand man.' Plumridge continued to snipe. 'Wined and dined you, did he?'

'No. He was grieving.'

'For his three hoods?'

'For his daughter Petra.' Tim looked down at the table. 'She was one of the dead.'

Silence.

'And in spite of that this Yuri still wants to do you favours!' Plumridge sounded incredulous. 'Are you sure his chalice is not poisoned?'

71

Yes, he was sure.

'Why didn't Yuri phone you?' asked Livy. 'Why the melodrama?'

'He knows all international calls are monitored.' Tim shrugged. 'He's very secretive by nature.'

'We can accept that,' said Williams, watching Plumridge take the last biscuit. 'But does the story make sense. Di?'

Dotty Di from DERA nodded briskly, setting her jowls wobbling. 'Yes. The Russians pulled most of their C and B capability back from the outlying regions to the motherland in the early nineties. Same as they did with their nuclear stuff. We knew of Aksay but we were never sure of its function.'

'So Aksay's just a repository. Not a manufacturing plant?' insisted Williams.

'Don't know, old thing, to be honest. So many places to look. So few people doing the looking. Our Ivan's a right little Hydra. Clock him at Stepnagorsk and he pops up in an apartment block in St Petersburg.' She saw the looks of incomprehension. 'Satellite pictures showed a standard Stalinist apartment block. It was only when Alibek came over that we found out the block was really a biological warfare research plant.'

'But what do you think's stored at Aksay?'

'Oh, anything, dear heart. Anything at all.' Diana beamed. 'Anthrax, plague, smallpox, Ebola, Lassa fever, encephalitis. A veritable Pandora's box.'

'Thank you, Diana,' said Williams with heavy irony. She continued to beam.

'We've tapped into Interpol's computers in Lyons,' announced Plumridge. 'Igor Botkin is associated with a particularly nasty bunch of past and present KGB hoodlums, politicians, crooked businessmen and thugs called the Moscow Narco Group. As an indicator of their size and power, they've a large base in Cam Ranh Bay in Vietnam where they bring in drugs from South America. The drugs shipment we failed to intercept is believed to come from them.' He brushed crumbs off his tie and could not resist glancing accusingly at Tim. 'Igor, nickname the Polecat, is thirty-five. Aggressive new kid on the block. Believed to be controlling the southern swathe of drugs routes around the Black Sea into Europe either for himself or for the Narco Group.'

'Quite capable of stealing whatever it is the Arab wants?'

'Absolutely. Though he'd probably bribe his way in and out. He could transport it to England using Narco Group's connections.'

'There's a new KGB liaison man coming over later this month to discuss joint action on the Mafiya threat,' announced Livy.

'Assuming the door's open to the sweet shop and Igor can get his hand in the jar, who's after the candy? Who is this Arab?' Williams answered his own question. 'The phone call to Jordan suggests a Palestinian terrorist group, but would they have the funding or the reach for such an operation?'

'They certainly couldn't put their hands on ten million dollars just like that,' said Livy.

'Has Cheltenham anything to offer on this?'

'You know we've had to cut back our signals and intelligence effort on Russia as part of the peace dividend . . .' said Bill Jones.

'Not as much as *we've* had to,' snapped Livy.

Bill Jones continued to smile affably. '. . . But since 2100 Zulu last night we've been listening closely to southern Russia . . .'

The black phone – the secure land line – rang. Williams picked it up and after a second passed it to Bill Jones who began making notes.

'Did you see the story in the papers about the dog who wouldn't move from his master's grave. Stayed there howling piteously for a week,' whispered Mickey to Livy Hull.

'No! Oh, poor thing. They're so loyal. More loyal than humans.'

'Not really,' said Mickey. 'They'd trapped its tail under the gravestone.'

'Beast.'

Bill Jones came off the phone looking pleased with himself. 'That was good timing. At 0930 Zulu today a man made a phone call from Rostov Intourist hotel to a private number in a suburb of Damascus, Jordan. He said in Arabic, "The gates of Gaza are open." A man at the other end replied, "God is good." A minute later the Damascus number phoned the Baghdad home of Rihab Taha, the wife of Iraq's oil minister, and relayed the message.'

'Rihab Taha received an award from Saddam Hussein last January for scientific achievement. We don't know why,' said Commander Penn.

'A man in Baghdad said, "Uday will be delighted."'

'Saddam's elder son?'

'I don't know. It would make sense. Saddam keeps everything important inside the family and Uday heads his intelligence networks.'

'Oops,' said Livy.

Mickey brewed gunpowder tea so strong it melted spoons and left an indelible brown ring on every cup and mug it touched. Williams loved it.

'Thanks. I'd brush up the ambush tale, Tim. Just in case you're ever asked officially. How you had a weapon to return fire, that sort of thing.' Williams gazed out of the window. 'Those two trains are very close together, aren't they?'

'Different sections of signal track, sir,' explained Mickey.

'Really. Do you think British Rail – or whoever it is now – would let us see round the signal box?'

'Shouldn't be a problem. If necessary I'll say it's a security exercise.'

'That'd be interesting.' Williams's eyes lit up. 'You're going to Rostov tomorrow morning, Tim. Sally is going with you. Sorry, Mickey, but language is more important than muscle in this case. Alison is getting you visaed up as we speak. Try to get hold of Yuri today. Bill Jones will help you if you have problems.'

He put his head into the corridor. Sally entered looking shy and diffident. She did not like these office games. She had told Williams she believed Tim was straight. As straight as a die, to use the phrase she had recently acquired. Good, said Williams. But let's not make a final judgement yet.

Tim, too, felt ill at ease. Williams must have briefed Sally before he'd told him. A strange way of doing things!

'I've a great cover for you, Tim,' said Williams. 'You're researching a TV documentary on Andrei Romanovich Chikatilo. Cannibal killer and mass murderer. Rostov was his stalking ground. Try to appear a little more loveyish. A word, Sally.'

'Coming.' In the doorway she paused and beckoned to Tim. She whispered, 'You don't mind, do you?'

'No. No, not at all.' What could he say? 'Would you like to have dinner tonight? To make up for last night's abrupt ending.'

'I can't.' Sally stared at the knot in his tie. 'I've got to pack, wash my hair and get myself together. We'll see lots of each other in Russia.'

Sally's presence on the operation nagged away at Tim all afternoon. At dusk Williams wandered in on some pretext to look at the trains. They were alone and Tim took advantage of the informality of the situation to ask Williams about Sally.

'I hope I'm not prying or asking questions I shouldn't,' he stuttered. 'But we are to be working together.'

Williams took a second to reply. He knew he was going to have problems finding the correct verb. Acquire, recruit, adopt, bought.

'She was um . . . looked after by old Teddy Millibanks, used to be station head Cyprus, blown up in Beirut a few years ago. Saw her through university and brought her back here . . . She does odd jobs for us. Satisfied?'

Williams was more or less convinced that Sally had not known that Teddy Millibanks, old intelligence hand and shyster, had concocted a cock and bull legend which he spun to the Israelis. Nor had she known he had used operational funds to pay for her education. It was only after he was killed that London learnt they had an adoptive daughter. Williams wished he knew more. Sally had been picked up in an Israeli raid on a terrorist safe house. She had not spat, hissed or clawed at her captors. She had been unusually compliant. Teddy had acquired her in one of those labyrinthine Levantine deals. Williams suspected that he had claimed she was a freelance agent in place. For some reason it suited the Israelis to pretend to believe him.

As it happened Tim and Sally almost met that evening. Tim worked late to finish a paper which had to be returned to DIS archives before he went away and Mickey offered to give him a lift towards Piccadilly on his way home. Approaching Eaton Square they pulled around a Jaguar parked outside one of the larger porticoed terraces. If Tim had turned his head he would have seen Sally in a fine silk coat over a low-cut black dress on the arm of a man who escorted her into the back of the car. Sally was dressed to kill. Shining hair, perfect make-up, silver choker. The Russian businessman was entranced. They dined at the Savoy, where Sally turned heads as they entered. Throughout the meal she was coquettish and challenging in turn. She ignored the lapses in the Russian's table manners and merely sipped at each of the three bottles of wine he ordered. She forwent the second glass of cognac. Sally declined his offer to go back to his hotel suite and instead offered him champagne at the specially appointed Belgravia apartment.

Inside the elegant living room she carefully locked the

door, not bolting it, drew the curtains, brought out champagne and glasses and slipped out of her dress all within two minutes. Naked apart from hold-up silk stockings and a black lace tanga, she eased off his jacket, hung it over a chair in one movement and continued to undress him until with a whoop of merriment she led him into the bedroom and closed the door. She insisted on having the lights on.

Five minutes later a tiny red light in the face of the bedside alarm clock came on and Sally began murmuring with pleasure. When she thought she heard the faintest of sounds from next door – it could have just been her imagination – she threw herself on him in a frenzy. After four minutes the red light went out.

When the man finished, he insisted on returning to his hotel. Post-coital triste, an incipient hangover and the darkness of the Russian psyche threatened to overwhelm him. Tomorrow, perhaps. Perhaps, said Sally, knowing she would not be here. When he left she picked up the phone, but they were safely away.

Sally stayed in the shower a long time, washing away the memory of the night. Not much longer, Williams had said. Not much longer.

Friday 6 March

'Watch your handbag. There's an Old Russian saying, "If Odessa is the mother of crime, then Rostov is the father".'

'Oh, yes.' Sally knotted the strap of her bag around her wrist. 'And which old Russian went round saying that?'

The operation had stalled but on a personal level it was amazing how easily they had slipped into each other's company. Comfortable and effortless like long-time lovers. Despite the expertise of Bill Jones's department, calls to Yuri Kornilov's Rostov home and to his dacha brought a number unavailable tone or no reply. Vagaries of the Russian telephone system. To arrive unannounced would be an act of discourtesy but Tim was running out of time and politeness.

They had arrived in Rostov a few hours earlier having endured the Aeroflot flight from Ankara in the company of a cockroach which kept Tim amused by dancing on his broken arm rest. Now they had left the fourteen-storey concrete box of a hotel to hunt for a telephone without listeners attached. Next to the hotel was a scruffy park with benches with deeply carved bottoms which suggested a more horizontal use, as Sally put it, and lingering couples who appeared to be waiting for dark to try them out. In the centre, surrounded by stagnant pools full of cigarette ends, was a monument to Sergei Kirov. His copper boots, jodhpurs and military tunic had oxidized grey-green and his hand was raised in greeting. His words on the base were in colloquial Russian.

Sally read out, 'Fuck me! We've had a brilliant result. To

be honest, it really makes you want to go on living and living.'

Tim peered dubiously at the quotation. 'Where does it say Fuck me?'

'It doesn't,' admitted Sally with a grin. 'Interpreter's licence. That's what he would really have said.'

'Didn't do him much good though, did it?' said Tim. Sally looked at him questioningly. 'He was assassinated, allegedly by Trotskyists but probably by Stalin who used his death as the excuse for a purge.'

'I didn't know that,' she confessed.

Tim felt she should.

At the edge of the park they found a phone booth. They had to step over smashed panes of glass, but the phone worked. Tim inserted kopek coins. On the third ring someone answered.

'*Da*.' Tim recognized the voice, a rasping file on metal.

'Bolt. This is Tim. Is Yuri there?'

'No.'

'I am in Rostov.'

'I will meet you under the balls at five.' The line went dead.

'Chatty,' commented Sally. 'What are the balls?'

'You'll see. We've time to kill. Fancy a walk?'

'Promise I won't get mugged.'

'I'll protect you.'

'My hero.' For a moment Tim believed Sally was going to take his arm and snuggle up to him. But the moment passed and Sally stepped ahead around a puddle. Tim felt she was there to keep an eye on him. She was his minder. He couldn't have asked for a lovelier one.

They came to Bolshaya Sadovaya, the long, straight, tree-lined thoroughfare which runs through Rostov. The buildings were a mixture of grey Stalinist boxes and painted cottages which looked as if they had come in from the country for market day and stayed. Here and there were dilapidated mansions in pale greens and cranberry reds, the

79

legacy of the wealth of the *kuptsi* – the legendary merchants of the last century.

It was treacherously mild. A false spring, as the receptionist had told Sally. There would be more snow yet. But for the moment everyone was out enjoying the fine weather. Young boys played around the cannons under the original fortress wall, while giggling schoolgirls in white bows licked ice creams and shouted at each other. Sally was an obvious foreigner. She stood out in her thick reefer jacket, long bright woollen scarf, designer jeans and a Paddington Bear hat.

'Chikatilo picked up some of his victims here,' announced Tim as they came to a large square with bus and train stations. 'If we're being followed this is a natural place for us to visit.'

'Are we being followed?'

'I don't think so, but as we're simple TV researchers we won't go into anti-surveillance drills until we need to.' His voice softened to ask a favour. 'I love railway stations. Can we have a look inside?'

'Why do you love them?'

'I don't know. People going somewhere new, lovers meeting, travelling hopefully, arriving.'

'You're an old softie really, aren't you?' She gave his arm an affectionate squeeze. 'Come on.'

The dirt and stench of the teeming station committed serial GBH on their senses. Rostov was the gateway to the Caucasus. Trains rattling south for the mountains of Turkey stopped here, as did the ones heading north to the great Russian plains. The vast, crumbling building with its corridors reeking of urine was a melting pot of unwashed humanity. Swarthy Azeri women in bright headscarves sat on the floor by bundles of belongings and screamed at their urchin children, peasants in dull brown suits and knitted Fair Isle pullovers squatted next to cardboard suitcases, while loud Georgians with white teeth and fierce moustaches called out to Sally. She answered them with a challenging look and grin. They fell silent for a moment before they burst out cheering and laughing.

'What did they say?'

'Oh, just an invitation?'

'What did you say?'

'To keep themselves for their goats, they weren't big enough for real women.' She smiled sweetly up at him.

Tim was dumbfounded. Sally hadn't broken step. 'But . . . but you didn't seem to say that many words.'

'Verbal shorthand.'

They stood on the busy bridge over the broad Don and gazed towards the endless steppes stretching away eastward while Tim explained that, never mind what the geographers said, locals believed Asia started here.

He turned off the main road down an asphalt path which wound past jumbled huddles of small summer cottages and through corridors of acacias to a complex of restaurants and cafés known as a relaxation station. Tim looked back. There was no one in sight.

'Chikatilo killed one of his first victims here. Larisa Tkachenko, seventeen. Wild and unruly. Wore a claret red jacket. He bit her nipple off.'

'Ooh.' Sally winced and unthinkingly rubbed her breast with the palm of her hand.

Dusk was falling. They made their way slowly back towards the lights of the city. A young boy was showing off, balancing around the rim of a fountain as his mother smoked and gesticulated to a woman with a pram. The boy was getting more daring, striving for attention.

'It's going to end in tears,' murmured Sally.

As she spoke the boy slipped, threw out his arms, overbalanced and toppled in.

'He's fallen in the water,' exclaimed Tim in his best Goons voice.

'Sorry!' Sally was laughing but not knowing why.

'He's fallen in the water,' repeated Tim. 'You know the Goons, Eccles, Bluebottle, Colonel Bloodnock, Moriarty . . .'

'No.'

'Peter Sellers, Spike Milligan, Harry Secombe. The Goons were the beginning of modern comedy.'

'Must have been before my time,' said Sally.

At five minutes to five they began to make their way across the central park past the giant unfinished theatre begun fifteen years earlier. Tim threw his arms around Sally.

'You could have warned me you felt this way.' Her voice was muffled, her face pressed into his anorak.

Tim released her. 'One last check no one's following.'

He stopped next to a giant equestrian statue commemorating the Red Cavalry which had liberated Rostov from the Tsarists.

'Under the balls?' queried Sally.

'Look up.'

'Oooh. What a big horse!'

Bolt was bareheaded and held his huge arms close to his body as if to fend off an attack at any moment. His top coat was open to show a dun-coloured sweat shirt and ill-fitting jeans. He gave a grave smile and made the effort to speak.

'The *vor* was called to a *bratski krug*, a circle of brothers, in Moscow to settle a dispute. He could not refuse. I have told him you are here and he will return tomorrow.'

Sally saw the scar across his neck and thought it must have been a brave man who did that. Or a desperate one.

They sensed his relief when they declined his invitation to join him for a meal and a drink. His duties done, Bolt lumbered back into the gloom.

A collection of vaguely drunk, overweight, peroxide blonde prostitutes hung around the hotel entrance. Inside a live band was torturing a Beatles number from a dais guarded by enormous speakers. Couples shuffled round the tiny dance floor. Sally and Tim made faces at each other and headed back to the bar at one side of the foyer. The only beer was Canadian Molson lager. Sally had mineral water and they shared a red caviar open sandwich.

'So how did Chikatilo manage to kill fifty-three?' she asked.

'Luck, police incompetence, the secrecy of the Soviet system.'

'Did he confess when they caught him?'

'Yes. He had a wonderful memory. He took detectives to graves of victims they didn't even know about.'

'Why didn't they know?'

'No one had reported them missing.'

The reception area was filling up with European businessmen returning from their efforts to buy, sell or plunder in the crossroads city, its hinterland full of uneconomic coal mines and heavy industry, all going bankrupt, all seeking saviours. Each businessman had a Russian partner or minder with him.

'What a dark country. What happened to Chikatilo?'

'He was executed in a prison in Novocherkassk about thirty miles from here.'

Devayt gramov. That's what the Russians call the execution. Nine grams. The weight of the charge of the short round fired from a specially adapted Makarov service pistol, Tim explained. Chikatilo enters a windowless room. He is told to stand on a line inside the door. Crouching on a ledge over the doorway is an Interior Ministry executioner. Chikatilo will see the blood channel gouged in the floor. Boom. The executioner fires down through the skull. The corpse twitches and lies still.

'You know some very peculiar things, don't you?'

Another wave of international businessmen entered the foyer, avoiding eye contact with the pimps, drug pushers and currency dealers lounging around the walls. A slightly-built Arab man was leaving.

'Fancy another caviar buttie?' asked Tim, but Sally was up and running, her handkerchief over her mouth, beads of sweat visible on her forehead. 'Are you all right?'

Sally was already up the first flight of stairs stumbling towards her room. Tim thought he'd give her a few minutes before he went to see how she was. He'd started his second beer when the mobsters surrounded his table.

Sally lay on the thin mattress, immobile in shock. She had only just made her room as the waves of nausea surged over her body like a spring tide. On her hands and knees she had crawled into the bathroom and stayed there a long, long time. Now she stared blankly at the ceiling, amber from the glow of the street lamps. She didn't want to close her eyes because she believed that when she did so, she would see the camp. She was fooling herself, she knew. The memory was pressed into her, a die on her mind, whether she closed her eyes or not. The sound of the siren and then her mother screaming. There had been loud bangs and she was frightened. She could not have been more than four. She thought she had no clothes on although that could have been a later embellishment. A thump and a blast of hot air and she was falling, falling – like in a dream, except it wasn't a dream. She'd woken up on top of old Yusef, who let her ride on his back and pretended to be a horse. She touched his face and felt the bristles and smelled the black tobacco in his crinkled hair. She'd thought he was asleep and tried to wake him in their black tent. Men were shouting and women wailing. The plywood and iron sheets were torn away and brilliant sunlight filled her blinking eyes. Her mother snatched her up and held her so close she could not breathe, so she became frightened again until they gave her sweetmeats and oranges to suck. The men, sweating, hawking and spitting out the dust, had taken their Kalashnikovs and trudged off towards the distant hills. The younger boys made rifles out of pieces of wood and killed Israelis among the shacks of tarred packing cases and canvas until their rifles had to be put on the fires for warmth at night.

The squalor, the long queues at the two water taps, the dirt, the stench, the barbed wire were as much part of her life as the burning sun by day and the bitter, biting cold at night, so cold the desert stones would crack like ice. She never had any toys, her mother told her later. She played with her fingers, weaving them in front of her face, now a palm's frond, now an octopus's tentacles, now a tank's tracks. She was paler than the others in the camp and taller, and from the age of six she had a crush on Mahmoud the Martyr as he called himself once he'd heard of the Arab heroes slaughtered in the hijack at Mogadishu.

She didn't question why she did not have a father. So many women were bringing up children alone that it was a vast collective, every woman mother to every child. Her own mother was sunburn red with blue eyes and high cheekbones. She couldn't remember how old she was when she first noticed her mother was unique in having blue eyes and she wished she had them too. The Russian Woman, they called her. The Russian woman who'd chosen to be Palestinian. And her daughter with the spindly legs and ready tongue. Once when her mother had fallen sick, yet again, with the bad water, her friends had gathered round where she lay on her pile of rags and told her she should go back to Russia. Never mind how bad things were there, they could not be as bad as here in the dun mountains. But her mother had said no. She had made her choice. Here she had lived. Here she would die. And Sally – although that was not her name then – had let out a long sigh of relief because she was already planning to hide away if her mother left. Hide so she could stay near Mahmoud.

The brown bear rose up on its hind legs to growl a warning as the three men in tracksuits approached with Tim. It was shackled by its ankle to a short chain attached to a steel stanchion. A red semicircle had been painted on the ground around the bear which began to box with its massive paws. The men closed round Tim and hustled him on.

Tim was curious rather than scared. He knew the Russian Mafiya killed as a first option rather than the last so when the men handed him a note from Igor Botkin asking, in

English, to meet him and pledging his safety, he had decided to accept. The journey had been in silence through dense forest on a dead straight road, the fire-breaks opening on either side as pale windows in the oppressive night. Floodlights snapped on as the Mercedes drove through the electronically operated gates and in their glare Tim made out an American ranch house complete with wagon wheel on the white stucco wall. South Fork meets South Russia.

Tim was escorted into the living room. Two of the men folded their arms and watched him while a thick-necked lout with almost white hair cut in a pudding basin style went to find their master. An interior designer had created the room in warm barley shades with long, low sofas arranged in islands around glass tables and huge standard lamps casting a subdued light. But Russian love of kitsch had got to work. A pair of buffalo horns protruded over crossed US cavalry sabres on one wall, with a fan display of Winchester rifles and Colt pistols on another. The largest TV set Tim had ever seen dominated half the room. In the other half, a tigerskin rug, complete with head, led the eye towards a specially lit framed object. Four pages of a American magazine feature on Igor Botkin had been mounted behind non-reflective glass. IN THE LAIR OF THE POLECAT. The main picture showed a handsome blond man lounging on a large silk bed with two Nordic beauties wearing very little except pouts.

'I wish they had not called me Polecat. That is what my enemies call me.' The subject of the picture was almost six feet tall and well built, with straight fair hair and firm jaw. But in the flesh the movie star looks were marred by empty blue eyes, devoid of pity or emotion. The eyes of a psychopath. 'My friends call me Igor. You will call me Igor and I will call you Tim.'

He reeked of cologne and wore nothing but a white towelling robe with *Georges V, Paris* on the pocket, a chunky gold Rolex watch and tasselled loafers. A hard man, a dangerous man. He held out his hand. Tim took it and, at the last microsecond, adjusted his grip so that when the bone-crushing pressure came, he was able to exert the stronger grip. A muscle in Botkin's cheek twitched in frustration as Tim applied enough pressure to prevent him getting a squeeze on. He released Tim's hand and nodded curtly.

'You speak excellent English,' said Tim.

'Thank you,' Igor preened, the test of strength instantly forgotten. 'It is necessary to speak English to be an international businessman. Scotch? Glenlivet, Glenmorangie or Chivas Regal?'

He filled cut-glass tumblers as two women wearing small scraps of leather appeared in a doorway. Igor barked at them and they disappeared.

'Did you meet Boyar on the way in? My men are scared of him. I don't know why. Come, bring your glass and say hello.'

The bear was sitting on its haunches gnawing a bone the size of a man's thigh. Igor picked up a six-foot pole sharpened to a point and prodded him. Boyar growled deeply.

'Boyar is an Asian Brown bear – the most dangerous in the world.'

'*Ursus arctos*.' Tim nodded. There were stories of Asian Brown bears killing cows and carrying the carcasses across rivers, walking on their hind legs. They could outstrip a horse over a short distance. He recalled the survival lecture when they'd been warned about the bear; part of the build-up to a job in Siberia which was luckily aborted.

'Heyaah! Heyaah!' Igor darted in and rammed the pole into the bear's belly. Boyar glared balefully at his tormentor. Igor, lips drawn back in a cruel snarl, clouted him on the nose. The bear exploded into action, hurtling with amazing speed towards Igor. The Russian knew the length of the chain to an inch. The chain snapped tight and Boyar, right hind leg stretched out behind, fell in a clumsy heap, growling in pain and confusion.

'Be rather more fun if he wasn't chained,' observed Tim softly.

Igor ignored the jibe. 'I introduce Boyar to those who owe me money.'

Suddenly he was bored. He threw down the stick and turned back towards the house. In the living room he downed the tumbler of Scotch in one gulp and refilled it before bothering to see if Tim wanted more.

'I heard you had arrived in Rostov. Your . . .' He searched for a word and instead mimicked pulling a trigger. '. . . are still talked about. I expected a bigger man. Not taller but bigger.'

Tim refused to rise to the bait. Instead he sat quite still, letting Igor extend himself while he stayed compressed and contained.

'I would like us to be on the same side,' continued Igor, flopping on to a sofa.

'I'm on no one's side,' said Tim.

'But you came to see Yuri Andreyevich. You see, I know everything.' Igor looked smug.

'So what do you do?' demanded Tim, beginning to have an uncomfortable feeling that he had been invited here as part of a larger game.

'I am a businessman. I buy, I sell, I build. This is the new Russia. The Russia of opportunity. I was a *fartsovchik*, a street trader, I sold jeans and videos. I made connections. Yuri Andreyevich does not understand. Money is power. Not respect, money.' Igor rose and stalked to stand beside his magazine article, his proudest possession. 'We live in cruel times. You have to be more than tough to survive. You think my boys are tough, I can lick any of them. You have to know what you want and be prepared to get it, even if other people suffer. Maybe you call this selfishness, but a person aware of his selfish nature is a person who knows himself. He is a person capable of finding harmony between his acts and his deeds. Enlightened selfishness is an improvement on the communist years.'

Tim was sure he would find the speech in the cutting. 'But is it a justification for crime?'

'My friend, Russia is criminal. State, commerce and criminal are as one . . . Now I have a surprise for you.' He pushed a button on the phone. A moment later a girl with a pale, oval face and flaxen hair walked hesitantly into the room.

'Tim. A countrywoman of yours. Emma Bagg from Wiltshire. Say hello, Emma.'

She smiled uncertainly at Tim.

'Hello,' said Tim.

'Emma is at Rostov university. She's my English teacher.'

Emma dropped her eyes and blushed.

'I help Igor with commercial and legal documents. His English is really very good.' She spoke with the soft burr of her county.

'I put a notice in the university and Emma applied. I chose her from hundreds.'

'Ten,' corrected Emma. 'And three were Sudanese.'

The charm left Igor's eyes. He stabbed the phone again and immediately the two women appeared in the doorway. Igor put a hand on each of their naked behinds and disappeared without a word. Envy and relief struggled for supremacy in Emma's face.

'He doesn't like being contradicted,' she explained with a tight smile. 'Don't mind his little ways. He's all right, really. What are you doing here?'

Tim explained he was researching a TV programme on Chikatilo and that he'd only arrived that day.

'What's the weather like back home?'

'Wet.'

'I had a letter from Mum yesterday. She said it hadn't stopped raining for a fortnight. I don't mind the rain if I'm all wrapped up, but it makes it miserable round the farm. The muck gets everywhere.'

'Your dad's a farmer?'

'Nothing so posh. He's cowman for Mr Truckle outside Warminster. My dad's always talking about buying a farm but he never does anything towards it. I suppose BSE was enough to put anyone off cows and that's all my dad knows about.' Emma caught herself. 'I'm sorry, I'm not normally a chatterbox, but it's so nice to have someone to talk to.'

Tim learned that Emma was on her foreign language year away from Bath University. She had come to Rostov on Don last September. To be honest, she'd be glad when July came. She didn't think she'd be homesick but she was. Daft, wasn't it?

Tim was intrigued by her relationship with Igor Botkin, who he was already thinking of as the Polecat. Was she his mistress? She made a most unlikely gangster's moll.

'He needed someone to handle his English and German business correspondence. I speak to him in English and I'm teaching him German.'

Tim glanced down at her slender hands. Unthinkingly, Emma pulled down the sleeves of her sweater to hide her bitten fingernails.

'Do you spend much time out here with him?'

'Sometimes.' Emma made a little face. 'It's more . . . homely than the hall of residence. But you? Who are you making the film for?'

One of the independents, he told her. It's all commissioned stuff nowadays. 'What's university life like?'

A bit boring, she confessed. And Russia itself was so drab. 'Everything's sort of second-rate and ill-fitting.'

When Tim smiled to show he understood she was quick to return the smile and he saw how lonely she really was. How desperate to have a friend.

Emma hoped to become a teacher, she said, but she had to get her degree first. Rather than talk about herself, she was eager to know about Tim.

'Are you here by yourself?'

'No. I have an assistant with me.' He wasn't sure Sally would approve of the description.

'Oh.' Emma's face fell. 'I could have shown you around.'

'There's no reason why we shouldn't meet.'

'Oh, yes. Yes, please. That'd be nice.'

Igor reappeared in the doorway needlessly readjusting his bathrobe. The subtlety of a peasant in the Winter Palace. Emma stiffened.

'What would be nice?' he demanded.

'We were arranging to have tea in Rostov,' explained Tim, rising to his feet. It was his turn to become bored with the game, whatever it was.

'I don't know if I can spare her.'

Tim could not tell if it was a compliment or a declaration of proprietorial rights. 'I must get back. Are you coming?'

'No,' said Emma. 'I can't.'

'I've brought this for your approval. It's still to be fired.' Peter Poynter held out a round terracotta face with protruding tongue.

'Thank you. What is it?' Livy Hull was still recovering from the shock of finding him waiting for her on the doorstep of her flat as she arrived home from work. 'An evil spirit? A demonical dryad?'

'Just a face.'

Livy took her time undoing the various locks, thinking quickly of what she would find on the other side. Christ, she hoped that bloke last night had been discreet and tidy. But then men didn't wear earrings to leave under the pillows. They left semen stains on the sheets.

'You know it's always lovely to see you, but you could have told me you were coming up. There are telephones.' Damn Peter.

'Anyone would think you aren't pleased to see me.'

'Oh *no*,' Livy said in her 'mummy's reading a bedtime story' voice. She wrapped her arms around his broad torso. 'I'd like to see you *all* the time. But I could have got food in especially and I *am* coming down to Dorset tomorrow – work permitting.'

His beard, full, long and coarse, the sort of beard an artist should have, irritated her skin.

'I heard from Ross in the second post. Or maybe the only post – in that dump . . .' He said to spite her for his lukewarm welcome. Livy stiffened. It was her dump, her pile, her village, her county. She could disparage it because she belonged to it. He was the lodger, the unpaying guest. Peter realized his mistake, for he held her briefly before moving to the window where his bulk blocked out the Telecom Tower and the lights from the Italian restaurant opposite.

'I'll get you a drink. Let me change first.'

How many toothbrushes were out? She flew into the bathroom. Just one. Everything seemed all right. No razor or male deodorant.

Into the bedroom. The bed was unmade. Livy brushed down the sheets of scurf and small tightly curled hairs, wrinkling her nose in disgust at herself. God, wasn't it sordid when you weren't doing it! She turned the pillows and hung up her suit jacket. Peter had come to the bedroom door.

'I know you're not interested but Ross has suggested an exhibition.'

'I am interested. You know that. Please don't be in a pet, pet. I'll get you a drink and you can tell me all about it. It sounds good news.'

'It'd be held in the Bond Street gallery.'

'That's excellent, surely,' called Livy, her head in the fridge to see how much ice was left. None. 'Only beer or wine, I'm afraid. I always let stocks run down at the end of the week.'

'Wine.' He flung himself into a rattan chair which creaked in protest. 'It's not that simple.'

'Why? You have enough to show, don't you?'

Peter snorted impatiently. 'Enough to fill the gallery

twice over. Paintings, pottery, sculpture. But you don't understand. Ross will want it underwritten.'

'Underwritten?'

'See. I knew.' Peter Poynter banged his hand on the chair arm in frustration. 'It's like insurance . . . if things don't sell. And it's wrong, wrong, wrong. How can young artists afford it? It stifles talent. Bloody commercial galleries.'

'How much?'

'I don't know. Five, seven, maybe.' More like ten thousand but he didn't say.

'And this has to be found before the exhibition can go ahead?'

'Yes.' He sounded hopeless, a pathetic figure slumped in defeat. 'I'll try to talk Ross round. After all he's the one who says my work is eminently desirable . . .'

'And how will he want the money?' demanded Livy quietly.

Peter Poynter took time to answer, staring forlornly at his glass, a picture of dejection. He didn't meet her eyes. 'Cheque, I suppose.'

'All right. We'll find the money.' Livy was being business-like. 'Tell him to go ahead. I'll find the money.'

And for the first time Peter smiled.

Saturday 7 March

The restaurant fell quiet as the *vor v zakonye* entered. The manager and waiters lined up to show their respect and several men left their meals to kiss him on both cheeks and touch his hand. Nodding solemnly at the murmured words of greeting, Yuri finally reached the private dining room and took his place at the head of the table with an icy composure. He wore a pale grey double-breasted suit which had been pressed to within an inch of its life, but looked too large for his stooped frame. His grizzled, steel-grey hair was cut Gulag short and he sat square in his chair, his gleaming shoes resting squarely on the floor. He placed Tim on his right and Sally on his left. He was pale from so many years in prison cells and his teeth were too good to be his own, she decided. Three men sat facing the doorway.

'Once bodyguards were for men who wanted to look big,' said Yuri. 'Now I cannot go out without them.'

Plates of salami, cold pressed meats, chopped eggs with pale yolks, rye bread and vodka were brought to their table as Yuri apologized for his absence. He could not explain why Tim had failed to get through on the telephone. He would investigate. He wondered aloud whether his summons to Moscow was linked to Tim's business. Sally obviously fascinated him. Suddenly he released a torrent of lightning Russian at her.

'No, I'm British,' she answered in Russian.

Again he bombarded her so quickly that Tim could not follow.

'No, I'm British.' Sally, eyes wary, smiled to humour the old man.

Tim recounted his evening with Igor Botkin.

'The world is changing,' Yuri announced when he had finished. 'The honourable profession of thieves is becoming cluttered with former party officials, hustlers, bureaucrats and traders. The youngsters have no respect. All they want is money.'

The traditions of the *Vorovskoi Mir* extended back to the eighteenth century, Yuri explained to Sally. A real thief was not allowed to marry or have a family. He could not serve in the army, hold a job, pay taxes, have a residence permit or possess personal property. Thieves in law sought respect and influence rather than luxurious lifestyles. It used to be harder to be a thief than it was to be a member of the Communist Party. A real thief needed three sponsors, the party only two.

'If I'd worn a red tie as a Young Pioneer – as every Soviet child should – I could never have become a *vor v zakonye*,' said Yuri.

'Tim mentioned you have tattoos,' murmured Sally.

'Hah!' A proud twinkle came into Yuri's eye. He pushed back his chair and slowly rolled up his trousers to show stars tattooed on both knees. 'They mean that I will never kneel to any man. They can kill me but I will never kneel down.'

He unbuttoned his shirt to show a picture of Lenin on his chest.

'In the old days we believed a Soviet execution squad would never shoot at a portrait of Vladimir Ilitch. Some thieves had Stalin on their backs. I have a knight wearing a tiger skin – the symbol of manhood.'

Tim was anxious to learn about the Arab.

'I was approached through an intermediary. We set up a *strelka* . . .'

'Little arrow?' Sally did not understand.

'Slang for meeting,' explained Tim with a deadpan face.

'. . . I believed it would be a *teneviki* or a *chorniye* . . .'

'Shadow businessman or black, street names for Azeris or Chechens,' translated Tim.

Sally stuck her tongue out at him. Bolt's mobile phone rang. He left the room.

'. . . but he was Arab. About this high. Clean-shaven. He was not nervous. I smell fear and there was none on him.'

Bolt returned holding out a phone. 'They've stolen it,' he croaked. 'Last night.'

Yuri took the phone and listened intently. Finally he glanced at his watch and said, 'Shakhti railway station. Two hours.'

'They've broken in?' demanded Tim.

'A flask containing germs was taken last night. Its disappearance wouldn't normally be discovered for days, but I have a man checking every morning. We are meeting him.'

Tim realized the Polecat had summoned him last night to make sure he was out of the way, to provide an alibi. And to mock him.

'Thank God for your informant.'

'God has no part to play in this atheistic country. I put a technician on my payroll when the Arab approached me.'

'Thank you, Yuri Andreyevich.' Tim left to make a coded phone call to London.

'He is a good man, your Tim,' Yuri confided to Sally.

'He is not my Tim.'

Yuri gave her an old-fashioned look. 'You should make him so.'

Sally was curious. 'Why are you doing all this for him?'

'Did Tim tell you about an ambush?' He downed a glass of vodka in one.

'He said there was a pitched battle. I'm sorry about your daughter.'

'Tim shot the man who threw the hand grenade and threw himself on top of Petra to protect her. It was a million to one chance that the fragment stayed so low. It entered her head as he tried to shield her. He was willing to give his life for her.' Yuri's impassive face clouded and hardened and Sally glimpsed the man who had fought his way to power in a dozen Soviet prisons. 'I have a debt of honour. A debt this *mussor* Polecat has despoiled. He thinks I am old, he thinks I am dead, but I only slept. Slept too long. Lenin said, "This is not the time to stroke people's heads. Today hands will descend to split open skulls." He was right.'

Shakhti means The Mines and the name explained its existence. Black tips of coal waste were visible miles away before they reached the outskirts of the dingy, grey town. Each single-storey house had a small pile of coal before the front door. Every window was shuttered. The grubby, green-painted railway station was at the end of Yuri Gargarin Street, a long way from the town centre.

Gennady Tsana, in a black fur cap with earflaps, sat at a corner table in the buffet picking nervously at a bread roll. He bowed over Yuri's hand and told his story as if he was giving a police statement.

'I am a technician first grade. Every morning it is my job to inspect the freezer cabinets. This morning I found one in cold room B had been tampered with.' Gennady took off his black-rimmed glasses and rubbed them on his tie.

'Where are the cold rooms?' demanded Sally.

'They are all in deep underground bunkers.' Tsana resented questions from the woman. He addressed Yuri Andreyevich. 'We do not see the sunlight. See how pale I am, like a miner.'

'There are guards and security?' asked Sally.

Gennady threw up his hands. Guards! They had not been paid for a month. They'd sell their rifles for a bottle of vodka. But there was electronic security with coded number panels, identification badges scanned by lasers and even a palm print system, although it had not worked for six months. Things had deteriorated, but it would still be impossible for an outsider to break in.

'Do you make biological weapons?'

'No. We only store the germs.'

Each cold room held large stainless steel freezers, he explained. Inside the freezers were locked racks of containers holding flasks a little smaller than that one there. They turned to see a traveller was having his thermos flask filled with black tea from an urn. Seeing them looking, a red-headed girl held up a basket of tired meat pies. Sally shuddered at the thought of what was in them.

'The outer containers are sealed with wax, but the cold has cracked the seals so now no one can tell if they've been opened or not,' continued Gennady. 'Because of this I arranged the tops in a pattern. This morning I saw one had been moved. I unscrewed the top. It was empty. Someone has removed the inner flask.'

Sally opened her mouth as a huge locomotive with a red star on the front thundered through on its way north. They waited until the interminable express had passed.

'Who goes into these freezers?'

Gennady shrugged. 'No one.'

'So what was stolen?'

'I don't know.' Gennady dropped his eyes. 'Everything is coded by the room and row.'

'Someone must know,' growled Yuri.

'The director and the senior scientists.' Gennady was desperate to please. 'But I am only a technician. I only know it as KH131. But I can tell you it was one of the smaller flasks so it must be extremely lethal.'

A grey commuter train was pulling in as they left the buffet, tubby babushkas in thick coats struggling to carry their bags down the steep steps from the carriages to the ground.

'Chikatilo used to pick up his victims on that train,' said Tim.

Sally didn't reply. She and Bolt accompanied Gennady back to Aksay to see if they could discover exactly what had been stolen. Tim travelled back to Rostov to report to London and Yuri, intent and tight-lipped, did not say where he was going.

*   *   *

'With respect, Coordinator. We don't even know there's anything missing,' pointed out Maurice Plumridge. 'We only have one man's story. He admits the seals were already broken. The inner container could have been taken a long time ago – if there was ever anything there in the first place.'

'It's in the informant's financial interest to say something's been taken,' concurred Livy Hull, cross that she couldn't now get down to Dorset. And she hated agreeing with Plumridge on principle.

'Commander?' Williams, annoyed at the coalition building up against him, tried to break the DIS man's silence in his search for allies.

'Don't know. Have to take the view of the man on the spot. That what he's there for.'

'The man on the spot can be too close. Loses his objectivity. He wants to believe his Joe.'

'Captain Platt wouldn't do that,' declared Mickey stoutly. He might be speaking out of turn, but someone had to defend Tim.

'I think I agree,' said Williams.

'It would be easy for Yuri to have invented the Arab's approach and then get the technician to embroider his story by saying something's been stolen,' Livy suggested.

'But why? What does he gain? He hasn't asked for money.' Williams leant so far back in his chair he could see the electric plug at the base of the wall. He felt his vertebrae click. 'Diana, does the description of this place sound genuine?'

'Oh, yes. I think so. I think so, yes.' Dotty Di from DERA had the unnerving ability to follow the arguments silently with only her eyes moving as she became more and more wound up like a clockwork toy. Then someone pulled out the key and off she ran. 'It's not how we'd do it, but there's always a danger of applying western standards to others.' She leant forward with a jovial smile. 'We weren't always as careful ourselves. Did you know during the war fifteen ladies from a Bristol soap factory filled five million linseed cattle cakes with anthrax spores without wearing as much as a face mask. And do you know, not one fell ill.'

'Thank you, Diana.' Williams pushed himself back to see if he could make another vertebra crack.

'The Cousins are still banging on about the missing nuclear bombs,' reminded Livy.

'Pswah.' Dotty Di imitated a Battleship-class steam loco-motive climbing Shap Fell. 'Child's play. The most recent piece of American modelling compares a Hiroshima-size nuclear device – that's 12.5 kilotonnes of TNT – 300 kilograms of sarin nerve gas and 30 kilograms of anthrax. Who do you think wins? The gas is a total flop. Kills sixty to two hundred. The bomb accounts for between 23,000 and 80,000, but good old anthrax wipes out between 30,000 and 100,000.'

'Do we always have to come back to anthrax?' asked a pained Plumridge. Felicity had not been best pleased when he had been called in on Saturday morning. She had expected him to watch the girls ride.

'It's the US military's preferred biological warfare agent, although I'm not sure I agree with them,' Diana added in a sotto voce aside.

'Why?' Williams couldn't help asking.

'Why is it preferred? Because it's a silent, invisible killer. You get 100 million lethal doses per gram – that's 100,000 times deadlier than any chemical warfare agent.' Diana positively beamed. Such sense. Better than silly old bombs with all the destruction and damage they cause. 'It's low technology and cheap, cheap, cheap. Anthrax is easy to produce in large quantities and very easy to weaponize. It's stable and it can be stored almost indefinitely. You can freeze-dry it in munitions or simply pump it out as an aerosol.'

'Why don't you like it, then?' goaded Plumridge.

Diana shrugged coyly. 'I personally think there are better

agents, but anthrax does the job. Inhaling just eight thousand spores is almost certainly fatal. That might sound a lot but they weigh less than one-millionth of a gram.'

'We don't know what's been stolen is anthrax. I assume there are other agents?'

'Oh dearie me, yes. Yes of course.' Her plump face shook with indignation. Nature manipulated by evil was infinitely varied.

'Talk us through the options, Di,' requested Williams, beginning to mentally compose his overdue letter of appeal to Greenwich Council. 'Briefly, if you will.'

Diana smoothed down her voluminous long skirt and chortled in delight at being invited to talk about her pet bugs. 'Viruses are the simplest forms of micro-organism. They are unable to reproduce themselves, so they colonize other cells. Some spread in the air, others in blood or body fluids. Viruses cause the common cold, AIDS, herpes, smallpox, rabies, Ebola and her gentler sister Marburg . . .'

Dear Sir, I respectfully submit . . . I may as well be polite to the sods *. . . that there are no reasonable grounds for the parking attendant to believe that the vehicle remained at rest in the parking place . . .* Use their convoluted language back at them . . . *in circumstances specified in the Road Traffic Act 1991 (as amended).*

'Bacteria are one-cell organisms which can be fought by antibiotics. Bacteria cause illness either by invading tissues or producing toxins, some do both. Bacterial toxins include botulinum, ricin, tetanus and food poisoning. Rickettsia are a sort of midway between viruses and bacteria. In people, rickettsia cause typhus, Q fever and psittacosis.'

On Wednesday, 4 February, I inadvertently scratched out the month of January on the visitor's parking permit. This was not an attempt to defraud Greenwich council nor could it be. The visitor's parking permit could not have been used previously. 4 January 1998 was a Sunday and I had scratched out the Wednesday. Nor could the permit ever be used again. 4 January 1999 is a Saturday. Could the parking attendant ever believe it would be? Bloody jobsworth.

'Botulinum toxins cause a type of food poisoning called

botulism. The strain known as type A is simply the most dangerous substance known to man. The lethal dose is 0.3 or 0.4 micrograms and there's no effective antidote.'

The others were fascinated in spite of themselves.

'How do you die?' demanded Livy.

'Horribly, my dear,' boomed Diana cheerfully. 'But the beauty is that it's so hard to detect. Four hundred people were affected in the food poisoning outbreak in Scotland in 1996, but it took days before health authorities could positively identify the culprit as *E coli* 0157 in meat pie gravy.'

'Why so long?'

'When a doctor sees a patient with food poisoning he tries to guess the bacterium from the patient's symptoms and his account. There's a delay while samples are sent to the Public Health Laboratory Service for analysis. Standard microbiological tests take about forty-eight hours because you have to mash up the suspected food to allow the bacteria to grow. The process needs to be done carefully when, as in the case of *E coli* 0157, only ten of the organisms are enough to cause infection and there may be thousands of other bacteria present.'

'There must be quicker ways to identify the bugs,' said Plumridge.

'Oh, there are – but they're not normally used. Where was I? Oh, yes. There's shellfish poison known as saxitoxin, easily produced and soluble in water. A dab on the end of a rifle-fired flechette would kill in, say, fifteen minutes.'

I have paid for the permit, consequently a parking charge in respect for the vehicle has been made. You will see from the envelope containing the PCN that the parking attendant timed the envelope at 16.51. The PCN is timed at 14.51. The discrepancy shows how easy it is to make such mistakes. In the light of that error alone, I submit that to press the charge would not only be oppressive but alien to natural justice. Bastards.

'But all these have to be delivered. They have to be *weaponized*,' said Plumridge.

'Oh absolutely,' beamed Diana. 'The obvious way is by

dispersal in air. Some particles will be killed in the explosion if delivered by bomb, others destroyed in sunlight or extreme temperatures, anything can happen. But they're so numerous and so lethal that the bacterial agent will always get through. Of course, the particle has to be between one and five microns to be breathed into the lungs.'

'Well, that's a relief,' cried Livy.

'Oh, no, no, no, dearie. A simple paint sprayer produces just the right size.'

Sunday 8 March

Emma watched Tim get out of the big black Volga and enter the hotel and wondered what to do next. She'd been waiting for what seemed like ages in the hope of catching him and now her nerve failed her. Come on my girl. Nothing ventured and all that. It was a measure of her loneliness and homesickness that she was hanging around at all. Her mind was ashamed at herself for her brazenness and weakness, her body dodged buses and lorries to get to the hotel before Tim disappeared. She forced herself to slow to a casual saunter. Tim was turning away from reception, his room key in his hand. He saw her instantly. Emma studied his face for a flicker of annoyance, but she registered only surprise and mild pleasure.

'Hello. I was passing so I thought I'd drop in to see if I could help. Maybe translate for you.' The words came out too quickly.

'That's good of you,' said Tim. 'But my assistant's bilingual.'

'Oh, sorry.' Emma was deflated. She looked so sad that Tim held her hand for a moment and proposed a drink. There was nothing for him to do. It was up to others. For the moment he was superfluous and he hated it. He fetched Molson beers and red caviar open sandwiches from the bar.

'You know, you don't look like a TV person,' said Emma.

'Why not?'

'You're too clean-cut, somehow. You're more like a soldier.'

'I don't know if that's a compliment or not,' laughed Tim, thinking he must change the subject quickly. 'Your parents must be very proud of you.'

'Yes. I'm the only one of the Baggs to go to university. My mum reckons I take after her side of the family. She had an aunt who was a teacher. My dad's chuffed to bits. I'm an only child, so I suppose I'm something of a daddy's girl.'

'How did you become interested in Russia?'

'I had measles when I was thirteen. I was in bed, bored, and I got my hands on *Crime and Punishment*. I was fascinated. I fell in love with Russia – the image, not the reality,' she added somewhat sadly.

'Don't you have friends at the university?' Her fingernails were chewed to the quick, he noted again as she lifted her glass.

'There was a German girl, Maria, but she left last month. There's Igor, of course.'

'Boyfriends?' He wondered again if Polecat was a boyfriend.

'Not really.' Emma blushed and reached up to brush away a strand of hair.

'That's a nice watch,' observed Tim, catching sight of a Cartier.

'Igor gave it me.' She blushed even deeper.

'You won't see many of those in Wiltshire.'

'No. Do you know Wiltshire?'

Tim stopped himself saying he had been on army exercise there. 'Not really.'

'Oh, it's lovely. Huge skies. I know there's huge skies here but they're different somehow. These are cold, ours are warm. Like the people. That's what I miss. The people and village life. Things like the Heytesbury Extravaganza.'

'Sounds posh.'

Emma burst out laughing. 'It's a village fair held on the junior school playing field. Me and my dad run the stall where you have to follow the electric wire with a hoop without touching it. Mum helps with the cakes. It's to get money for the fireworks.'

'What fireworks?'

So Emma, face alight, told Tim of the big bonfire the

village held every November except last year when the man who was going to light the fireworks had a heart attack and now, because it's public, you must have someone with a proper fireworks certificate, or something like that and everyone was disappointed. She'd come home from college specially. In the holidays she sometimes worked behind the bar in the Prince Leopold in a nearby village. In summer she helped out at Bill Puddy's pony trekking . . .

As Emma talked away, Tim realized she had left all her best times behind in Wiltshire. You could take Emma out of Wiltshire. You could never take Wiltshire out of Emma. She was talking about Russia.

. . . They'd said Russian was the language of the future. But it wasn't, was it? Not any more. English was. And she already spoke that. Even though she spoke Russian and knew Rostov, she was a stranger here. She spoke of the dark, cruel Russian psyche. Hard on their animals, hard on their people. The least human race I know, she said.

Finally she caught sight of Tim's watch and said with a start that she had to leave. She didn't want to, but this was the one day of the week she saw her professor. Tim volunteered to walk her back and was rewarded by a grateful smile.

Bolshaya Sadovaya used to be called Engels Street, said Emma, pointing out places of interest. Tim, who knew most of them from his last visit, felt a fraud. He hadn't told her he had been here before and it was too late now.

'That's the public library on the corner of Voroshilovsky Prospekt where Chikatilo used to go to read the newspapers.' Emma was eager to help. 'Is this sort of thing useful?'

'Very,' replied Tim.

Emma thought it would be nice to hold hands but she did not suggest doing so. She walked very close to him, brushing his sleeve with hers. He had put her on the inside of the pavement. Very gentlemanly. No one had ever done that before.

'See that building over there.' Emma indicated an elegant four-storey mass of brown stone, taking up a whole block. 'This side's the main police station, the other half is the KGB or whatever they call themselves now.'

Standing near the KGB entrance, Igor Botkin was talking to a short, very broad man with the stamp of authority. Igor, bareheaded in a long black leather coat, seemed to be telling a story, for the other was listening and laughing, his head thrown back.

'There's Igor,' said Tim.

'Oh, yes.' Emma seemed disconcerted. 'He's with his KGB colonel friend. His name's Linnikov. He often comes out to the dacha. I think they must be business associates. I . . . I won't interrupt them.' She increased her pace.

The university's main building was white, modern and low. It was impressive from a distance but as they got close Tim saw the large jagged cracks in the steps, the windows grimy with dust and the façade mottled with damp and neglect.

'Thank you for walking me back.' Emma sounded very formal. She had not spoken much since they'd seen Igor. 'Can you find your way all right?'

She was not willing to let him go yet. There were words still unsaid.

'I'll see you again, I hope,' said Tim.

The tension was broken. 'Oh, yes. That'd be lovely. I'll leave a message at the hotel if you like. If I can do anything to help, anything at all, just let me know. Here's my address.'

She had it already written out. She slipped the piece of paper into his hand, kissed him on the cheek and ran up the steps.

Poor, pale, whey Emma, thought Tim as he made his way back. What a nice kid. So lonely. Know how she feels.

Yuri's dacha was old and made almost entirely of wood, with a primitive lavatory and a shower that only worked while you held down a chain. The floorboards were covered by coconut matting and the walls were prickled with large nails to hold various artifacts from hunting rifles to cooking ladles. A bottle of vodka, half empty or half full depending on whether you were an optimist or pessimist, sat on the oilcloth-covered table.

Sally and Tim arrived at the same time.

'Any news?'

'None,' replied Sally. 'Gennady still can't get at the records and he's scared of reporting something's missing in case he's suspected.'

'London aren't exactly pulling their hair out. Perhaps it's the weekend.'

'I've had a visit from my friend Colonel Linnikov,' announced Yuri. 'He says the Polecat is hiding the Arab in the city. He'll make a run for Odessa tonight guarded by a large escort.'

'Is this Linnikov short and broad?' demanded Tim.

Yuri nodded. 'Like a barrel.'

'Two hours ago I saw him laughing with Botkin outside KGB headquarters,' protested Tim.

Yuri handed them vodka glasses almost absentmindedly. He lifted his, held it high in a silent toast, then drained it in one and hurled the glass violently into the stone fireplace where it smashed into pieces. His eyes blazed.

'Of course you saw Linnikov with the Polecat. They work like that,' spat Yuri, linking his index fingers. 'Linnikov was born a Cossack, but he's sold out to Moscow. Now he's supposed to be one of the KGB's crime experts. Huh! He is more bandit than all of us together. He wants me to walk into a trap. The Arab escapes in another direction and my *razboiniki* get killed. A double victory for that scum Polecat. He will take over in Rostov.'

'We could turn the tables on the ambushers,' suggested Tim.

Yuri smiled. 'No. You're going to the real ambush.'

'And me,' said Sally.

'I don't know, little kitten.'

Sally put up such a fierce and determined argument the men gave in. She did not tell them she had more experience of ambushes than the pair of them put together.

Dad would have finished milking now. Emma, in her mind's eye, saw the milking parlour on a winter's night. The cows lined up under the naked electric light bulbs, steam rising off their stippled black and white flanks. The smell of manure and warm milk and the crackling frost in the yard. She returned to her dull little room in the hall of residence. One wall was filled with photographs of her mum and dad, Poppy the cat, Winnie her horse, her friends from the village, groups from university, one of her with her collie Jack in front of their bungalow. One of Boyar the bear. She wished Igor would not be so cruel to him, prodding him like that. Animals had a natural dignity. It wasn't right to keep him chained up.

Yes, dad would be coming home from milking and mum would be baking, filling the bungalow with warm homely smells. She'd be doing her homework ready for school in the morning. The evocation decided her to write home and tell them about Tim.

There was a perfunctory tap on the door and Igor strode in.

'Don't you ever knock?' Emma was annoyed at him barging in on her dreams rather than into her room. 'I could have had someone here.'

'I have a fax from Germany that needs translating. Wait outside,' he told his bodyguard leering over his shoulder. 'I shall not be long.'

Emma sat at her desk and read the fax. It set out proposed delivery dates and prices for a shipment of whisky in return for oil. She began typing a translation in Russian. Igor stood behind her. She stiffened at his touch and whispered, 'Please', when he first cupped her breast but she did not stop him undressing her as she worked, typing

109

away even as he made her rise to pull off her jeans and knickers. She refused to allow his brisk caresses to spoil her concentration, so her indifference made him angry and he viciously squeezed her nipple.

She gasped. 'Let me finish this.'

Later he complained that English women were cold. Clean but cold. Not like Russian women who reek of sex, sweat and perfume. When he had gone she put on her housecoat and went down the corridor to the bathroom. She hoped the water would be at least lukewarm.

The snow was easing, just the occasional flake swirling out of the darkness into the headlight beam like a tracer bullet. The two men in the cab of the military ambulance chain-smoked and listened to the whir of the cross-country tyres over the forest road. In the back under the dim red light, Tari sat on a stretcher wincing at his minder's snores and calculated how long it would take to reach Moscow so he could speak to his daughters. He thought of them often in this sullen and alien land. He pictured them playing together in the hills above the camp, always cheerful, always laughing. He hoped they were not miserable in Baghdad. The mission had been a success. The Iraqi money would buy surface to air missiles for the true Palestinian freedom fighters. Give the Israelis and their own traitors something to think about. Gaza International Airport! Crap. He'd bomb it to hell and back. That would teach Arafat and his clique to make peace. They were too busy feathering their own nests to remember the poor and the homeless; the dispossessed millions. He would remind them. Linnikov would be able to help get the missiles. The drumming of the tyres lulled him to sleep. He closed his eyes and smiled at his girls.

He awoke as the driver jabbed the brakes, once, twice. Tari slid open the flap to peer into the cab and grabbed the wooden packing case by its rope handle. Through the small windscreen he saw a militiaman, red band around his hat, holding up a lamp and waving to them to slow down. Ahead he made out the reflection of a flashing blue light through the trees.

'Tell him we are on a special mission. We cannot stop for anyone,' hissed Tari. The militiaman stood aside and they coasted around the corner.

A car lay on its side. A police cruiser blocked the rest of the road. Another militiaman was walking towards them.

Tari's nerve endings tingled. It smelled wrong. It was too neat and tidy. There were no marks on the road where the car had skidded, no trail of debris. All too organized. He made up his mind. Ten yards ahead a track led off into the trees.

'Don't stop. It's a trap. Take that track on the left. Go!'

Tari clung to the box as the ambulance accelerated, skidded, bounced off a bank and jolted up the rough path between silver birches. The snow twinkled in the starlight. Through the trees Tari made out two horsemen standing perfectly still, their long white capes covering their mounts' backs. They had carbines over their shoulders and the horses breathed clouds of steam into the night air. Tari was still blinking at the sight when he saw the tree trunk across the track. His minder clicked off the safety catch of the Uzi machine pistol.

'Now!' The green ambulance lurched past and a second tree crashed across the track behind it.

'Go. Go.' Tim wrenched open the front door and rammed his Kalashnikov in the ribs of the driver. Do not shoot unless you have to, he had instructed the assault team. Hit the flask and we die. Surprise, speed and violence were all. Tim grabbed the driver desperately trying to turn the steering wheel and heaved backwards. The passenger was screaming defiance. A metal door slammed and a short burst of automatic fire came from the rear. Young Sasha staggered round the side. He leaned against the side of the ambulance and slid down on to the snow. Tim swore. He had taken the cab because he believed the Arab would be there. He was wrong. He chopped the driver with the rifle stock and ran towards the rear of the ambulance. He gathered himself to burst around the corner when someone big and heavy crashed into him. The man smashed a machine pistol into his face. As he dropped Tim lashed out and caught the man's legs so he too fell. They lay ten feet apart in the snow. Tim was aware of the other's breath vaporizing in the cold air. For a microsecond they stared at each other, then both began to bring up their weapons to bear. Tim cursed the longer barrel of the Kalashnikov. It was all happening in slow motion and Tim was losing the race. The muzzle of the Uzi gaped like a tunnel. Hell!

Crack. Crack. The man's cheek exploded in a bloody cloud of bone and tissue. Sally stood wide-eyed, both hands around a small Biretta automatic.

A figure, wrapped up in top coat, scarf and hat, shot out of the back of the ambulance clutching a wooden box. There were shots from the front and the sound of breaking glass.

'Stop him.'

Tari had one thought – to escape. Escape with the flask. The trees were all around. Even with the eerie light from the snow, if he could only gain the undergrowth . . .

Tim made a despairing lunge to ankle tap the fleeing figure, who stumbled and almost fell. Tari put his hand on the ground to steady himself. Tim grabbed at the rope handle.

The Arab kicked Tim in the head. Ignoring the blows, Tim flung himself forwards to grasp the handle in both hands. He jerked hard. The box slipped through Tari's gloved fingers.

Tim lay panting on the ground as the swaddled figure raised a gun and pointed it at his head.

'Shoot him, Sally.'

A horseman galloped towards them waving a carbine. His mount shied at Tim who dropped over the virus to protect it. The horse reared and wheeled. There was a flash, a shot and the rider screamed in pain. In one movement Tari pushed the wounded man out of the saddle and scrambled up.

Tim grabbed his Kalashnikov and fired two snap shots. He missed. He rose on one knee, breathed deeply and tracked the Arab fighting to control the plunging horse. He slid nicely into the foresight. Tim took up the first pressure on the trigger.

Shit. Sally was running in front of him between his rifle and his target. She was firing wildly.

'Sally. Get down.'

Too late. The horseman galloped off between the trees. With hoarse cries two other riders set off in pursuit.

'Are you all right?' There was genuine concern in her voice. She knelt beside Tim and gently dabbed at his bloody mouth with her handkerchief.

'Thanks for that.' He squeezed her shoulder. 'Where'd you get the gun?'

'I persuaded Bolt. It wasn't difficult.'

Sally began shivering. Her hands trembled and she hid them in her pockets. Tim rose and wrapped his arms around her. How small and slender she was. Vulnerable somehow. Sally put her head against his chest and wept.

Beside them the small wooden box sat upright in the trampled and bloody snow.

Sasha's body lay in a pine coffin on a trestle table with two candles at his head. The oil lamp hanging from the roof cast soft shadows around the shed where the men scuffing the black earth floor were already on their second bottle of vodka.

'Our comrade Sasha.'

'Sasha.' They downed their glasses in one.

Sally bowed her head before the open coffin. Viewed from the left side Sasha might have been sleeping. Only from the right could you see the puckered hole in his temple and the brown blood which still seeped out. What a waste of a young life. Good-looking boy. Didn't look as if he had ever shaved in his life. His comrades had placed a spray of red forest berries on dark foliage around his head. Sally found it was beautiful and very sad.

'In Russian, red – *krasnii* – shares the same semantic root as the word for beauty – *krasivii* – and in the older version of the language they were synonymous,' she explained to Tim. 'Brown – *korichnevii* – is close to fundamental or root – *karennoi*.'

'Sasha was a true *patseni*, a warrior,' proclaimed Yuri. 'He fought for his fellows. He gave his life for his fellows. His family will not want. We shall look after them. What is more important than anything else, more important than money, is friendship. The more friends a person has, the better he is. That's what gives us strength.'

'*Pravilno batya*. That's right, father!' The dark shapes raised their glasses once again, gigantic shadows looming across the rough walls. An incense burner swinging from the rafters made the air heavy and fragrant.

'Always help one another, stay close to each other. This is our dignity as *blatnye*. Everyone will fear us. No one will break us. Together we are strong.'

'*Pravilno batya*.'

'The communists succeeded in grinding into dust the intelligentsia, the White Guards, the Church, the Monarchy. They destroyed everything for the sake of their own ideology, but they failed to destroy us. We shared comradeship and we rejected materialism. Our worth was measured differently. We outlasted Stalin, Lenin, all of them, because we were crystal pure. We were frozen between death and growth, but we survived.'

His men banged their vodka glasses in agreement as Yuri fought to persuade himself as much as his men that they still had a role to play in a world which was changing and leaving them behind. And that Sasha was not a twenty-year-old wide boy but part of an ancient tradition and to die as he did was honourable.

But Yuri was an anachronism, Tim knew. The power of the *vors* was failing before the onslaught of greed and corruption. The fall of communism was responsible for the rise of the new Mafiya, but the schism had begun in the gulag scab wars of the 1950s between those who had fought against the Germans in the Great Patriotic War and those who believed putting on a uniform was a betrayal of their principles. They identified themselves by their tattoos. Blue for the traditional gangsters. White for the budding crime tycoons. The scabs – *suki* – who survived the wars broke their ties with the old criminal establishment. When they were released they became black marketeers, ideally placed to capitalize on the post-communist corruption and chaos. They cared nothing for tradition.

'This new Mafiya has no culture,' insisted Yuri. 'They think because they have merged with the governing apparat no one can fight them, but they have lost the most precious thing. The respect of the people.'

From under the coffin he brought out the wooden box with the rope handle. It was some fifty centimetres high and shaped like one of those boxes which hold expensive bottles of port. Yuri prised it open with his jackknife. Woodchips tumbled out exposing an aluminium container. Wedged tightly inside that was a cross between a cocktail shaker and a thermos flask. Over the yellow and black international symbol for a biohazard was a handwritten name in black ink. Yuri solemnly handed the flask to Tim.

Monday 9 March

'Where are the girls?' yawned Plumridge.

'Where do you think they are?' shot back Felicity, putting breakfast dishes in the dishwasher. 'Move out of the way.'

Plumridge, bleary-eyed and heavy-legged, was not up to guessing games. But he wasn't brave enough to take on his wife when she was in one of these moods either.

'I don't know,' he said meekly.

'Tabitha's cycled down to the stables to put out the feeds before school and Phaedre's gone to her harp class. You'd know that if you'd come in at a reasonable time last night.'

'It was only around ten o'clock.'

'It was half past ten and you were reeking of whisky,' snapped Felicity.

'There's a flap on in Russia.'

'There's always something,' she sneered. 'And don't stand there like a useless lump. If you want breakfast you can get it yourself.'

There was a crunch of tyres on the gravel. Felicity instinctively inspected herself in the small kitchen mirror and pulled a strand of hair behind her ear. Even at eight in the morning she wore light make-up.

'Good. It's the man from the garage for the Range Rover. I got him at home yesterday. At least someone's efficient around here.'

She swept out as Plumridge helped himself to the remains of the carton of orange juice and dropped two pieces of sliced bread in the toaster.

'What's wrong with the Range Rover?' he inquired when she returned.

'The horse box virtually came off yesterday. It almost put us in a ditch, but of course you don't care because you weren't here.'

'There must be something wrong with the towing mechanism.'

'Of course there's something wrong with the towing mechanism. Don't be even more stupid than you normally are.'

'More money,' sighed Plumridge.

His wife slammed shut a cupboard door with enough force to make his plate rattle. 'It's my money. Just remember that. If we had to rely on your salary I don't know where we'd be. So don't start . . .'

Monday. Bloody Monday. Except it wasn't really the start to the week because he'd not had the weekend off.

'How am I going to get to the station without the Range Rover?'

'I'll take you in the Golf, but you'll have to go now because I'm picking up Tabitha. You can stuff your face in the car. Hurry up.'

'Our Timmy's come up trumps.' Williams was delighted. He even smiled benignly down at an early tourist boat. His hopes that the others would be equally pleased was about to be dispelled.

'About time,' said Plumridge sourly, still smarting from his breakfast humiliation.

'Do we know what exactly he's snatched?' demanded Livy Hull.

'Not yet. Communications are not secure. Just a call to Moscow. Not even Tim. A Russian voice.' Williams assumed a suitable bass. 'Bin-go. Bin-go.'

'So we don't actually know where Tim is at the moment. Or whether he and the girl are even alive . . .'

'Oh, really!'

'The code word could have been extracted from them,' said Livy. She was not in a good mood. Peter Poynter had

117

returned to Dorset at the weekend, leaving her alone in London. Angry with Peter in particular and life in general, she was grateful for anything which gave her the chance to work out her frustrations.

'Being a little fanciful, aren't you?' snorted Williams.

'What if we set up an escape route for them and the flask and it's not them,' persisted Livy. 'We'd find we'd invited the Trojan horse into the citadel and it had staggers.'

'Don't forget, legally Tim is guilty of being an accessory after the fact. He is in possession of Russian state property,' pointed out Plumridge.

'You're not suggesting we give it back, are you?' exclaimed Williams. Ten floors below the London fire brigade boat *Phoenix* was slowly heading upstream.

'This development has caught us by surprise,' admitted Plumridge. 'We didn't know he was going to use his initiative in such a dramatic way.'

Present Plumridge and Livy Hull with a gift horse and they'd reject it for having bad teeth, fumed Williams. Dotty Di was fidgeting, eager to be included.

'Can we destroy the flask, Diana?' demanded Williams.

'Oh, absolutely. But I'd like to know what I was destroying. Different organisms have varying susceptibilities and resistances.'

'Fire?'

'It would need to be very hot.'

'A furnace?'

'Oh no.' Diana winced. 'The flask would explode in an open furnace. It would have to be destroyed in a sealed incinerator. If the virus gets into the atmosphere . . . Oh no.'

'Down a drain?'

This time Diana actually shuddered. 'God forbid.'

'Well, we can't give it back,' said Williams, becoming increasingly annoyed at what he saw were sophistic considerations. 'Tim can hardly drive up to the gates of this blessed place and say here's your germs back. Look after them better this time. The way the Russian mind works, the guard would open it to make sure Tim hadn't nicked a gram or two.'

'And he can't leave it in his friends' hands. That would be unthinkable,' declared Plumridge.

'We'd love to know what these naughty Russians have been up to,' coaxed Diana. 'Then we could work on an antidote.'

'Do we have the moral authority to ask Tim to carry this flask? Think of the dangers inherent on the journey. Imagine if it slipped out at Moscow airport . . .'

'The Americans once released harmless bacteria in Washington airport as an experiment,' beamed Diana. 'It ended up in 200 different cities throughout the States.'

'What about sending an RAF plane to Turkey to collect it?' asked Diana.

'Whose budget?' snapped Plumridge.

'We can't bury it, we can't destroy it, we can't give it back. Anything else we can't do?' demanded Williams with heavy irony.

'We can't do nothing,' smiled Diana.

'It would be wrong of us to take a unilateral assumption of moral or legal responsibility for the flask,' concluded Plumridge.

Pompous oaf. You're paid to take decisions, not run away from them, thought Williams, continuing to smile benignly.

'I'll prioritize it at Steering Committee this afternoon, although it'll mean a delay in bringing back Tim and Sally. Every hour they're out there increases their danger.'

Yuri's men brought two messages from the hotel to the dacha where Tim and Sally were staying. A fax from a British merchant bank in Moscow asked for more details of the consignment and hoped that transportation could be delayed for twenty-four hours, and a handwritten note from Emma said she was sorry she had missed Tim when she'd called and hoped to see him before he left.

'It's a trap,' declared Yuri as Tim prepared to drive to the university.

Tim didn't think so. He believed Emma was lonely and homesick. But he had been betrayed by a woman before.

'You can come if you wish,' he told Sally.

'Wouldn't dream of it. Two's company, three's a whatsit.'

'Emma's very sweet.'

'So are almonds, but you can choke on them.' She put her hand on Tim's arm. 'Take care. I know you feel sorry for her, but make sure you're not walking into an ambush.'

Three bodyguards accompanied Tim. One went ahead and knocked on Emma's door, announcing there was a call for her on the communal phone in the alcove under the stairwell. Emma, face alight, ran down the corridor, the soles of her slippers slapping on the linoleum floor. Tim watched from a distance as she picked up the receiver. Her anticipation gave way to confusion and then disappointment when she found no one on the other end. The messenger gave Tim the thumbs up.

Three minutes later Emma was plugging in her electric kettle, making sure she had enough powdered milk and delighted to sacrifice the last of her Tetley tea bags. She wished she had biscuits but she hadn't entertained a guest in her room for ages. Tim sat upright on the edge of the bed trying not to let the barrel of the Makarov automatic dig into his kidneys.

Emma darted to the door and locked it. 'People have no manners around here. They're always barging in unannounced,' she explained blithely.

She wondered if Tim would take it as his cue to crush her in his arms but instead he told her he'd be flying back to London soon. Her face fell.

'I'll write if you like,' he said.

120

They exchanged addresses. There were pauses when each searched for something to say but the harder they tried, the more shy they became.

Emma cursed herself for not being a forward hussy like Maria. She would have had Tim in bed by now. Emma hadn't even sat next to him. She wanted to touch him, kiss him, hold him, but her natural reticence meant she did not know where to start. If only he'd make the first move . . .

As the minutes passed she became increasingly anxious that the opportunity for a wonderful memory was slipping away. And Tim, fond, pitying, protective Tim, did not have a clue of Emma's desires. Instead his mind was on the unfinished operation, angry at London for dithering and hoping they'd make up their minds sooner rather than later. The longer they delayed, the more time Polecat had to strike back. Tim wished now he'd grabbed the flask and kept running – all the way to the British embassy in Moscow. Then let the diplomats sort it out.

'When are you next home?' he asked.

'I'm hoping to get back for the Easter holidays if I can get a cheap Aeroflot flight – otherwise I won't be able to afford it until July. My best friend is getting married and I'm a bridesmaid, but that's a lifetime away.'

'It's not so long. It's amazing how quickly time goes.'

'Only when you're enjoying yourself,' she said.

All too soon Tim announced he had to leave. No, thank you. Two cups was enough. I really must go. He sounded genuinely reluctant. When she helped him on with his anorak, Emma stood so close that all he had to do was incline his head and kiss her. As their lips touched she threw her arms around his neck.

'Perhaps I'll see you in England?'

'Stay in my place in London, if you're passing through . . .'

'Can I? That'd be brilliant.'

'Yes of course. Take care.'

'And you. Take care. Have a safe journey.'

Emma managed to close the door before the first tear trickled down her cheek. She sniffed in derision at herself. A stupid cold little girl. Igor was right. A real woman would have known how to seduce her man.

Tuesday 10 March

The snow was falling again. Soft, stealthy flakes which felt for their faces and caught in their eyelashes. Silently the stark memorials, grand mausoleums and rectangular headstones were being softened and rounded. Their feet scrunched on the gravel.

'That could have been me,' said Tim, looking at the coffin ahead. 'I actually thought I'd had it. For the first time I reckoned my end had come.'

Sally, small and dainty in the cortège of bulky overcoats wending its way through the cemetery, tucked an arm through his. Although Tim did not know, she had saved not one life but two.

'What was it like?'

'I remember being frustrated and annoyed because my first instinct had been not to carry a Kalashnikov. Too cumbersome.' He squeezed her arm. 'Thank you. Where did you learn to shoot like that?'

'Finishing school.'

She had fired her first shot with the same model of Biretta. In those days it had seemed enormous and heavy. The first time Mahmoud touched her was to move her shoulders into the correct position and lower her into a crouch with both arms extended. Feet apart, evenly balanced, both eyes open, push pull with your hands. She jerked at the trigger and the sound of the shot deafened her. The tin can leapt in the air. She had been thirteen. She did a dance of joy and threw her arms around his neck. He had taken the pistol from her and scolded her for capering with a loaded weapon.

Six men walked ahead carrying the coffin, draped in

nature's own shroud of snow. Tim had been surprised when he learnt the men came here once a fortnight to visit their dead. 'For us it is a ritual,' explained Yuri. 'To show our respect for those who taught us and went before.'

'Sorry I went to pieces after the ambush,' said Sally.

'There's nothing wrong with that. I know blokes, hard as teak, who throw up afterwards. Just reaction. No one can help it.'

Sally had thought she would never stop shaking. That was always my weakness. The others used to laugh at me but I can't help it. At the time I'm like ice, but later I turn to slush.

They stopped a respectful distance from the mourners surrounding the grave. Some carried pictures of the dead boy. Sasha's mother and sisters, swathed in black, clung to each other, swaying in grief.

Sasha's body was lowered in the grave to the wails of the womenfolk. The priest began intoning in a vibrant baritone . . . there was a deep roar and the earth heaved upwards and sidewards. Sally felt she was inside one of those little plastic snowstorms and someone was shaking it violently. The blast hurled her off her feet behind a granite headstone which protected her from the falling masonry, debris and severed limbs.

The two light blue Toyota Land Cruisers turned off the potholed main road into the shade of the residential avenue. Last week's rain had cut deep ruts and troughs into the gravel shale, making the black saloon which had followed them wallow on its soft springs.

'Yeh, I see him,' growled Shane Cosker into his mobile phone to the second Land Cruiser. The Australian head of the eight United Nations inspectors grimaced in frustration. 'Hey, you guys, Bad Penny's turned up again.'

'Aw shit,' exclaimed Tennessee Joe Bradley, their American biological weapons expert. 'You can bet a dime to a dollar he's on the radio to his pals ahead. What I'd give to get this job done properly for once without these ragheads fucking us around.'

'Remember, guys, stay loose. Don't let them get to you. Whatever happens keep your cool and smile, smile, smile. Shit!' They bounced into another axle-bending hole. 'Left here.'

The crumbling villas in the Baghdad suburb had once been painted genteel pastel greens, blues and pinks, but the colours had faded and the façades were stained with damp. Ornate ironwork balconies had rusted, gardens were overgrown and untended and a wooden shutter hung limply by one hinge.

'Must have been nice around here once,' observed Cosker.

'If Saddam ever plays ball and the sanctions come off, I'm going to get into the Iraqi paint industry on the ground floor.'

'Is it easy to make paint?' asked Cosker.

'About the same as anthrax,' replied Tennessee Joe. 'Hey! Isn't that it? What's going on?'

Three men were urgently carrying boxes of files from a villa to a waiting van. A second black car suddenly emerged from a side road and cut in front of them before slowing to a crawl.

'Oh, for fuck's sake!' cried Cosker, leaping out of the cruiser. He was past the secret police car before its occupants realized what was happening.

A short man pushed a box into the back of the van, picked up a plastic briefcase and began walking briskly away. Cosker recognized him from his photograph in their office.

'Dr Shakir Akidi. We are from the United Nations Special Commission.'

The man hesitated, partly turned. One of the guards screamed at him in Arabic.

'Dr Akidi, please come back. Under the United Nations Agreement I have authority to interview you.'

125

The second cruiser halted ahead of the scientist. The inspectors began to climb out – and the world went ballistic. The nearest Iraqis sprinted up to the UN men screaming and spitting with rage, the secret police formed a cordon around Professor Akidi and the van drove off, its back door flapping open. An open army lorry skidded around the corner in a cloud of dust.

'The cavalry's arrived.' Cosker knew who they were before he saw their insignia. Troops of the 2nd Battalion of the Special Republican Guard, responsible for protecting Saddam Hussein and his family. The soldiers, brandishing rifles, piled out of the lorry to surround Cosker and his team, jostling and shoving.

'Under the powers vested in me by the United Nations, I demand to interview Dr Akidi and inspect his papers.'

'Not possible,' shouted an Iraqi officer who could have been Saddam's twin. 'You leave.'

Cosker scowled down from his six feet four inches. 'This is a violation of the February agreement between UN Secretary General Kofi Annan and President Saddam.'

Dr Akidi was hustled into a black car, clutching his briefcase. Cosker stood powerless as the car took off, wheels spinning on the gravel.

Cosker swore under his breath. UNSCOM had received a tip-off that Iraq officials had lied about their work with ricin, a deadly toxin derived from castor beans. The Iraqis had first denied using ricin in weapons, then, under pressure, claimed its use was solely defensive, before finally admitting packing it into 155mm artillery shells. Cosker suspected Iraqi scientists under Shakir Akidi, a British-trained biology professor, had made much more ricin than they admitted. The scientists had harvested castor beans round the clock after the Desert Shield military build-up began. Somewhere there was a hidden stockpile.

Cosker and his team were not going to find it today.

An angry muttering crowd goaded on by the soldiers was gathering around the UN men. A woman pushed a stick-thin infant in Cosker's face. The baby scrunched tiny fingers into hollow eye sockets and sobbed quietly.

'Murderer,' she screamed. 'He needs medicine. He is hungry. You will kill my child. Murderer.'

Something snapped inside Cosker. He grabbed the Saddam lookalike and held him to face the crowd.

'When he and his master tell the truth you will have food and medicine,' he shouted. 'They lie and you suffer. Tell them to stop hiding weapons of war. It is the fault of Saddam Hussein if your children die. He is the one who is killing you.'

Shit. He'd gone too far, but this job got to you. Especially when you knew that medicines allowed into the country never reached the needy. Instead they were siphoned off by Saddam's cronies and resold on the black market for vast profits. And Saddam was deliberately not selling all the oil he was permitted so his people stayed hungry and he could blame the United States.

It couldn't continue like this. Something was going to give.

Wednesday 11 March

'To sum up, Russia is in danger of becoming a Mafiya state – the first time in history there has been the wholesale criminalization of an entire society. A criminalized Russia constitutes a direct threat to western national security by fostering instability in a nuclear power. Every pore of the state mechanism is steeped in corruption.'

Special agent Wash K. McSweeney paused and looked up from the lectern. In the front row Haydn Williams remembered to blink intelligently. God, how the Cousins liked to witter on, using ten words, and long ones, when one cogent one would do.

'The daily toll of contract murders is a reflection of the fundamental lawlessness that has entered into the governance itself. When bureaucracies become as corrupt as the Russian ones have, those inside who strive to be honest encounter an impossible dilemma. They are not faced with a few bad apple colleagues. Crime and corruption are the rule – honest men are the exception. But the Russian Mafiya gangs, the most violent, and potentially the most powerful group of organized criminals in the world, are not the core of the crisis. They are its product. Russia has become fundamentally corrupted to the point where the normal business of the state, of law enforcement, of the judiciary and of commerce cannot be undertaken without at least the possibility of reference to corrupt or criminal interests.'

McSweeney turned over the last page. Williams silently cheered. They'd finally taken the decision to bring out Tim, Sally and the flask through Odessa, where a British-officered Liberian freighter was delaying sailing for twenty-four hours with engine problems. It would call at the

Turkish port of Trabzon and from there they would fly home courtesy of the RAF. Williams wished he was in his office overseeing the operation. Protocol demanded his presence here.

'Russian organized crime is already a global problem. If their gangs help foreign crime networks gain access to nuclear materials, then the scenario becomes truly frightening. Last July two Lithuanians were caught trying to sell Russian tactical nuclear missiles in Miami. Finally, on the evening of 12 January this year, a militia officer found a body sprawled across the front seat of a Zhiguli automobile in a central Moscow car park. The corpse's head hung out of the driver's window punctured by three bullet holes. The car park belonged to the Interior Ministry. It was a casual piece of brutal effrontery – as if the murderer was saying, "What can you do about it?" Thank you.'

McSweeney sat down to a ripple of applause. One hour and fifteen minutes. Williams's left buttock was numb. He wished Five would provide softer chairs for these occasions.

'I noticed you ducked the KGB's part in the criminal conspiracy. Sword and shield or the biggest crime gang of them all?' murmured Williams, shaking the American's hand.

'Hey, man, get off my back. What I think don't matter and what the Agency thinks is not for the ears of a white man.' McSweeney grinned. 'Good to see you.'

'The West Germans are closing down their links with the Russians. They reckon the Mafiya has penetrated deep inside the Kremlin.'

'What the BND does ain't nuttin' to do with me,' said McSweeney in a deep southern drawl. In a normal voice he added, 'Don't go away. Need a quiet word.' He turned to speak to an assistant commissioner from Scotland Yard.

'What did you think of the lecture, Mickey?' asked Williams.

'I liked the story of the Russians swapping their prostitutes for Mercedes cars from German gangs.'

'You wouldn't really rather have a Mercedes than a

woman, would you, Mickey?' demanded Livy Hull. 'Think of the cost. It would be much cheaper to service a woman.' She realized what she had said and burst out laughing.

They waited in the foyer of Thames House for McSweeney. Discreetly lit photographs of former director generals of the Security Service lined the walls. Williams was intrigued to see the light above Roger Hollis was flickering again. A celestial judgement? Hollis had long been suspected of spying for the Russians. Legend said the flickering light was a coded signal that the case against Hollis had been proved. Electricians said it was faulty wiring.

'I was surprised at the turn-out,' said Livy, recovering from her faux pas. 'I thought Five were so wrapped up in Ireland that they had mutton stew on the canteen menu and attended compulsory ceilidhs every Friday night.'

'They're into the future,' explained Williams. 'If there's peace in Ireland, they'll be needing a job. International crime is a lovely bailiwick. Needs lots of loot and bodies to police it. Ah, Wash. Are you going to walk with us, boy?'

'You should never call a black man boy. But in your case, Haydn, I reckon you know no better. So how's the Welsh Wizard?'

'Struggling to make sense of the world, as ever.'

They were an odd couple. McSweeney, a six-foot-three former line backer for Washington State, and Williams, thin with unfashionably long silver hair and glasses, looking more like Lloyd George than ever. Livy tried to imagine guessing their relationship if she saw them together for the first time. She failed.

'You were interested in a certain vessel. *The Sheila-Na-Gig*?'

'Was I?'

'Hey, man. Reciprocity. Remember.'

'I know of an eternal reciprocity of tears. But aye, I was. Totally clean.'

'She certainly wasn't two days before.'

Williams looked up like an inquisitive sparrow. 'Are you sure?'

'When she left Bremerhaven she was loaded and I mean loaded. You remember that storm? Reckon that suited her fine. Reckon she cross-decked then or even landed her cargo. My best guess is the drugs were put ashore in Holland.'

'This is one hundred per cent?'

McSweeney stopped for a moment. 'Why'd she change her plans, eh?'

'I hear you boy. I hear you.'

'Boyar. Boyar. Eeyah! Eeyah!'

'Please, Igor, don't. Don't be nasty.'

He ignored Emma's pleas and again viciously rammed the sharp stick into the bear's stomach. Boyar was on his hind legs, head twisted on one side, snarling helplessly. He swung a massive paw and growled. If he had connected he would have taken off his tormentor's head, but Igor stayed just outside the red circle.

Emma blinked back tears of pity. 'Why do you do it? What's the point? You'll make him hate you.'

He shot her a look of pure contempt. 'You think he doesn't hate *you*? If I step in the ring he will kill me, but if you go near him he'll kill you also, even with your kind heart. He thinks all men are evil. But if you have no fear let's see how close you can get to him. As close as you got to your friend Tim, yes?'

'What?'

Igor suddenly stood behind her grasping her shoulders. He pushed her towards the bear.

'What did you tell your friend?'

'What! Nothing.' Emma was confused. 'Tell him what?'

'Don't lie.' He crushed her shoulders with his powerful hands.

'Stop. You're hurting me.' Emma could not understand why Igor had turned against her. What had she done wrong?

Boyar roared, straining at the chain which secured him to the post. He balanced on a hind leg and a foreleg. The other shackled hind leg was stretched out behind him, one fore paw flailing at the couple.

'When did you see Tim?'

'Monday. He came to the university. He said he was going back to London. Please, Igor. Please.'

She was panting in fear. Boyar's black eyes stared deep into her own. Emma put her hands to her throat and tried to flatten herself back against the monster inching her towards those great razor-sharp claws.

'What did you talk about?'

'Nothing,' she gasped. 'We didn't talk about you if that's what you think. Why?'

Boyar was puzzled. He'd seen many struggles when Igor and his thugs shoved other men towards him and they had screamed in fear. The fights excited him. But he knew Emma. She spoke to him softly and gave him meat when he was hungry because the others forgot. He sat back on his haunches, feeling the pain from the steel band biting into his leg, and regarded her with his head on one side.

'Hah!' Igor pretended to hurl her to the bear, then at the last minute snatched her back. 'So what did you talk about?'

'Home.'

A band of gypsies in bright reds, greens and yellows milled around in the light spilling from the doorway to the separate foreigners' check-in at Rostov airport. Russians who had to pass them to get to their entrance gave them a wide berth.

'They are thieves,' explained Yuri from the back of the car. 'They swarm over you and the next thing you know they have taken your purse, your watch and the gold fillings from your teeth. They are there to help you. I have other men around the airport, but I hope the Polecat will have followed the false trail we laid. You will be safe when you take off.'

Yuri declined to leave the car in case he was spotted. Tim shook hands. Sally gave Yuri a kiss on the cheek and a wan smile. She envied Tim his focused stillness. There was something reassuring about his calm. The gypsies parted like a multi-coloured wave to let them through into the dimly lit hall. They presented their tickets and explained they only had cabin luggage to an indifferent Aeroflot stewardess. The security X-ray machine was switched off and no one took any notice when the metal detector frame beeped as Tim walked through. They found themselves alone in a drab green room which had not been swept in a week. There was no bar or tea stall, just hard benches around the walls and another surly hostess counting and recounting airside passes. Tim sat in the corner with the briefcase on his lap. The case was chained to his wrist. It contained, if anyone looked, a brightly wrapped cylindrical present and a paperback book.

'We're sitting ducks, aren't we?' Sally felt she should whisper.

'It's the obvious place to snatch it back,' Tim agreed.

Sally was so tense she thought she was going to be sick. 'We could have been armed if we'd known how slack security was.'

'Bloodthirsty little beast, aren't you?'

'I reckon I'm owed my pound of flesh after that bomb,' she declared, instinctively touching the purple and yellow bruise on her forehead. Her chin was a mess of small cuts and abrasions where she had pitched head-first in the gravel. She and Tim had escaped lightly. Six had died, including two cemetery workers. Sasha's mother, sister and the priest were seriously ill.

It was war.

A man opened the door leading out to the aircraft. Sally stiffened. He spoke briefly to the hostess and disappeared.

'It's all right.' Tim squeezed her hand. She frowned up

133

at the clock for the third time in a minute. The old board showed flights to Moscow, Kiev, Yeblochnaye and, at the bottom, Odessa. Departure was due in ten minutes. But the minutes were passing like hours. Sally could not sit still. She imagined that at any second the door would fly open and a gunman burst in, spraying the room with machine gun bullets.

'Did you see the competition in a Russian magazine to find a new symbol for the country?' Tim asked, feeling her rigid alongside him. 'The Brits have roast beef, the Swiss have the cuckoo clock, what did you think the Russians came up with?'

'Dunno.' Sally was not in the mood to play guessing games.

'The Kalashnikov. Invented in 1947 and still killing people around the world today. Vodka was second. Fancy the hammer and sickle being replaced by the gun and the vodka bottle.'

'Really.'

'Some suggested a prostitute, seeing how women and raw materials are Russia's main exports. Did you know all European prostitutes in Turkey are known as Natashas?'

'Fascinating.'

The departure board began clattering. The flight to Odessa was boarding. The stewardess barked at them, but they were made to wait five minutes before setting off to walk across the tarmac to the waiting aircraft – an ageing Ilyushin copy of the Boeing 737. Every yard was a death sentence for Sally, imagining the gunman on the spectators' terrace staring along the barrel with her in his sights. Every second she expected the blow in her back as the bullet tore through her body. More likely they would kill Tim first. She had a spare key. She knew what she had to do. Unlock the handcuffs, take the briefcase and run. Leave Tim. Wounded or dead, she must leave him and run. Sally climbed the steps as if ascending a scaffold.

The evening flight was only two-thirds full. They slid into their seats towards the rear. Bolt was already sitting behind them. Crates full of empty beer bottles were stacked across the forward port emergency exit. Sally searched in vain for a seatbelt, but she did not care. She was safe. As safe as anyone was flying Aeroflot. She closed her eyes and let out a huge sigh.

As the Ilyushin trundled down the runway gathering speed she felt relief break over her in a lovely warm wave.

'This is the most dangerous time,' announced Tim.

'Shut up.'

'Apart from landing, of course.'

'I'll kill you.'

'You're not really scared of flying, are you?'

'No. Only of crashing.' The Ilyushin lifted off and Sally did not know whether to hit Tim or kiss him.

They were still climbing as Tim explained 1998 was the year of the Devil so they would see an upsurge in satanic rites. '1998 is three times the mystical number 666 – representing the Antichrist. In 1332 it's said the Devil ruled the earth for six days.'

'The little imp,' said Sally.

Suddenly there were shouts. A man in a balaclava ran past waving a pistol. A shot, a scream and hoarse cries. Tim slid down in his seat. Sally stood up to see what was happening and glimpsed a struggle near the cockpit before Tim hauled her down. Another shot, nearer this time, and the cabin lights went out. Tim hit the buttons over their heads to turn off their reading lights. He pushed the briefcase down next to the fuselage. The aircraft pitched up and then its nose dropped. Tim slammed his right arm across Sally to hold her in her seat as her stomach bounced along the ceiling. She let out an involuntary gasp as overhead luggage lockers broke open and bags and coats tumbled through the cabin. Women screamed and moaned. One started praying in a loud voice. There

135

was a single shot behind them. The plane levelled out and when the cabin lights went on they saw two men in jeans with balaclava masks. The nearer one held a Russian army grenade in one hand and a small revolver in the other. The pin of the grenade was still in place, Tim noticed. The address system crackled.

'This is the captain. Please keep calm.' His voice was taut with controlled fear. 'Stay in your seats. The aircraft has been taken over by armed members of the Kurdish People's Party . . .'

'Do as you are told and you will not be hurt.' A new voice. Ragged and uncertain. A dangerous voice, Tim reckoned. The speaker was not in control of himself. He would not have the authority to control the situation without resorting to bloodshed.

Williams stood watching the lights of the trains, thinking it was more pleasant to look at them than suffer being packed in one. Mickey New was asking if he had seen the Hitchcock film on TV the night before. Both were by way of being film buffs.

'Not last night, but I think I know it by heart.'

'You remember the bit where Cary Grant is clinging to his girl's hand to stop her falling off Mount Rushmore while hanging on himself and the baddie comes up and grinds Grant's hand under his heel?'

'Yes.'

'How long do you reckon you are from the end of the film at that point, guv?'

Williams considered. 'Five minutes?'

'Think what has to happen. The villain Martin Landau is trying to kill Grant. Grant has to save himself and Eva Marie Saint. He has to find the vital microfilm. Number one baddie James Mason is captured and Grant and his lady get married and the two of them head back East. So how long do you think it takes on the screen?'

'Ten minutes,' guessed Williams.

'Forty-three seconds.'

'What!'

'It's true. You start with Landau's shoe crunching on Grant's fingers. A shot rings out. The shoe begins to slide away. The statuette that Landau's holding drops to the ground and breaks open to reveal the microfilm. Cut to good guy Leo G. Carroll, who is thanking a police officer with a rifle. Behind them stands Mason, flanked by two other police officers. Cut to Grant and Eva, him saying yes you can do it and her saying, no I can't. Then a great shot of him pulling her up except it's on to the top berth in a train and he's calling her Mrs Thornhill – his name. Forty-three seconds. The film ends as the train roars into a tunnel. Genius.'

Mickey grinned. It was not often he could get one over on Williams.

'All right,' said Williams, his competitive instincts aroused. 'What did Hitchcock use to represent the birds in the flying sequences of *The Birds*?'

Alison and Bill Jones burst into the office. 'I told you he'd be here,' gasped Alison.

'There's a situation in southern Russia,' announced Bill Jones. 'Just had an alert from Cheltenham relay from Cyprus. The pilot of Aeroflot flight 721 has informed Rostov ATC that armed terrorists have taken over the plane.'

'Tim's flight!'

'It's a hell of a coincidence,' admitted Bill Jones.

'They don't exist,' barked Williams. 'What do we have?'

'Two or three armed men, claiming to be members of the Kurdish People's Party. Not a known group – but that means nothing. The captain says they want to go to Iran.'

'It must have happened very soon after take-off if they're still under Rostov ATC.'

'They hadn't reached cruising height.'

'So what will the Russians do?' asked Mickey. 'Scramble fighters to bring them down?'

'Unlikely, unless we offer to pay for their fuel,' replied Williams.

'There's been no increased radio traffic on their air force nets,' said Bill Jones.

'So what did Hitchcock use?'

'Cake crumbs,' replied Williams.

Sally shrank lower as the masked figures ran up and down the aisle shouting and brandishing their pistols. She remembered Tim's hurried advice. Do not stand out. You do not want to be noticed. Fade into the background. Become a seat.

'Face front. No talking.'

'Reminds me of school,' muttered Tim.

The stench of vomit and excreta filled the cabin. Behind them came a steady *drip drip*.

'Face front,' screamed a hijacker. There was a thud and a woman began moaning in pain.

'Aren't you supposed to have special pistols inside airliners?' asked Sally.

'Yes, low velocity so they don't puncture the skin of the aircraft.'

'Do you think they have those?'

'No.'

'Me neither. Tim, I'm scared.' A pause. 'Aren't you?'

'Yes, of course.'

'Then sound bloody scared then.' She hit him in the ribs. 'Please be scared – for me.'

Alison lifted Williams's forgotten cigarette off the edge of the table where it was charring a groove into the polished top. Williams was already lighting another one.

'He's 200 miles outside the Black Sea military zone. He enters that and there could be fireworks,' said Bill Jones, a line to GCHQ to his ear.

138

'As long as they don't shoot it down. Be prepared to tell Russian Southern Command what's on board if they scramble.'

'If they want to go to Iran, why don't they change course?'

Williams inspected the large wall maps of South Russia and the Middle East. 'We can force them down if they reach Turkish airspace.'

'I'm not sure the Turks will be too happy about that,' said Livy Hull.

'We have RAF Tornados there to enforce the Iraqi no fly rule. We'll get two up under NATO aegis.'

'It's still Turkish airspace . . .'

'The captain's sent out a Pan,' announced Bill Jones.

'A what?'

'A Pan message. It's the emergency level beneath a Mayday. He says a shot has severed a fuel line. He's going to put down on a deserted military field. Correction . . . mothballed, a mothballed base called Tsimbalsaya.'

Mickey was already tapping away at a computer using two fingers.

'Allow me.' Alison pushed him aside.

'Are you cleared for this?'

She gave him an old-fashioned look and soon diagrams of military airfields and missile sites in South Russia began scrolling down the screen.

The aircraft banked and began losing height. Beyond the scratched windows there was nothing but black night. Without stars to aid him, Tim had no idea which way they were heading. The landing gear rumbled down and locked into place.

'We're landing,' he whispered. 'I don't think we're back at Rostov. I can't see any lights.'

They had not been airborne more than fifteen minutes. The cabin went dark again. A baby screamed as the change in air pressure hurt its ears. Sally swallowed.

'This is the worst part,' he said.

'You're a sadist.' She felt for his hand in the darkness and held it, listening intently for changes in engine power.

For all they knew they were descending to their deaths.

'Remember the survival position. Hands on head, forearms in front of your face, high heels off, glasses off, pens out of top pocket, false teeth out. Are they false?'

Tim was surprised when Sally kissed him on the cheek.

'They're arguing. The pilot's demanding the airfield turns on the runway lights and they're refusing. Someone's switched on a VOR beacon and a basic ILS. In theory he should be able to follow the glide slope. He says he can see the field. He's going to land.' Bill Jones's knuckles were white as he grasped the receiver.

An enlarged printout of Tsimbalsaya airfield, satellite photographs of the base, a large-scale map of its surrounding area and a map of southern Russia took up most of one wall.

'He's on final approach. Four miles out. Someone on the ground says he's too low.'

'It'll be a miracle if we get out of this alive,' whispered Sally as the engines suddenly surged with power.

'Why do people believe miracles are only good things? We reckon it's a miracle if a tree falls on a windless day and misses a little old lady by a yard. But what if the little old lady cycles down the avenue of trees every day for twenty years then one day a tree takes a dislike to her and decides to flatten her. Isn't that also a miracle?'

Sally had never known Tim talk so much. His reaction to danger was to become wryly humorous. She was wondering if this lighter Tim was the real one when the engines screamed and the Ilyushin flew into the ground.

The aircraft bounced back up into the night sky and tried again. This time the nose wheel held as the Ilyushin bucked and careered down the uneven runway. Reverse thrust opened up with a roar.

'Keep the position. The nose wheel might fold,' instructed Tim. He wrapped himself around the briefcase on his lap.

'They're down. They're down.' Williams was aware of a collective exhalation in the room as if everyone had been holding their breath for too long. 'What now?'

'The haggling begins. The hijackers will demand a second plane. The Russians will try to stall. The hijackers will lay down deadlines. The Russians will string them along as long as they don't start killing passengers,' explained Livy, who had been on a hijack exercise. 'That's what we would do. Maybe the Russians are different.'

'They aren't known for their patience or willingness to negotiate with terrorists,' agreed Williams.

'They've switched to a land line. There's a KGB colonel popped up from somewhere,' recounted Bill Jones. 'He's taking control of the operation. He's telling Rostov that the terrorists have chosen the wrong airport. He has a surprise in store for them.'

'Sounds like some local hero who wants to make a name for himself,' scowled Williams.

Tim reckoned they had been on the ground for between three and four hours. The hijackers had forced everyone to hand over their watches. Sally had taken his off his wrist so he would not have to show the briefcase tucked down at his side. They had also taken everyone's passports. The terrorists had stared at them specifically and Sally found herself hoping the British Government was sympathetic towards the Kurds. It was hot in the cabin and the baby continued to howl against a chorus of sobs and wailing. The dripping behind them had finally stopped, but the sour stench of vomit was growing thicker. The hijackers spent most of their time in the cockpit or at the front of the cabin; unusually they had not addressed their hostages.

141

Before they had been ordered to pull down the window blinds, Tim had caught sight of a high barbed wire fence and trees. It appeared they were on the outer perimeter road of a large airfield. It would have to be military.

He considered his options. It did not take long. If he'd been armed and did not have the flask . . . But he wasn't armed and he had the flask to guard. He was helpless.

There was a movement outside the fuselage. A scraping at the outer skin. Tim tensed. There it was again.

'Be ready to get down.'

'Wha . . .'

Boom. Crash. The emergency exits above the wing exploded inwards. There was a smart crack and choking smoke billowed through the cabin. The rip of a light machine gun came from the front. Someone in a gas mask, para smock and old cracked boots grabbed Sally, manhandling her out of her seat towards the exit. She was thrown from hand to hand until she was flung out. Tim kicked down the empty seat in front of him, scrambled over it and did the same again. The smoke was so thick he couldn't see across the aisle. It stung his eyes and he clamped a handkerchief over his nose. Don't hang about. Just go. He reached the exit and jumped. The ground rose up in front of him. Tim made a good parachute landing, even weight on both feet, absorbing the shock in his knees, and rolled to one side. He breathed in the night air, began to stand up and then the ground came to meet him again.

'Why did you kill those guys? They were on our side.' Igor Botkin shifted in the passenger seat of the speeding Mercedes to peer at the shadowy figure sitting upright in the back.

'The authorities needed bodies. They have bodies.'

To shoot three of your own men just to make a cover story convincing. What ran through this guy's veins? Iced water. It would not do to let this little Arab see he was impressed.

'Why didn't you kill the Englishman and woman?'

'Why?' echoed Tari. This man was as stupid as he was arrogant. 'At the moment it is a small domestic hijack. No one in the West is interested if a few Russians and Kurds kill each other. But kill the English man and woman and you have an international incident.'

But she was not an English woman. Tari resented Polecat's chatter. He needed silence to put his thoughts and emotions in order. She had not seen him at the airfield. He had stayed well back and no one had witnessed his surprise. Salilah! He remembered how she had broken her nose. She was a wild leggy colt desperately wanting to be one of the boys, to share their weapons and their training, to be tougher, keener, harder than any of them. On the assault course she took incredible shortcuts to keep up with the stronger boys of her age. Salilah did not have time to swing hand over hand along the horizontal ladder. She had tried to run along the top. Her foot slipped and she'd smashed her nose. She had clung on, blood pouring everywhere, turning her face into a red smear. But she had finished inside the set time.

He had taught her to shoot after she had gone on and on, following him everywhere, arguing, cajoling, stamping her foot in frustration, even kicking him. The other boys had found her persistence amusing and in the end he gave in. She had hit the target with her first shot. She had whooped and done a dance of joy still clutching the loaded weapon. A funny skinny kid who had grown up to be a beautiful woman – and she'd never had her nose fixed.

Polecat fell silent under the other's scorn but finally his resentment broke to the surface like a poisoned gas bubble. 'You think you're so clever but you couldn't have done it without me. Linnikov was brilliant.'

'He was being well paid.'

'Yeh, what about seeing some of this money?'

'Five million dollars will now be deposited in the Nicosia bank. You will get the other five million when the virus is in my hands in England.' Tari wished he could take the virus with him. Not let it out of his sight. But it was too dangerous. If he was intercepted and caught, then the flask would be recovered. The Iraqis were right to keep them apart and not reunite them until everything was in place.

'I'll leave it in its gift wrapping. A present from me.'

'As you wish.'

There was a chilling sense of purpose about the Arab which annoyed Polecat. Tight-arsed bastard. Polecat took a large drink from his hip flask. As an afterthought he offered it to Tari.

'I do not drink alcohol.'

'What are you? Some kind of fanatic in a holy war? What do you call it, a jihad?'

'No,' replied Tari with an enigmatic smile. 'My war is holy only to my people.'

'You're a terrorist?'

'It depends which side you are on. Some follow me. Others hunt me.'

'Is there a price on your head?' The absolute stillness from the back made Polecat say quickly, 'Only joking. All outlaws together, heh?'

Yes, there was a price on his head, but he'd already paid a higher price when the Israeli helicopter had attacked his car.

Now the idiot was boasting.

'I've killed eight men. How many have you killed?'

'I do not count. I kill only when I have to.'

'Yeh, so do I. I had to kill the last guy because he wouldn't sell me the land next to the hotel I'm building.'

'But his widow did, didn't she, boss,' cackled the driver.

Polecat laughed harshly. The Mercedes swung out to overtake the small convoy of army buses carrying the passengers of the downed jet back to Rostov.

'You want the flask in London. Boy, you must really hate the English.'

'Not really.' Why didn't this thug shut up. He didn't hate

the English. Any more than he liked the Iraqis. But my enemy's enemy is my friend. As simple as that. America supported the gangster state of Israel. He hated Americans – but not the English. Despise them, yes. Hate them no.

'You're a mercenary like me,' judged Polecat.

'I believe in something. You believe in nothing but empty greed.'

'There is nothing empty about greed.' Polecat took another large swig. 'Greed gets money, money gets power, power gets more money. It is a wonderful ascending circle.'

You moron, thought Tari. Money is not power. Sovereignty is power. Land and its integrity. That is worth fighting for – not money. He could not be bothered getting into an argument.

'You know the flask has to be there within a fortnight.'

'No problem. I already have a good idea.'

The Russian pretended to be his own man, but Tari had been briefed by Iraqi intelligence that he was merely an arm of the Moscow Narco Group. He did not trust Botkin. Anyone who felt it necessary to call themselves the Polecat had to be inadequate. Tari would rather have dealt with the *vor v zakonye*. But he sensed the old man had not wanted to become involved – and he had badly miscalculated trying to divert half the operational funds towards the Movement. It was ironic that he had had to pay Polecat the full ten million dollars.

'As long as the flask is kept in the proper condition. It must not be damaged. It must be kept frozen.'

'I know. But the shortest way isn't always the best. Trust me.'

I wouldn't trust you any further than I could throw your pet bear, thought Tari, but I have no option.

Friday 13 March

'Thanks for the VIP treatment. I've never been through Heathrow so quickly,' said Tim.

'Coordinator's idea, boss. Thought you both deserved it.'

'So I'm not going to be shot on my own quarterdeck then?'

'Don't be daft,' grinned Mickey New. 'You ain't got a quarterdeck. No. Mr Williams reckons it was a set-up.'

Tim exploded. 'Of course it was a bloody set-up. How many assault teams carry bolt cutters and club the passengers as they escape?'

'The official line is that KGB special forces happened to be training on the airfield which is how they could mount a rescue so quickly.' Mickey glanced in the driving mirror. Sally had fallen asleep in the back of the Range Rover threading its way up the M4 towards London. 'There's also a press blackout – officially not to give other Kurds the same idea.'

'I feel bad about Bolt. They must have killed him in the first minutes. The only casualty among the passengers. What a coincidence.'

'I bet your mate wishes he'd never got involved.'

'Yeh.' Tim had been thinking along the same lines. Yuri's debt of honour was more than repaid. 'So what's happened while we've been away?'

'Not a lot. Ireland's teetering on the brink of peace. Mike Atherton's about to step down as England captain and the Hammers had a good win. Alison goes on about having to do the work of two as Maisie's still off sick but I think she enjoys feeling important.'

Williams was waiting for them at the security screen on the tenth floor. He shook Tim's hand and kissed Sally on both cheeks. He wore his suit jacket, which gave a formal air to their reception.

'Your report from Moscow's stirred things up a bit. Dotty Di can't wait to get her hands on you.' Williams gave an apologetic smile. 'I'm afraid it's going to be a full session of the Grand Inquisition. Don't worry.'

The first thing Tim saw in the windowless conference room were the two empty chairs at the head of the table – for the accused. There were glasses of water in front of them, so obviously they were expected to do a lot of talking. Tim was struck by the air of aloof indifference which greeted them. Only Dotty Di beamed her tight-lipped smile and nodded like a wobbling woodpecker towards them. Next to her was a stranger; a Slav by his raw cheekbones with huge transparent ears. Mickey stood at ease inside the closed doors.

Tim recounted the hijack up to the point where he was knocked unconscious and awoke to find himself being half-carried, half-dragged to a waiting Red Army bus. The briefcase had vanished. For dramatic effect he held up the handcuff and the severed chain. Livy Hull took it from him and the others passed it round the table as if by handling it they could feel the resonance of the hijack. Sally had not seen anyone attack Tim nor grab the briefcase because she had been hustled away into a hangar. Yes, Tim agreed with Plumridge, he had thought the hijack had been suspicious, especially when the hijackers made no attempt to speak to the passengers, but what could he have done?

'Quite,' agreed Williams. 'We can assume the Russian state wasn't behind the seizure. They could have simply arrested Tim.'

'Someone went to a lot of trouble and expense,' observed Livy. 'Only the KGB or Federal Security Bureau possesses that amount of muscle.'

'Who were they working for?' demanded Plumridge.

'Whoever paid them. Remember Hindawi's message from the grave.'

Diana could contain herself no longer. 'What about the flask? What did it look like?'

'Like a cross between a thermos and a cocktail shaker,' replied Tim.

'A Dewar flask. What did it say on it?'

Sally borrowed Alison's notebook and printed in large Cyrillic letters. 'Марбург У'.

'Oooh, ooh.' Diana was quivering in excitement. Next to her the Slav's cheek muscles perceptibly tightened. 'You're sure? Absolutely sure?'

'Yes,' said Sally. 'Marburg U.'

'Oooh. It's a nasty one. Nasty is not the word. Oh, dearie me, no. No, not at all.'

'Diana,' said Williams in his best bedside manner. 'Would you like to tell us about Marburg U, whatever it is?'

'Marburg is a filovirus. Latin for thread. There's no treatment or cure. It's among the oldest things on earth – and so deadly it's beautiful.' Dotty Di's thoughts were like the runaway train that went over the hill.

'Diana!' Williams spoke as if he was admonishing a feverish child.

'Where do I start? Where do I start?' She took a deep breath. 'Marburg first appeared among workers in a vaccine producing plant in the West German town of Marburg in 1967, hence its name. The same epidemic also popped up in Frankfurt and Belgrade. The thirty-one cases struck terror because of the disease's ferocity, the speed with which it spread and the way the victims died. Basically the poor things bled to death. The virus destroys the organs so tissue turns to jelly. Despite the best care in the most modern hospitals in the world, seven victims died within sixteen days. Almost one in four. That is fearsome.' She held up a chubby index finger. 'Yellow fever kills one in twenty and we thought that was an especially lethal virus – but

Marburg! And the amazing thing is – no one knows where it comes from.'

'What do you mean, no one knows where it comes from?' demanded Plumridge.

'The original epidemic was traced to a batch of infected Uganda monkeys. The virus erupted out of the African jungle, killed and disappeared again. Everyone believed the outbreak was a one-off, but eight years later an Australian backpacker caught the Marburg virus in South Africa. He was tended by a team of fifteen top, and I mean top, doctors and scientists. He died within four days. Marburg keeps claiming lives, but we cannot find its reservoir species.'

'Sorry?'

'Remember I said that a virus is a parasite,' explained Diana. 'It needs a species of insect or warm-blooded animal where it resides and where it reproduces. The relationship between the virus and its reservoir is commensal, that is, one organism benefits without harming the other. When the reservoir species comes in contact with another animal, such as a human being, the virus jumps ship. It attaches itself to the new animal and tries to turn it into itself. Invariably the virus destroys its new host.'

A heavy silence hung around the table.

'How big are these viruses?'

'My dear, 100 million could cuddle up nicely on a full stop.'

'How is the Marburg transmitted?'

'Friends at USAMRID, the US Army Medical Research Institute of Infectious Diseases, conducted experiments in 1986 which convinced them Marburg can be transmitted by air. Basically they put an infected monkey and a healthy monkey in cages at different ends of a room and the healthy monkey crashed.'

'You said Marburg was a filovirus. Is that special?' demanded Williams.

'There are only three in the world. The other two are Ebola Zaire and Ebola Sudan. One outbreak of Ebola Zaire killed nine out of ten, but the victims weren't getting top-class hospital care. Left alone, it's possible Marburg is Ebola's gentler sister. But we didn't leave it alone. At least our Russian colleagues didn't, did they, Gavin?'

The Slav shook his head in solemn agreement.

'My colleague and friend Nikolai Ustinov was working at the Vector plant at Novosibirsk in April 1988 – ten years ago next month.' He spoke slowly, not from language problems but to weigh each word carefully. 'He was accidentally injected with Marburg. For the first time we saw the effect on a fellow human being. Scientists such as ourselves are used to the viciousness of nature, but none of us was prepared for the way he died.' He paused, breathing through his nose. 'We were ordered to take Nikolai's organs and blood and fashion a new type of biological weapon. Some of us felt this was not right.'

'Gavin came over the following year,' interrupted Diana.

'The new strain exceeded all expectations,' he continued. 'When we tested it on monkeys we found it was several hundred times more lethal than anthrax. We called this strain Marburg Variant U. This was what is in your flask.'

'Which we lost,' snapped Plumridge.

'We didn't lose it,' Sally snapped back. 'It was stolen from us. We snatched it at gunpoint in the first place. No one seems to remember that.'

Plumridge jerked as if he had been stung by a wasp. His face darkened in anger.

'Fair point,' said Williams. 'Let's have a break for a minute. Gavin, thank you for your contribution. Diana, will you stay?' In the corridor, he whispered to Sally, 'Well said, but go home and get some rest. I'm afraid you won't be cleared for the next part and I don't want to give Plumridge the opportunity to point it out. Write your report at home.'

'Okay. Bye, Tim. Thanks for everything.' Sally gave him an unexpected kiss on the cheek. 'See you soon.'

'Oh, yes. Bye.'

'You two got on all right?' asked Williams as they watched Sally enter the lift.

'Absolutely, sir. She's a very plucky girl,' replied Tim staunchly. He did not mention the strange gaps in Sally's knowledge which had been bothering him. The latest had been Sally's failure to know there could only ever be three ridings in Yorkshire. Tim thought everyone knew that old chestnut. She was also remarkably ignorant about the Eagles pop group, silver sixpences, Windscale and Sergeant Pepper.

Plumridge and Hull hove back from their respective offices. 'Right. Ready for round two . . .'

'The question is, Coordinator' – Plumridge steepled his fingers – 'is this flask intended for Britain or Baghdad? That's the nub, isn't it?'

No, it wasn't the nub. Williams found himself disliking Plumridge's second-class intellect hiding in a double-breasted suit. Time he impressed a little. Time to strut his stuff, as the Cousins liked to say.

'Let's consider what we have, shall we?' Williams flashed a mirthless smile. 'This began with an intelligence report from an Iraqi scientist that Saddam Hussein planned to smuggle biological weapons into Britain. The agent initially was probably going to be anthrax and the means, perfume bottles. The source, al-Hindawi, was arrested but managed to smuggle out the message that if Saddam felt threatened he was prepared to employ the Samson Option, a recognized terrorist scenario. The Samson Option is not an act of a sane or rational man. But Saddam is neither and the noose is closing slowly but irrevocably around his neck. When he feels sufficiently threatened he will employ that option. Now consider – al-Hindawi would have been interrogated. If he disclosed his previous revelation, and we must assume he would under torture, then it's logical for Saddam to change the biological weapon and the method of putting it in place. A Palestinian, almost certainly employed by Iraqi intelligence, steals a flask of Marburg virus, one of the most lethal biological agents in the world. He does so with the help of the Russian Mafiya. He wants the virus transported to London. On those premises I think we can say within the parameters of probability that the Marburg and the Samson Option are connected. And the Russian Mafiya will be instrumental, in some way, in getting it to Britain. Does that answer your question?'

Plumridge could only open and close his mouth like a fish flapping on a beach. Livy Hull smirked at his discomfort. Williams pressed on.

'How will the virus be kept, Diana?'

'Hard to say, old thing. Gavin believes they'd probably store it in blood serum in glass vials. If you want to keep it simple but effective, just mix it with water in a spray.'

'I assume the virus has to be kept frozen?'

'Viruses thrive in egg yolk,' chortled Diana. 'Nowhere happier, but the flasks will generally be stored in a super freezer at around minus 160 degrees Fahrenheit.'

'How long can the virus survive outside that temperature?'

'Up to ten days perhaps, depending on circumstances. Viruses are primitive. They have a great determination to survive. If only one hundredth or one hundred thousandth survives you have a mega disaster such as Britain has never experienced.'

'But surely a terrorist won't have the knowledge or facilities to use the Marburg virus to threaten London,' carped Plumridge.

'Do you know Kathleen Bailey? Was with the US Arms Control and Disarmament Agency? She reckoned you could build a major biological arsenal in a room fifteen feet square with £5,000 worth of equipment.'

'Is that true?' demanded Livy.

'Typical American hyperbole,' retorted Diana. 'I could do it in the kitchen with the price of a week's shopping from Sainsbury's.'

'Any thoughts on methods of dispersal, Di?' asked Williams.

'Overflying London would be the obvious way. A similar projection of spraying anthrax from the air over Washington DC on a cool, clear night with a light wind estimated around three million fatalities. One million more than a nuclear attack.'

'Surely most of these bugs will die on the way down,' protested Plumridge.

'It was assumed only ten per cent of the anthrax survived. Five per cent of the remainder died off each minute. Of course, our Marburg will have been genetically engineered to make it resistant to light and pollution.'

'Can you do that?' demanded Livy Hull.

'Easily. You simply transplant the genes of the virus into a radiation-resistant pathogenic organism. It's very simple . . .' She seemed about to embark on an explanation.

'Yes, thank you Diana, we have the picture,' said Williams.

'If this hits the fan . . .' said Livy.

'If this hits the fan, dear, you'll witness the biggest social upheaval since the Black Death.' Diana gave a satisfied chuckle at the thought.

Plumridge was late for lunch with his wife. He knew she would be cross. The fact that he'd been tied up would not matter a jot.

'But you could have made an excuse and left,' she complained. Her mouth, normally prim, now appeared perfect for sucking lemons.

'How could I, dear? It was very high-powered. I couldn't slip out.'

A bottle of Pouilly Fumé and another of sparkling mineral water were already open on the restaurant table. More wine had been drunk than water. The Swaine Adeney bag at Felicity's side suggested yet another equestrian purchase. Plumridge was afraid of his wife. He had confronted that realization some time ago, but recently the fear was corroding into hate. And there were their two daughters who despised him while swallowing up every penny he earned. He knew all about the monstrous regiment of women!

Felicity was holding up *Horse and Hound* magazine. 'We've found just the thing for Tabitha. Fifteen one. Eight years old. Experienced hunter. Very gentle.' She saw the look on his face and slapped down the magazine so the cutlery rattled. She was quick to get her retaliation in first. 'I don't know why I'm telling you this. I know you're not interested.'

'How much?'

'That's all you think about. Money!' Felicity indicated to a hovering waiter that she was ready to give her order. Plumridge hurriedly opened the menu. 'Oysters, then the monkfish with sundried tomatoes and basil.'

Plumridge, to save time and effort, ordered the same. He was already trying not to glance at his watch. He really was too busy for long lunches, but Felicity took his protests as a personal snub. She again admonished him for being late. She had to get back home. Something to do with the pony club or bridge club or some bloody club.

'How much?'

'Five thousand.' He winced. 'Maurice. It's a bargain. Anyway we're going to see her tomorrow. Near Fordingbridge. Tabitha's really excited. If we get a favourable vet's report . . .'

He was being presented with a fait accompli. No one had mentioned this new pony last night when they had all sat around the table on one of the rare occasions when the whole family was together – apart from gymkhanas.

'Not a word. She's looking forward to it.'

Plumridge thought others in his office would not believe it if they saw him now. What had happened to his confidence, his management skills, budgetary control, dogmatic self-belief and determination? All bluff and braggadocio – blown away to a wraith of smoke by a shrew of a rich wife and two demanding, exacting, greedy, grasping daughters. Little darlings.

'And just remember, it's not your money. It's mine.'

'Sounds as if you were done up like a kipper, boss,' declared Mickey as he fought to get to the bar in the converted fire station. He was brought up short by the young man in front of him who answered his mobile phone instead of trying to get served. 'Excuse me mate. Do you want a drink or a bloody chinwag?'

The man took one look at Mickey and edged out of the way. Finally Mickey emerged with two pints and found space against the wall.

'Yeh, I reckon you were well and truly stitched. While I remember, Mr Williams has called for all the papers on the *Sheila-Na-Gig* op and the Cyprus laundering scam to take home.'

'How do you know that?'

'I happened to be conducting a covert operation to liberate some of Alison's sugar when I saw the flimsies. It's all on the QT.' Mickey raised an arm. 'There's Cautious Kenny. You'll like him. Me and his lad were in 40 Commando together. Kenny's a card.'

A man aged around fifty in a British Warm overcoat and brown trilby hat threaded his way through the crowd. He had a bulbous nose and an unseasonal tan.

'Pleased to meet you. Any friend of Mickey's is a friend of mine. I'm going to buy you a drink. Just had a bit of a result, didn't I? It's a long story but . . . a connection told me of a nag going out in a maiden at Windsor last week. You wouldn't touch a maiden normally. This nag was at nixes – nines – but the connection had been kosher in the past. So I did a twoer. Bosh, one thousand eight hundred quid better off. Always worth going to the track, save on tax.'

Tim slowly realized Kenny was talking about horse racing.

'There was no one to collect the cup for the filly in the

winning enclosure, was there? Maktoum wasn't there. Probably didn't know she was running. Henry wasn't there and I felt sorry for the travelling lad. He's done the biz and there's no one to share his hour of glory. In the bar after I gave him a good drink to say thank you. This morning, the lad came on the dog to tell me of one running at Doncaster. Never have spotted it. Led the procession home. Bosh. Thank you very much.'

'What does Kenny do?' laughed Tim as Kenny bought a round despite their protests.

'Sits at the end of a bar and makes phone calls.'

Kenny was back almost immediately, somehow holding pints and whisky chasers and a large gin and tonic.

'Cheers. Makes up for yesterday, don't it? Didn't think it would drift, did I?'

Tim found it hard to keep up with Kenny's knack of beginning a sentence in the middle of a thought process.

'I had this steamer, right? Only late, wasn't it? Tens in the morning linen. Too many faces went shopping for it as soon as the offices opened. The offices sent it down the line to the course and by the time the bookies opened their tissue it was carpets . . .'

Tim frowned.

'Threes. Three to one. I took it off the shoulder, didn't I? Eleven to four. Bosh. Lost a quarter a point. Just as well I only had a monkey on it.'

'So you missed out £125,' said Mickey. He translated for Tim: Cautious had had a tip on a horse whose odds had shortened from 10–1 in the morning papers as punters backed it heavily. 'Tim's just back from Russia. Do they have racing there?'

'Don't know,' said Tim sourly. 'But if they did, it'd be bent.'

'Funny you should say that. There's a lot of Russians around the East End at this moment in time. Real flash geezers and loaded. Heavily into property. They don't know what to do with their dough. One's bought into a book of a pal of mine at Lingfield tomorrow.'

'How do you mean?' asked Tim.

Cautious hesitated. 'Say you think the favourite ain't going to win. You go to the boardsman and say I'll put £10,000 or whatever into the book. The money gives the bookie the opportunity to offer a fraction more than the man next door. If he can offer 11/10 when all around is offering evens, he'll attract money. If the favourite goes down, he wins. If it comes home, he pays out.'

'Can anyone do that?'

'Highly illegal.'

'But it happens?'

Kenny nodded in a majestically knowing fashion and produced two metal badges for Lingfield Racecourse. 'These any good to you? It'll be a good early season meeting. I'll be there, so we could have a drink.'

'Not for me,' said Mickey. 'I've promised to take my nipper to the London Dungeon. Why don't you take Sally?'

'I wasn't planning to see Sally.'

'Now you've got an excuse,' said Mickey, who saw more than he let on.

Sally paused, her fingers resting above the keyboard. They weren't going to like it, but it was the truth – as far as she knew. She felt fond of Tim. Although he appeared a little out of fashion, there was much truth and valour in him. Where did that come from? He had a strangely gentle interior for one who had chosen, and excelled in, a violent profession. But it didn't pay to get involved in this game. The phone interrupted her thoughts.

'Impressions? Intuition? Facts?'

'Honest. Decent. He's very good, isn't he?'

'Yes. He's the best we've had.'

'Sorry to disappoint you.'

'Nothing to be sorry about. I'm glad. But it wouldn't have been the first time a victim had planned his own robbery.'

'Not in this case.'

'Okay, but don't give up yet. Stay close.'

'Funny you should say that.' An idea was creeping into her head. A silly idea. A nice idea. Sally enjoyed the microsecond's warmth of anticipation before unpleasant reality reimposed itself.

'Don't forget Arabella has a box tomorrow.'

'I'll be there, but please . . .'

'You know how important it is to find this virus. I'm convinced the Russians have a part to play. Valentine's almost ours. Please . . .'

Sally paused.

'One last time?'

'One last time. *Nos da.*'

Haydn Williams picked up the first of the buff-coloured folders, weighed it carefully in both hands and put it back on his desk. He unlocked Tim's room and stood looking down at the orange threads of light lining up at signal gantries like runners on their marks. All those thousands of people returning to their suburban homes, planning their weekend. Work in the garden, watch a soccer match, decorate the spare room – certainly not brief the Home Secretary that a biological weapon was probably, only probably, about to be brought into Britain. The Home Secretary would have to issue an all-ports alert. Totally pointless, but he'd cover his back in case things went pear-shaped later.

Williams smiled wryly at the idea of the individual trains as facts of different lengths which had to be marshalled so they ran on the right lines, all going in the correct direction, arriving regularly and without crashing into each other. He reckoned Waterloo's signalling system was coping better than his brain. And it was all interconnected. Like current events. All interconnected. The missing drugs, the Marburg, the Samson Option.

. . . And the treachery.

The one thing he did not want to think about. The

one thing he had to think about. Someone in London was taking gold. Russian gold? Iraqi gold? KGB gold? Mafiya gold? Someone in their community. Cypher clerk or director general? Secretary or department head? Computer programmer or analyst?

How had they known Tim's flight? It would be comforting to believe the leak came from Yuri's gang. But there had been the recent row of operational failures. Taken together it suggested something else. Something more unpleasant.

He didn't need this problem. Not now. Not with the Marburg loose.

It didn't rain but it poured, as his mam used to say.

For some inexplicable reason, he boarded his thought train on a branch line. He almost began with the failure of recent operations. But then it occurred to him to take a lateral approach and look at similar operations which had succeeded. The interception of the *Simon de Danser* had been a brilliant piece of intergovernmental cooperation against the South American cartels and the Azeris, even though the prosecution failed because of Customs blunders. Then they had a string of successes against the Chechens. But to balance their successes there had been the money transfer from Moscow, via Budapest and Cyprus, which fell off the screen as it approached the City of London, the cock-up in Beirut and the *Sheila-Na-Gig*. Only against the Moscow Narco Group did they fail.

Williams sifted through the three-dimensional kaleidoscope of possibilities, probabilities, denials, half-truths and suppositions. Overlapping circles of interest, straight lines of power, triangles of financial frolics through the Virgin Islands, Colombia and Moscow. And someone somewhere talking to the wrong people. A puzzle of a hundred variants and only one common denominator. Betrayal.

The Russians were pivotal, he sensed. They would lead to the Marburg. They would lead to the traitor. Stay close to the Russians, Sally.

*   *   *

Tim wrinkled his nose. Something was different. An elusive hint of perfume lingering in the hallway of the old house. It was vaguely familiar, but he had the sense of smell of a log. The scent preceded him as he climbed the stairs, his travel bag over one shoulder. By the second landing he remembered he had no food at home and slowed while he wondered whether to go back to the kebab shop. He was still debating when he reached the fourth landing and he was plunged into darkness. He took two more steps before he saw a sliver of light coming from under his door. For three minutes Tim stayed absolutely motionless, breathing easily through his mouth, head to one side to pick up the slightest sound. Keeping to the side of the stairs he tested each one in turn until he was outside his door. Someone was moving inside the flat. Tim considered what he could possibly own to attract a burglar. Nothing came to mind – and that meant whoever was in his flat wasn't there for the video. He was there for Tim.

The sounds were coming from the kitchen area. Good. The nearer to the door the better. Tim slipped his key into the lock. It turned. The intruder was either an amateur or he wanted Tim to walk in. Tim exploded through the door.

He had his arm around the woman's neck and his fist drawn back for the punch under her right ear when Sally screamed and dropped the plate she was washing up. It bounced.

'You'll give someone a heart attack doing that.' She twisted her head to see it was still attached. Refusing to be ruffled by Tim's dramatic entrance, she picked up the plate and put it on the draining board.

'Christ, Sally. I could have killed you.' Tim slowly took in the fact that she was doing the washing-up in her reefer jacket, sleeves pulled up to the elbows.

'Isn't there any heating in here? It's freezing.'

Tim obediently turned on the gas fire. 'Sally . . . ?'

'How could you let this place get in such a tip? You must

160

have had this milk before we went to Russia. There's a mug containing the primeval soup from which all life evolved. I can't get it clean.'

'Sally. What are you doing here?'

She indicated the plastic carrier bags at her feet. 'I thought I'd cook you a meal, but I can't do anything until I've cleared up. I boiled the kettle for hot water, so don't just stand there – get a tea towel and start drying. There's two bottles of Sancerre which should go in the fridge . . .'

'Sally . . .'

'That's unless this is a gin-free zone in which case you can open one now.'

Tim brought in his bag containing a duty-free bottle of vodka. On the way back he examined the lock.

'Sally . . .'

'We're having snapper with ginger and garlic followed by some yummy cheeses . . .'

She had her back to him, bustling around the sink. He slowly turned her round and held her by the upper arms. 'Sally. HOW DID YOU GET IN?'

'Oh.' Sally made her lower lip quiver. 'Thought you might ask that.'

'And?'

'Just a knack I picked up.'

'At finishing school?'

'Yep.' She opened her eyes wide, a smile twitching at the corners of her mouth. 'At finishing school.'

How did she know where he lived? 'But you can't go round breaking into people's homes to cook them supper.'

'Why not? It would make one of those silly TV programmes.' She returned to washing dishes. 'Why don't you get a cleaner?'

'The place isn't big enough to need one and I never get round to it myself. I . . . um . . . I don't have anyone round here so . . .'

'Don't you have a girlfriend?' It was the first time she had asked him outright.

161

'No. Not really. No.'

'I'd have thought you would have.' Sally found herself wondering what sort of girl Tim would be attracted to. Someone bright and lively to balance his own sombre moods, sexy, because she was sure he had a great body, intelligent, a daredevil, a looker. She stopped, recognizing she was describing herself.

'Have you a CD player for some music?'

'Not even a gramophone. The little dog ran away and took it with him.'

'Sorry?' Sally didn't understand.

Tim pulled out a small shortwave radio from his bag. 'What sort of music?'

'Don't mind. You choose.'

Somewhere among the twelve bands Tim found a jazz station which turned out to be French. Sally shed her outdoor coat and bustled round, demanding utensils and condiments, tutting in exasperation at Tim's bare cupboards, then magically saving the day by delving into her bags. She peeled potatoes and tipped the skins on top of a torn-up letter in the rubbish bin. She was surprised by Tim's spartan existence. Most young officers shared flats or houses, but Tim lived all alone in this sad garret. It was as if he was deliberately cutting himself off from the world. There were no personal touches. No letters or bills, just a yellowing pile of evening papers. She peeped into the bedroom and took in the single pillow on the double bed. She was hunting for table mats in the big solid oak sideboard when she saw the photograph lying face down. She picked it up and examined the two rows of grinning young men in jungle fatigues, holding automatic weapons.

'Your army mates?'

'My troop.'

'You're all so young.'

'That was taken two years ago.'

Tim had aged a lot in that time, Sally thought. The face

162

in the photograph was carefree and proud. Now it was troubled and watchful.

'He looks a fun guy.' She indicated the man directly behind Tim.

'He was known as the Brigand.' Tim could not help smiling. 'He was a right scallywag. Life was one long laugh to him.'

Sally picked up on the past tense. 'Is he dead?'

'He drowned. So did Squiffy, the guy on my right.'

'What happened?'

'They were crossing a river in flood. The . . .' Tim searched for a non-military word to describe the piece of equipment. 'The shackle securing their line to the bank failed and they were swept away.'

And I failed to check it. If there was one thing they learnt in the Regiment it was check, check and check again. But he'd been thinking of Linda. Bloody Linda. The Brigand was buried in St Martin's in Hereford, but Squiffy's body was never found in those mountain torrents. They'd been in Serbia illegally. They could not hang around and so they had to give up the search. It hurt.

The inquiry decided the accident was a one-off which no one could have foreseen. It had been Squiffy's task as sergeant to check the equipment. But Tim knew if he had double-checked, as he normally did, he would have spotted the fraying line on the karabiner.

If he had not been thinking about bloody Linda.

Squiffy's brother blamed him and Tim had told the inquiry he held himself responsible. Some found the stance admirable, others considered it weird. And when he continued to wear his hair shirt in public, the latter opinion became the majority. It had led to him being moved up to London. No room for mea culpas in Stirling Lines. A good soldier, they said, but prone to take things personally.

'I'm sorry,' said Sally. 'Your job's very dangerous, isn't it.'

'You reduce the odds by training. It should have been prevented.'

Tim concentrated on finding two matching knives and forks and Sally snatched a glance at him.

You loved those men, she thought. They were yours. You loved them like a father and you feel you let them down. Sally knew he blamed himself, she had read the report. But the report did not tell of the raw, stark pain which pierced Tim. The pain which had scoured and etched his face in the past twelve months.

Saturday 14 March

Tim and Sally met Cautious Kenny in the champagne bar talking to a bulky man with a rubicund face and wearing a flat cap. Tim introduced Sally and Cautious cleared his throat to formally introduce them to his bookmaker friend.

'This is Charlie Gates. He's trading as F & W Whitton today. Champagne, or is it too early?'

'It's never too early for champagne,' said Sally with a throaty chuckle.

It had taken most of the two bottles of wine the previous night before Tim built up courage to announce that he had been given two passes to the races and if she wasn't doing anything . . . Although of course he understood if she was . . .

Sally had hesitated for only a moment before saying she'd love to come. Then she had been in a hurry to leave, announcing she had things to do if she was spending the day out. He phoned for a taxi and accompanied her to the kerbside. They parted with a friendly kiss.

In the cab, Sally examined her feelings. He had failed to make a pass. How gentlemanly. How disappointing. But for the best. Definitely for the best. She registered the uncomfortable feeling that it would be very easy to fall for Tim. Against all her precepts and fine intentions, she knew if she didn't watch her step she was going to become emotionally involved. Not a good idea. It was one thing to begin by obeying orders, another to end up obeying the heart.

As soon as she arrived home she made a phone call.

Now she sipped her champagne and wished she had got

hold of Tim before he left home to dissuade him from wearing sports jacket and cavalry twill trousers. He looked exactly what he was. An off-duty army officer.

Charlie and Cautious began talking about bagmen, runners and odds in a language of their own so Tim and Sally went to visit the paddock to see the runners in the first race. They arrived as the thoroughbreds were being led in by their stable lads. Sally was struck by the racehorses' long-legged elegance.

'Aren't they beautiful? That little one's pretty. The one with the sheepskin noseband.'

A small bay with the number 3 on its saddle-cloth pranced towards them.

'Oh, you are lovely,' crooned Sally as the horse tossed its head in her direction. 'He winked at me. He was telling me he's going to win. He knows a friend when he sees one.'

Tim consulted the form in the race card. 'Not according to this. Unplaced the last three times out. It says: "Room for overall improvement. Must find something extra if going to realize last season's early potential."'

The jockeys walked in their heel-down scurry out to the middle to shake hands with the self-conscious group of owners and their wives and receive last-minute instructions from their trainers.

'I don't care. I'm going to put a bet on him.'

Sally enjoyed the hustle and bustle of the racecourse. Ruddy-faced men wearing brown trilbies sauntered from the paddock back to the stands, some carrying binoculars with dozens of coloured badges from previous meetings tied to the straps. Young women, done up to the nines, tottered and teetered on high heels over the grassy areas and wished themselves back in the hospitality boxes. On the rails dividing the public area from the members' enclosure, sober young men in suits murmured into mobile phones. This is where the big bets are laid, Cautious explained. No money appeared to change hands and the air of discreet business contrasted with the surging throng around the bookies on their boxes. Boardsmen, Cautious called them. Sally placed £20 on her outsider at 12–1.

'You've got to spekulate to akumilate, my son,' she told Tim in a fair impression of Cautious's East End accent.

They watched as the bay took the lead two furlongs out and, urged on by the jockey and Sally's cries of encouragement, held on to cross the finishing line by a short head.

'I knew this was going to be my lucky day,' cried Sally, leaping up and down. She hurried off to collect her winnings.

Cautious greeted them in the champagne bar. 'How did you get on?'

'She only had £20 on the winner at 12–1,' said Tim.

'He told me he was going to win,' explained Sally, eyes sparkling. 'I know about these things.'

'*He* is a filly, miss,' corrected Cautious Kenny.

Sally burst out laughing. 'All girls together, then.'

They toasted Sally's win before strolling around the public areas. Near the paddock, Tim spotted Maurice Plumridge and his wife Felicity, looking like an advert from *Horse and Hound* in a green Loden coat and large silk scarf over her shoulders. He shied away from meeting them and steered Sally into a bar where a group of large men were all shouting at the same time. He realized with a start they were speaking Russian, and told Sally what Cautious had said about Russians buying into Charlie's book.

There were eleven horses in the Handicap, but it was clear from the odds that there were only four horses in the race. Tower Bridge was the favourite at 5–2. F & W Whitton was offering 11–4 and was doing brisk business. Glendoul and Roger's Heir were on 7–2 and Castle Maid at 5–1. The others were priced at longer odds.

'Do you really think Tower Bridge will be beaten?' Sally asked Cautious.

'Yeh, I do, princess. He's carrying top weight and the going's too hard for him. He's a good nag, but I don't think the handicapper has done him any favours. I reckon both

Glendoul and Roger's Heir are in with a chance.' He blew his nose loudly. 'Glendoul's on a good mark at present – three pounds lower than when he won last year at Kempton. Roger's Heir has got the pedigree, but I reckon the distance is a bit too much for him unless the stable are trying to push him out.'

Charlie was still doing brisk business, but as Sally looked, he reached up and rubbed out the 11–4 opposite Tower Bridge on his board before chalking up the same odds as the others.

'Why's he done that?' demanded Sally.

'Racecourse security would think it a bit odd if Charlie offered better odds than everyone else all the time so he moves it around, doesn't he?'

Two minutes later he put the odds back up again.

'Why don't the other bookies match his odds?' Sally was fascinated by the mathematics of the betting.

'They don't want to increase their liability on one horse in case they can't lay it off. They have to balance their book,' explained Cautious. 'Charlie's only giving better odds because the Russians have put extra dosh in his satchel. If too many other bookies match his odds, he'll push it out by another quarter of a point.'

'Does it really make that much difference?' asked Sally.

'If you lay, say, £4,000 on at 5–2 you get back £10,000. You do it at 11–4, you get back £11,000. Which are you going to take?'

As the horses began cantering down to the start, there was a flurry of activity as the bookies shortened the odds on Tower Bridge. From 5–2 he was 9–4 and then 2–1. Most bookies wiped his price off their boards. When the price went back up, it was down to 7–4.

'What's that mean?' asked Sally.

Cautious grimaced at the tictac men frantically sending their messages. 'A lot of money's just gone on Tower Bridge. Someone thinks they know something. They think he'll win.'

Tower Bridge, a rangy chestnut, cantered down to the starting post, his jockey in red and yellow with a red cap chatting to Glendoul's rider alongside in black and white colours. The grey, Roger's Heir, followed them.

'They're wrong. The white one will win. He's the perkiest,' declared Sally, disappearing to put on her bet.

Tim watched Sally through his binoculars, then stiffened. Felicity Plumridge was marching purposefully between the lines of bookmakers. As she drew level with Charlie, he rubbed out 7–4 against Tower Bridge and chalked up 2–1, a quarter-point better than anyone else. In the distance the horses were being loaded in the starting stalls.

Mrs Plumridge spoke earnestly to Charlie who nodded. She handed over a large wad of notes which he passed to the clerk who put it deep inside his satchel. Pale and intense, she strode back towards her box.

Charlie glanced in their direction. He touched the tip of his nose with his middle finger, palm outwards. His right hand came over to touch his right shoulder. Then he banged together his fists before describing a large circle.

Cautious did a quick intake of breath.

'A punter's gone five large on the favourite.'

The course commentator's voice crackled over the loudspeakers.

'They are under starter's orders and they're off.'

Sally returned breathlessly to give Tim a peck on the cheek.

'For luck,' she explained before focusing on the race. The field stayed bunched together for the first half-mile before the pace began to tell and first one and then another fell away until by the mile marker there were just five horses left in the leading bunch.

'Castle Maid is in the lead being pressed by Roger's Heir and Glendoul. Tower Bridge is running strongly on the outside.'

'Come on Roger's Heir,' shouted Sally.

'Tower Bridge is putting in a challenge. It's Tower Bridge on the outside.'

169

Tim could see the red cap of his jockey out in front pushing on the horse with his hands and legs. The early leader fell back.

'And it's Tower Bridge by a length as they approach the two-furlong marker.'

For a second Tim swung his glasses away from the galloping horses towards the box where Felicity Plumridge stood like a rock pressing her binoculars to her eyes. Others around her were shouting for their horses but she stood distant and immobile. Tim switched back to the track.

'And it's Tower Bridge, Glendoul and Roger's Heir. It's between these three. One furlong to run and it's Tower Bridge from Glendoul and Roger's Heir and Roger's Heir is moving up . . .'

Sally did not need the binoculars. She could hear the drumming of hooves as the three horses thundered down towards the finish. It happened so quickly. With only a hundred yards to run the grey surged past Tower Bridge. The chestnut's jockey brought down the whip to urge on the favourite but he had nothing left to give.

The three horses swept past.

'Bosh. Weighed in, my son.'

Sally leapt at Tim, wrapped her legs around his waist and kissed him on the mouth. She jumped down lightly and without rearranging her dress gave Cautious a big hug, kissing him on both cheeks. He blushed scarlet. Tim remembered Mrs Plumridge. She was standing stock still, staring at the winning post.

'First, Roger's Heir. Second, Glendoul. Third, Tower Bridge. The distances, half a length and a short head.'

'So, how much did you win?' demanded Tim.

'Oodles and oodles,' laughed Sally.

In the bar they watched a video of the race while Cautious again explained why he knew Tower Bridge would not win.

'Too much weight. Knew he wouldn't have the legs,' he smirked. 'Our Charlie's happy as a sandboy. He's well up.'

'Isn't it exciting,' exclaimed Sally, breathlessly.

'Sport of kings, princess. Sport of kings,' proclaimed Cautious expansively. 'Now if you'll excuse me, I've a little bit of business to conduct. Enjoy yourselves.'

As soon as he left the bar, Sally leant over and kissed Tim.

'Just thought I'd do that.'

'I'm glad you did.' For a moment their eyes met and softened. Tim found he was holding his breath. A microsecond which he desperately wanted to last a long long time. Sally too, had opened her mouth a fraction as if she was about to say something.

'Sally! Darling!'

Tim swung round and found he was looking at a member of the starved chic aged anywhere between thirty and forty-five, with a tight, sunburnt face, an artificial glossiness and teeth too white and even. An actress who had side-slipped into marketing was his instant judgement.

'Arabella. Hello. Would you like a glass? Tim, if you would . . .'

Tim took his cue to get an extra glass. Surprisingly, he caught the barmaid's eye straight away. Sally and Arabella were deep in conversation.

Sally was saying, 'What else could I do? If he'd seen me . . . Hello. That was quick. I'm sorry, I should have introduced you. Tim Platt, a colleague. Arabella Chambers, an old friend.'

He was a colleague now, he noted.

Arabella held out a doll's hand. 'Actually I'm hosting a box here. Corporate hospitality, overseas clients, you know the sort of thing.' She was struck by an idea. 'Why don't you join us? Lots of lovely nibbles and buckets of shampoo.'

Tim waited for Sally to decline. Instead she said gaily, 'We'd love to.'

If she saw the cloud of disappointment cross Tim's face, she ignored it and Tim could do nothing but nod in pathetic

171

acquiescence while he seethed at having to share Sally with a crowd of businessmen.

'We won't stay long,' she whispered as they followed Arabella. 'Just to be polite.'

The box was not at all what Tim had expected. It was full of drunken Russians and florid Londoners talking out of the side of their mouths in the way long-term prisoners acquire. Empty champagne bottles sat under a table. More was chilling in ice buckets alongside bottles of whisky and brandy. A rough and ready form of corporate entertaining. It was clear why Arabella had invited Sally. There were only three other women and these men needed to flaunt themselves and their power before an audience.

'Don't tell anyone I speak Russian,' murmured Sally before Arabella swept her away. Tim, left by himself, wandered to the front of the box to watch the horses go down to the start of the next race. When he next looked around Sally had come alive as though someone had turned on a light deep inside her. She sparkled so that the other women, bright brassy blondes, appeared dim by her side. The Russians flocked round her.

Tim poured himself a whisky.

''ere, this is a private party. Can't remember inviting you,' growled a big man with broken veins under rheumy blue eyes, a huge cigar and the paunch of an out of condition bouncer.

'I'm with Sally.' Tim indicated in her general direction. 'Arabella invited us.'

'You look like a copper to me.'

'Afraid not.' Tim lifted his glasses to watch the horses entering the starting stalls.

'Oi, sunshine. I'm talking to you.' Tim's indifference had lit the man's drunken short fuse. 'What do you do then?'

'I'm in the Army.'

'I buy and sell fucking squaddies,' sneered the man. 'Piss off out of it.'

'I don't think so.' Ice was beginning to crackle through Tim's veins. That old flash of temper which used to land him in trouble before he learnt to harness the explosive violence. In the last year he'd believed the spark had been extinguished for ever. He slowly extended his fingers, stretching them as far as they would go, and exulted in the charge building up inside him.

'Oi, everyone, listen. Fucking shut it,' hollered the man. 'Who invited this fucking toe rag in 'ere with his fucking airs and graces? Cos he's going out on his arse.'

Arabella was instantly at his side, placatory hand on his arm. 'Behave yourself, Ronnie,' she chided. 'Tim is a captain in the SAS. He's my guest.'

Tim groaned inwardly. Why the hell had Sally said anything? He knew from bitter experience it would inflame the situation. Sally was pretending this was not happening, head close to a cocky-looking Russian.

'They're off.'

'Think yourself hard, do you?' jeered Ronnie. The others were taking an interest, hoping for a punch-up. 'Try to hit me. Go on. Hit me.'

'I've no quarrel with you,' said Tim, turning away to watch the race.

'Don't fucking turn your back on me, sunshine.' Ronnie grabbed his shoulder and spun him round. 'Hit me. Go on, fucking try.'

Tim was still turning as he raised his left hand and clicked his fingers. Ronnie's eyes followed the hand and Tim, in slow motion, reached up and flicked the end of his nose. The box bellowed in laughter.

At the back of the box, Sally told the Russian, 'My telephone number is for my friends.'

The Russian fumbled in an inside pocket of the expensive, ill-fitting suit and held out his fist. He took Sally's hand, held it upwards and dropped an uncut diamond into her palm. 'Now I am a friend, yes?'

'Yes,' said Sally. All eyes were on the confrontation

173

between Ronnie and Tim. She quickly wrote down a telephone number. 'Now I must go.'

Ronnie's eyes were watering. He had been humiliated in front of his mates, in front of his guests. No bastard ever got away with that.

'Ready?' asked Sally, appearing at Tim's side.

'You're not going anyfuckingwhere, sunshine.' White spittle bubbled at the corners of Ronnie's mouth and the red blotches on his cheeks had joined up into a crimson slash. He was raging. Drunk and raging. He was going to kill the bastard who had made a fool of him. No one, but no one messed with Big Ronnie Sparks.

Tim too felt angry, angry at Sally for deserting him. But his anger was like tempered steel against the other's molten rage.

He shrugged and raised his right hand in a slow parabola. When it was level with Ronnie's face he again clicked his fingers. Ronnie's face jerked after the hand and Tim, who had shifted his weight, hit him with a left cross on the point of the jaw. His fist, travelling no further than nine inches struck like a piston. Ronnie crumpled. For a moment the only sound was that of an empty champagne bottle slowly revolving.

'Some people never learn,' said Tim. 'When the finger points at the moon, the fool stares at the finger.'

He looked around, deliberately challenging eye contact, then took Sally's arm.

'I'm sorry to have spoilt your friend's party,' he said bitterly when they were outside. It was the first emotion he had allowed himself for some time and it tasted like bile in his mouth.

Sunday 15 March

'Hello. Back for more.'

'I told you, I will fly every day I can. Soon I'll go solo and then watch me.' The grinning Arab made zooming motions with his hand.

Cheryl, the flying club secretary, inspected her rota. 'I'm afraid Chris, the chief flying instructor, isn't here today. Eddie will take you up. He's taxiing in now. Did you remember your German log book?'

Tari slapped his palm to his forehead. 'Dolt. Idiot. I would forget the hump on a camel. Tomorrow. I promise tomorrow.'

'There's no hurry. We can always transfer the hours later.'

A bustling, curly-haired man in white shirt with two gold bars on his epaulettes pushed open the glass door to the clubhouse and began to fill in the flying sheet on the counter.

'Eddie, this is Ali. Your next pupil.'

'Pleased to meet you.' Eddie did not look up. 'Get yourself a quick cuppa and I'll be with you in a minute.'

Tari wandered past the coffee machine into the deserted bar and began inspecting the cut-off ties on the wall.

'Christ, Eddie,' hissed Cheryl. 'This is the guy who paid the two grand up front.'

'Bloody hell! Yeh, right.' Ooops! Unless you had a rich mummy and daddy the most common way to get up the hours needed to apply for a commercial pilot's licence was to instruct. And flying instructors' jobs weren't that easy to come by. Lose this one and he'd never get to read *Flight Magazine* from the front – only from the back where jobs were advertised. He reached under the counter for the confidential pupil's notes.

Makings of good pilot, Chris had scrawled. *Must concentrate. Needs constant supervision or he'll commit suicide – and kill you. KEEP SWEET.*

Tari was standing at the sliding glass window watching a Cessna 150 stagger into the sky.

'Sorry about that,' said Eddie, all charm and bluster. 'Too much paperwork. You've flown in Germany, Cheryl tells me.'

'Yes, but I had to move to London before I could go solo.'

'So you've come here to carry on?'

'Only one place to learn near London. Biggin Hill. Battle of Britain. Spitfires.' Tari spread out his arms and began zooming around the bar making sounds of aero engines and machine guns. He ended with an explosion and a terrific crash on to a plastic settee.

'Um, yeh. Yeh, right,' said Eddie, thinking, *Christ, this guy's a fruitcake.* 'All right. If you'll do a walk round to make sure both wings are there and we have enough petrol, I'll nip to the loo and we'll go flying. You have done a walk round, haven't you?'

Tari nodded enthusiastically.

By the time Eddie climbed into the right-hand seat a few minutes later he had already gained the impression that Tari was large, round and jovial. Instead he found a slight figure with deep brown eyes grinning manically.

'Biggin Hill. Good morning. Golf Bravo Juliet Kilo Foxtrot.'

'Kilo Foxtrot. Good morning.'

'Biggin Kilo Foxtrot. We'd like some circuits, please sir.'

'Kilo Foxtrot. Three in the circuit at the moment. Right hand. Runway two one. QFE niner niner seven. QNH one zero one seven.'

'Two one. Niner niner seven. One zero one seven.' Eddie, doing it by the book, scribbled the figures on to the perspex cover of his map. He unnecessarily turned the knob on the altimeter away from the correct setting so Tari could reset it.

'So what have you done?' asked Eddie.

'Circuits, cross-country, tight turns, engine failure on take-off. Honestly, I am very close to going solo.'

'Okay, off you go.'

Tari kicked the brakes free and inched forward the throttle, jabbing hard on the left brake to bring the nose on to the centre line of the perimeter track.

'Where are you from?' asked Eddie once they had established a moderate speed.

'Qatar. In the Persian Gulf. My father is in the construction business. He builds palaces, hotels, oil wells.' He laughed at his own joke.

Tari went through his pre-flight checks, talking to himself in sing-song English. 'Now I turn the key one two and watch. Revs fall less than one fifty. One two now one. Drop. Good. High revs, good. Id-ling good. Carb heat, good. Petrol pump, yes, flaps, yes, wiggle wiggle.' He pulled and turned the yoke and turned his head to see the rudders react to his foot pressure. 'Yes sir.'

'Very good,' commended Eddie.

They taxied up to the hold on runway 21 as a Robin yawed towards them, crabbed sidewards, bounced and took off again.

'Bloody shit,' exclaimed Tari. 'I tell you what. I will demonstrate a short field take-off, okay?'

'Okay,' agreed Eddie, remembering Ali's file. 'But watch your airspeed.'

'Bet you I am airborne by the numbers.'

Eddie mentally measured the relatively short distance to the figures painted in the middle of the runway. It was feasible – just.

'Kilo Foxtrot, cleared for take-off.'

'Kilo Foxtrot, roger,' said Eddie.

'Brrm,' purred Tari. They turned on to the centre line

and Tari stood on the brakes while he slowly increased the power until the airframe vibrated. He transferred his feet to the rudder bars, holding the TB9 against the torque of its engine as it rolled forward. As they gathered speed, he let down more flap until they were fully extended. On the numbers, Tari hauled back on the yoke and they went up like a lift.

'Whee,' cried Tari. 'I win.'

'Watch your airspeed.' Eddie thrust the yoke forward to stop the aircraft falling out of the sky. They lumbered along barely above stalling speed until Eddie brought up the flaps to 30 degrees and established their climb at 75 knots. At 300 feet he handed her back to Tari. Chris had been right about keeping an eye on his pupil. He could kill them both.

'No need to fly bomber circuits,' Eddie instructed as they turned downwind at 800 feet. 'Keep it tight. You're doing excellently.' He was, too. After the initial lunacy he had settled into a proficient pilot. He flew by his fingertips, adding only small increments of power and making gradual changes of direction. All very subtle and smooth. Eddie began to feel confident enough to begin chatting.

'What are you doing over here?'

Tari grinned self-consciously. 'I was supposed to look after my father's business interests in Germany but I met a Catholic girl in München.' He giggled. 'I had to leave. My father would go mad if I married a non-Moslem. So I came here and soon I start business school. Until then I am looking for opportunities. How much is a small plane? Say like this or the older one, the ST150.'

'It depends on what it's got in the way of avionics. Any-where from ten to sixteen grand. Maybe more. Thinking of buying one?'

'I could be.' Tari fell silent. It was obvious to Eddie that the Arab liked the idea.

After thirty minutes Eddie became bored and suggested they do some cross-country. Unusually for the time of year there was fine weather cumulus away to the east and he

178

thought his pupil would enjoy playing in the clouds. He dialled 117.3 for the Detling beacon on the edge of the London TMA and told Tari to hold track for the beacon.

How different it was flying here, thought Tari, looking down at the rolling green fields and small lush villages joined by neat tarmacked roads. Here and there were large secluded houses with swimming pools and tennis courts. No endless gritty desert, no sudden red dust storms, no plodding strings of camels casting long shadows. Everything was softer, easier, flabbier. Like the people.

When they were overhead Detling they climbed up above 3,000 feet into the clouds where Tari made more machine gun noises and pretended to swoop on invading Messerschmitts.

'This is wonderful. Truly wonderful,' he enthused. 'The clouds look so solid. Like walls of wool. Then puff, they are no more than vapour.' They flew along a vertical gorge of cloud; one second they were shrouded in swirling wraiths of mist, climbing over a downy hillside, the next they exploded into bright sunshine.

During their return flight Tari began talking about owning a plane of his own. Would Eddie keep his ears open? He would be grateful he said, very grateful.

As he drove away, barping the horn of the new black Mercedes, Tari waved cheerfully once, pressed the button to wind up the window and seemed to deflate. He didn't know which was the more taxing, play-acting or flying.

Cheryl, waving goodbye, had the strange thought that the Arab's still, watchful eyes did not fit in with the rest of his jolly, laughing countenance.

It was only at the end of the day as Eddie drove home in his old Ford Escort that it dawned on him how well Tari had handled the plane among the clouds. Not like a learner at all.

Monday 16 March

'I'm sorry Haydn, I simply cannot believe it.' Livy Hull tugged crossly at a pearl earring. 'Are you honestly telling me that a serving, dyed-in-the-wool KGB hood with one foot firmly planted in the Moscow Narco Group wants to come over? Why?'

'I don't know. He made contact with your service,' replied Williams, rubbing in the fact that her colleagues in Six had not told her of the approach from codename Valentine.

He also did not tell her that, in a roundabout way, he had suggested that route to Valentine.

'Maybe he's had his hand in the till. Stashed the money over here and now wants a new ID to enjoy it,' smirked Plumridge, enjoying Livy Hull's discomfort. 'In return for which he'll shop his partners in crime.'

'Do we want any more KGB hoods? I thought they were falling out of trees.' Livy was not willing to forgive the slight.

Williams shrugged and kept his thoughts to himself. It was not easy debating values of agents when you knew so much more than you could say.

'Is Valentine *genuine*?' Livy took off her glasses and scowled myopically.

'Someone made the approach,' lied Williams patiently. Why did she have to be so bloody-minded? 'We don't know if it was a fishing expedition, a licensed operation or a bit of freelance banditry, but our masters are of the opinion that we should listen to what Valentine has to say.'

'How was the approach made?'

'Livy!' said Williams reproachfully.

'All right but why go to Vietnam to talk to him? Why doesn't he just get on a plane and fly to London? I *mean*, he must have a passport.'

'American drugs intelligence believes a huge cocaine shipment recently passed through the Colombian port of Buenaventura,' said Plumridge. 'The Cartels have strong links with the Moscow Narco Group. Valentine's presence in Vietnam makes sense if the group is shipping the cocaine through its base at Cam Ranh Bay.' He crossed an ankle over a knee and leaned back expansively. 'His presence there actually lends him credence. Yes, I like him.'

'Phuh!'

'When's the new KGB liaison expert on the Mafiya paying us a courtesy call?' demanded Williams.

'Primakov? Middle of next week,' replied Livy, still glowering at Plumridge. 'Why?'

Williams sucked the earpiece of his glasses. 'I'd be interested to hear what Valentine has to say about him. He doesn't show up in any registry or database.'

'So?'

'So. I'm curious why he's using a work name when he's a legal. No pictures of a Colonel Primakov, either. For all we know we could be emptying our drawers to a thief in the night.'

'Oh really, Haydn. Sometimes your paranoia goes too far.'

'That's what I'm paid for. Perhaps our Tim will recognize him from his adventures in Russia.' Williams found a silver hair on his shoulder and held it up to examine its length.

A bleeper sounded in Livy's large black handbag. She fished it out and held it up close to her eyes. Her face remained expressionless.

'Well, I've made my feelings known.' She rose, smoothing down her skirt. 'I think you're barking up the wrong tree. Excuse me.'

'Crabby today, isn't she?' observed Plumridge, always more

equable when others around him were angry or put out.

'If she'd waited, I'd have told her the all-ports alert is going to be announced Wednesday.'

'By the way. I have something to show you.' Plumridge passed over the buff envelope he had been holding.

Williams pulled out a selection of twelve by ten photographs. They showed Tim at the front of the box at Lingfield races.

Oh, bloody hell! Williams lit a cigarette to play for time and wondered why the right hand never knew what the left was up to. He carefully scrutinized each frame. Fortunately the camera had not been able to penetrate to the rear of the box.

'We'd better have Tim in.'

Tim promptly admitted being at the races with Sally. 'She bumped into an old friend who invited us to the box. We didn't stay long. It was full of East End villains and Russian thugs.'

'Have you reported this contact?' demanded Plumridge, who knew he hadn't.

'No.'

'Why not?'

'I didn't think it was important.'

'Don't you think others should be the judge of that?'

'Did you see anyone you recognized?' asked Williams in a softer voice.

'You mean at the races?'

'Of course at the races,' barked Plumridge.

'No, sir.' Tim addressed Williams. 'That is, apart from Plumridge and his wife. I hope she had a profitable day?'

Plumridge bridled. 'What do you mean by that?'

'Betting on the horses.'

'My wife does not gamble.' His mouth snapped shut.

Tim, smarting from Plumridge's brusque treatment, said innocently: 'I was sure I saw your wife place a bet. She was wearing a green Loden coat and silk scarf.'

'You must have been mistaken.'

Williams's eyes flicked between the two like a snake's tongue.

'Sorry.' Tim's insolence was tangible. 'Your wife must have a double.'

Our Tim's standing up for himself, approved Williams. Not before time. Is Sally giving him confidence or is his natural loathing of Plumridge finally surfacing?

'I don't suppose you've come across a KGB colonel calling himself Primakov on your Russian adventures, have you, Tim?' asked Williams, changing the subject.

Tim thought. 'No, sir. What does he look like?'

'Wish I knew.'

When the others left, he shook his head in despair and pulled out the letter from Greenwich Council he had received that morning.

Thank you for your recent communication regarding the above Penalty Charge Notice . . .

Why did these illiterate morons feel the need to use capital letters?

The contents of your letter have been given careful consideration . . .

Rubbish. They'd had his appeal just two days. A mere blinking of the eye by Greenwich Council's own mean time. They couldn't wait to put the boot in. And ungrammatically.

. . . The above vehicle was parked in a residents bay displaying a visitors permit which was dispalying an incorrect month ie January instaed of February.

Nor could they be bothered to check their spelling

Having considered the facts, the Council regrets to inform you that it is satisfied that the Penalty Charge Notice has been correctly issued and payment of the charge is now due. The boxes on the visitors permit displayed in the vehicle were incorrectly scratched and, therefore, the permit was invalid.

Terrible English. Williams read on. He could either accept the Council's decision and pay the penalty – if paid within 14 days the discounted price of £20 would be accepted. Never.

You have the right to pursue a formal appeals process. You should be advised however that taking the issue through the appeals procedure would lose you the opportunity to pay at the discounted rate. The formal procedure is set out in the Road Traffic Act 1991 and must be strictly adhered to . . .'

Who had rejected his appeal? There was no signature. Merely some scrawled initials. What a shoddy, Kafkaesque way of dealing with the public. The arrogant indifference of the council official infuriated Williams. Not to know one's judge was alien to the precepts of justice. Only the Inquisition were masked. His blood boiled over.

'Alison. Get me a copy of the Road Traffic Act 1991, there's a smashing girl.'

Williams called Tim into his room late in the afternoon. The past few hours had been busy ones. Pieces of the jigsaw had slotted together; others had slipped apart. Plumridge's guess about Vietnam had been prescient. Livy Hull came in to say the DEA did indeed anticipate a drugs movement through Cam Ranh Bay in the next few days and requested a Brit on side.

'Don't mind Plumridge,' Williams reassured Tim. 'You couldn't have known what you were walking into. How were the races?'

'Fine, thank you.'

The fight had been a small blot on a good day. Sally had been so sweet and apologetic, ardent to make up. She had clung to his arm and begged his forgiveness. 'If I'd known I wouldn't have gone within a thousand miles of those awful people.' Tim couldn't stay angry with her. They had dinner in a small Thai restaurant and Tim hinted that they might meet on Sunday, but she headed him off at the pass by making it clear she would be tied up all day. She wasn't around today either. Shame.

'The men you found yourself with on Saturday were London villains and Mafiya connections, local criminals happy to help Russians launder their money in property

184

or whatever for a healthy cut. Most of the Russians were, we think, from Ekaterinburg but there may have been one or two from Moscow,' said Williams, putting a cassette into the video player. 'The gangs talk to each other if there's profit in it. See if you recognize any of these from the races. This was taken yesterday.'

The video had been shot through a peephole of a parked van. It showed a small crowd of men waiting under the pavement awning of an expensive restaurant. Two smaller swarthy men who could have been Latin Americans joined them and they all went inside. The watcher was shooting through the plate glass window. A crowd of men at the bar. Indistinct figures of women in the background. The video became a series of stills taken inside the restaurant.

'That one there,' pointed Tim. 'Long face, holding a glass.'

'Good,' said Williams, contentedly.

A new scene. A bedroom. The camera high up, pointing down on to the bed. The same man again, now in his shirt, unbuttoned to the waist. A woman's arm came into view. Williams moved in front of the set.

'We don't need to see this, do we?' He turned off the TV, leaving the video running. 'You're going to Vietnam. The Cousins intend to electronically tag a shipment of cocaine, jarking, I think you call it, and they're demanding a demonstration of commitment from us, say Six. You will lend your expertise as an ace jarker.'

'Right, sir.' Tim made to stand up. Williams had not finished.

'But that is not why you are going to Vietnam – whatever the Cousins may think.' Williams reached for the phone. 'Let's get some tea organized and I'll tell you about Valentine.'

It was a masterclass in disinformation. In confiding that he believed the Moscow Narco Group were to be instrumental in moving the virus, Williams made no mention of his hidden reason for Tim's operation. Ten minutes later he concluded by saying, 'Your job is to bring Valentine home. Your priority is the Marburg. The drugs are secondary. I want you to ask Valentine two questions as a token of his earnest.'

'Yes, sir.'

'What does he know of the Marburg? The flask may already be in Vietnam to be included in the shipment. Then again, if the drugs are destined for Europe they'll cross Russia straight through Polecat's territory. Does that make sense?'

'Yes, sir. But you said you had two questions.'

'Did I?' Williams appeared abstracted. 'Oh, yes. Ask him the real name of Colonel Primakov. I need those questions addressed immediately so I'm sending Sally with you in case Valentine's English is not up to it. Try to look disappointed, boy.'

Tuesday 17 March

'But why can't we go out? I'm bored.'

'Soraya's not very well, are you?' The nurse frowned at the little girl's flushed cheeks. 'You were ill in the night and you've still got a temperature.'

'I'm better now, honest, Fatima. Please. Please. Can we go and play in the garden?' Her fingers were fidgeting like demented worms.

It wasn't healthy for the girls to be cooped up in this Baghdad villa all day, but the garden was a dangerous shambles, strewn with masonry and rubble from the cruise missile attack on the neighbouring airport. The wrecked underground shelter with its crumbling concrete and jagged steel wires was an irresistible magnet – and a death trap.

'Here.' Fatima thrust a pot of water at the unshaven guard. 'Put this on the fire and make sure it boils.'

'It's not necessary.' He made no effort to take the blackened pot.

'Do as I say or I'll throw it over you.' Fatima, eyes blazing, stamped her foot. 'And then I'll tell your officer what an ignorant pig you are.'

In the overgrown garden the guard built up the fire from pieces of charred and splintered wood and spat into the pot.

Leila was bossing her younger sister around as usual. They were having a dolls' tea party and Fatima watched closely to make sure they did not put tap water in the dolls' cups and drink it. Soraya was being hyperactive and fretful at the same time. She was normally such a happy little girl. Bright as a button and so advanced for three.

Fatima was fiercely protective of her charges. Poor little orphans. That's what they were in all but name. Their mother dead and their father away fighting the Zionists. He would be furious when he found they were being kept in a virtual prison guarded by a surly dolt from the secret police. The last villa had been better, but two days ago they had been moved here next to the Republican Guards compound. The drains smelt, the lights only worked for a few hours every evening and she did not trust the water. The sun came out.

'Shall we take our dolls for a short walk?' Fatima glared at the guard, daring him to deny her. She didn't like this district. Too many soldiers and cruel men, but the little girls did not mind. Anything away from the boredom of the dusty villa. And the fresh air would do the girls good.

They walked out into the street to find a tall Westerner wearing a blue baseball cap surrounded by armed soldiers.

Shane Cosker was coming perilously close to losing his temper – again. He and his team had received a tip that the 2nd Battalion of the Special Republican Guard had carried germ agents in refrigerated coolers from a military training centre to al-Bakr University. They had tried to spring a surprise inspection to uncover records of the transfer. But soldiers at a security checkpoint refused to let them through. Now other military units rushed out to surround them.

'You leave. Leave,' screamed a furious officer. 'This area is off limits. You are next to a presidential villa. You are not allowed to be here. Go.'

'I have the right to inspect these army buildings.'

'You have no right. You have no right to be in my country.' The officer with green epaulettes was working himself up into a fury.

An army truck pulled away to reveal a line of soldiers passing bulky objects wrapped in black plastic bags over the wall from the headquarters into the presidential villa.

They were bigger than log books. Hell! They were the right size and shape to be the coolers themselves.

'What are those men doing?' demanded Cosker, chewing gum hard.

'You leave.' The officer screamed orders and soldiers advanced on them, rifles held across their chests.

'Come in. Come in.' Fatima gathered the two girls to her side like a mother hen. The UN party reluctantly climbed back into their Jeeps, Cosker tight-lipped and white with fury. 'We'll go and play indoors. It's not nice out here.'

Wednesday 18 March

Sally stood on the balcony wearing only a thin tee shirt and looked across Ho Tay lake which stretched ahead, placid and unruffled. Tim was asleep in bed with the single cotton sheet pulled up to his chin. The air conditioning was on its lowest setting and the large ceiling fan on high so that it sent out gusts and eddies, lifting the sheet off his body. Tim, who claimed he could never sleep on flights, had passed the time reading a guidebook. Now he was catching up before they set off to find Valentine – or Valentine found them.

Unable to sleep, Sally regarded the absolute stillness of the lake and felt sad and strangely reflective. It occurred to her that her life resembled an unequal musical stave.

One line, the top one, ran all the way from her birth and held the sum of Sally's knowledge and experience. Only Sally knew that one.

One, a long time ago, had covered her childhood – or childhoods, because there was more than one in the refugee camps and the training camps.

The line that began when she fell in love with Mahmoud.

The line which ended the day the Israelis handed her over.

The line when she paid her dues, still continuing, but please God not for much longer. And the final line? That was the future. That was waiting to be written.

I am both victim and high priestess, she told herself. Miles from home, the home I don't have. Miles from me, the me I don't know.

A ridiculously young guard in bright green army fatigues with outsize red epaulettes hollered at an even younger boy in a wooden boat. The boy was rowing an old man with a wispy white beard to cut weed from the shallow bottom. When they drifted close to the hotel, the guard began throwing stones. One struck the old man on the back and dropped into the boat. The old man did not turn round, merely touched the point of impact with his hand. The boy shipped oars, picked up the stone bigger than his fist, shouted at the guard and hurled it back. It plopped harmlessly into the water. The guard jeered and threw two more stones.

Thang Loi hotel was modern – for Hanoi – and functional, made out of slabs of white concrete, stained by the damp heat. It was alleged the floor plan of the four-storey hotel had been copied from a one-storey Cuban hotel, which explained why there were doors which led nowhere and corridors ending in blank walls.

There had been a moment's embarrassment while a receptionist with bright red fingernails and an impish grin informed them that the reservation from London had only specified one room and the hotel was full.

'Are you sure?' inquired Tim, looking sheepish.

The receptionist, whose name badge said Bach Ha, shook her waist-long black hair. 'Yes, afraid so.'

'I'm comfortable with that,' smiled Sally.

They had been very chaste. Sally had gone into the bathroom first and emerged in her sleeveless tee shirt. Tim wore his boxer shorts. Sally felt sleep gathering around her. She slid the window shut and climbed into the nearer bed. Despite the fan, it was too warm with the tee shirt on. She pulled it off and stuck her arms and legs out of the sheet. Slowly, subconsciously she divested herself of most of the sheet so when Tim awoke she was almost naked. He lay and looked at her for a long time.

'This is the right place so we'll wait until two o'clock and follow instructions.' Tim shifted uncomfortably. 'I feel I'm in Lilliput.'

They perched on tiny red plastic stools only inches above

the ground. From the café they gazed across Truc Bach lake at hoardings advertising Carlsberg lager set among the flame trees on the distant bank.

Sally was discovering that Tim was obsessed with maps and guidebooks. 'Truc Bach means white silk,' he read. 'There was a palace here which was turned into a reformatory for deviant royal concubines who were condemned to weave very fine white silk. By the way, we're millionaires twice over. I changed $100 at the hotel and got one million two hundred thousand dong. Did you know there are no coins in Vietnam?'

'Fascinating.'

They had woken to find an unsigned note at the hotel reception. They were about to follow its instructions.

'Two o'clock. Let's go sight-see.' Sally raised an arm and two pencil-thin cyclo riders in green pith helmets and Hawaiian shirts performed a suicidal U-turn in front of a dilapidated bus and pulled up, gesturing feverishly for them to climb aboard.

'One each,' decided Sally. 'They're not used to Western-sized people.'

The cyclos consisted of a back-to-front tricycle with the cyclist behind the forward-facing passenger seat. They set off towards the old quarter of the city, riding through narrow streets whose names – Paper Street, Rice Noodle Street, Fried Fish Street – once reflected their business.

'This is a nice way to get around,' called Tim. 'You feel you're part of street life.'

'You also feel that there's nothing between you and your Maker,' replied Sally as a moped sliced across their front.

There were very few cars, just lingering herds of bicycles and buzzing Honda motorcycles, each carrying at least three people. Tangled electric wires drooped between rusty pylons like untidy lengths of noodles. Small crowds squatted at open-fronted corner cafés, dipping into rice bowls with their chopsticks. The pavements were cracked and uneven and the buildings low and pleasantly shabby. There were relatively few Westerners. After an hour's tour, Tim found a restaurant in a tiny room upstairs in the old quarter where they were the only diners. They drank Halida beer and feasted on sweet and sour fish, prawns in a delicate ginger sauce and slices of beef with dark, strong spinach.

'We're making ourselves pretty visible,' said Tim. 'I just wish Valentine would contact us.'

'It's a funny feeling knowing there's someone out there watching you.'

'Maybe there's not. Maybe this is a wild goose chase,' said Tim. He hoped it wasn't. As he was leaving, Williams, in a rare moment of complicity, had murmured how much he was relying on Valentine coming over. The Arab and the Marburg had dropped out of sight. Valentine was their only lead.

He counted out a pile of the ragged notes for the bill. The boys were waiting for them. They pedalled past the cold concrete cube of Ho Chi Minh's mausoleum and stopped at the tranquil oasis of the Temple of Literature before heading back across the railway line into the French quarter. Here the teeming streets became broad, leafy boulevards of ochre apartment blocks with green shutters and red-tiled roofs and once elegant mansions in need of a scrape and a coat of paint. They could have been in a rundown provincial French town *circa* 1914 if it were not for the pigs that lay squealing in long wicker baskets and a class of fifteen small schoolchildren, neat in blue uniforms, all clinging to the same cyclo.

'The school bus,' declared Tim. The afternoon wore on and still Valentine did not make contact. They had to be clean of any tail by now. Tim was getting a sinking feeling that Valentine was not going to contact them that day. Okay. He could wait. He wasn't sure Williams could.

Sally watched Tim anxiously scanning any Westerners who came near them in the hope it was their contact. She felt guilty. She could describe Valentine to him – in great detail – only she was not allowed to. Poor Tim, an innocent abroad.

Night fell quickly and by eight o'clock the streets were largely deserted. Near their hotel, they came to a beer garden set behind a dusty hedge. Tim gave the cyclists $10 each. They accepted the notes palm upwards before folding their hands as if in prayer and bowing with simple dignity. A boy led them along a tunnel of high shrubs to an opening. They found themselves in a tiny clearing with a bench and small table right on the side of yet another lake.

'A canoodling bar,' laughed Sally. 'These communists aren't that starchy after all.'

The night air was so soft that Sally wanted to rub it between her fingers. Unknown golden stars twinkled in the velvet sky. Tim drank in the redolence. 'In such a night Troilus methinks mounted the Troyan walls, And sighed his soul toward the Grecian tents where Cressid lay that night.'

'I didn't know you were poetic.'

'It's not me. It's Shakespeare.'

'You're a very unexpected man,' observed Sally and for once her English let her down.

A frog began to croak in the floating lily bed. It was answered by first one then another and another until the whole lakeside reverberated with deep-throated sounds while Tim and Sally held hands with the innocence of children.

At the reception desk Bach Ha handed them another note in the same handwriting.

'When did this arrive?' demanded Tim.

'A boy brought it, maybe two hours ago.'

'Not a Russian?'

'Russian.' Bach Ha looked puzzled, then her face cleared. 'No. Two *Lien Xo* call this afternoon but you not here. They go away.'

'How did you know they were Russian?'

'*Lien Xo* in my country a long time.'

194

'They ask for me by name?'

'Yes. You Mr Platt, right?'

Tim and Sally looked at each other. It didn't make sense. Valentine would not bring a friend if he was going to defect. But who else knew they were here?

Tim passed the note to Sally. 'We're getting the runaround. He wants us to go to China Beach.'

'Where's China Beach?'

'Almost 500 miles south. How do we get there, Bach Ha?'

She indicated an airline computer in the back office, out of place among the Dickensian ledgers and bundles of coarse, yellowing paper. She tapped away at the keys. 'You fly Danang, but tomorrow flight full.'

There were options, she explained. The Reunification Express left for Ho Chi Minh City nightly at 1am. It would reach Danang at . . . she looked up a battered timetable . . . 3am the day after tomorrow. There was an express bus that left at 6am. That took just 24 hours on a good day. 'It's quicker if you hire a car. Only maybe sixteen hours.' There were no self-drive cars.

'Tomorrow you enjoy yourself. I book you flight next day.'

'We'll think about it,' said Tim. 'Shall we go to the bar?'

'I'm awash with beer and I'm still jet-lagged. I'll go to bed, if you don't mind. You have a beer if you want one.' Sally wanted to get into her own bed and pretend to be asleep by the time Tim came. She wasn't ready for his advances. Not yet. Not ever, if she was strong enough.

Tim leant on the bar and tried to work out the ramifications of the Russians' visit. Maybe Valentine's fellow mobsters had found out he planned to defect. They were on his trail. Was that why Valentine wanted them to move on? But how did the Russians know to ask for him by name? How did they know where he was staying? Perhaps Valentine had been clever. Perhaps he had used his colleagues as unwitting dupes. Then again, perhaps he was about to double-cross Tim.

A green gecko clung to the ceiling waiting for an insect supper over the heads of two Taiwanese businessmen drinking bottles of Heineken. An English grammar book lay face down on the corner of the bar.

Bach Ha materialized. 'What you want?'

'You're a barmaid as well?'

'Yes. I do everything.' She bobbed her head, grinning happily.

Tim took a Halida beer and pointed at the English book.

'It's mine,' said Bach Ha. 'Once we all learn Russian. Now we study English.'

The Taiwanese belched their way out. When Bach Ha went to clear away their glasses Tim saw for the first time that she was perfectly proportioned but tiny. She came up to his chest and her waist was the thickness of his thigh.

'You are very short,' he smiled.

'No. You are very tall,' she corrected. 'Where is your lady?'

'She's gone to bed.'

'You no go to bed with her?'

'No, I drink a beer.'

Bach Ha nodded, thinking it over. Then in a coquettish gesture, she pulled her long hair across the lower part of her face so only her bright impish eyes were on display. 'Good. You drink beer and talk to me in English. Maybe I give you free beer for English lesson. Yes?'

'Yes,' said Tim.

When he finally came to bed, Sally was sleeping with deep rhythmic breaths. She had thrown off the sheet down to her waist. He did not wake her.

Thursday 19 March

Tim was waiting in reception for Sally to join him for breakfast when he saw the two men emerge from a red Japanese car. They both wore jackets despite the early heat. The nearer one was vaguely familiar. Tim wondered if he had been on the video? But the second one! His heart missed a beat. It was the same thick-necked thug with white hair who'd taken him to Polecat's dacha near Rostov. What the hell was going on!

Tim dashed to the desk. 'Bach Ha, are those two men coming up the path the same ones who asked for me yesterday?'

Bach Ha looked out into the sunlight. 'Yes, I think so. Yes. The man with white hair.'

'They are very bad men.' Tim thought desperately. 'You must say we are not staying here. Say we have taken a car to Halong Bay and we come back tomorrow. Do you understand?'

She nodded gravely. 'Yes. Take your passports quick.'

Sally was hopping along the covered walkway from the bedrooms trying to avoid stepping on the cracks in the concrete. Tim could not reach her before the men arrived at reception. He backed towards a lacquered screen gesturing madly. The men were at the doorway. Please look up. Please. Sally finally raised her eyes to see Tim waving like a lunatic. She frowned in incomprehension. Tim jabbed a finger at reception and she saw the two men. She did not know why Tim was hiding but that was good enough for her. At the last second she darted behind a large plant.

Bach Ha approached the men, smiled, listened and

regretfully shook her head. She indicated the rack containing guests' passports and shook her head again, more forcibly this time. The men appeared not to trust her for they left the desk to inspect the tourists and businessmen having breakfast. A wave of arriving Germans swept into reception so that when the men went to resume their questioning, there was a two-deep wall of flesh between them and Bach Ha. She smiled apologetically and continued taking the Germans' passports. The men walked to their car, glanced back once and drove off towards the centre of Hanoi.

Tim explained briefly to a shaken Sally that the white-haired Russian was the Polecat's lieutenant.

'How did they find us?' Sally had turned pale.

'God knows, but we can't stay here. Are there flights anywhere near Danang, Bach Ha?' demanded Tim, scanning the guidebook.

Sally could not wait to get away. As the white-haired man had pushed through the crowd, his jacket had opened and she'd seen the handle of a pistol. Something was going on she didn't understand. She had an uncomfortable feeling it was some sort of game of cat and mouse. And she was definitely the mouse.

'I will look on computer. Come.' Bach Ha led the way into the back office. 'You go to Hué? It's only 100 kilometres from Danang. Flight at 12.30. Yes, there are seats.' She tapped away with the long red fingernail until she was satisfied.

They paid the bill in US dollars and Tim added $50. She tried to give it back. 'For you,' he said quietly. Her eyes widened and she whispered, 'Thank you.'

Poor Boyar. Emma threw him a piece of meat and the bear sat upright on his haunches, the chunk between his claws. Poor Boyar. Poor Emma, too. Since Tim left she felt more homesick than ever. She awoke every morning with a dull ache in her stomach. She could not wait to get home. There was nothing to look forward to here. She stuck it only because to quit would be letting down her parents. Tim had been a fleeting bright spot in a dull sky, but since he'd gone, the night had grown darker. Igor the Polecat had turned against her. He was very excited about something to do with the Far East, but he did not use her to translate his letters any more. He made it obvious he did not trust her. She thought it unfair. She hadn't discussed his business with Tim, but now he went out of his way to snub and belittle her.

He would summon her to the dacha only to keep her hanging around for hours while he stayed in the bedroom with his two whores. Once they had come out and watched a porn movie, the three of them, almost naked, fondling each other on the sofa. Emma, red-faced and angry, had left the room. Another night Igor had mockingly suggested she join them and then accused her of being frigid when she refused. His men jeered at her and tried to paw her as she passed. The atmosphere had changed. She didn't feel safe in Polecat's dacha.

'Emma. Emma. Where are you? Come here.'

The Polecat was with two men she had not seen before. One stared at her in such a way she felt cold fear.

'I don't need you tonight.'

'Then why did you bring me out here?' she had the courage to ask.

'Give me the watch,' he demanded.

'Why?' Emma put a protective hand over the Cartier watch.

'I want to get an identical one for the daughter of a business associate. You can have it back.' Igor held out his hand.

Emma did not believe him. She hesitated only for a moment.

'Here. Take it.'

In the darkness of the porch Igor kissed her with an unusual passion, squeezing her breasts and kneading her pubic bone as if conducting an inventory. Touching the places which belonged to him.

'Goodbye.'

The driver did not drop her outside the university block as he usually did but at the crossroads a quarter of a mile away, claiming he had another errand to run. Emma did not mind. She was glad to get out of the hot stuffy car with its stench of black tobacco and sickly eau de cologne. As she walked through the night she knew she would never return to the dacha. She hoped Boyar would be all right. To cheer herself up she'd write a letter home to her mum and dad when she got in. She'd posted one to Tim that afternoon. She hoped he'd reply. It'd be lovely to stay with him. She was still fondly imagining a romantic idyll together as she stepped off the pavement in the dark stretch where the street lamps had failed. She did not see the black car until it was almost upon her.

'You want taxi?' An unctuous man in a blue suit two sizes too big weaved and ducked before them. 'I know good hotel. Where you go?'

Tim and Sally watched four boys push a trolley carrying passengers' luggage to the brick shed which pretended to be Hué airport.

'China Beach,' said Tim.

'Very long way. Eighty dollars.'

'Seems a lot,' said Tim.

'Don't be mean. We can afford it,' chided Sally.

'It's not the principle, it's the money.'

'Seventy-five dollars.' The man led the way to a white car with a bright blue offside wing, grafted from another car. 'Water buffalo,' he explained.

'It's going to be dark when we get there,' said Sally. 'Let's have a flying tour of Hué before we set off.' She was safe for the moment and her good spirits bubbled back to the surface.

'You were wrong then, yah.' Sally dug Tim playfully in

the ribs as they passed large circular pits. 'They weren't bomb craters after all. They were graves. Don't know nuffin, do you? Admit it!'

'We were flying over the demilitarized zone and they looked like craters. It seemed logical.' Tim tried to suppress an embarrassed grin.

They drove through a gate in the high ramparts into the inner city called the Citadel. 'The Communists held Hué for twenty-five days during the Tet offensive,' read Tim. 'By the time it was retaken by the Americans and South Vietnamese, over 100,000 had died.'

They left the car to walk into the Imperial Enclosure and on into the Forbidden Purple City where the emperors' concubines lived. The site was covered in long, rough grass and vegetable allotments. A few crumbling stone balustrades and tumbled carvings were all that remained of imperial glory.

Sally, who had finally got her hands on the guidebook, demanded to see a famous parrot in a nearby pagoda.

'He can say *"Thua thay co khach"* – Master, there is a guest. That's very good isn't it? Better than I could say.'

'But he's Vietnamese. Bet he'd have trouble with *"Ilkley Moor baht 'at"*.'

'He also says *"A Di Da Buddha"*. What a funny thing to say. Sounds like a football chant. I wonder what a *Di Da Buddha* is?'

Tim tutted in exasperation. 'It's pronounced ah-zee-dah and it's the Buddha of the Past.'

'Oh! How do you know this?'

Tim gave an eloquent shrug of his shoulders as if to say: Doesn't everyone? She thumped him with her fist.

'It's on the next page,' he confessed.

'Lady. Parrot dead,' said the driver, so instead they visited the tomb of Tu Duc – a vast, serene enclosure covering temples, lakes and courtyards.

'He had 104 wives, an untold number of concubines and no kids,' read Tim as they stood among frangipani trees. 'Every meal, he had fifty chefs prepare fifty dishes which were served by fifty servants. His morning cuppa was made from drops of dew on lotus leaves. In fact, he wasn't buried here at all. He was buried secretly elsewhere with his treasure. The two hundred servants who planted him were executed to keep the secret.'

'Well, if he's not here, we may as well go,' said Sally.

The road led through suburbs of brightly painted bungalows with rusty corrugated iron roofs and neat gardens. One or two old men wearing French berets lifted their arms in tired greeting. At a broad, still river they waited for a snub-nosed tug which belched thick diesel fumes as it pushed a metal pontoon ferry. The land slept under a solid red sun. Mild cows grazed, small pot-bellied pigs rooted by the water's edge and chickens scratched in the dirt around a weathered brick shack with a palm leaf shelter. An hour later they recrossed the same river on a high bridge. They were by the coast and the waters opened into a lagoon where hundreds of stakes formed arrowhead traps into which the fish would be swept by the incoming tide.

It began to rain. Slowly at first with drops the size of a baby's fist, then increasing in tempo until they felt they were sitting under a waterfall. The driver pulled in as the rain sheeted across the countryside blotting out rice fields and distant hills. It cleared for a moment and they saw the sea frothing and churning before the curtains of rain closed in again. After ten minutes it became a steady downpour. Darkness fell and they drove through the empty streets of Danang and out again to the stolid Stalinist monolith that proclaimed itself to be the China Beach Hotel.

It was seedy, dismal and depressing. They were left to find their own rooms along dimly lit corridors and past a kitchen billowing with steam and reeking of boiled cabbage. Tim's room had a single damp grey sheet, there were cigarette burns on the cheap table and only one light worked. Sally did not suggest sharing.

Tim waited for Sally in reception and wondered why they had been given such shoddy rooms when the place seemed half empty. He caught a glimpse of Sally standing on the steps outside. She'd been quick. Obviously she had not wanted to linger in her room either.

'What a hole.'

'*Comment?*'

The girl turned. She had an olive skin and Roman nose – but from the back she was the spitting image of Sally.

'Oh. I am sorry,' stuttered Tim. 'I thought you were . . . um . . . You have the same hair . . .'

'*Quoi?*'

'You look like my friend.'

'*Non. Pardon.*' The French girl decided Tim was not trying to pick her up and smiled. At that moment Sally emerged. Tim grinned inanely and fled to her side.

'Huh! I leave you alone for two minutes and you're off chatting up strange women.'

They strolled slowly through the small aircraft hangar of a dining room, looking for anyone who might be Valentine. Tim remembered there was a second restaurant near the beach. The night was pitch black. The storm had moved south but rain still dripped off the trees. They skirted around large puddles, hearing the crash of the breakers before stumbling over the low wall of the restaurant garden. It was deserted apart from a bored waitress doodling on her order pad.

'How did the Russians know to ask for me by name?' mused Tim, returning to the subject they had nagged at off and on all day.

'How did they know where to find us?' repeated Sally.

'Perhaps one of those two thugs was Valentine. We don't know what he looks like.'

'No, we don't,' lied Sally as the waitress placed huge prawns, pork with lemon grass and fried rice in front of them.

Tim warmed to his idea. 'If Valentine had persuaded his

203

mate to come across, it would be a clever thing to do. Turning the hunter and the hunted into one.'

Sally bit her tongue and concentrated on a procession of ants which climbed up the damp wall and on to their table where they organized themselves into working parties to carry away the spilt grains of rice. She put down tiny pieces of food and tried to keep her eye on one at a time but they were so busy that she kept losing her chosen ant among the throng. When they had eaten the waitress came to collect the dirty plates and rice bowls. Before Sally could stop her, she wiped the table in a broad sweep, brushing away the ants and all their industry and enterprise. Sally felt foolishly sad.

They were walking through the grove of casuarina trees back to the lights of the hotel when a man's voice said, 'Mr Platt. Please do not turn around.'

Sally gasped. The voice came from behind and to their left where the trees were thickest.

'I am sorry to put you to so much trouble, but you understand I have to take precautions.' A reedy voice speaking mannered, accented English. 'You understand we are only looking at each other at the moment – or rather I am looking at you.'

'I have two questions to ask you,' said Tim, speaking to the darkness.

'Not until I have assurances from you.'

'Yes,' said Tim. Sally squeezed his hand.

'I want a guarantee that funds I shall move to Britain will not be seized.'

Promise him everything, promise him nothing, Williams had said.

'Why should they be?'

'You have new laws regarding seizing assets arrived at, how shall we say, unusually.'

'That should not be a problem.'

'I will want a formal undertaking. I will become German with valid passport and documentation. Your department will rent me a suitable house in Southern Ireland, near Kinsale, for the twelve months.'

'Again, that should not be a problem, but I will ask London.'

'I want your word.'

'I have to ask London.' The wind changed and Tim smelled cigarette smoke. There was a silence. When Valentine spoke again his voice had become cold and dismissive.

'They sent a messenger boy.'

'I will have a reply for you by tomorrow.' Tim parried the insult.

Valentine appeared not to have heard him. He continued his dictation. 'I have a girlfriend in Moscow. She will come with me, although she does not know yet. You will extract her when I am ready, maybe two weeks. No longer than three.'

'I'll put the request.' Tim's night sight was improving. He turned his head a little. 'I have to ask you . . .'

'She will not leave without her dog. There must be none of this quarantine business. Is that understood?'

'Yes.' Tim had had just about enough of being treated like a little boy.

'Tell London my terms,' said Valentine curtly. 'Tomorrow go to Hoi An, about twenty kilometres away. Be at the floating restaurant at dusk.'

'I've questions to ask you,' insisted Tim. 'And there's something you should know. Two Russians came to our hotel in Hanoi. They knew my name. Are they connected with you?'

Silence. A drip of water fell off an overhanging branch, hit Tim's neck and trickled down his back. 'Valentine?'

'He's gone,' said Sally.

Friday 20 March

'Do you think Tim's got that right? It seems a very strange thing to demand. If those char wallahs in the Home Office ever find out, they'll take our charter away.'

'But Haydn, dear, you don't have a charter,' pointed out Livy.

'I had a pal who was a pilot in the RAF. More of an acquaintance really,' began Plumridge, stretching his Oxford blue braces with his thumbs. 'He was coming to the end of a tour in Germany and couldn't stand the thought of his dog, corgi I think it was, going into kennels for six months, so he smuggled him into an old Devon, remember them, ten thousand rivets flying in close formation, and found an excuse to come over to UK. Landed at RAF Manston and when the silly beggar was the furthest point from the control tower pushed the dog out. The dog thought he was being abandoned and chased the plane all the way to the hangar. Caused no end of a stink. No idea what happened to the dog.'

'I wouldn't put a dog of mine in a quarantine kennel for six months,' said Livy to the surprise of both men. 'You hear such terrible things. I read of a dog dying because he swallowed half his mat and no one noticed. It's a scandal.'

'You don't think that Valentine's plea might be a nice little touch designed to appeal to a nation of animal lovers?'

'I think it demonstrates genuine concern. Valentine is obviously a man who thinks ahead.'

Williams nodded. 'Tim can find out whether the girl-friend has a passport or if she has time to get one. I'd rather she came out legally. A land route would be best with the dog, but we'll go into details later. We're not dealing with Gordievski here, after all.'

Livy gave a little smile at the reference to the famous SIS coup when they smuggled the KGB London chief out of Moscow after he was recalled, correctly suspected of being a British agent. He'd gone for a morning jog under the very noses of his watchers and popped up in a safe house in Hampshire.

'I assume we'll let the Cousins in on Kinsale for a share of the rent. Wash McSweeney loves all things Irish, so I reckon Valentine is in for a long interrogation.'

'That reminds me,' said Livy. 'The Cousins have been on. They're asking when we intend joining them. They reckon the shipment's due at Cam Ranh Bay any day.'

Williams groaned. 'I hope Tim isn't going to have to abandon Valentine for this operation. I don't know why they can't do it themselves.'

'The all-ports alert has found nothing so far,' complained Plumridge.

'Did you expect it to?' Livy examined her nails, blood red today.

Alison tapped on the door. 'The car's downstairs, sir.' She saw Williams's blank look. 'Drinks with the KGB Mafiya liaison man at Thames House, then lunch at Rules, you remember.'

'Oh, yes. You two coming?'

Plumridge nodded, grateful for the lift, but Livy shook her head. 'I'll miss the drinks. I've got to see a man about an exhibition.'

The three walked out of the lift together. Williams and Plumridge slowed to watch Livy go up to a big shaggy bear of a man who glanced pointedly at the clock over the security desk.

'I'll catch you up,' she called to Williams. 'Order me oysters and the lamb, rare.'

'Another working lunch.' Peter Poynter could not keep the sneer out of his voice.

'As a matter of fact it is.' Livy bridled. 'And really, Peter, it's nothing to do with you. I'm missing part of it to do you a favour, a big favour and I'm not having it.'

She took off her glasses and scowled at Peter like a cross myopic dormouse.

'I'm sorry, Livy. I'm so anxious to get everything sorted out and I was hoping we could have lunch together. Just the two of us.' He knew that would soften her. 'You don't have to come to the gallery if you're busy. I'll have a glass with Ross. You really don't have to.'

'I'll come.' Livy might be in love, she might be sexually infatuated, but she wasn't silly. She wanted to see where her £10,000 was going. 'I'll come to Bond Street and then go on. After all, I want a receipt for my money.'

In the back of the taxi, she leaned across and playfully squeezed his balls.

'Ooh, look. A Chinese fishing net. Isn't it beautiful?'

Sally stopped her bicycle by scraping her feet along the road. The fine netting hung like a spider's web suspended on four poles above the green waters of the inlet. Sturdy red and blue wooden fishing boats were tied up three abreast at the quayside, and on the wide Thu Bon river men and women crouched in the sterns of slim canoes, laden with bananas and palms, paddling first on one side then the other.

'And there's your double.' Tim spotted the French girl with the dark hair.

'She's not a bit like me,' objected Sally. 'Look at that nose.'

'From the back. Same height, hair, same white trousers.'

'She's a size 14 if she's an inch.'

Tim gave up. They sat at a table on the water's edge across the narrow quay from an old merchants' house and godown which had been turned into a restaurant. A studious, bespectacled man in his early forties took their order for beers in impeccable English.

'What a lovely town,' observed Sally.

'The fighting passed us by, so Hoi An has not changed much since it was a major seaport rivalling Malacca and Macao,' he said. 'Have you seen our fine old houses?'

'All we've seen is the big hotel and four private mini-hotels and they're all full,' replied Tim. There had been a fax from London waiting for them at the hotel. But no room. Tim and Sally left their bags and hired bikes.

'Many Chinese visitors have come for the festival, but I have a room if you want one,' said the man, hesitantly. He pointed to a window under the red-tiled roof looking across to the small island. 'Would you like to see?'

Sally took in the big sagging brass bed, richly stained floor boards, rattan chairs and the blue and white china basin and jug and fell in love with the room.

'It's gorgeous.'

'Thank you. My name is Nguyen Duy Van. Please call me Van.' He paused. 'You must understand this is not official. I have no licence for foreigners.'

Tim returned to the hotel to collect their bags and carried them up to the room. The bed, he noted, was not that big. When he lay on it, he rolled into the middle.

'I'll sleep on the floor,' said Tim as a canoe containing white ducks, tied in pairs by their feet, glided soundlessly past. Some of the ducks stretched out their necks to drink.

'You don't have to.'

'Oh.'

They spent the afternoon strolling around the quiet town, visiting garishly decorated Chinese congregational halls and ancient merchants' houses with their dark wooden rooms. Half an hour before dusk they arrived at the small floating restaurant, moored at the end of the quay where the river narrowed and green foliage overhung the water. Tables were placed around the edge of the circular covered raft. A basic kitchen with primitive toilets, stacks of cold drinks and a huge old-fashioned refrigerator took up the middle.

They ordered beer and watched a pot-bellied piglet and a puppy playing together, rooting in a pile of peelings before the piglet became bored and trotted up the steps into a house. They were still smiling when they saw Van and an erect woman wearing a black western-style dress and a string of pearls. Tim waved.

'My mother, Madame Nguyen,' introduced Van.

'And how are you enjoying our backwater town?' Her English was sculpted rather than spoken.

'It's lovely.'

'Yes, it does grow on the visitor. The pace is so much slower than one is used to, even in Vietnam. A Gordon's gin and tonic,' she told the waiter fawning at her side.

The elderly woman possessed a proud severity and unblinking eyes that made Tim want to check that his flies were done up. She was not a woman one would lie to.

'Your English, if you don't mind me saying so, is perfect.'

Mme Nguyen bowed graciously and fitted a cigarette in a holder for Van to light.

'My mother was professor of European languages at Hanoi University,' he explained.

'I have retired, although I advise the Government on language teaching courses. English is really my third language. French, of course, is my second after the vernacular. I was educated at the Sorbonne – briefly.'

She possessed the clarity of diction and the fluent cadences of a BBC wartime announcer.

'You read Wilfred Owen's poetry.' Mme Nguyen addressed Tim.

'Yes, I have a book with me,' said Tim, realizing that the old woman, who delighted in holding centre stage, had been through his belongings.

'I happened to see it as the girl unpacked for you. At my age this is permitted.' She dropped her eyes in a semblance of apologetic flirtation. 'I used Owen to demonstrate the anti-heroic mode in Western poetry. Some of our rulers said I was wrong.'

'What happened?'

'Bac Ho was on my side so I continued my lectures. It was not so easy after he died. Fortunately my Russian is also excellent,' she added dryly. 'Now I must be going. Thank you for the drink. Maybe I shall see you later this evening.'

The restaurant owner scampered to the edge of the gangplank to bow her ashore.

'What a fascinating lady,' observed Tim. 'I wonder if she really did know Ho Chi Minh?'

'Very powerful lady,' said the owner, taking away her glass. He did not elaborate.

Over the palm fronds the sun careered downwards in a blood red ball. Tim and Sally sat in silence, deep in their own thoughts. Tim was thinking about the fax from London.

All proposals okay. Imperative you get answers before going too far down road. You have authority to negotiate. Your cousins expect you any day.

Tim told himself the Russian had to come up with some answers this time. He'd allowed Valentine to seize the initiative at China Beach. He'd set the agenda and told Tim what to do. This time Tim would not be such a pushover. He slapped an insect nibbling his bare arm and the owner promptly lit a moon tiger on their table. A Canadian couple paid and left and they were alone.

A sultry, brooding calm lay over the river as if a thunderstorm was about to break. Large pods hanging on a tree came alive and rustled and squeaked before flying upstream.

'Fruit bats,' announced Tim. 'They're harmless.'

Sally shuddered.

The sun cast longer and longer shadows until it suddenly disappeared.

'He's late.'

'He's being careful,' said Tim.

'What happens if he doesn't show?'

211

'We wait.'

Tim and Sally took it in turns to try to make small talk.

'He seemed so positive,' mused Sally, her arm dangling over the rail.

'Are there crocodiles in Vietnam?'

'Dunno. You've assumed custody of the guidebook. Why?'

'Because there's one drifting under your hand.'

Sally shrieked.

A dark shape bumped against the raft's floats.

'It's not a crocodile. It's got hair. Oh my God!'

Tim leaned over the edge. He found himself looking at Sally's double floating face down in the gently swelling water.

Colonel Primakov was loud and laughed a lot. He laughed at his own jokes and everybody else's – even when they were not making any. He seemed as broad as he was tall and he had a gargantuan appetite for drink, food and life. He tucked his napkin into his collar and agreed things in Russia were not good. Forty per cent of private business, fifty per cent of banks and sixty per cent of state-owned companies were allegedly controlled by the Mafiya. He lifted bushy black eyebrows in appreciation of the jugged hare. The claret was superb. Another bottle? Why not? There were an estimated nine thousand criminal gangs in Russia. The Chechens and Azeris were the worst. What about the Moscow Narco Group, asked Williams. Primakov shrugged and began to speak of the increased links between the Russians, the Italian Mafia and the South American drugs cartels. Cooperation between law enforcement agencies was needed. International co-operation to combat international crime.

But are things really that bad, inquired Livy. Primakov flashed her a smile. Certainly. Counterfeit money, dirty money, drugs, weapons, prostitution flourish. Drugs like amphetamines and ecstasy are being manufactured in former Soviet pharmaceutical facilities by highly trained chemists. Heroin is flooding from the Caucasus through southern Russia, moving the centre of gravity of drug production from the Golden Crescent markedly nearer to London; soldiers are selling their guns for bribes, superpower technology is being diverted to forge bank notes so convincing that foreign banks cannot tell them from the real thing.

Boy, they had a battle on their hands! But together they would fight them and beat them. They had to share their intelligence. That was the key. He set about demolishing a syllabub.

Primakov was telling them what they already knew, Williams noted. He had fallen silent to watch the Russian. Primakov gave the impression of a bluff, honest soldier; brawn rather than brains, but Williams saw how he concentrated on Livy, encouraging her comments and answers while seeking to minimize his own softly persistent interrogation. He was obviously a ladies' man because Livy was responding, flirting subtly with her eyes.

It was as though there was a hole in the room when Primakov left, escorted to his car by Williams. He had nodded a curt farewell to Plumridge but lingered over Livy's hand, brushing it with his lips in a surprisingly light way. Livy found herself wondering what Primakov would be like as a lover. Brutal, direct, powerful. An ox of a man. Sometimes that was what she wanted.

'Do you really think she looked like me?' Sally finally came out with the words.

They could still make out the body in the moonlight, drifting slowly downstream. By the same moonlight, Sally was chalk white and the planes of her face were hard and flat.

'From the back she was a dead ringer.'

'She's dead all right. Shouldn't we do something?'

'We can't get involved.'

213

'You're right.'

Tim was surprised at Sally's matter-of-fact manner. He did not know she had shaken hands with death more often than he had; seen more dead bodies, been accountable for more killings.

'But why would anyone want to kill me?'

'Only Valentine knows we're here.'

Tim was puzzled. It was a rigorously observed rule that members of rival intelligence services did not kill each other. After all they generally had more in common than they did with their respective masters. The unwritten rule had been drummed into Tim when he had joined Williams's outfit.

'Why would Valentine want to kill me?' Sally brought out a handkerchief and began winding it around her fingers. 'Who knows what I look like?'

'Polecat's men,' suggested Tim. It made sense. The KGB would not break the rules. It was not in their interest. Today's killer was tomorrow's target. But the Mafiya! They killed as a first resort. 'Perhaps they were hunting Valentine, came across her, believed she was you and killed before they realized their mistake. If they have realized their mistake.'

'What a terrible reason to die. Mistaken for someone else.'

'Is there a good reason to die? Shit! There, coming down the hill. The white-haired man.'

And walking equally purposefully up the quayside was the other Russian from Hanoi. They both wore jackets and kept their hands close to their pockets. Tim and Sally slid back into the shadows in the centre of the raft and watched as the two men met at the bend of the road.

'Oh Christ. They're coming here,' whispered Sally.

Tim's brain was racing. 'We need a diversion. You.'

'Thanks.'

'Sit under that light with your back to the gangplank.'

'Do you want me to wail like a ghost?'

But Tim had already vanished into the shadows. She heard a scuffle on the roof before, nerves tingling, she slipped into the seat.

The footsteps on the wooden gangplank stopped with a muffled curse. Sally thought she knew what the tethered goat felt like during a tiger shoot.

The white-haired man crossed himself. The other pulled out a gun from his pocket. Whitey shook his head and drew a stiletto blade from an arm sheath. He gestured for his partner to move anti-clockwise around the raft. Tim tracked him across the roof until he was level with the refrigerator and dropped lightly behind him. The Russian felt the rush of air and half turned. Tim wrapped his left arm round his neck and punched him hard under the ear. He lowered the Russian to the deck and found a small Chinese automatic in his pocket. The owner watched expressionlessly from the kitchen. Tim held his finger to his lips and squeezed past.

The Russian was less than six feet from Sally, the wicked blade glinting in the moonlight. Tim brushed against a wok. Clang. Whitey spun round. Tim darted in, chopping down on his right wrist with crossed fists, jarring the Russian's arm so he grunted in pain and dropped the knife. Tim half-turned, jabbed his elbow into the Russian's throat and scraped his heel down his shin. As he jerked forward Tim punched him on the point of the jaw. Whitey's head whipped back, cracked into a post and he sprawled senseless.

'Brave girl.' Sally looked up with a strange expression as if she was about to burst into tears or laughter or both. The owner was still standing impassively in the middle.

'Bad men,' said Tim. '*Lien Xo*. Bad men.'

'You friend Madame Nguyen. No problem.'

'I hope I haven't made trouble for you.'

The owner showed Tim the cleaver he was holding behind his back. 'No problem.'

Tim dropped the knife and guns in the river, explaining

215

to Sally, 'They could have been used to kill your double. They could incriminate us.'

They hurried back along the quayside. As they pushed through the crowded path between the fish stalls, littered with fish heads, rotting vegetables and pools of fetid water, Tim spotted two heavily built Western men coming towards them. He quickly steered Sally into Van's. When they recovered their breath they called their contact in Hanoi from the phone in the corridor behind Van's restaurant.

'This is most irregular.' The upper-class voice drawled and crackled down the line. 'I'm under instructions to fax you at the hotel.'

'But something's happened,' insisted Tim.

'This is an open line.'

'But . . .'

'Listen.' Seething, Tim listened. 'You must go and see your cousins tomorrow. The chap you want has gone to Dalat. Got that? Dalat. Seems to be giving you a bit of a runaround, isn't he? Understood? Good.'

The line went dead.

'Fuckwit.'

'That's the first time I've ever heard you swear,' smiled Sally weakly, slumping against the wall.

'I don't like you going to Dalat by yourself. I wish I hadn't thrown those guns away.'

'Don't worry. I'm a big girl. By the way, where is Dalat?'

Tim consulted the guidebook. 'Another 500 miles to the south. It's a hill station built by the French at the turn of the century to escape the heat of the lowlands. We go to Nha Trang together and then split up.'

Van agreed. 'The best way is to take a train from Danang to Nha Trang. You can hire a car there to drive you to Dalat. Long-distance buses and trains start early in the morning. Train is better. If you want I will send a boy to Danang to book your seats on the train.'

Sally grabbed Tim's arm and pulled him around the corner. The four men were sitting down at a table across the road.

Van went to serve them. When he returned he looked grave. 'They are searching for you. They have your descriptions. I said I had not seen you. They did not know I understand Russian. Talking among themselves, they said they will kill you when they find you.'

'Is there something you wish to tell us?' Mme Nguyen stood at the foot of the stairs, severe and compassionate at the same time. 'We would like to help but we need to know what is happening, you understand.'

Tim and Sally looked helplessly at each other. Tim thought it was time to put their cards on the table. They had nothing to lose by trusting the old woman.

'I cannot tell you everything,' Tim began. 'But the Russians are smuggling drugs into your country. We are trying to stop them.'

'You are police?'

'Sort of.' It was close enough to the truth, he told himself.

'You are honourable.' Mme Nguyen decided. 'The men outside are scum.'

'They're going to search the town until they find you,' said Van.

'Perhaps we should go to Danang tonight,' said Sally. 'It's a big city, we should be able to lose ourselves there.'

'No,' corrected Van. 'Here you are among friends. Friends are very important when you are being hunted.'

'To have the population on your side is two-thirds of the struggle,' agreed Mme Nguyen.

'Were you in the Viet Cong?'

'Wasn't everyone?'

Later that evening Mme Nguyen, wearing another plain black dress, dined with Tim and Sally in their room. Van carried in table and chairs and they sat by the window. They feasted off grilled river fish in a sweet ginger and garlic

217

sauce, unlike anything Sally had tasted before, duck breast with pickled vegetables, fiery pork cubes, spinach and long flat noodles. Mme Nguyen produced two bottles of Chablis and Van brought out his best crystal glasses. Sally watched the full orange moon rise over the palm trees of the river island and felt the balmy air. They lit two oil lamps and the polished brass bed glowed red in the warm beams. She felt safe in this house.

Mme Nguyen spoke of her friendship with Ho Chi Minh with light-hearted reverence.

'He was forty years older than me. He was like a father. He was a father to his country. He encouraged me to study in France even though our countries were soon to be at war. He liked the French. He even tried to like the Americans but they wouldn't let him. Whole sentences in our Declaration of Independence are the same as the American Declaration of Independence. He asked for American help, but they ignored him.' She put the tips of her fingers together and rested her chin on the pyramid she formed. 'He knew France was a spent force. In the confused days at the end of the Second World War, he allowed French soldiers back to get rid of the Chinese who had invaded the north. He said he preferred to sniff French shit for five years than eat Chinese shit for the rest of his life.' She smiled at Sally. 'Does that disgust you?'

'No,' Sally replied. 'No, not at all.'

'Of course Ho Chi Minh was only a nom de guerre.'

Tim felt he was being asked to supply his real name. 'Um . . . Nguyen Tat Thanh.'

'Are you related?' asked Sally.

'No,' laughed the old woman. 'Six million Vietnamese share the surname Nguyen.'

Finally she rose. 'In the morning I shall accompany you to Danang to see you safely on the train. It will take me back to the old days.'

When Van had cleared away the chairs and table and closed the door, Tim and Sally looked at each other.

'I'll sleep on the floor.'

'No need.'

'Are you sure?'

'Tim?'

'Yes.'

'Why don't we just go to bed and see what happens?'

Sally and Tim made love in the big brass bed and tried to be quiet and lay in each other's arms listening to the sounds of the house.

Tari found the tour of Wembley Stadium boring, but as the world symbol of English football it was an ideal target. He regretted there were no matches being played there in the near future. Anyway, there were problems of dispersal and escape. No one in Baghdad had given it that much thought. Iraqis never bothered with the small details by which an operation succeeded or failed. Tari believed in meticulous planning. He would be flexible, prepared to move sidewards, even backwards, before moving on, always moving on. That's why he had been on tours of the English National Opera and the National Theatre. Tari was not interested in western sports or decadent opera. They were merely venues; sites for demonstration – if Baghdad decided to take that route. Personally Tari favoured an all-out strike. Total warfare. Total fear.

Driving back from Wembley, Tari detoured to park outside a modern block of flats in Highgate. Since he'd seen Salilah after the hijack she had moved in and out of his thoughts. He knew where she lived – or had lived when they'd first brought her to England. London's Arab world was a small place. Palestinian agents, posing as students, had met her in her early days as a translator – before she had been warned to distance herself totally from her past. They had followed her home. Such small pieces of information were useful. They had told Tari.

He was surprised to find her name on the topmost of the intercom buzzers. There was only a slender chance of seeing her, he recognized. She was probably at work. He had nothing to say to her, anyway. He did not know why he was waiting – but wait he did. He parked on double yellow lines while traffic wardens walked past and stared curiously. Tari smiled and they sauntered on. He was pleased his cover worked so well. The English class system!

Across the road newspaper placards outside a newsagent proclaimed *Peace in Ireland?* He knew how the IRA had paralysed London with the odd bomb here and there. Not many dead. They had forced the police to seal off the City, the smallest unattended package closed a railway station and a suspiciously parked car caused traffic chaos. Even hoax calls brought pandemonium.

Think what he would achieve – all with one small flask. In an experiment London Underground had sprayed harmless bacilli in Colliers Wood station in the south of London. The bugs were found eighteen stations away. Devastating. If he did something similar in the West End – maybe in Oxford Circus tube station – the impact would be colossal.

Until the flask arrived, he intended to keep a low profile. Tomorrow another piece of his cover was arriving; another piece falling neatly into place.

After twenty minutes Tari gave up waiting and drove off. He was thinking of the future. He didn't see the little girl toddling ahead of her mother until she stumbled over the pushchair she was wheeling, lost her balance and lurched into the road. Tari hit the brakes. The girl disappeared under the front of the car. Her mother screamed. He was out and picking her up in a second. She couldn't be more than three – the same age as Soraya. She had blonde hair and wore a pretty blue frock, now smeared by dirt and oil.

Tari held her and the girl gave an almighty wail. Her knees were grazed and bleeding but she was more scared than hurt. Her mother fussed around her while apologizing incoherently.

'I'm sorry. You can't take your eyes off them for a second. She had reins but she doesn't like them. There, there, darling. I would never have forgiven myself.'

Traffic was building up; a crowd was gathering. Tari did not want to be the focus of attention. As he drove away he found his hands were shaking. He pulled into a tree-lined street and stopped. While he collected himself his thoughts inevitably slipped to Leila and Soraya – his two gems. They were his heart, his life, his weakness, said some. Against all precepts of tradecraft he carried their pictures. He pulled them out now and gazed at them. Scamps. Imps. Angels. And at the back of his mind that implacable nagging worry, a presentiment that something was wrong. He had tried to dismiss his anxieties as the fussing of an old woman, but something told him it was the sixth sense, that bond which was said to exist between a young child and its mother. And he was mother and father to both. Had one been killed, run over as he had almost run over the little English girl, or were his fears merely transferred insecurities about his operation? For his peace of mind he had to know. He was parked ten yards from a phone box and he had bought a new phone card only that morning. Providence. He was meant to phone.

The number dialled out immediately. A lout answered the phone. He asked for Fatima.

'Who wants her?'

'Her brother.' Silence, then, 'It's me. Don't say anything.' A sharp intake of breath. 'How are the girls?'

A moment's hesitation. 'They're fine.'

Something in Fatima's voice scared him.

'Tell me.'

Fatima breathed down the phone. 'I'm worried about the little one. She was feverish and running around too much, but now she's lost her energy and her colour isn't right.'

'What does the doctor say?' demanded Tari.

'It's not that easy.'

'Yes it is. Tell them you need a doctor. A good doctor.'

Shit. The telephone was devouring his card. There wasn't much time left. 'Tell them I said so. Let me speak to the girls.'

A pause, then Leila was shouting excitedly down the phone. 'Daddy, daddy is that you? We miss you.'

'How are you?' Of all the things he wanted to say, all the emotions choking his heart, he could only come out with banal questions.

'We don't go out to play much and Soraya is very quiet.'

In the background he could hear the voices of Fatima and the man raised in argument.

Fatima came back on the phone. 'He says you must go and never call again. You are breaking rules.'

'Tell them, tell them . . .' A wave of incoherent fury swept over Tari. 'Tell them they can go fuck themselves. Until I know Soraya has been seen by a doctor, the best doctor, they can go fuck themselves. Tell them . . .'

The line went dead. Tari found his hand clutching the receiver was clammy. Beads of sweat covered his face even though the day was cold. He wiped the receiver.

Saturday 21 March

Dawn came suddenly. Slanting rays of light caught the tops of the waving palms on the island opposite, the night faded to grey and a delicate shell pink settled over the water where solid firm shapes of small boats were already moving.

'Good morning.'

'Good morning.' The small embarrassed smile of first-time lovers.

'Did you sleep well?'

'Hmmm, apart from someone waking me up a couple of times.'

'You didn't seem to mind.'

'You can wake me up whenever you want.'

There was an urgent tapping on the door. 'Breakfast,' called Van.

They regarded each other with regret. 'There'll be other times?'

'Yes,' replied Sally. The smell of coffee on the cool morning air and the first peep of the sun's rays dappling over the green river were forging a memory that she thought would stay for ever.

They set off just after five o'clock in a battered, high-sided truck. Van drove, with Mme Nguyen next to him. Sally and Tim crouched at one side of the cab. They had been driving for less than fifteen minutes when a white car sped up behind them, its driver leaning on the horn. It was crammed with Russians.

By the time they pulled up at the vegetable market near the station in Danang, the sun had climbed high into the sky, bringing a hot and humid day. Van and Mme Nguyen set off to reconnoitre. They returned to report that two of the men were on the platform outside the foreigners' waiting room while the other two were standing on the far side of the track by the first-class carriages. It was impossible to board without being seen.

'They don't know for certain you are booked on the train. They are covering every eventuality,' said Mme Nguyen. 'They will go to the airline office once the train leaves.'

'Can you distract their attention?' asked Tim.

'Vietnamese trains travel very slowly, especially in towns,' said Van. 'We use railway lines as paths, so the engine driver has to crawl along. Recently a thief stole a German's bag from a moving train. The German jumped off the train, chased the thief, caught him, recovered his bag and made it back on to the train.'

The train gave three long blasts and two dirty green diesel locomotives slowly emerged around the side of the station.

'We've missed it,' cried Sally.

'Don't worry. You will see,' replied Mme Nguyen.

The men returned to their car, watched the long line of dusty carriages slowly disappear from view and drove away down Quang Trung Street.

'Now we catch the train.' Mme Nguyen pulled a red and gold armband out of her bag. 'People's Committee of Quang Nam-Danang Province,' she explained.

In the distance the train was sending out piercing blasts as it crept between the tightly packed shacks. The truck shuddered into life and pulled away with a grating of gears. They turned out of the town and drove along a road running parallel with the railway line. When they were alongside the cab of the throbbing locomotive Van sounded the horn and waved the red and gold armband out of the window at the driver. When he was sure he had been seen, he pulled ahead of the train and stopped.

'Come,' cried Mme Nguyen, pulling on the armband.

She strode imperiously to the railway and stood in the

middle of the track with her hand raised. Tim and Sally watched spellbound as the massive locomotive slowed to a halt. A guard approached Mme Nguyen and bowed. They had a brief conversation and the guard bowed lower.

'He will show you to your compartment,' she called above the pulsing roar of the engine.

'Thank you.' They shook hands.

'Do not thank me. I have not had so much excitement in years. It is good for my old bones.' Her eyes twinkled.

From the train they waved farewell to Mme Nguyen and Van. Both raised their hands in dignified salutes until they were out of sight. Tim and Sally found they were sharing a compartment with a Vietnamese couple learning English from a basic primer. The man gave Tim his card: Dr Pham Tan Hung, Deputy Director, Centre for Preventive Medicine of Vietnam Railway. Tim smiled and spent the next hours correcting their pronunciation of *high jump* and *tendon* and *Olympic*.

'It's a shame we don't have this compartment to ourselves. We'd get lots of points for doing it on a Vietnamese train,' mused Tim regretfully.

Sally raised her eyebrows, which he hoped signified her agreement.

She looked out of the window, marvelling at the different shades of green and the endless paddy fields with water buffaloes, white ducks and peasants wearing straw non hats. When she left the compartment she discovered they were in an oasis of peace compared with the second-class carriages, which were a cross between noisy picnic sites and a busy market where families and groups shared meals, played cards and talked loudly all at the same time.

They agreed that she would try to stay in the Palace Hotel on Dalat Lake. She would agree to Valentine's demands, but she had to insist on answers about the Marburg and Colonel Primakov. She would immediately contact their man in Hanoi with his reply.

'I wish I was coming with you. You don't know what this Valentine might be like.'

Oh yes I do, she thought.

'I'll be all right. You go to Cam Ranh Bay, whatever that is.'

'It's a huge natural harbour. The Russian Baltic fleet rested there on its eight-month voyage from Kronstadt to its destruction by the Japanese in 1905. Imagine sailing 18,000 miles to meet your doom.'

'I think I know how they felt,' replied Sally, who reckoned she had been travelling all her life.

They dozed and woke as the train came out of a tunnel. They were moving at walking pace, feeling their way along narrow tracks cut into the cliff side. Beneath them was the perfect crescent of a sandy beach, deserted apart from a few fishing boats drawn up at the water's edge. Tim slipped into a pleasant reverie about spending weeks there, living in primitive fishermen's huts, back to nature. The clouds grew heavy. Peaks ahead and above them were shrouded in mist and in the distance, a rocky headland disappeared in sheets of rain.

It was still raining heavily when they arrived at Nha Trang at 4pm to be swamped by a crowd of touts offering hotels and taxis.

Tim held Sally's face gently in his hands and kissed her forehead.

'You take care.'

They lingered over their goodbye, unwilling to let go of each other. Finally Tim let her arm slip through his fingers, feeling a wave of immeasurable sadness. He took a deep breath and asked a taxi to take him to Cau Da where his cousins had a villa.

'And when was this call made?'

'Yesterday afternoon, Coordinator. It was low grade but it showed up on the Iraq monitors.' Bill Jones felt he had to explain. 'You'd be amazed how many calls there are to

Baghdad. We know most of them, but we couldn't place this one.'

'I see it was made in Dartmouth Park Hill.' Williams inspected the transcript headed by the ten letter and number code. 'Any significance?'

'Not that *we* know,' continued Bill Jones. 'But what makes it interesting is that our language people are convinced the caller is a Palestinian. Different Arabic.'

'"You must go and never call again. You are breaking the rules,"' read Williams. 'Then he says, "Tell them they can go fuck themselves. Until I know Soraya has been seen by a doctor, the best doctor, they can go fuck themselves. Tell them . . ." I assume they cut him off.'

'Absolutely,' said Bill Jones. 'By this time he's raging.'

'The reference to the rules suggests he's on some sort of operation.'

'His case officer must be going spare. He'll want to rein him in,' said Livy.

'I think he'll call again unless he comes to his senses and uses cut-outs.' Williams sighed deeply. 'Do we know of an Iraqi illegal out of Palestine?'

Plumridge shook his head. 'No. This is a new one on us.'

'And?'

'We're doing our best, but Ireland's got priority. SB are trawling through the dissident groups, Shi'ites and Kurds. We've triggered all the phone boxes in the exchange and surrounding ones. Anyone dialling Baghdad will show up instantly.'

'Where did he call?'

Bill Jones shook his head. 'Private number near the airport.'

'We cannot afford to ignore the Palestinian connection. It's the only lead we've got to the Samson Option.'

'It was only Tim's gangster friend who mentioned an Arab. There's little collateral that he actually exists. Colonel Primakov didn't place too much reliability on that Yuri character, whatever Tim Platt says,' objected Plumridge. 'Pleasant chap, Primakov. Great sense of humour.'

'I thought he laughed rather too much, personally,' said Williams. 'He never came out with a straight answer. Still, Livy made a hit with him.'

'I did not.' Livy, caught unawares by Williams's sally, felt the rush of blood to her face.

'He phoned your home one night,' smirked Plumridge.

'What!'

'We tapped his calls. Shame you were out. Missed opportunity there, eh?'

Sunday 22 March

'We called Cam Ranh Bay Vietnam's Hawaii because of the beaches,' declared Jedd Fry, chewing gum with the measured action of a contented ruminant. 'We built the port, the airstrip, the dry dock, and when we left the Russians just steamed in and didn't even say thank you. Hell, this was the largest Soviet naval base outside the USSR.'

'The area was famous for its tiger hunting back in the 1940s,' volunteered Tim, lying next to him. A quarter of a mile away two giant cranes, casting cones of amber light, were lifting containers off the black bulk of the *Maria Vega IV* and swinging them on to the quay where over-sized fork lift trucks scuttled back and forth. On the military side of the harbour, two grey Vietnamese gunboats and a corvette were tied up alongside a mole.

'Shit. I hope there aren't any here now. These mosquitoes are bad enough. Ain't got nothing like them back in Oklahoma. No, boy.' He raised his binoculars. 'Now ain't that strange.'

Tim slowly scanned the dark countryside to his right and then to his left, knowing they were most vulnerable when they concentrated on one object to the exclusion of everything else.

'What?'

'For the last three nights there's been a marine guard in that green hut by the gate. Didn't do much because there was nothing to guard. Today the *Maria* sails in and they vanish.'

'Bribed to look the other way?' suggested Tim.

'What are they looking the other way from? This is just a merchant ship unloading its cargo. *We* know she's

229

carrying enough cocaine to refloat the Russian navy – they shouldn't. Ah, there's the container coming off now. Svenson Lloyd with a blue square painted on her.'

Tim didn't ask how Jedd knew. He watched as the container was picked up and then he continued covering every inch of the dockside through his glasses. At first he thought he imagined it. A tiny flare of light lasting less than a second. A pinprick glow. Someone lighting a cigarette.

'First-floor window. Fourth from left. Window's open, too.'

'Why would a guy smoke in the dark?' mused Jedd. He shifted his bulk and concentrated on the administration block. 'He's got a good field of fire. You're the fighting man. Where would you place others for maximum effect?'

One man in the admin block, certainly. One across the way to rake the other side of the containers. And a stop group in the guard house. Let them in but never let them out. The cranes. Of course. Great elevation and a perfect field of fire. Push the intruders towards the killing ground. Where are you? Where are you? Gotcha.

'Third crane. There's a guy there who's never heard of cam cream.'

'Gee. What d'you know? An ambush?' Jedd Fry didn't seem too concerned.

'This is going to make life more difficult,' muttered Tim almost to himself. 'More difficult, but not impossible.'

'Do you know how we test the weather in Oklahoma?' chewed Jedd. 'Every house has a crowbar hole. Before you go out you put a crowbar in the hole to test the wind. If it bends that's normal. If it breaks, you stay at home.'

'Are you saying we should stay at home?' Tim found difficulty following Jedd's homespun philosophizing.

'Hell no, boy. This is going to work in our favour – although you'll be as much use as a parasol in a twister. Always did wonder why your people were so darn keen to get in on the act.'

'Hang on. It was Langley who insisted we came.'

'Someone's been pulling your tassel, boy.'

'Seriously, Jedd. I was told you asked for help to jark the container.'

Tim's tone made the big man put down his glasses. 'Someone somewhere is playing games, old buddy. *I, we* are not going to jark anything. We may have pulled out of here twenty-odd years ago but we left behind complete networks. These things tend to run themselves, become self-perpetuating if you know what I mean. There's men down in that harbour about to earn their corn. They are the fish in the sea. We are the lighthouses that stick up out of it. *They* are planting the transponders.' He paused. 'But there's one thing I don't understand, boy. You turn up and so does the opposition.'

'What do you mean?'

'Those goons weren't there yesterday. It's as though they knew you were coming today.'

A cold stillness settled over Tim. If he was expected here, then Sally would be expected in Dalat. Hell's teeth.

'Jedd, have you got a spare vehicle?' Tim was suddenly impatient. 'I must get to Dalat.'

'Is that where your lady partner's gone?'

'Yes,' Tim was forced to admit. 'She could be walking into a trap. I need a car, fast. A motorbike would be better.'

'No sweat. Let's go.'

'I owe you,' said Tim as they crawled through the long grass towards their lying-up position.

'Hell you do. I could be in an Iraqi shithole jail or worse if it wasn't for you. Let's go rescue your partner, partner.'

Sally made herself easy to find. She checked into the Palace Hotel at the side of the lake which stretched for almost a mile in a boomerang shape through the heart of the sprawling hill station. She ate in the restaurant by herself and sat at the bar until ten o'clock when she went to bed.

Next morning came clear and bright. Looking out of

231

her window, she thought she could have been in Surrey. European buildings were scattered among the gentle folds of the hills and a golf course sat on the far side of the lake. Only the peaks of Lang Bian in the distance suggested something more dramatic. The air was cool at 4,500 feet. In the crowded market she bought the largest sweater she could find, a stuffed kangaroo which hummed 'Waltzing Matilda' and a plastic bird which picked up toothpicks with its beak and which she thought would go really nicely in Tim's grotty flat.

She half wished they hadn't made love. She told herself she was going to have to be firm. The night in Hoi An was a one-off, a momentary weakness. No one could have spent a night in that magical room and not made love. It would be different in cold grey London. She knew how much Tim wanted this operation to succeed. She wanted to help him, to see Valentine safely back in London. It would be Tim's triumph. She'd kiss him on the cheek and fade out of his life. Because if she didn't go soon, it was going to be hard. Bloody hard.

Sally wandered around the tourist spots until in the afternoon she hired a Honda 90 for five dollars and rode off past carefully tended cabbages, spinach and carrots set out in neat rows in the rich red earth to see the last emperor's palace. She was disappointed at its 1930s suburban style, but a fantastic hotel with tiny rooms set in concrete giraffes and toadstools, and giant spiders' webs made of wire, restored her faith in Vietnamese taste.

And everywhere she looked for Valentine. Where was he? It was easier for Sally. She knew what Valentine looked like. So did Tim, although he didn't realize it. She wanted Valentine to appear when she was by herself. She had been nervous in case he made some snide reference or innuendo about their time together in London in front of Tim. She hoped he did not expect a replay. He wasn't having one.

But where was he? Her mind started playing tricks on her. She felt she was being stalked by an invisible man.

232

Valentine was watching her at every turn but she couldn't see him. Stop it or she'd work herself up into a nervous frenzy. She put a brake on her imagination.

Williams's fervent words kept running in her mind like a loop of tape. *Valentine. He's on the inside where two circles overlap. Where the Mafiya meets the KGB. We need him. He will come bearing gifts. We need those gifts. He could hold the key to the Marburg, the key to the sickness in our organization.*

That's why she had gone into the box at the races, accepted the diamond, given her body. Just part of the wooing of Valentine.

At dusk the flights of broad steps from the market to the upper town were transformed. Trestle tables and benches appeared on the flat spaces between the flights. Stocky women in woollen hats rigged up electric lights from car batteries and metal cauldrons full of duck, chicken and quail eggs simmered over glowing charcoal. Aluminium basins of clams, snails and whelks bubbled and steamed. Sally shivered despite the sweater and the plump, apple-cheeked girl in a red anorak motioned for her to move closer to the brazier. She slid up the bench and thought how the Vietnamese reflected the vegetables they grew. On the plain they were thin and reedy like rice shoots, while in the hills they were sturdy like their crops of potatoes and cabbages.

Her loneliness pressed in on her. Much of her time at the camp had been spent waiting. There too the streets had possessed a lamplit darkness and a half-moon drifted above the hills. And in her heightened state of awareness, she was again in the makeshift town where women had bruises of grief under their eyes and pale blue lights burned over the rusted doors of the air raid shelters. Rock music and patriotic music and the murmurs of old men. The buildings deliberately ramshackle because they were not allowed to build permanently in case they forgot their true homes. At the same time it was daylight and she was gazing towards the range of brown hills to the south and west where silver planes left vapour trails high in the forget-me-not sky and the faces which stared at them were fixed in hatred. The flickering memoryscope brought her pictures of army trucks under camouflage netting and a procession with hand-embroidered banners and Jerusalem represented by the Mosque of Omar in gold paper and sea shells. Tractor-drawn floats, with bigger girls in khaki fatigues baton twirling with Kalashnikovs, the fighting youth with strips of red keffiyeh around their heads. Lamb and rice and cheesecake. Targets of man-sized cutouts of snarling Americans and rolls of brown sticky paper to patch up the holes. Belches of martial music to wake you in the morning. Daily readings of condemnations of Zionism, Egyptian treachery, capitalist exploitation, western imperialism and Zionism again.

And Mahmoud, coruscatingly intense and ravenously passionate.

A tiny waif with direct eyes and two metal claws on withered biceps approached Sally. One claw held a clear plastic bag with small denomination notes. Sally opened her purse and dropped in a tatty banknote. The girl gave a resigned sigh and moved slowly down the steps, frail and pathetic in her ragged green dress.

Sally believed she had been generous.

'How much did I give her?' she asked Apple Cheeks, who had been watching.

The girl held up a twenty-dong note.

'I didn't, did I?' Sally was aghast. That was less than a penny. She stood up, searching among the pools of light for the small figure. Apple Cheeks pointed towards the vegetable stalls at the foot of the steps. Sally found the crippled girl squatting by two peasant women huddled alongside piles of cabbages.

'I made a mistake. Here, please take this.'

The girl held out her claw and Sally dropped four tightly folded notes into the bag. In the distance she heard the sound of a helicopter.

'I'm awfully sorry.' Sally hurried away. She did not see the girl offer the bag to one of the women, who reached in and extracted the 5,000-dong notes – the largest notes in circulation. Twenty thousand dong. Just over £10. As much as the little girl would beg in months.

Sally returned to the bench where Apple Cheeks was dishing out steamed clams. She was debating whether to be brave when a bony shank rubbed against her thigh. The little girl slid up the bench next to her.

'This is Chi Bo,' announced Apple Cheeks.

'Hello, Chi Bo.'

The small dark face split into a beaming smile. Sally's first instinct was that she had come for more money, but Chi Bo grinned happily up at Sally and launched into a spate of Vietnamese.

'Chi Bo say you good woman. She say many many thank you.'

'*Cám on*,' said Sally, using every word of her Vietnamese.

'*Cám on rât nhiêu*,' chanted Chi Bo. With Apple Cheeks interpreting, Sally found out that Chi Bo was seven years old and both her mother and father were dead. The little girl gazed up into Sally's face in adoration.

'Are you hungry? Would you like food?'

'Chi Bo always hungry,' laughed Apple Cheeks, giving her a plate of open clams. Chi Bo's eyes travelled from the clams to Sally. Not knowing what was expected, Sally extracted one from its shell and held it to Chi Bo's lips. She pulled it into her mouth and kissed Sally's fingers. Sally found it a desperately humbling experience.

'Now Chi Bo wants to show you.'

The waif leaned into the table, turning her body so the claw on the upper right arm could pick up the clam shell. She twisted her head and raised her stump so it just reached her mouth. Sally grinned at her victory and Chi Bo's dark eyes sparkled with happiness. Suddenly her gaze switched from Sally to something over Sally's right shoulder. Sally turned to follow her eyes. The first two Russians from Hoi

An were standing behind her. Sally shrieked and leapt to her feet. As they darted towards her, Chi Bo, sensing they meant harm, snatched up a bowl of scalding water in her claw and dashed it in the face of the white-haired one. Sally was off and leaping down the steps four at a time. Chi Bo tried to throw a kettle at the men. One picked her up by her neck and hurled her away. Apple Cheeks struck him across the head with a ladle as he crashed past. Sally dodged into the covered market, hearing harsh shouts and Chi Bo's thin screams. She weaved through shoppers in an alleyway of red slabs of meat hanging from rails above butchers' stalls. A hand flailed at her sleeve, missed, grabbed her sweater at the back. Sally spun around and went for the Russian's eyes with her nails. The other man twisted her arm behind her back. Chi Bo screamed for help from the entrance. Screamed again. Everyone was staring. Two butchers, clutching bloody cleavers, were advancing around their stalls towards them. Sally got her teeth to the Russian's hand and bit with all her might. She kicked, twisted and then she was away. Running for her life. Out into the night, leaping over piles of rotting vegetables and garbage, past crushed cardboard boxes and potato peelings. Behind her the hubbub was dying down. She slowed, desperately dragging air into her tortured lungs. When she thought it was safe, she leaned against a wall, panting for breath. She had to get back to the hotel and safety. She would phone Hanoi from there. She had no idea where she had run. The lake was probably behind her so it would make sense if she went around the market by the dark back roads.

Sally collected herself, jogged around the corner and crashed into a Russian. She screamed. He slapped a hand over her mouth and she viciously bit into his index finger. A stinging blow to her head and she tasted her blood in her mouth. Still she twisted, turned, bit, scratched, kicked and fought as the two men half-carried and half-dragged her to a car. She landed a wild swing with the flat of her hand. In return the white-haired man punched her hard in the side of the head, so she reeled and her ear caught fire. Dimly she heard Chi Bo's cries in the distance. There were people running, the thud of bodies colliding and she was released. As she stood swaying, by the faint light of a street lamp, she believed she saw Tim battering the white-haired Russian in insensate fury, his lips drawn back like a wild animal's. Alongside him a man mountain was pounding the other Russian against a wall. There was a moment's silence and she collapsed sobbing into Tim's arms.

Tuesday 24 March

'Wanker!' Mickey New braked as the car on the inside lane accelerated to prevent them joining the motorway. In the back Sally felt sleep creep over her. A bleak, drizzling London dawn was breaking. In here was lovely and warm. She snuggled down and let her eyes close.

'Sorry the flight got in so early,' said Tim as Mickey pulled around the offending car and accelerated towards London.

'Don't worry, boss. I went for a run before I came to collect you.' Mickey chuckled. 'Did I tell you what happened to a mate of mine called Tom Petrie? He fancied doing the London Marathon, so he starts training. He gets to work at seven so he's out running before it's light. He lives near this loony bin, right. One morning he's jogging along when PC Plod draws up. Hello, hello, hello and what are you doing? Training, says Tom. Plod looks at Tom, looks at the mental hospital and asks, "What will you be doing for the rest of the day, sir?" News editing the currant bun, says Tom. Wallop. He's in the nick before anyone's thought to ask if one of the inmates is missing. Only problem – Tom was the news editor of the *Sun*.'

Tim smiled, feeling the prickling grubbiness of the long flight catch up. He envied Sally's ability to drop off anywhere. Others in the Regiment could switch off, nap and switch back on recharged. He went straight through on nervous energy.

'There's a report that a man's body's been found in Hoi An,' said Mickey.

'Woman's body,' corrected Tim.

'No. Definitely a man's. We thought it might be Valentine.'

238

Tim frowned. 'Was he identified? Any further details?'

'Not as far as I know. Just one line from a news agency. If our man in Hanoi has followed it up, I ain't heard. The all-ports alert was secretly issued while you were away. Except it's in today's papers. It was a *Sun* exclusive, but the others caught up.'

'Your mate . . . ?'

'No way. But Plumridge and his lot were having the vapours last night and everybody's doing a soft shoe shuffle about anthrax. There's today's *Daily Telegraph* behind you.'

An all-ports alert had been issued last Wednesday, read Tim, after intelligence reports that Saddam Hussein threatened to smuggle deadly anthrax bacteria into Britain disguised as duty-free goods, including perfume and alcohol.

'That's not right,' said Tim. 'We don't know for certain it's anthrax. Why not say it could be Marburg?'

'Too bloody scary,' replied Mickey.

Tim read on. The Home Office – not known for its willingness to talk to the press about anything – had gone out of its way to wheel out experts who scorned the efficacy of anthrax delivered from perfume sprays. What would Iraqi agents do, they mocked. Stand on the tops of high buildings with scent aerosols full of the poison?

Official spokesmen blurred when the threat was made and insisted Saddam's threat was not a specific one against Britain but against 'the enemies of Iraq', which included the US and NATO allies who threatened military action against Baghdad last month over UN weapons inspections.

There was no mention of the missing Marburg U virus.

No mention of the Samson Option.

'They're playing it down like mad,' summed up Tim when he had finished reading.

'They don't want to panic the public,' explained Mickey. 'They argue that most people have heard of anthrax. They think it's something cows have, so it's not as frightening as something new and terrible like Marburg.'

Tim threw the paper on the floor in disgust.

'You know we went back to Cam Ranh Bay that night,' he said. 'Just to trail our coats. Almost got slotted.'

'Hardest thing in the world to deliberately ponce around,' declared Mickey.

'Too true.'

It had been a nerve-racking few minutes. He and Jedd Fry had allowed themselves to be seen as they burrowed through the scrub towards the perimeter fence. Luckily the gunmen had been trigger-happy. Maybe they had learnt what had happened in Dalat and they weren't taking any chances. Tim heard again the rounds zipping past in the foliage, the heavier thuds of tree strikes. One burst whistled over his head, parting the leaves with the air pressure, bullets buzzing like bees. Thwock. Thwock. The sound of the round punching into the thick moist wood was like that of a bullet hitting a man.

They'd withdrawn, laughing insanely in relief.

'Anything else happen while I've been away?'

'Cautious had the Gold Cup winner at Cheltenham. Cool Dawn at twenty-five to one. He's a very happy bunny.'

'What about the factory?'

'The bigwigs had lunch with a KGB crime liaison colonel. Plumridge took your umbrella and never brought it back.'

'Did you meet the KGB man?'

'Briefly, when the Coordinator showed him around. Nice guy, always laughing, built like a brick shithouse. Alison's got it on her. Maisie, the temporary secretary, came back to work at the end of last week. Yesterday she went back to her old department because they are so short staffed. Alison's livid. Ripped my balls off for leaving a file in our room over lunch. She's had her hair done. You'd have thought that'd put her in a better mood but the only one who can do any right is that smarmy creep Plumridge. She's always doing little errands for him.'

Sally woke, stretched and yawned luxuriously. 'You can drop me at Hammersmith.'

'We'll take you home,' said Mickey.

'No, really,' insisted Sally. 'In this traffic it'll take hours.'

Mickey absolutely refused. It was Tim's turn to doze as Mickey cut in and out of rat runs and back doubles until magically they arrived on the heights of Highgate.

'See, I told you it wouldn't take long,' he said proudly.

Sally directed him to the small red brick block of flats.

'This yours?'

'Yep. Top floor. You must come up and see my vista sometime.'

'I'd love to.'

She gave Tim a swift peck on the cheek, waved gaily to Mickey and disappeared through the front door.

Tim had vaguely hoped that she would invite him in. Unreasonable, he knew. All she'd want to do was unpack, do her washing and catch up. But . . . but . . . on the flight, they had held hands and once, while she slept, quivering in her dream, she had dug her nails so deeply into his palm that the marks were still there.

'Williams wants you to look at pictures of Arabs in case you'll spot someone you saw in Russia, but he said for you to get your head down first,' said Mickey. 'This afternoon will do.'

'Doesn't he want Sally to look, too?'

'He didn't mention it.'

The flat was dusty and damp and reeking of cat's pee. Tim struggled to push up the sash window. A gust of fine rain blew in. He put 50p in the meter and turned on the gas fire, shivering with cold and tiredness. He dropped his dirty shirts on the floor and hunted under the bed and in cupboards for a trapped cat. He sniffed again. Perhaps it was dead mouse. He shook his head over his dreadful sense of smell. The damp had lifted the walnut veneer off the tallboy. Tim tried to press it down and frowned at the grime. He must get a cleaner. An hour or two a week. That's all it would take. Some little treasure who would fetch basic groceries like bread and milk, do his ironing and bring him meals he could reheat. In his dreams!

He cut the mould off a piece of cheese he found in the fridge and bit into it. Rock hard. Kicked his dirty shirts to join the pile left from before he went away. He'd have to go to the launderette soon or they'd get as mouldy as the cheese. Perhaps tomorrow. Always tomorrow. He continued chewing while sifting through the mail he had found on the hall table. Bills, junk mail, one from Russia. The neat upright script of a schoolgirl. Emma.

He climbed into bed, arranged his pillows and began to read.

Hello. I was thinking of home and I thought of you. I hope you do not mind me writing to you. It was lovely meeting you in Rostov. I have such happy memories of the afternoon you came for tea. For a globetrotter like you, it was nothing but my social life hardly sparkles and meeting you was a lovely experience.

Reading that, I know you could take it the wrong way. Please don't. You know what I mean.

I hope the research went well. Please tell me when you think you might start making the documentary. If I am still here, perhaps I could help in some small way.

I've not seen much of Igor since you left. In a way that's a good thing but it means I have more time on my hands. To be honest, sometimes I hope he will call even though I don't really like him. I don't want this to be a depressing letter, and it's not meant to be, but somehow I feel I can be truthful with you. I feel you know me.

Oh dear! Tim read on.

Emma was planning to go to a foreign students' social evening and she was having tea with her tutor tomorrow. Her mum had written that beef and lamb prices were falling again and farmers were in for a rough time, but you wouldn't think so considering the price of meat in supermarkets. She'd found a cheap flight so she hoped to make it home for Easter. If it wasn't a terrible imposition, could she possibly stay with Tim?

> I hope you don't think I'm forward but it would be great to see you when I'm in London. I promise I won't get in your way. I could buy you a meal to say thank you. Or if you like, I'll cook one.
>
> Of course I fully understand if you can't put me up or if you'll be away when I'm passing through.

He winced at the way she was bending over backwards to give him a way out.

> Please write when you have a moment. The first thing I do every day is to check my pigeon hole for mail. If you're too busy to write a letter, a postcard will do.
>
> I have to go. Igor has sent word he wants to see me at his dacha. I want to get this off tonight. The sooner I post it, the sooner you might reply.
>
> All the best, your friend, Emma.

Poor Emma. The pages reeked of loneliness. She had used her best Basildon Bond writing paper and a fountain pen. There was something terribly sad and poignant in her gauche naïveté. Tim promised himself he would write back in the next few days. And he'd phone. She'd like a call. It'd be a nice surprise.

Sleep overcame him, but not a happy sleep. A hollow sleep, with grey dreams of yearning. Large monochromatic skies and a flat landscape. It was a dream he could not remember when he woke, but it left him with an uncomfortable feeling.

Three hours was a long time to spend staring at hundreds of pictures on screen. Visa application photos, prison mugshots, video snatches, enhanced crowd scenes. Any Arab you may have seen in Russia, said Williams. Let your thoughts coast. Don't concentrate. See if you can trigger some hidden memory. It's a long shot, but humour an old man.

So Tim sat in the comfortable chair in the windowless room in central registry listening to the murmur of the air conditioning and the hum of the AppleMac computer and tried to stay awake as face after proud, unshaven face unrolled on the screen. He tried to remember if he had seen any Arabs in Russia. Yes, he had. There had been one in Emma's block, complete with keffiyeh. Two portly sheiks in djellabas at Moscow airport, and there was one in the hotel in Rostov. Going out as a crowd of businessmen came in. Just as Sally was taken ill. He would not recognize him if he came and sat opposite him. Tim let his mind wander. He didn't have a lot to go on. He believed he had caught a glimpse of an Arab after the hijack. At the time he'd thought he was a fellow passenger, if he had thought anything at all after the blow to his head. But he couldn't remember seeing him later – and they had been the only foreigners on the flight.

Tim's eyes were on stalks by the time he felt a tap on the shoulder and turned to find Williams smiling benignly down at him.

'Any luck?'

''Fraid not. There was one I recognized but it turned out his mug shot was in the papers after he drove a suicide bomb truck. You should give Sally a go. She'd have had a better look at the guy after the hijack.'

'Give her a day or two to get over the flight.' He didn't tell Tim that Sally was deliberately kept away from Arab and

Israeli operations in case she should feel divided loyalties. 'Let's go outside. You can't smoke in here.'

They joined other smokers sheltering against the drizzle around the edge of an internal courtyard. 'The Cousins are ecstatic about the Cam Ranh Bay operation. They reckon they've got the shipment on a long piece of rope. Just ready to haul it in whenever they want to.'

'You know they didn't want us there,' said Tim.

'Who told you we weren't wanted?' demanded Williams, fumbling to produce a box of Swan Vesta matches.

'Jedd Fry.'

'The man in the field is often the last to know.'

Tim nodded ruefully. 'Have we heard from Valentine?'

'No.' Williams rasped the match. 'Looks likely the body in Hoi An was his.'

Tim took his courage in his hands. He wanted to talk about the Vietnam operation. His latest failure. He wanted to explain and justify, but he was worried it would appear that he was making excuses. Tim felt guilty about the failure – although he was personally convinced there had been nothing he could have done to salvage the operation.

He spoke quickly. 'Everywhere we went in Vietnam we found the opposition or they found us.'

Williams shook out the match, made to throw it on the steps and then returned it to the box. He glared at Tim as if daring him to say more.

Tim ploughed on. 'It seemed they knew what we were doing before we did.'

'We were naïve in allowing our signals traffic to be virtually en clair. We thought we were dealing with a load of hoodlums. We didn't know they'd call on KGB expertise. It shows their links are closer than we feared. We won't repeat that mistake.'

Williams saw the doubt in Tim's eyes.

'I've ordered an inquiry into our communications management and procedures. Between you and me our chap in Hanoi was out of his depth. He didn't have a clue. I'm going to bring him home once the dust settles.' He took Tim's arm. 'Don't think about it. Don't hold any inquests or post mortems. Let it rest. Least said . . .'

'Yes, of course.'

'I'm afraid you're going to have to trust me, Tim. Me and no one else.'

Tim didn't understand what Williams was talking about but he nodded anyway.

Wednesday 25 March

Tari did not believe what his cut-out told him. Max sounded convincing, but it was his job to sound convincing: basically *he did not know*. How could he? It was five days since Tari had learned that his daughter was unwell. Since then Max had made all the right reassuring noises but he was just passing on what he was told. What did he really know, sitting in that overheated flat in Frankfurt? The assurances were too glib, too pat somehow. Tari's suspicions were aroused. Fuck the rules. He had to know about Soraya.

He exchanged his black clip-on tie for a heavy silk one. He put on an overcoat, glasses and trilby. With his knife-edge creases and polished black Oxfords he could have passed for a specialist with a plate in Harley Street. Tari had made his decision in the small reaches of the night when he was unable to sleep. He might have taken up the Schmidt woman's offer – he enjoyed the superiority of fucking European women, especially blonde ones – but he was preoccupied and instead rebuffed her. He considered whether to seek anonymity in crowds or risk an isolated phone box in the countryside. On the whole he favoured the loneliness of a busy place, a rush-hour crowd worrying whether their train would be on time and if they would get a seat. It helped that it was raining. No one looked twice at the figure behind the misted-up panes in the old-fashioned red telephone box outside Faversham station.

The electricity was on for once and Fatima was boiling goat's milk for Soraya when the phone rang. It rang and rang. Fatima peeped out of the kitchen into the hall where the gorilla was supposed to be on guard all the time now. There was no sign of him. Perplexed and feeling she was

247

doing wrong, Fatima tiptoed towards the phone and picked it up. 'Hello.'

'Fatima, it's me. How is Soraya? Has the doctor been?'

Fatima was so surprised to hear his voice, she answered directly. 'Soraya's not well. She has a fever and she's weak . . .'

'Hasn't she seen a doctor?' His voice rose to a scream so she had to hold the receiver away from her ear.

'He has been. I asked him what was wrong but he could not be bothered to talk to me. He said Soraya needs drugs to get better, but because of the Americans there are no drugs. I'm very worried. I'm giving her milk and honey. It's all I have.'

'There are drugs, but they are stolen.'

'He said there were none.'

'He lies. They can get them if they want. Tell him . . .'

Fatima screamed.

'We assume the guard came back at that point,' said Bill Jones. 'You can read the transcript, but I thought it would help to hear the call.'

'He's pretty desperate, isn't he?' exclaimed Livy Hull. 'Calling the same number again. Breaking every rule in the book to find out how his sick daughter's getting on. Would you do that for your daughters, Maurice?'

She knew he would cheerfully break their necks, but it would be churlish to say so.

Plumridge ignored her. 'What was he doing at Faversham station? Catching a train to London?'

'Hardly,' retorted Williams. 'He'd know we could have met the train when it arrived if we'd been on the ball.'

'We weren't expecting a call from Kent,' apologized Bill Jones. 'We've now programmed to intercept all international calls, triggering on "Soraya" and "Fatima".'

'The caller sounds young. Youngish anyway. So does Fatima. Who is she? Not the wife, surely? More like a nurse or a nanny.'

'So where's the wife?' demanded Livy, dressed today in the long black and white dogtooth jacket she believed made her arty and accessible. 'Why are the kids in Iraq?'

'Hostages,' ventured Plumridge. 'Remember Saddam's predilection for human shields.'

'Or to ensure our man does what he's told. Behaves himself and follows the plan. There is more.' On cue Alison swept into the conference room and placed new transcripts on the table. Williams pressed the play button on the console at the side of the interpreter's booth.

Again the room was filled by the Arab's voice. This time he was speaking to an answerphone. There was no message, just a single beep and the voice harsh, cracking and spitting in its fury. They examined their transcripts, trying to match the words to the rising anger.

'Tell Uday that unless my daughter gets the drugs she needs then the operation is off. Do you understand. Off.' There was a vital urgency in his plea for comprehension. His voice dropped half an octave and became hard. 'If anything happens to her . . . if she dies . . . then the wrath of Samson shall descend upon you and your kind.'

'The wrath of Samson,' repeated Williams dreamily.

'And this time we know the number,' crowed Bill Jones. 'It belongs to the Directorate of General Intelligence run by Saddam's elder son Uday.'

'When was the second call made?' demanded Plumridge.

Williams smiled like the cat who had had not merely the cream, but had licked the butter churn as well. 'Fifteen minutes after the first – just ten miles away – from a phone box on the westbound services on the M2.'

'A compromise between emotion and training,' judged Livy. 'With emotion getting the upper hand. He must be desperate to make that second call.'

'The call takes seven seconds,' said Bill Jones. 'Our trick cyclist found enormous stress patterns which the speaker is trying hard to subsume.'

'But why is he in Kent? Has he been abroad since the

first call?' Livy enjoyed speculating on Five's turf. 'Is there a connection between the first call in London, Faversham and the service area?'

'Don't know, as yet. We're checking the ports.'

'A preliminary psychological profile,' said Williams picking up another paper. 'Doting father . . . Acts as mother as well as father . . . Only allowed weakness . . . Maybe compensating for the death of the mother for which he might feel responsible . . . Death of wife might be driving him . . .' Williams put down the profile. 'Makes cheerful reading. Sounds like a fanatic with only one weakness – his daughter.'

Stan Bagg fingered the collar of his shirt and felt that the knot in his black tie was still in place. His open, ruddy face spoke of an outdoor life and Tim could tell he was uncomfortable in a suit. From the puffiness around his eyes Tim guessed he had been crying recently. Here was a man of few words and few visible emotions, feeling more pain than he knew existed. Tim didn't know what to say. Mr Bagg had phoned Tim's flat early that morning. After listening Tim had given him directions to the anonymous building. At lunch time he found him waiting in reception. Tim took Emma's father to the pub they used as a local, where he apologized for dragging Tim away from his work.

'I wouldn't have troubled you, but Emma wrote such nice things about you that her mother and me felt you ought to know. Half-pint please. I've never been a drinking man and I've lost whatever appetite I possessed.'

Tim signalled to the barman and wondered what to say to console this decent man who had come to tell him Emma was dead.

'Reading between the lines, I think Emma was lonely in Russia,' said Mr Bagg. 'It's such a long way away and Emma's never been a great mixer. She had her friends, like, but she tended to stay inside her own circle.'

'She enjoyed talking about home,' said Tim.

'Ay, she was a home bird. Her mother was that proud of her. . . This has broken her heart, this has. Fair broke her heart . . .'

His voice tailed away as Mr Bagg stared sightlessly into the distance and Tim knew he was speaking about himself.

'What actually happened?' asked Tim, gently.

'She was walking back to the hall of residence last Thursday night. A hit and run driver. It was instantaneous.'

'That's good,' murmured Tim.

'Yes, she suffered no pain. Probably didn't know what happened. Not a bad way to go, if you have to. But you shouldn't go at that age.' His face tried to be angry, but it collapsed under the weight of grief and appeared merely tried and bereft.

'I'll come to the funeral, if I may.'

'Thank you. Thank you. Emma would have liked that. I don't know when it will be. The Russians are taking their time releasing her body.'

'Why?'

'I don't know. That's why I came to London, to ask the Foreign Office to help speed things up.'

'And?'

'I saw a very nice young gentleman. He explained the embassy in Moscow would make representations on my behalf, but of course he couldn't promise anything.'

I bet he couldn't, thought Tim. Emma's dad would be putty in the hands of some smarmy git at the FCO. Mr Bagg would tug his forelock and apologize for wasting their time and they would pour balm on his grief and after two minutes subtly glance at a wristwatch to show the interview was over. Back upstairs the official might write a note before recommending no action or just forget about it. And down in Wiltshire Mrs Bagg, her hopes and pride in her only child extinguished, would grieve day by long day until her daughter's body was returned.

The hell she would.

'I'll see what I can do to help,' promised Tim. He was rewarded by such a gentle smile of gratitude that Tim decided that if he accomplished nothing else this month he would get Emma's body back home.

'Ay, ay, all right. I'll speak to someone as soon as we get back. Now stop going on and smile for the camera,' ordered Haydn Williams as they stood together on the steps of the cream-painted terraced house in one of the endless streets behind the Natural History Museum. The door snicked open and Tim found himself in a featureless hall staring at a large booth of tinted one-way glass. The keep. Behind the bullet-proof glass men with their own independent air supply guarded the front door. Any terrorist group foolish enough to try to storm Mossad's London out station would be cut down by machine gun fire before they reached the stairs. From the street, the houses on either side bore different companies' nameplates. Inside the three were linked and a close observer would have noticed that no one ever went in or out of the other two doors. Not that an observer would have been allowed to spend much time lingering outside the terrace before the Met's diplomatic protection group began asking quietly persistent questions.

'David Levy. Tim Platt,' introduced Williams.

'Welcome.' A firm handshake, olive Levantine features and an intense, intelligent face.

'So you vant our help again? Oy vey. What is a poor man to do? Always you come, always we help and do we get a call, a thank you?'

'David's a great fan of *Fiddler on the Roof*,' said Williams drily. 'I get the same routine each time I bring a new colleague here. He forgets I knew his father at Cambridge and young David used to stay with us in Greenwich when he was a penniless student. How is Sam?'

'Talking about giving up his chair. He says he's getting old. All he wants to do is fish.'

'I'll believe it when it happens. Sam Levy's professor of moral philosophy at Berkeley,' he explained as Tim marvelled how many people the little Welshman knew.

They were given identity badges and David escorted them through a sort of airlock into empty high white corridors. They went up a back staircase into a small room which smelled of warm dust and hummed with banks of what appeared to Tim to be hi-fi systems and computers.

'Male. Palestinian. Young, you believe. Most are – they don't live very long.'

Williams handed over the tape. 'You have ten seconds of voice there. You said that should be enough.'

A technician inserted the tape into a machine and green and red lights began blinking.

'May I ask what's happening?'

'This is an analogue to digital converter. It chops up the tape into 44,000 segments per second. Each segment has a different shape. A voice print is made up of these shapes,' explained David. 'It's like a fingerprint. No two are the same. Experts used to believe that a voice print was not as exact as DNA or the pupil of the eye, but we've proved it is. Every voice has a wave shape made up of points. You compare fingerprints by matching given points. It's the same with a voice print. The more points we have to compare, the more exact the match.'

Mossad's voice bank was the envy of every other service, Williams had lectured on the way over. Quantico was running like merry hell to catch up, but the Israelis had seen the value of identifying the enemy by voice much sooner than anyone else. It stemmed from the proliferation of Arab terrorist groups. It did not do to retaliate against the wrong faction. So Mossad's listeners were second to none. No scrap was too small. No trifle overlooked. They recorded everything and filed it away. And as technology advanced they found they were sitting on a goldmine of information and their database ruled the Middle East. Now other services came cap in hand, trading secrets for access.

So it pained Williams, the most generous of men apart from sharing intelligence, to have to tell Mossad about the mysterious Palestinian on his patch. He did not mention the Marburg, of course, nor the Samson Option – which might still be a little stirring of the waters by Mossad itself. He merely said a Palestinian illegal was making phone calls to a intelligence officer's home in Baghdad. That was enough to make the Israelis curious.

'We'll take a sample, compress it and encrypt it so it makes no sense to anyone who might be listening and send it down an ISDN line to Tel Aviv.'

'If he's on the database, how long will it take to get a match?' inquired Williams.

'This time of day . . .' David tilted his hand back and to. 'About three or four minutes. There's a new brute of a computer which can do around a thousand searches a second.' He caught the technician grimacing. 'I don't think that's classified.'

They waited in silence, staring at the hourglass symbol. It took just under three minutes before a fuzzy picture began scrolling on the screen.

'Yep. Yep.' David Levy whistled softy. 'There's a prize for you. Thinking about him only recently. I'm glad he's on your turf.'

'Why?' demanded Williams.

'Because he's not doing any mischief in my part of the world.'

Thursday 26 March

'The truth? The truth is I believe she is not going to make it. There is too much damage to the lungs. If she had been given antibiotics sooner, it might have been different. Who saw her?'

'Al Sayeed.'

'That bloated incompetent buffoon . . .'

'Sssshhh. Keep your voice down.' The man with the professional tape recorder over his shoulder glanced nervously around the hall to see if the guard had heard. 'You know who Al Sayeed is related to.'

'Why didn't he prescribe?' demanded Dr Aziz.

'He says he didn't have any drugs available. I'd bet he sold them on the black market before anyone bothered to tell him this little Palestinian girl was important. If he'd known Uday was interested he would have acted very differently.'

The doctor swore. 'I've given Soraya an injection to front load her course of drugs but I'm not hopeful. For your purposes I've also given her adrenalin. That'll kick in very soon so you should begin your interviews now while she is still quite poorly. She'll feel gradually better over the next hour. Then you'll have a happy, healthy little girl for a while before she goes downhill again.'

Upstairs the radio recordist knelt by Soraya's bedside, watched anxiously by Fatima and Leila. 'How are you feeling?'

'Better than yesterday, thank you,' said Soraya.

The journalist spoke into his tape recorder. 'Tell us what happened, Soraya.'

'I wasn't well,' piped up the little girl. 'I was tired. I

255

couldn't go out to play. A man in a white coat put a needle in my arm. It hurt.'

'Were you brave?'

'Yes, but I cried.'

'How do you feel?'

'I don't know. I want to get up.'

'This is Fatima. She is Soraya's friend and nurse.' The sound recordist nodded to Fatima.

'I was very worried. Soraya obviously needed medicine but it was not available because the Americans want our children to die. Bless the members of the Ba'ath party under our glorious leader Saddam Hussein who scoured the land until they found what Soraya needed.'

Soraya put down the script and the man turned off the recorder.

'Good,' he said. 'In a few minutes, Soraya, you can go and play with Leila.'

Later as the girls giggled and played in the garden and every sound was recorded, Fatima could not believe her eyes. Soraya seemed to have come back from the dead.

'Soraya's sparkling,' she remarked.

'Say that into the microphone.'

It made for good radio. Soraya and Leila's thin high voices chattering on endlessly; now bursting into song and laughing aloud. It presented an aural picture of happiness and health. Finally the journalist from the Ministry of Information was satisfied he had enough for a number of short programmes charting Soraya's recovery from sickbed to perfect health.

'When will these go out?' asked his cousin, the doctor.

'The first tomorrow or the next day. The others will be transmitted depending on the medical timescale. Maybe a happy ending in about a week.'

'She will probably be dead by then,' said the doctor.

'Any chance of a brew? Good man. At least I can smoke in here without being treated like a bloody pariah.'

Neither Tim nor Mickey smoked, but that never seemed to occur to Williams, who used their office as a refuge from the anti-smoking strictures of Alison and Livy Hull. In return he connived in Mickey's illicit electric kettle to the extent of warning Mickey when surprise fire and safety inspections were due.

'That was smart work with Yuri, Tim. You can tell I'm of a generation who grew up without electronic mail and world wide webs.'

Tim smiled modestly. It had seemed an obvious solution to e-mail the Palestinian's picture to Rostov, where Yuri had positively identified him as the man who approached him.

'I could have seen him at the hotel, but I wouldn't swear on oath. No leads at this end, sir?'

'Unfortunately not. Immigration and SB have no record of anyone remotely like him entering the country,' replied Williams. 'But he has got in. So how did he do it? What ID is he using? Where's he staying? Most importantly, is the virus with him? What's the SBS motto, Mickey? Not by strength but by guile. Something like that?'

'That's what the public thinks,' grinned Mickey. 'Inside the squadron we have another. No sky too high, no sea too deep, no muff too rough, we dive at five.'

'Yes, well, thanks for sharing that with us. But it is guile, isn't it?' Williams abstractedly tugged at a lock of white hair. 'Do you remember what David Levy said, Tim? "We don't really know anything about this Joe but we feel we know him very well." So what do we know?' Williams began talking to himself while staring at the early morning trains lining up to deposit their loads of commuters into Waterloo. The others listened in respectful silence. 'He's brought up in the Palestinian refugee camps, trained in Yemen and probably in North Korea. Aged around thirty. No one even knows his real name. Used to call himself Mahmoud and more recently, Tari. Hard-line Palestinian extremist. Will never agree to the state of Israel in any shape or form. Up to his elbows in gore. The usual run of terror bombings and killings but interestingly specialized in political assassinations in the early nineties using some girl, maybe his wife, as a honey trap. Rather puts him above the average terrorist fanatic. Wife killed in Israeli helicopter attack two years ago. She was driving his car. So he feels guilty.' He realized ash had built up on the end of his cigarette and turned to look for an ashtray. The movement made the ash break off and fall to the floor. 'Sorry. Is that why he phones? The first call was from a residential street. Why is he there? Why was he concerned? Is this the latest in a number of calls begun elsewhere? I don't think so. It sounded from the reaction that he'd just broken the rules for the first time. All of a sudden he becomes the sort of Joe who drives case officers to drink. Does he have a case officer in Britain or is he being run on a very long leash? Is he being serviced by the Russian Mafiya and British criminal connections?' Williams paused. 'I think he was travelling to or from somewhere when he made the first phone call. It's unsettled him and he has no peace of mind until he phones again. Why rush hour, Mickey?'

'He knows there'll be lots of people around.'

'Yes.' Williams seemed pleased with the answer. 'It's late morning in Baghdad. Does that matter? Probably not. But why Faversham of all places?'

'Because he's not far away,' hazarded Tim.

'It offers the best compromise.' Williams nodded. 'He was in control then, but fifteen minutes later he makes another call. By now he's hopping mad – but he still remembers his training. He does not reveal his home ground. He goes on the motorway. He could be en route to London, instead he's moving further from his base.'

'He could have phoned from Dover or Folkestone,' objected Tim. 'That would make us think he's going abroad and then he could head back to London.'

'Yes. Yes, I see that,' conceded Williams. 'But ports are high-risk places with tight security and closed circuit cameras. I don't know.' He threw up his arms in a gesture of surrender.

No one spoke.

'I've a hunch,' confessed Williams finally. 'A feeling in my water and I'm trying to rationalize it. I just sense he's near where he made that second call, that he's near Faversham. Sorry, I'm not a paragon of logic, am I?'

'Always go by your gut feeling,' said Mickey stoutly.

'Ay.' Williams came to a decision. 'Ay, I shall. Thanks boys.' He threw open the door. 'Alison. Get the Chief Constable of Kent on the phone.'

Eddie the flying instructor gave a big thumbs up at the side of the runway. Left alone in the cockpit Tari took a large breath and wondered how deep acting went. The first solo was a momentous step in any pilot's career. Grizzled Jumbo pilots with tens of thousands of hours in their log books could still talk you through their first solo. Tari remembered his. He still felt a nervous flutter. Calm. Be calm. And don't be too good.

Easy does it. Maybe a little stagger. Three hundred feet, flaps up, fuel pump off. Five hundred feet turn to starboard and continue climbing. Over his right shoulder he saw Eddie, now just a dot, walking back towards the clubhouse.

He had considered not flying until he heard how Soraya was being treated but it would have been unprofessional to abandon his timetable. He would put everything in place, go all the way – and then put it all on hold. But his threats were not idle ones. If anything happened to his little girl, he would take terrible revenge.

Downwind he allowed himself to drift up to 850 feet. That would be expected. Ahead, to the north, he could see the grey smear of London. A short-haul jet was climbing out of City Airport, passing over the squat needle of Canary Wharf. Part of his mind ran through his downwind checks. Brakes off, undercarriage welded down, mixture rich, pitch fine, hatches and harnesses secure. The rest of his mind ran over the operation, as he did ceaselessly all day, every day.

Now he had a base, solid communications through Max, and a cover. All he lacked was the flask and that was due to arrive soon. Only he knew where it was. He and that oafish Russian mobster Polecat.

A Beechcraft was on long finals so he extended his downwind leg before turning and trimming out for 70 knots.

'Biggin. Foxtrot Zulu. Finals full stop. Contact one ahead.'

'Foxtrot Zulu Biggin. Roger.'

He made a perfect landing, allowing himself to show off. They would think it was luck. Only he knew how well he could fly.

'Foxtrot Zulu. Well done.' The tower congratulated him.

'Thank you. Thank you very much.' He allowed his voice to be grateful and animated.

Eddie was waiting outside the clubhouse and Tari slipped into character, grinning broadly and punching the air in celebration.

'That was incredible. I didn't want to land. I wanted to fly for ever. Let's celebrate. Champagne.'

'Why not?' said Eddie, who had finished flying for the day. Tari insisted on Cheryl, the secretary, doing the honours. Everyone in the clubhouse was invited to toast Ali's success.

'To flying,' he cried. 'And happy landings. Many of them.' He made a big fuss of filling in his log book with the details of the flight. In the Special Remarks column he printed FIRST SOLO in large letters and underlined them twice.

'I have decided I will buy my own plane,' he confided to his instructor.

'Funny you should say that,' murmured Eddie, who had been hoping Tari would raise the subject. 'There's an ST150 in the hangar at the moment which I think might be up for sale.'

'Wow. Let's look. We'll take champagne for the mechanics.'

Eddie pointed out the aircraft with red and blue trim. Its engine cowling was open and a panel missing out of the port wing.

'Romeo Romeo. Yes!' enthused Tari.

'It's owned by two blokes. Only one's about to go to New Zealand to work and the other's not that fussed about keeping it on by himself. He's knocking on a bit and reckons he can always hire a club aircraft to keep his hours up. She's done some hours, but the airframe and engine's been regularly maintained.'

'Oh yes.' Tari walked around the aircraft touching wing tip and elevator. It was obvious he was falling in love. He inspected the cockpit and Eddie saw he was imagining flying. 'How much?'

Eddie made a sucking noise. 'Should be able to pick her up for around twelve grand. I know the guys, I might be able to get a bit off.'

'Oh, Eddie, would you? I mean that would be great. Twelve grand's no problem. When could I know? Ah. Wait.' He held up a finger, a frown filling his beaming face. 'Would I be allowed to go solo in her?'

'Yes, in theory,' smiled Eddie. 'Remember your air law. You are not allowed to carry passengers until you have passed your General Flying Test, but there's nothing stopping you flying yourself. Insurance might be a problem, though.'

'Poof. I shall sort out insurance and soon I shall pass my GFT. I have a great instructor.' He put his arm around Eddie. 'My friend, I tell you what. I will pay you twelve K for Romeo Romeo. Cash. You buy it for whatever you can and I will buy it off you. It is my thank you for my first solo. Now we have more champagne.'

In the celebrations no one noticed that the Arab did not drink.

*   *   *

'Hello, stranger.'

'Sally, hello. Where are you?' Tim juggled with the fork and the can of cold baked beans, finally tucking the receiver under his chin.

'I'm oop north,' she said with an attempt at a Yorkshire accent. It was also an attempt to mask the strange nervousness she felt as she had waited for Tim to answer.

'I tried your home a couple of times but all I got was the answerphone. I didn't leave a message.' Tim was unwilling to let Sally know just how often he had called.

'I'm sorry. I wanted to get away for a few days. I should have told you.' Sally in turn did not want to confess that she had needed time on her own to work through the experiences of Vietnam and her feelings for Tim; feelings which should not exist. From the eagerness in his voice, she guessed he felt the same. Oh, this was silly. You didn't go falling in love in her job.

It needed one to retreat, one to be more hesitant and colder. It would have to be her.

'Having a nice time?'

'I'm staying with a friend in the Lake District. The scenery's stunning.' And I'm thinking about you.

'Good.'

He suspects I'm with a boyfriend and he's hurt. You have no rights over me. I can do what I want.

'My girlfriend's at work in the day so I take her dog out for hours. We walk to different pubs for lunch. You'd love it.'

Why did I say that. Sounds almost like an invitation.

'Yeh. I enjoy walking with dogs. Beats marching with a company.'

'How are you keeping?' What a constipated conversation.

'Fine. Working hard. Lots of developments. Can't tell you on the phone but we've ID'd the Arab guy. He's over here.'

Sally's mouth opened in a silent scream.

'Some sad news. Emma was knocked down and killed by a hit and run driver.'

'Oh, no. I am sorry. Poor thing.' She paused. 'I'm back at the weekend . . .'

'Shall we have dinner?' asked Tim quickly. He found himself holding his breath for her answer.

'Why not? We'll treat ourselves.'

'It'll be my treat.'

It was German counter-intelligence who made the significant breakthrough.

As Williams said, everyone gets one lucky break in an operation. The talent comes in recognizing where and when. He also said that the call showed Arab intelligence organizations are monolithic and meddlesome.

Others feared that Iraqi anxiety came from the knowledge that Saddam was about to do something which might rebound horribly. They wanted their Doomsday weapon in place before they embarked on a military adventure. This scenario preoccupied Western analysts for an anxious two weeks. Williams had other priorities. Find the Marburg virus.

The breakthrough involved a fat German slob and laziness. It wasn't the fat slob who was lazy. Max, however people objected to his personal hygiene and habits, was meticulous. A bit player but with professional aspirations. The laziness was on the part of the Iraqi intelligence clerk in the Paris embassy who used the same mobile phone to call Max to pass on messages on three occasions in three days. Unforgivable, said the German listeners. The man should be shot.

Until then Max Tragl had escaped the notice of the BND. The Vice Squad in Frankfurt knew all about him and his shabby overheated flat above the jazz bar in Saxenhausen. They knew about his international contact agency – and his porn enterprises. But they had not suspected that he was a post box for the Iraqi intelligence agency until that clerk used the same mobile. And then they acted quickly.

The phone rang. Max heaved his bulk out of the sagging, overstuffed armchair, brushed the S&M magazine off his elephantine lap and waddled across the room. He hoped it was not that madman in England. Not again. He had passed on exactly what he had been told. It did no good ranting and raving. The Iraqis could be ruthless bastards. He'd known them slot agents for less.

He recognized the sibilant voice of the man in Paris.

'Ici Cummerbund. When does our friend expect to meet Samson?'

It was not an unlikely conversation to have over the phone to such a place; the caller speaking obliquely, a false name, the true meaning of the message coyly hidden.

Max scratched his groin. His shirt had come open exposing a triangle of waxen fat. He screwed a piece of fluff out of his navel, examined it and flicked it away.

'I will ask him.'

'I have a new phone number for him. Ready? Two eight three one six four five nine seven four five. He will hear the news he seeks.'

Max repeated the number.

Across the cobbled street two men in white shirts and dark ties watched the spools of their tape recorder revolve.

You could wait weeks for the smallest piece of tittle-tattle and then you could not hope to understand its significance. But they had a lucky break.

Max, consulting his communications schedule of times and numbers, found he could speak to the madman in England in thirty minutes.

Tari was pretending to speak into the receiver while holding down the bar. He would allow only two minutes. The phone kiosks he had chosen were all the old-fashioned enclosed red boxes.

One ring.

'Yes?'

'The moon is bright . . .'

'And the stars shine.'

Ridiculous recognition phrases.

'When will you meet Samson?'

Tari felt a blast of anger. The bloody cheek. He should tell them to go to hell until he heard Soraya was well. He controlled his temper and forced himself to answer.

'By the end of the month.'

'I have a number for you. Ready. Two eight three one six four five nine seven four five. You will hear the news you seek.'

Tari put down the phone and smiled up at the tower of Salisbury Cathedral.

Max disappears from the story. Much to the BND's chagrin he was not destined to play a major role in the intelligence effort against Saddam. His body, even more obscenely bloated, was found downstream in the Rhine two weeks later. It is not known if Iraqis, Israelis or porn racketeers were responsible.

Under the existing agreement monitored calls to Britain were routinely passed on to Cheltenham. In mounting excitement the voice was authenticated as Tari's. The code breakers cracked the numbers without looking up from their crosswords.

Haydn Williams made no secret of his satisfaction that he had guessed correctly. Another strand added to his myth.

Livy was sceptical. 'Why does he come out with the word "Samson"? Rather blatant, isn't it?'

'Only if you know its significance. They obviously don't know that we do. At least we have that on our side.'

The meeting Williams chaired between his department, Six, Five, SB, Metropolitan and Kent police was optimistic in the light of the phone calls. Although Williams confessed at the outset they were 'tap dancing on water' with just a blurred seven-year-old photograph and a vague description. The operation was codenamed Patchwork and the computer randomly named the subject 'Barbel'. Williams liked the name.

'*Barbus barbus*. Britain's rarest native fish,' he told Tim. 'The barbel was generally confined to rivers flowing into the North Sea. Now it's found almost exclusively in the Trent and Thames.'

They agreed to describe Barbel as late twenties, early thirties, dark hair, brown eyes, light build and around five feet nine or ten. The operation would be a compromise between thoroughness and discretion. The search would be widened outside the usual run of hotels, B and Bs, boarding houses and hostels to take in caravan parks, mobile home sites, university halls of residence and holiday cottages. No reason was to be given for the inquiries.

Try estate agents and letting agencies, said Williams. Is Barbel buying his own food? His daily bread? Or is someone looking after him, feeding him, housing him? Buying more food than usual. Are there newcomers in tight-knit communities? Let's get out on the streets and country lanes and find out. Let's ask postmen, newspaper boys, milkmen, ladies who run village shops and men who drive country buses. Canterbury with its fluctuating tourist population would provide the easiest cover, although Barbel could have tucked himself away in the smallest hamlet or isolated farmhouse. Even on a boat on the Medway.

If Barbel was found he was not, repeat NOT, to be approached. If Barbel was scared off, the scarer would end up as a night watchman. Five's technical branch undertook to secretly tape any potential suspect. Engage him in conversation, record his telephone calls. Just get his voice on tape and as surely as a fingerprint they would know it was Barbel. Then the second part of the operation would come into play. Three teams from Five's surveillance department were on alert. Country clothing, Barbours and cords, wellingtons and labourers' overalls. Bring your dogs, even horses. Kent County Council vans, post office vans, horse boxes and tractors were ready.

'We have four days to find him,' said Williams. 'Four days before the Marburg arrives.'

'I don't want to worry anyone,' said Livy Hull, 'but Saddam last night made a speech for domestic consumption threatening to withdraw recognition of the boundaries with Kuwait. He also hinted at demanding reparations for the damage done in the Gulf War. He knew the speech would be picked up internationally.'

'Is he about to start muddying the waters again?' demanded Williams.

Livy shrugged elegantly. 'There's worse. We've an unconfirmed report the Iraqis have acquired Chinese missiles with the range to reach Tel Aviv. If Saddam launches a pre-emptive first strike on Israel and the Israelis retaliate – and nuclear retaliation can't be ruled out – then the Middle East will go up in flames.'

'Cheering news,' murmured Williams.

*   *   *

First returns were not encouraging. An inordinate number of French, Germans, Dutch and Danes had rented accommodation in the search area. The villages, they thought, would be the easiest to comb. It was an estate agent in Canterbury who offered the name Frau Schmidt from Hamburg, who had taken the Old Rectory in Boughton under Blean for two months.

Police Constable Simon Richards knew Boughton – a long ribbon of a village running along what had been the London to Dover road before the bypass was built and Boughton went back to sleep. At the end of the village, past the Woodcutter's Arms, the road climbed a steep hill to the highest point in east Kent. During the war radar masts had peered watchfully out to Europe and their massive concrete bases could still be seen in the clearings in the woods beside the road. The Old Rectory stood in three acres just under the brow.

That morning, PC Richards was still enjoying the warm glow of learning he had passed his sergeant's exam. Life was good and getting better. He and Jayne had been married only a month ago and after tonight's piss-up with the lads he was taking a week's leave to decorate their new house in Canterbury, especially the nursery.

His police car bounced over the potholes in the drive up to the big house. Too big for one woman, he thought, but perhaps this is what she was used to. After all she had a driver.

'He's one of them chauffeurs with a uniform and a hat. Ever so smart, he is,' said the lady behind the local post office counter. 'Saw him parked outside when she came in yesterday. Friendly enough, only mutton dressed up as lamb, if you know what I mean.'

The woman who opened the heavy front door was not mutton dressed up as lamb. Ilse Schmidt was a perfectly preserved thirty-five-year-old who was determined not to age a day past twenty-eight. Her skin was stretched tautly over fine high cheekbones and she wore her long straw-coloured hair up, conveying an image of a cultured, cold Nordic beauty. Tight black trousers and a bright baggy rollneck sweater completed the picture.

She led the policeman through the high hall with a sweeping staircase into a living room which could have hosted a five-a-side soccer match. Through the french windows he could see out on to lawns and a paddock stretching as far as the dual carriageway cutting. There was a low log and coal fire in an alcove and she invited him to be seated.

Just a routine check on European nationals staying locally and also a crime prevention call, he explained, his flat hat on his knee. 'Are you here on holiday or business?'

'Both, really.' Her English was good. 'My husband is being transferred from Hamburg to head the London office. I've come ahead to find somewhere to live. This part of England is very attractive, but it is difficult to commute. Commute, you say, *ja*?'

'Yes.'

She smiled in a brittle sort of way. 'Would you like a coffee or maybe tea? I do not make tea well. You would be better with coffee.'

'No, thank you. I must get on. May I see your passport?'

'Yes. Yes, of course.' Frau Schmidt seemed surprised at the request. 'But we are all Europeans now, yes?'

'Yes, indeed,' replied PC Richards, copying down the details. 'So you don't think you'll be buying anywhere around here?'

'No. I think I have made a mistake. I will look in Surrey where the trains are faster.'

'We have a bad service in this part of Kent,' agreed PC Richards. 'Are you alone here?'

'No. I have a Turkish driver. He works for my husband, but Hans Dietrich did not want me to be alone. He's not here but no doubt his passport is upstairs: would you like to see it?'

'Thank you.'

Frau Schmidt disappeared and returned moments later with a Turkish passport.

'Benny's been with us for two years. He is very reliable. Are you sure I cannot get you a drink? Maybe a beer.'

PC Richards looked up from transcribing the details of the Turkish passport and sensed a hint of an invitation for something more than a drink. Ilse Schmidt was standing in front of him, hands resting on the backs of her hips, legs slightly apart. Head on one side.

'I'm on duty, thank you.' Time to get out of here. Now he looked closely he could recognize the neuroticism in her face. Her eyes were too bright and the mouth could easily transform from sternness into a pouting leer. 'Are you satisfied with the locks on your windows and doors?'

'Oh, yes. This house is like a fortress.'

'Good. Well, thank you.' He made towards the door. This would be one to tell the lads tonight. How a blonde beauty tried to lay him, him a newly married man. You met all sorts in this job, you really did.

It was only when he told the story in the police club that he wondered if the chauffeur was there to check up on Ilse Schmidt or whether he was her lover. Then he began to puzzle why the Mercedes car was in the drive if her chauffeur was out. The passport details had checked out; so had the references she'd given the estate agent. But it began to worry him.

'Do you have to do that?'

'You should try some.'

Ilse Schmidt plucked open the flap and carefully spread out the packet to expose a small pile of white powder. Using a corner of a gold Amex card she began transferring the cocaine on to the back cover of a glossy magazine. She used the edge of the card to reduce the small lumps into powder. She continued to caress the powder with the card, chopping, flattening, arranging the line until Tari thought he would scream at her.

'What did the policeman want?'

'He was checking on foreigners and he wanted to know if I had locks on my doors and windows.'

Tari did not know whether to be suspicious. Where he came from identity papers were inspected every day. It was normal for police to demand to know who was staying in a house. But was it normal here?

'Don't do any more of that stuff. We must go out.'

Ilse purred and slid her hand down over her breasts to her stomach. Cocaine always did this to her. Made her warm and sexy. It also made her increasingly desperate for sexual release. The Palestinian was already turning away.

At the garden centre he bought a large spray container with a tube leading to a nebulizer and a few other bits and pieces. In the hardware store they picked up a small electric motor and a pump. Back at the Rectory, Tari experimented. In theory it should be a simple matter to secure the container in the back of the aircraft and run the pump off the battery to push the liquid along the tubing to an aerosol nozzle near the tail. At dusk he took Ilse outside and made her stand downwind while he experimented with the spray. She was stoned and she stood giggling with a joint behind her back while the mist fell on her face.

When he was satisfied he allowed himself to share a joint with her in front of the fire. Kif was smoked in the camps so he did not consider it to be harmful the way he despised cocaine, but he would not smoke until the day's work was over. Ilse blew smoke into his mouth and undressed him. When they were both naked he pushed her back on the carpet and took her directly and brutally in a mechanical act where the only pleasure was the release. Ilse, whimpering, fought to contain herself until she saw his face begin to contort and then she screamed and beat him with her fists.

Later he attached a piece of blue plastic sacking to the barbed wire alongside the A2 so it appeared as if it had snagged there on the wind.

Saturday 28 March

Soon after daybreak a small-time criminal driving from Canterbury to the Medway, as he had been paid to do twice a day for a week, spotted the plastic sheeting. At lunchtime he left his car unlocked in the car park next to the whelk sheds in Whitstable. When he returned he checked that a solidly wrapped parcel had been taken from the boot. He had no idea what it contained. He only knew he had been given it by a mate who did business in the East End.

Tim's only reminder of his twenty-ninth birthday came from an old aunt whose sole interest in life was to send cards. She never missed a birthday, anniversary, illness, recovery, new house, new baby, new job or redundancy. Tim wished he had not received a single card, then he could feel really sorry for himself. As usual he did not have time to go for a run. He told himself he'd go tomorrow. Like going to the launderette – tomorrow. Fortunately he didn't have to train hard to stay in shape, but he would have to get his clothes washed because he could not afford to keep buying new shirts and underwear.

He didn't intend to announce his birthday. He wasn't the sort to go around dropping hints or buying cakes for the office. He might tell Sally tonight, then again . . .

Alison smirked as he came out of the lift. She had her hair up and wore a string of artificial pearls over a black rollneck even though it was the weekend. She looked as if she was going up in the world. Certainly not the down to earth secretary who used to have dirty-joke-telling competitions with Mickey.

'The Coordinator is waiting to see you.' She made it sound very formal.

'Now?'

'Immediately.'

'What's up?'

But Alison was already picking up the phone to announce his arrival.

Williams was behind his desk with a dour-faced man with an axe of a nose standing behind him. The man stared at Tim and Tim appraised him in turn. Rumpled white shirt, specks of dandruff on a shiny suit, nicotined fingers. Someone more used to the coalface than the Athenaeum.

'Alison. Three teas please, like Mickey makes them. Tim, sit down. Happy birthday.'

'Thank you.' How did he know?

'Overrated things, birthdays. Never bother with them myself.' Williams did not introduce the other man, who continued to regard Tim with a steady gaze. 'Do you have a safety deposit box, Tim? Think carefully before you answer.'

'I don't need to think carefully. I know I don't. Why would I need one?'

'People in our line often squirrel bits and pieces away for a rainy day. The odd load of dosh, a passport, a gun. It's done all the time. It comes with the job. I've had a few stashes in my time. Probably still do if I could only remember. It's the instinct for self-preservation in a bad world.'

'No,' repeated Tim, emphatically. 'Why do you ask?'

Williams glanced at the other man as if expecting him to speak, but he continued to look boldly at Tim as though his stare alone would bring a confession. Tim, feeling his anger rising, turned to stare back, locked the other's eyes with his own and let his gaze rest on infinity. He could do this for hours. Well, seventeen minutes was his record, achieved in a foxhole in the bleak Bosnian mountains with his troop sergeant when not a lot else was happening. You were allowed to blink but not move your eyes. Silence fell in the room. Tim wondered what Williams was doing. Looking amused probably. Tim heard the clock tick. The silence grew. He was drifting off into another world, thinking of Sally and their evening ahead. The deadlock was broken only by Alison's arrival. She moved between them to put down the mugs and the man's eyes flickered in her direction. A small victory but an important one. He counter-attacked.

'Am I being accused of something?'

'No, Tim. You're not,' said Williams. 'I think there's been a crude attempt to smear you, but it's so crude that it's puzzling.'

'And after the Bettaney affair we can't afford to ignore the obvious,' said the other man in a lowland Scots accent.

'Bettaney actually shoved secret papers through the letter box of the KGB resident in London, who ignored them because he believed they were from an agent provocateur,' explained Williams. 'Since then if we look a gift horse in the mouth, it is only to examine his teeth. Tell me about your financial assets, Tim.'

'They're not a lot. Current account, Cheltenham and Gloucester building society account – from Hereford. I've got a TESSA and a few shares in BT and British Gas from the time we had a stock market craze in the Regiment. We were going to make our fortunes, but we soon got bored. There's a few grand in the building society because I sold my old MGB when I came to London. I've still got a half share in a house near Hereford, a mortgage, oh, and a motorbike and that's about it.'

'One bank account, only one building society account. Nothing in the Channel Islands, Bahamas, the Virgin Islands?'

Tim couldn't help himself. 'Don't be daft!'

'I agree,' said Williams. 'Daft. Sorry, Tim. Mac?'

'Ay. Ay.' The Scot slowly agreed. 'But why?'

'Excuse me but this is all rather Kafkaesque, isn't it,' complained Tim.

'Yes. It is, isn't it? That's exactly what it is,' chuckled Williams. 'Sorry. I'll buy you a lunchtime beer for your birthday as Mickey's not here.'

He did not explain further.

In the pub Williams told Tim that he had pulled strings on behalf of Emma Bagg's father and as far as he knew the paperwork had been completed. He gently probed about the Vietnam operation and Tim's relationship with Sally. Tim confessed he was seeing Sally that evening.

'Excellent. You two should get out and enjoy yourselves,' enthused Williams while silently cursing Teddy Millibanks for carelessly allowing himself to be blown up. There were still parts of Sally's life that remained a mystery. Millibanks had known things about Sally which she didn't know herself. And she was close enough. Protecting herself under layer on layer while offering such an apparently open face. He hoped Tim would not get hurt. No one got close to Sally. She didn't allow them to.

'By the way, the container from Vietnam has been flown to Rostov. Interesting eh?'

Williams liked to lob in little bombshells of information and watch them explode over people's minds.

Tim frowned. 'Polecat must be involved.'

'He's pivotal to all this.' Williams had come to the same conclusion. 'He's the one who first stole the Marburg, the one who controls the drugs routes through southern Russia, and it was his men who pursued you in Vietnam. Everywhere you look you see the grubby fingers of Igor Botkin, aka Polecat. What's Yuri doing in their own private war?'

'He's biding his time,' replied Tim. 'I think he's hoping to catch him off balance.'

When they arrived back there was a message that the container had already left Rostov. If its waybill was to be believed it was due to reach Amsterdam on Monday night.

'You think the Marburg is in the container?' demanded Tim.

'We know from the phone intercept the virus is arriving in Britain within a few days. The timing's right and the rest hangs together. Take Mickey and find out.'

In his office, Williams made sure he would not be disturbed and made a painful phone call. When he'd explained what he wanted there was silence on the line.

'Please, don't you think I've paid my dues by now?'

'This will be the last one. Promise.'

'You said that before the races.'

'You know how important this is. I wouldn't ask you otherwise. And I promise.'

'Promise. Really promise.' There was a crying urgency in her voice.

'Please.'

'All right.' The words could have been wrung from her by torture. 'Tim must never find out. Never.'

'How could he? I promise you this is the last time. You've paid your dues, Sally.'

'*Idha 'at Al-Jumhoriya Al Iraqia Fi Baghdad.*' Radio Baghdad's call sign was followed by a blast of martial music. Tari locked the short wave radio on 97.45 kHz and bit his lower lip. Ilse Schmidt was gazing into the fire with unseeing eyes and a vacant smile on her face. Tari drummed his fingers on the back of the red velveteen chaise longue and curled his lip in contempt. If Ilse did not curb her drug habit once the operation was under way, she would be a liability. He did not like liabilities.

He listened impatiently to exhortations to stand fast behind the glorious leader Saddam Hussein in the battle against American imperialism. More diatribes of hate and paeans of praise for the Ba'ath party and Saddam. The announcer became more specific.

'*Our children are dying because the great Satanic enemies America and Britain will not let the free countries of the United*

277

*Nations lift the unjust stranglehold on our great nation. Our
children are dying because our enemies deny them medicines and
drugs . . .'*

Tari scowled at the lies. Iraq was permitted to export
enough oil to pay for vital medicines and food. For the
first time Tari objected to the propaganda, furious that
Soraya was caught up in the lies. He returned from his
silent vilification of Saddam to hear the announcer say:

*'Our glorious leader Saddam Hussein looks after his children in
the face of Yankee oppression. Three-year-old Soraya was close to
death before dedicated doctors and caring Ba'ath party volunteers
joined forces to find the vital drugs she needed. Dr Aziz . . .'*

'Why was she close to death? Because you pigs were
allowing her to die,' stormed Tari.

A different voice. Deeper, more authoritative. *' . . . Diphtheria is a potentially fatal disease affecting the membranes of
the nose, throat and larynx. If not treated a membrane is
formed across the throat obstructing breathing. It also causes a
degeneration of the heart muscles. Years ago diphtheria caused
many deaths, especially among the poorer people, but modern medicines and antibiotics mean that we can control the
disease.'*

The announcer again. *'Soraya is resting in a bedroom in
a Ba'ath party villa in Baghdad. She is being looked after by
her nurse and friend Fatima. Her sister Leila waits anxiously
for news.'*

The doctor. *'When the diagnosis of Soraya's illness was
confirmed the Ba'ath party pledged that she should not die,
despite the barbarities of the American oppressors. Party members
scoured the country, emptying their own medicine chests to help
little Soraya. Finally a suitable antibiotic was located.'*

Announcer: *'Soraya, little one. How are you?'*

'*I didn't feel well . . .'* Tari gasped with pleasure at Soraya's
voice. *'. . . A doctor came in a white coat and put a needle in my
arm. It hurt.'*

'*Were you brave?'*

'*Yes. But I cried.'*

The doctor: *'We stabilized Soraya and arrested her decline. Her temperature fell and she became more alert.'*

Fatima: *'I was very worried. Soraya obviously needed medicines, but they weren't available because the Zionist Americans want our children to die. Bless the members of the Ba'ath party under our glorious leader Saddam Hussein who searched the land until they found what Soraya needed. Now we trust in Allah.'*

Announcer: *'We'll come back soon to see how Soraya is progressing. Until then, goodbye, Soraya.'*

'Goodbye,' piped up the little girl and Tari punched the air in victory.

They would not broadcast the beginning of a running story unless it had a happy ending. He had disobeyed orders and maybe there was still a price to be paid for his actions, but Soraya was all right and that was all that mattered.

Now he could get on with the operation.

The same transmission also played on the radio in the small office alongside the Tigris half a mile downstream from the Presidential compound. Shane Cosker pushed back his United Nations baseball cap and glowered at the small man seated before him.

'Let me get this right. There was a fire in the top drawer of that filing cabinet and all the documents relating to the coolers and dryers were destroyed. Right?'

The slow-moving ceiling fan failed to ripple the thick night air. It hung sulphurous and stifling, so that they felt they were breathing a tangible commodity like gelatine. Sweat mingled with grease on the man's receding hairline. He licked his lips nervously.

'Yes, sir.'

'But nothing else was destroyed? There is no fire damage to the office . . .'

'No, sir.' His eyes kept drifting to the two members of the Special Presidential Guard with their green lanyards and green silk scarves standing stony-faced behind the tall Australian.

'There was not even any fire damage in the other three drawers.'

'No, sir.'

'And how do you think it happened?'

'The will of Allah.'

'The will of Allah!' barked Tennessee Joe Bradley. 'Those coolers and dryers were used in your Mukrah installation for the creation of bacteriological weapons . . .'

'No, sir.'

'The papers relating to their purchase and their subsequent movement around the country were contained in that drawer. And now they have been destroyed.'

The lights flickered in the uncertain power supply. Cosker could feel rivulets of sweat running down his spine. With an effort he crossed to the olive green filing cabinet and pulled open the top drawer.

'Did you destroy them?'

'No sir.' The clerk's eyes pleaded with the guards for help.

'Do you believe in spontaneous combustion?' Cosker held out a handful of charred paper and ashes.

'Sir?'

What was the good! The clerk was obviously more frightened of the guards than he was of Cosker. They were not going to go and the man would not speak while they were in the room. Cosker had lost again.

Williams listened to a simultaneous translation of the broadcast. As it ended he quietly congratulated Bill Jones on the codebreakers' work.

'The numbers referred to date, time and frequency. It helped to know Baghdad Radio's wavelength. After that the rest fell into place,' he replied modestly. 'The broadcast was obviously in response to those demented phone calls.'

'He took a risk but it got action,' mused Williams, walking around his office with a heel to toe movement. 'How many agents in the field could demand – and get – their own radio programme?'

'Not many,' replied Bill Jones.

'Exactly. Iraqis have topped agents for lesser displays of insubordination. Tari must be very highly prized. They are desperate to keep him sweet.'

God, she's beautiful. So bloody beautiful. Waif-like. Her silly broken nose and funny lips. He'd seen an old film with a star with lips like Sally's. Leslie Caron. That's who she was like. Bet she wasn't a tenth as sexy as Sally. Sally must have sensed Tim's adoration or become aware of his scrutiny for she blushed. For the first time in the meal, Tim felt tongue-tied despite their two bottles of wine. Sally leaned across the table and took his hand.

'Isn't there something you haven't told me?'

For a second he thought he was back with Williams asking about some hidden bank account. 'No. No, I don't think so.'

'What day is it?'

'Saturday.'

'Fool. Whose birthday is it?'

'Oh.' Tim gave a self-conscious smile. 'Mine I suppose.'

'You don't make much of a fuss of yourself, do you?'

'It's not important.' No one else had ever made a fuss of him so he didn't.

'Here.' Sally handed him a brown envelope. 'For you. Happy birthday.'

Inside the envelope was a first-class Eurostar return to Paris and another envelope.

Sally grinned. 'You're always staring out of the window at trains.'

'You're trying to get rid of me.'

Sally winked. Inside the second envelope was a receipt for a room in a Montmartre hotel.

'A ticket and a hotel room?'

'Funny that,' said Sally brightly, holding up a rail ticket. 'I've got exactly the same.'

They leaned across the table and kissed.

'Springtime in Paris.'

'Have you been to Paris before?' Sally was curious.

'Once.' It was said in a dead, hollow way that made her frown.

'With the blonde girl?'

'What?'

'There's a photograph of a blonde girl in your flat. Sorry, but all women are curious.'

Tim didn't know she had seen the picture of Linda. 'That was over an age ago.'

Her look said he was lying.

'Fifteen months ago. She wrote recently but she's trying it on.' He swallowed nervously.

'Were you badly hurt?' asked Sally, wondering if she had stumbled on the reason behind his distrust of women.

'No,' lied Tim. She caught his eye. 'Yes. I suppose so.'

'Do you want to tell me . . .'

'Not really . . .' But he did. The whole story. Well, not the whole story but the facts. Her lips compressed when he recounted how Linda had taunted him with the colour of the baby and slowly he ran out of words. She squeezed his hand in reassurance and sympathy.

'Is that why you came to London? To get away?'

'Yes, but not from . . . Remember I told you of the two blokes who died crossing the river. I can't get it out of my mind that it was my fault. I was thinking of Linda. I didn't check.' Tim made an impatient gesture. 'It doesn't matter what any inquiry says, I feel guilty. I tried to get away but I only brought my guilt with me.' Soon he would have no secrets left.

He downed his glass of wine and a Thai waitress shimmied forward. 'Can I get you another bottle?'

'No, thank you,' decided Sally. 'We're going.'

'They were good mates. They're on the clock tower because of me.' He saw her incomprehension. 'The names of the Regiment's dead are inscribed on the clock tower in camp. When someone dies we call it beating the clock.'

'Oh, Tim, Tim, Tim.'

They helped each other up the stairs to his flat. They were both drunk and giggling and telling each other to be quiet. The cold and the damp enveloped them as they tumbled breathlessly through the door. Sally shivered.

'Let's get to bed before we freeze.'

'Forward hussy.'

Sally reached up and kissed the tip of his nose. 'Just as well or nothing would ever happen.'

'Once bitten . . .' he mumbled.

'I'm not here to bite you,' said Sally softly, taking his face and making Tim hold her eyes with his own. Just then Sally wanted to protect him against the ills and storms of the world. It wasn't supposed to happen like this.

Monday 30 March

'Know much about art, Haydn?' Livy glided up, canapé in one hand, glass of wine in the other.

Williams stopped himself wincing in front of a garish green canvas which reminded him of nothing so much as one of the bowls of faggots and peas he used to have as a boy on seaside visits to Porthcawl.

'Um, no. No, not really.' The catalogue proclaimed the work as *Forest Bark II*.

They regarded the oil side by side. Williams knew Livy was waiting for words of praise, but for the life of him he could find nothing charitable to say.

'Enigmatic,' he declared finally before escaping next to Mickey, who was standing before a bent piece of tin called *Man the Nomad* with his arms crossed and his finger to his lips as if auditioning for the part of an art critic. The price tag said £2,500.

'Load of bollocks, ennit,' bristled Mickey. 'Two and a half grand. My nipper does better than that at school.'

'You're a philistine, Mickey,' smiled Williams, silently agreeing with him.

'Nah. I'm a West Ham supporter. But honestly, guv. What do you reckon?'

'The same as you,' muttered Williams, holding the catalogue in front of his face as he remembered at the last minute that Livy could lip read. He supposed the works had to be all right, otherwise they wouldn't be exhibited in a Bond Street gallery – but their appeal was beyond him. He hoped he wasn't expected to buy something in a head of department gesture. 'Whatever happened to the trip to the signal box?'

Mickey slapped his forehead. 'I'm sorry, sir. It completely slipped my mind. We've been so busy with one thing and another.'

How it could have slipped Mickey's mind when he saw the trains every working day was a mystery to Williams.

'How're you getting on with Greenwich Council?' asked Mickey quickly.

'I've appealed to the London Parking Adjudicator.'

'I didn't know there was one,' said Mickey as a girl with aristocratic features and an incredibly high brow offered glasses of warm Chardonnay.

'Nor did I, but I've given him chapter and verse. I've pointed out that the only parking tickets I ever get are all issued by the same jobsworth. I reckon he's got the hump because I always successfully appeal – usually in forthright language. I've said I want to appear before the Adjudicator in person and asked that Greenwich provides evidence to show what proportion of the oaf's tickets are actually upheld.'

'Are you being represented?'

'I think I can represent myself against Greenwich Council's parking department, don't you?' said Williams in a surprisingly hurt tone.

Livy Hull was pleased at the turnout. A large number of colleagues, friends and relatives had responded to the three-line whip. Everyone seemed to be paying Peter's work a grave amount of attention and respect, even if few, if any, works were actually being bought.

Maurice and Felicity Plumridge had their heads together in animated discussion before a large abstract in purples and russets. Not that they had noticed.

'What do you mean he's got a cough? We all get coughs,' objected Plumridge.

'Equine cough is more serious. The horse can't be ridden and we just have to hope the vet can pull him through.'

'I thought the vet had given him the all clear before you

bought the bloody thing,' protested Plumridge. 'You said you'd only buy him if he had a clean bill of health.'

Felicity Plumridge gestured impatiently. 'These things happen.'

'We've only had the bloody horse a fortnight. Sue the vet.'

'Don't be absurd. God, this wine's revolting. If they have to serve such cheap muck they could at least try to hide its flavour by chilling it.'

'So you're saying we wasted five thousand on a bloody useless horse. We might as well have spent the money on this pretentious crap.'

He became aware of Livy Hull's presence at his shoulder.

'Seen anything you really like, my dear?'

From her assumed Dorset accent, he feared she had overheard his comments.

'Some are very . . . striking,' fumbled Plumridge.

'But not really to one's taste,' proclaimed his wife.

'Of course,' drawled Livy. 'So personal, isn't it. Art in the educated eye of the beholder.'

The only one who seemed to be taking the exhibition seriously was Commander Penn. He stood in front of *Forest Bark II*, his head on one side, and tried to explain to Williams why it did not work. 'The composition, you see. I think I understand what he's getting at, but the line and the balance are all wrong. The eye is distracted from, not drawn to the subject. And this brushwork is positively art school level . . .'

'So how would you appraise Livy's chap, as an artist . . . ?'

Commander Penn made a rueful sucking noise. 'Pedestrian, I'm afraid.'

The artist was closeted with the gallery owner Ross and a few of their cronies in the furthest corner from the door, making no effort to circulate.

'It's not my part to persuade philistines to appreciate art,' he hissed in reply to Livy's entreaties. 'The artist creates. Others sell.'

The Chardonnay was arriving less frequently and the order forms, left negligently on a small table by the door, stayed suspiciously blank. Alison arrived, demure in a black two-piece woollen suit which showed off a surprisingly shapely figure.

'Which one shall I buy you?' joked Mickey, coming up behind her.

'None, thank you,' she said, trying surreptitiously to concentrate on the row between Plumridge and his wife.

'No. We are not insured for these sort of things. He may get better in time, but he will not be sound this summer and Tabitha needs a pony. We'll have to get another one, that's all there is to it.'

Tim, arriving to collect Mickey to go to the airport, clocked Alison's interest in the quarrelling couple. As he was leaving he also clocked Livy Hull discreetly sticking a red dot on the bottom of a truly hideous painting.

'Bit different from last time, eh, buddy?' Jedd Fry grinned at Tim as they climbed into the back of a Dutch police patrol van to carry them unobtrusively across the huge container compound on the Nordzeecanaal. 'By the way, how's your lovely lady? Got over her fright?'

'She's not my lady but she's fine.'

'Bullshit. I saw you two together. I want an invite to the wedding, you remember that.'

Tim did his best not to blush.

Jedd Fry did not know it, but there were two separate operations on the go that night. Jedd's task was to verify the cocaine was in the container. Tim's was to find the flask of Marburg. Once the cocaine had been confirmed, Jedd intended to bail out and leave it to undercover customs agents to track it to its destination.

Tim and Mickey were going to return later that night – without the help of Dutch customs.

Williams was looking forward to producing the Marburg

at tomorrow's JIC like a conjurer producing a rabbit from a hat.

The stuff legends were made of.

If the flask was not in the container – then they didn't have a clue where it was.

'It threw us when they flew it to Rostov. Sure weren't expecting that,' agreed Jedd. 'But the little old bleeper kept on working even when they transferred the load to a new container. That's normal, breaking up and re-forming loads. We even got a picture of the container on the ground at Rostov.'

'You followed it all the way?'

'Sort of. We only managed route checks from Odessa to Lvov and through the Ukraine, but once it crossed the Polish frontier we had it in sight the whole time. Yeh, boy. The whole time. Through Cracow, Dresden, the Ruhr and boy, were they burning rubber! Two drivers. New Mercedes rig. Fair tired out our watchers.'

The van halted under dimmed lamps in a far corner. They shook hands with Bob, their Dutch customs liaison officer. Two hundred feet above them in the cabin of a jib crane Mickey was sweeping the site.

'We have plenty more,' said Bob, breaking the customs seals on the container.

Jedd Fry held a small direction finder in his hand.

'Ajax will find it for you,' said Bob.

The spaniel sniffer dog stood alert, stump of a tail quivering in anticipation. On command from his handler, he began snuffling busily along the loads inside the container. At one he rose on his hind legs and whimpered before moving on to the next. His floppy ears dragged along the floor and his rear was in continual motion, almost a case, thought Tim, of the tail wagging the dog. He darted to and fro until he reached the end wall – then he sat down, tongue lolling.

'Ajax,' commanded his handler. The dog rose and obediently began again sniffing at the loads, but without the same enthusiasm. The dog was going through the motions. I've tried but there's nothing here, he was saying. Believe me.

'Ajax's trained to find heroin and cocaine. He's our best dog,' explained his handler, at the end of his second trawl. 'If he says there's nothing here, then there's nothing here.'

'But there must be,' protested Jedd. A series of high-pitched beeps from the direction finder merged into a continual tone as he inched towards the rear. He stopped before the last pallet but one, which held three large packing cases with Vietnamese writing stencilled on them. 'Here. I told you.'

He broke open the top one. Inside were tightly packed duvets. Each one carried a label proclaiming in English that it was stuffed with genuine wild goose feathers.

'Someone's got a sense of humour,' said Tim sourly.

An anaemic blonde girl in tanga and bra gyrated briefly in a half-hearted attempt to catch their attention, then gave up and drew on her cigarette.

'Turn you on, Mickey?'

'Nah. It's too clinical, ennit.'

Tim knew what he meant. They pushed their way along Oudezijds Voorburgwal through crowds of curious onlookers staring at girls in narrow glass-fronted booths each the width of a telephone box. Behind every showcase was a small bedroom and wash basin. Clinical, as Mickey said. Along the canal side, the pale yellow glow cast by the traditional iron street lamps high among the leaves of the plane trees was swamped by the harsh red neon sex signs. Around the buttresses at the back of the Oude Kerk four large black women in white underwear were squabbling on the cobbles outside their booths.

It was gone midnight, but Amsterdam's red light district was just warming up. Three Spanish girls stood debating whether to enter the Sex Museum. The plainest seemed the most eager. Tim and Mickey found the Yam Yam sex club next to the Chinese church. The club had large pictures of couples coyly copulating under the banner: Real hard fucky fucky. Yuri was sitting at a side table in the downstairs bar guarded by two minders.

Mickey was initially surprised how small and compact the Russian was. He quickly realized it was only a superficial appraisal. Stern, grizzled Yuri possessed the type of steely determination he had known in his first sergeant major. A wee Jock who looked as if he'd be blown away on a breeze. The hardest bastard he had ever met.

'I thought you were in Rostov,' said Tim in simple Russian.

'I'm in Amsterdam because the Polecat is here,' explained Yuri. 'Where he goes, I go. We have much unfinished business.' Mickey, not understanding a word of the conversation, watched a naked long-legged girl slide up and down a steel pole. 'Would your friend like to see the sex show while we talk? It is not a problem. A friend of mine owns this place.'

Yuri barked commands and a half-naked girl came to escort Mickey upstairs. 'Don't let on to my missus, will you, boss?'

Yuri filled small glasses with vodka. 'You got my message. Good. But I did not expect you so soon.'

'I was in Holland.'

'Your visit is to do with drugs?' suggested Yuri.

'We hoped we'd find the stolen flask in a shipment of cocaine,' confessed Tim, thinking Plumridge would go ballistic if he could hear him.

'And you did not?'

'No. Why is the Polecat in Amsterdam?' It crossed Tim's mind that perhaps he was going to accompany the virus to London.

'There have been rumours that Polecat is involved in a drug shipment worth millions of dollars. I watch him. Suddenly he leaves Rostov. I follow.' Yuri knocked back the vodka in one and refilled his glass. 'He's visited a boat in the port of Hoorn some forty kilometres from here. She's called the *Archangel* from Hamburg, but there's no record of such a ship. She would reach England easily.'

'You think the Polecat has stashed the drugs on board?'

Yuri shrugged again.

'Thank you, Yuri. Once again I am in your debt.'

'The Polecat will not return to Russia.'

'How do you know?' Tim asked before he saw the expression on the old man's face. 'Oh!'

'Let us find your friend.' Yuri led Tim up a flight of back stairs and into a room where young men and women were in various stages of nakedness, either undressing for their public acts or putting their clothes on afterwards. On stage a lissom black woman and her white lover reached the end of their choreographed sex act. Through a gap in the curtains Tim watched as rows of Japanese businessmen craned their heads in formation. As Brown Sugar pumped out its final chords, the black girl brought the man to climax over her breasts. The Japanese exhaled a collective sigh. The naked couple scuttled quickly off stage and disappeared into separate showers, ignoring each other.

Tuesday 31 March

Williams put down the phone in his office and felt a sick wave of defeat wash over him. The Max phone intercepts had spoken of the virus being in Britain within the month – and this was the last day of the month. He seethed at his own blind willingness to believe all their eggs would be found in the one basket. He had been outwitted and now he was left empty-handed. He had been so convinced the Marburg was in the container. It all made perfect sense. Had someone been very clever or had he been stupid? Hell's bells. Where did they go now?

He was still looking down on the empty railway tracks when Tim's second phone call came. The news about the boat animated him. He was still convinced that the Polecat's presence in Amsterdam at the same time as the container was not a coincidence. Maybe the boat was the missing link. Analysts from Criminal Intelligence were hauled from their beds to tell Williams that the London street price for cocaine had not changed in the past month. That meant that the *Sheila-Na-Gig's* cargo had not reached the dealers. Either someone was stashing it so as not to depress the market price or it had never arrived. At the same time there had been reports of market distortions in Paris and northern France as well as the Rhineland.

Could the load have been switched to the Continent? demanded Williams.

The analysts hummed and hawed. Possible, they said. All things were possible, but it would need a sophisticated international wholesale distribution network.

Isn't that what you feared would happen if power-ful Russian Mafiya organizations forged links with pan-European crime gangs? Williams reminded them.

Yes, they conceded.

And ergo, if the *Sheila*'s last cargo, originating from the same Moscow Narco Group, had been switched to Western Europe, this current consignment would be targeted at Britain?

Quite possibly, they agreed.

All well and good, thought Williams, finally putting down the phone, but where the merry hell is the Marburg?

Tim was lying under a bush in the park alongside the small harbour at Hoorn and waiting for daybreak. He shivered in the thick dew and thought back to the first of his phone calls with Williams when he announced the container had been clean. It was like breaking the news of a death in the family.

The Markermeer emerged from the darkness as a flat grey looking-glass. Tall masts of sailing schooners along the outer mole formed a fretwork against the rising sun, and alongside them an ancient round keep stood guard above the lock. There was no mistaking their target. A large motor vessel with raked masts tied up in the Binnenhaven, the small inner harbour. Her lines became clearer in the gathering light.

Mickey swore. 'Bloody hell, boss. That's the *Sheila-Na-Gig*.'

'What!'

'She's had a lick of paint and they've put a small inflat-able on her stern but it's the *Sheila*. She can't draw anything like we thought or she couldn't reach here.'

'So?'

'So. You remember when we lost her in that storm,' mused Mickey. 'We reckoned she could have sheltered behind the Friesian Islands or cross-decked the drugs?'

'Yeh?'

'She received two messages which still haven't been deciphered. They could have told her we were waiting . . .' Mickey was unfolding a map of Holland and measuring distances with his thumb. 'A hundred-and-twenty-mile round trip and we lost her for the best part of a day. She could have been here before we even knew she was missing. Hell, she could even have dumped her drugs in this sleepy little place. Hardly your high-security Europort, is it?'

'But why make the dummy run just for the sake of it?' demanded Tim.

'She was expected so she came,' argued Mickey. 'If she hadn't arrived we'd have gone searching for her and maybe found her where she didn't want to be found.'

The yacht lay lifeless and still. As daylight grew they were forced to abandon their hiding place and retreat to the other side of the keep.

Tim reported their discovery. Williams must have pressed the panic button, for five minutes later they were ordered away from the harbour while the local police began inquiries and Dutch undercover squads moved into position.

At a small, spotless hotel in a side street they breakfasted off boiled eggs, ham and cheese before slipping into blissfully crisp sheets.

They were woken with a message to meet Bob at the Grand Café La Bascule in the town square at midday. There was a wedding taking place and they strolled into the cobbled square behind a dainty carriage drawn by two black horses accompanied by grooms in burgundy red livery.

The big Dutchman was sitting at an outside table having problems with a cup of cappuccino. He wiped the froth from his long moustache and polished his steamed-up glasses while explaining the café had once been a weigh house, in the days when Hoorn was a home port of the Dutch East India Company.

'You'd think it'd be too small,' objected Mickey.

'Not at all. Cape Horn is named after this town and Abel Tasman, who gave his name to Tasmania, was born here,' smiled Bob. 'To business. The boat arrived at dusk a couple of days ago with a skipper we believe was our friend de Koch and a deckhand. Your Russian Polecat was here yesterday with a woman, very attractive. They spent some time on board before leaving in the evening. We've staked out the harbour and a diver's examined her hull. So we wait.'

'Who's the geezer?' demanded Mickey, peering at the large statue of a bearded man with one hand on his hip and the other clutching a sword. Someone had draped an orange banner around him in anticipation of the forthcoming World Cup.

'That's the local hero Jan Pietersz-Coen.'

'And what did he do when he was at home?'

'Supported Holland,' said Bob.

It was the first time Stan Bagg had flown. It wasn't that he was afraid of flying – it was simply that he had never needed to. When Emma was growing up they had gone to the same caravan site in Swanage every year. Last summer vacation she'd been working in Bath. At her insistence, he and Kath had splashed out on a coach trip along the Rhine. It had been very pretty and their natural friendliness had overcome their suspicions of foreigners. So although Stan could boast he had been abroad nothing prepared him for the terrifying confusion, the queues, the stern armed guards and the Cyrillic script at Moscow airport.

Williams had been as good as his word. A young diplomat from the embassy smoothed the way through customs and immigration and drove Stan to a small hotel. He spent a miserable evening. He had never been so far from home. He began walking around the streets to try to get a flavour of the country Emma had chosen to embrace, but the roads were enormously wide and there were few shops or buildings whose purpose he could recognize. There weren't even any pubs. He was soon back alone in his sparse room.

The next morning he shaved carefully, feeling under his left ear for the bristles he always missed, put on the carefully folded and pressed white shirt and polished his shoes. Finally he did up his black tie. He wished Kath had come with him, but he accepted it was a man's job to bring home their daughter's body. He was ready a good half an hour before the same fresh-faced young man collected him. In the car Stan expressed his gratitude so frequently that the diplomat was prompted to reply that they were only too pleased to be able to help. At the same time he wondered why this farm labourer was getting VIP treatment.

At the airport Stan was escorted airside to a locked cold room, as bleak as the milking parlour in February. He placed his hand on the pale pine coffin in greeting and in farewell and swallowed back his tears.

He was last to board. The senior stewardess met him at the door to the aircraft.

'Would you like to sit here? It's more comfortable,' she said, indicating the front row of the business section.

'It's more expensive, isn't it, my dear?'

'Don't worry, Mr Bagg. You sit here. We'll look after you.'

'I don't want to be any trouble.'

How helpless and sad he looks, she thought. You met so many people flying. Most passengers were pleasant enough blurs, one or two were complete swine and then once in a blue moon you came across someone like poor Mr Bagg. Reeling from his loss, out of his depth. And so grateful for whatever she did.

When they took off, he gave a great big sigh. And the stewardess, sitting on the rear-facing jump seat opposite, felt her heart go out to him.

He picked at the foie gras, the poulet chasseur and the charlotte russe until, in a moment's inspiration, she asked him if he'd like one of the sandwiches made for the crew.

'Yes, please.' He devoured a round of cheese and a cup of tea, staring out of the window at the blue, blue sky. After the meal service the stewardess sat by him and said how sorry she was.

'Do you have a picture?'

Of course he did. His favourite. Emma standing at the gate to the home field, with her horse Winnie looking over her shoulder. Taken on the farm.

'It was all very sudden. A hit and run driver. She didn't know anything. She didn't suffer . . .'

No. The ones who are left are the ones who suffer, thought the stewardess.

'. . . Apparently her injuries were severe. We've been advised it's better not to open the coffin. We'd like to see our little girl again, but she won't be there, will she?'

'And you've got your memories.'

'Ay. We have those. The coroner's officer has said there'll be no need for a post mortem. Cause of death is clear enough. We're grateful for that. Her mother can't stand the thought of her being cut up. Let her rest now.'

'Yes.'

'Emma's being buried in the same church where my folk have been buried a century or more. One day her mother and me will join her.'

The stewardess dabbed at her eyes. And her a hard old cow of twenty years' flying. Tosh!

She asked Stan Bagg if he minded waiting until last and the other passengers glanced curiously at the ruddy-faced man in the black tie. When he made his way out he shook everyone's hand. It was all she could do not to hug him. By the time he saw the hearse drawn up under the nose wheel of the aircraft there were already flowers around the coffin.

The hotel had been built as a rich merchant's house in Amsterdam's Golden Age in the seventeenth century. Rembrandt had painted *The Militia Company of Captain*

297

Frans Banning Cocq and Lieutenant Willem van Ruytenburgh in a first-floor room facing the Amstel River. Tari, playing the role of curious hotel guest, stopped to gaze at the reproduction of *The Night Watch*, flanked by vast floral bouquets, on one wall of the room. It did not move him. He read about Rembrandt's revolutionary interplay of light and shadow and wondered what all the fuss was about. Art left him cold. It was for those who had the time and money to indulge themselves. There were more important issues to take up his time – like the fight for justice and land for his people in a world governed by oil and realpolitik. An ornate grandfather clock gently chimed the half-hour as he headed for the stairs. He checked himself. Anyone walking up was unusual – worthy of notice. He pressed the button for the lift.

Polecat lay back on the huge golden bed and smirked in memory of the last few hours and in anticipation of the next few days. He had every reason to feel smug. He was enjoying the reality of the adage that nothing succeeds like success. He had acquired a beautiful new woman – and soon he would be richer by five million dollars. This evening he would use that money to complete the payment on his part of the cocaine shipment. The first five million he had received for the Marburg had allowed him to buy his way into the magic circle. Put up or shut up, they'd said and he'd put up. The second instalment would close the deal. Once the cocaine was cut and moved down to the middlemen he'd be looking at a three hundred per cent return. Thirty million dollars. He raised his right arm and punched the air in victory. At last. He would annihilate Yuri Andreyevich Kornilov and his sad little men with their sad old-fashioned ways.

There was the splash of the shower before the bathroom door closed and he wondered if he should have got her out of the way while the Palestinian called. Why should he? If you had it – flaunt it. And he had it. Power, riches and a beautiful woman. He bristled at the memory of how the little Arab had laughed at him, mocking him for his ostentation. He wouldn't sneer now. The money he'd hand over would make Polecat a prince among men. He decided to show the woman the five million dollars and let the Palestinian see his lover, to demonstrate his class of woman. He would have admiration from both of them.

A tap on the door brought him out of his reverie. He pulled on a white towelling robe and slipped a small Starr revolver into his right-hand pocket. The tap at the door again. More impatient this time. Through the spy hole Igor saw the distorted face of the Palestinian.

'My friend. Welcome.'

Tari kept one hand on the door knob as his eyes swept the large room with its vases of flowers and gilt table lamps. He was wearing a long blue raincoat over a suit, but the arresting touch of genius was the conference identity card still absent-mindedly pinned to his lapel. He scowled at the sight of the champagne bottle and two flute glasses.

Igor misunderstood his disapproval. 'Today we celebrate.'

Tari stepped inside the room. 'We have nothing to celebrate.' His distant tone made Igor hesitate.

'What do you mean? You have $5 million for me. That is the agreement.'

'It has not arrived . . .'

'But it is arriving in London, today, as we speak.'

Tari shrugged. 'It should have been there already. You have been wasting time with drugs . . .'

'I promise you it has not been a waste of time.' Igor's smirk faded as he saw the frost in the other's eyes.

'You were told you'd be paid when the flask is in my hands – not before.'

'But . . .' Igor needed that money today.

'My masters are not pleased you departed from the timetable for your own ends. They think you are not to be trusted.'

'What the fuck do you mean? I got the flask for you. Not once but twice.' Igor's features thickened in anger.

'I've done my part; I want my money. If they don't pay up they'll never . . .'

'Never! What will *you* never?' sneered Tari, deliberately turning his back on the Russian to stroll over the thick carpet to the window. A long, glass-topped tourist boat was gliding silently under the bridge over the Rokin. Another was turning into the broader Amstel. He put his hand into his breast pocket. 'Here are the details of the new bank account in Nicosia. Number, name and password.'

'Good,' gasped Igor.

The Palestinian had been pulling his wire. Bastard. He'd make him pay for that, but he had to get his hands on that five million or he'd forfeit the first five million – and appear a loser in eyes of the Moscow bosses.

Tari read his thoughts. 'There's just $100 in the account – enough to open it.' He was almost whispering. 'You will have the five million dollars when I have the Marburg. Not before.'

Igor had gone pale. Flecks of foam appeared at the corners of his mouth. His lips drew back in an animal snarl. 'I'll break your fucking neck . . .'

The bathroom door opened. Sally stood there. Her hair was tied back and her face was flushed from the shower. A short white towel tied around the top of her breasts ended high on her thigh and hung open at one side.

Igor felt a surge of electricity leap between Sally and the Palestinian. He sensed rather than saw the mutual look of recognition and disbelief.

It was a trap.

'You know each other!' he howled.

Igor backed away towards the bed, tugging at the revolver in his pocket. The foresight snagged on the towelling. Tari sprang at him, grasping the Russian's gun arm. Igor was bigger, but Tari had a wiry, sinuous strength that belied his slender frame. Igor was forced to let go of the gun. He pushed Tari away and plunged his hand back in the pocket. The gun was still caught. He twisted it and the hammer also snagged. The mobster swore. Again Tari was on him. Igor was forced to use his hands to protect his eyes from Tari's vicious gouging. There was no science in Tari's assault – a mindless explosion of passion. In such fighting Igor knew he would win – in time. He prized away Tari's hands and short-armed him to the face. In the seconds bought, he delved again in the pocket, grasped the gun around the trigger guard and yanked with all his might. The cloth ripped. The hammer was free. Igor tore the pocket inside out, still the front sight snagged in the twisted material. It was a race to free the gun before the next attack. Tari was on him. Igor kept his hand on the pistol and strove to turn it towards Tari. His free hand battered the Palestinian in the face and blood spurted from Tari's nose. There was a muffled shot.

For a second, or maybe in Sally's mind eternity, the two men stood and swayed together, two soldiers impaled upon each other's bayonets. Then the ashes of death crept over the Russian's face, a pulse of blood trickled out of the corner of his mouth and ran down his chin. He slumped against Tari and slid to the golden carpet. His right heel beat a tattoo of death.

'You,' breathed Tari.

For a second the hatred deep in his eyes made Sally believe he was going to kill her. When she opened her eyes he was wiping the surfaces with the towel which had been wrapped around the neck of the champagne bottle.

News of Polecat's killing reached Bob that afternoon. Tim recalled the old thief in law's words and cursed Yuri for not holding off longer.

'Know anything about this?' asked Bob.

Tim shook his head.

They waited until dusk before establishing a cordon around the *Archangel* and boarding her. The only traces of drugs on board were a crumpled wrap which had once held a gram of cocaine and the roaches of four reefers.

In the closet in the front stateroom they discovered a brand-new American army issue Nuclear, Biological and Chemical protection suit, known as an NBC suit, or more popularly a Noddy suit.

Wednesday 1 April

The call came as Tim was reaching for the phone to ask his bank, in some way which would not make him sound like a right nutter, how many accounts he held.

'Hello, Tim. Tim, it's Linda.'

An icy hand grasped his heart. 'How did you get my number?'

'A friend gave it me. How are you? Are you all right?' He had forgotten how melodious she could make herself when she wanted. He remembered to ask how she was.

'Oh, all right. I survive,' she replied in a little voice, adding a sigh for maximum plaintiveness. 'But are *you* well? Are *you* looking after yourself?'

Tim did not understand this preoccupation with his health. 'Yes, thanks.'

'Did you get my letter? It's almost a month ago . . .'

'. . . um . . .'

'I told you I lost that office job. I worked for a hire company for a while, but they went bust owing thousands. I managed to walk off with a computer. I got some promotion work at a caravan show at Birmingham NEC. Then I went round the pubs pushing cigarettes, but it's fallen off now. But you're all right? Not a major yet or whatever.' Linda giggled. She was obviously nervous and making an effort.

There was a pause. It occurred to Tim that there could only be one reason why she was phoning. She wanted something. He did not intend to make it easy for her. He was surprisingly calm; in control of himself and, by extension, in control of the conversation.

'I had friends staying, but I'm by myself now,' she continued.

'Does that mean the complaints about the loud music have stopped?'

A sharp intake of breath. Tim grimaced at his own malevolence.

'I said I'm on my own.' Linda sounded really brittle now. 'You're never coming back are you?' There was a long silence. 'I think we should sell the house. I'll move into a small flat. After all, the house is too big for one and it's silly to have money locked up in property.'

That phrase didn't sound like Linda. Someone was coaching her. Tim was suddenly alert. He had deliberately avoided thinking about selling the house. He knew he'd go back to Hereford when his tour of duty finished in a couple of years. Maybe by then, when the wounds were not so raw, he could live there.

No, if he was honest, he never wanted to set foot in that house again.

'I don't know,' he hedged. 'I hadn't thought about it.'

'You could buy my share of the equity.'

There was Linda using unfamiliar words again. Tim wondered if she was by herself on the other end of the phone.

With a flash of intuition, he asked, 'Why? What's wrong?'

'The bloody building society is on my back, that's what's wrong,' she snapped. 'They're threatening to repossess the house.'

'What do you mean, they might take it back? They can't.' Tim didn't understand.

'We're behind with the mortgage payments,' Linda admitted in a strangled voice.

Tim was growing angry. The house was in their joint names.

'I've been paying my half of the mortgage. Linda?'

'Yeh, well. Like I said, it's not been easy.'

304

'But you had friends in there paying rent. And the bloke . . . ?'

'He didn't give, he took,' snapped Linda bitterly.

'But all the rent money . . .'

'Doesn't matter.' Linda was on the attack. 'An estate agent reckons we can probably get around ninety for it. Let's take it and split it – then you won't have to talk to me any more.'

'But we've got a seventy-five-thousand mortgage.'

'Yeh, so. We'd make fifteen and that's seven and half each. That'll go towards my flat.'

Tim quickly took stock. He had put in his £10,000 savings as a deposit while she had only offered £500. He had been paying £400 a month. To sell now would leave him with less than he'd put in.

'Have you paid anything at all?' Tim guessed she had not paid a penny. He felt the hairs on the back of his neck rise in anger.

'I've told you, it's been hard. I've had other things to spend my money on. Don't be horrid to me.' Now she was a little girl wheedling for sympathy.

'I'm not being horrid, Linda. Nor are we going to sell the house. Get a job, pay off the arrears and we'll talk about it. Not before.' He put down the phone amazed at his own strength of character.

Sally looked Haydn Williams squarely in the eye and said, 'When I came out of the bathroom, he was dead on the floor.'

Williams balanced an unlit cigarette upright on his desk. 'Dutch liaison say their SOCOs reckon there was a woman in the room. Left nothing behind, I hope.'

'If you mean fingerprints, no. I wiped everything. I even removed hair from the shower, whether it was mine or not.'

Williams nodded approvingly. 'So you heard nothing?' he repeated.

It was the third time he had asked and Sally wondered what he knew or suspected. She was determined not to be rattled.

'I was in the shower. The bathroom door was solid. It was closed. I didn't hear him. He didn't hear me.'

'Him?'

'Or she or them. We always assume a killer to be a him, don't we?'

'Do we? A bit unusual that he, she or them didn't search the rest of the suite. Most natural thing to do, you'd have thought.'

'No,' disagreed Sally. 'The most natural thing would have been to get away.'

'That would depend on why the Russian was murdered and what the murderer was after, if anything. Small calibre Starr revolver. A woman's gun.'

'I didn't shoot him, if that's what you're implying. That wasn't my job, was it?'

Williams leant back in his chair and tugged at a lock of silver hair behind his ear. 'A tiff? A falling out? No?'

'No!'

'No.' Williams swung forward to rest his forearms on the desk. 'I believe you. Shame though, especially after he took you on board the *Sheila*. Those drugs are out there somewhere and so is that damn flask.'

Sally shifted uncomfortably. 'Haydn, you did promise. Remember. I've paid my dues, haven't I?' From being proud and defiant, she became a supplicant. 'I didn't know Teddy had taken that money, did I? You investigated. You believe that I didn't know.'

'I believe.' He wished he knew more about old Teddy Millibanks' dealings – but it never did to look too closely at the bargains struck in the Middle East.

Tim saw Alison's overnight bag behind her desk when he went to scrounge some milk.

'Going anywhere nice?'

Alison pushed the bag out of sight. 'Only to see a girlfriend. You and Mickey are going to have to start buying your own milk. I can't keep supplying the whole office.'

Tim was trying to get a better look at the set of twelve by ten glossies Alison was sliding into a stiff envelope as Sally came out of Williams's office. It was the first time he had seen her since she'd left early Sunday morning to pack for her trip. His heart did a high kick.

'Hello,' she smiled.

'Hello. Fancy lunch?'

'It's only eleven o'clock.'

'Oh.' Tim was crestfallen. 'By the way, it's Emma's funeral tomorrow morning. I thought I'd go down to Wiltshire.'

'Would you like me to come with you?'

Tim nodded appreciatively. 'Thank you.'

'I may as well stay in your flat. It's handier for the M3,' said Sally in a businesslike tone. She grinned impishly as she saw the words sink in. 'If that's all right?'

'Oh yes. Of course. Um . . .'

'We're going to have to do something about that place. Is it worth our while trying to cook in? Do you have anything, say like salt?'

Tim thought. 'I've four tins of corned beef and three bottles of brown sauce.'

'You're hopeless,' she said fondly. 'I'll call you later.'

Tim went back to his desk with a warm inner glow. He made himself stop thinking about Sally and concentrated on why a KGB colonel from Rostov, friend of the Polecat and in league with the Moscow Narco Group, had been photographed arm in arm with Williams.

Morning prayers were brief – and depressing. Police and customs had drawn a blank in their hunt for codename Barbel. The search was expanding from east Kent up to London. The Met were conducting house to house enquiries in a half-mile radius of the London phone call.

SB was working overtime on all known Iraqi agents and sympathizers. Five was trawling its contacts in the maze of Middle East groups. Six was getting overdrawn in the favour banks with friendly services begging interviews with recent Iraqi defectors.

No one anywhere seemed to know anything about the Samson Option.

Williams hid his intense frustration under a patient smile, feeling in his stomach that the Marburg was now in the country.

Saddam was continuing to sabre-rattle by putting more buildings off limits to the inspectors. At the same time the US was making hawk-like noises as it became clear not only that the UN Secretary General had been conned by Saddam in the recent peace agreement, but that he in turn had misled the American Secretary of State.

Bill Jones reported that there had been another broadcast from Radio Baghdad charting the illness and recovery of little Soraya.

'She's still weak but she has enormous spirit,' announced Bill Jones. 'Her nurse calls her the bravest little girl in the world. The doctor is careful to point out that she is receiving a full course of antibiotics – obviously a message to her father. Her sister Leila has figured more in the last programme.'

'Is that significant?' demanded Williams.

'My people say it suggests the broadcast's being scripted. Time for a new character – and here's Leila. And medically her progress is almost too even. There should be hiccups. Not literally of course.' He guffawed.

'As we know Barbel is listening to these broadcasts, they may also be a way to transmit orders to him,' pointed out Williams.

Commander Penn sat pensively, no doubt thinking of that morning's strong rumour that DIS were to bear the brunt of the summer spending cuts. Williams did not have much sympathy. DIS, numerically the largest of the intelligence agencies, had slumbered through the build-up to the Falklands War and snored well into the Gulf War. It was about to pay the price for oversleeping. Then there was the farce of their new £34 million computer which was two years behind schedule and didn't work. It was going to be scrapped and an off the shelf system bought for £6 million. That balls-up hadn't reached the public yet.

Livy Hull wore a mannishly cut charcoal grey trouser suit which emphasized her bony frame, and an air of smugness which annoyed Plumridge.

'How's the exhibition going?' he asked, suspecting that it was not going at all well.

'Fine,' she lied blandly. 'How's the cough?'

'Cough?'

'I gathered Tabitha's new pony has equine cough. Can be nasty, you know.'

'Keeping horses is an expensive business.' Plumridge instantly regretted his admission.

'Don't I know it. The old man was master of the local hunt for donkey's years. Damn near crippled him financially. The old stables are empty now,' she added wistfully. 'Oh, Haydn, Colonel Primakov has come up trumps with a Chechen mob trying to slide into a private bank on Jersey. They were planning to link up with some Birmingham characters in a nice little money laundering scam. Primakov has chapter and verse of the Russian end. Our chap in Moscow is chuffed to bits.'

'Good,' said Williams automatically.

After the meeting Williams thought he'd see how the trains were doing. His few moments of restful contemplation. Others practised yoga. He had the trains. On Alison's unoccupied desk he saw a green flimsy of files removed from the registry. Jesus Christ! It was the list of files he had taken home. What was the girl thinking of leaving that lying about? Anyone, everyone could have seen it as they left his office.

'Alison!' He held up the flimsy. 'What are you doing?'

Her eyes rounded in shock or fear. He noticed she had on more eye make-up than normal.

'Where did you get that?'

'On your desk. What are you thinking of?'

'Oh, I'm sorry.' She looked helplessly round to see what else she might have forgotten.

'That new girl didn't last long. Shall I get you some help from central?'

'No, I'm all right, sir. Really.'

Alison was changing, noted Williams. Changing right under his eyes, but gradually so that he had not noticed. She'd become quieter. She didn't go for after work drinks with Mickey and the pavement artists downstairs as she used to. She'd smartened up her appearance, too. Become more feminine. He would speak to Plumridge to get her vetted again, quietly. If there were changes in her life, he needed to know.

Mickey almost knocked him over as he hurried out.

'I fixed it last night,' he said quickly. 'We've a VIP visit to the control room at Waterloo next week.'

'Excellent,' enthused Williams.

Tim was already looking out of the window. The photograph was bothering him, but it didn't do to ask too many questions around here. There were subscription lists from which he was excluded and clearance levels which he was near the bottom of. And there was the perpetual ethic of Need to Know.

In this case Tim felt he needed to know why a Mafiya bigwig had his arm around Williams on the steps of their building.

'Excuse me, sir.' He mustered up his courage. 'May I ask a question?'

'Ay, as long as you don't expect an honest answer,' replied Williams gruffly.

'There was a picture on Alison's desk . . .' he faltered.

'There's a lot of bloody things on Alison's desk.'

'There's one of you with a KGB colonel . . .'

310

'How do you know he's a Russian colonel?' demanded Williams sharply. 'He's in civvies.'

Feeling he was digging himself a deeper hole every time he opened his mouth, Tim stuttered, 'I saw him in Rostov.'

'Did you?' whispered Williams. 'Yes . . . ?'

'He's a contact of the Polecat. I saw them laughing together on the steps of KGB headquarters. Emma said they were business associates. He tried to put Yuri off the scent when Polecat stole the flask the first time.'

'Did he now!' Williams gripped Tim's forearm. 'And did he have a name?'

'Linnikov. He's a Cossack.'

'Not Primakov?'

'No. Linnikov. I'm definite.'

Williams released Tim's arm and stared sightlessly down at the trains. Occasionally he pursed his lips as if about to speak. Suddenly he swung back to face him.

'How are you enjoying our secret world, Tim? Are you enjoying it?' he demanded abruptly.

'Oh yes, sir.' The enthusiastic junior officer.

'Don't feel out of your depth? Worry about what you don't understand?'

That was a harder one to answer. 'Er. No, sir.'

'The best dim sum in London is at the New World in Chinatown. I'll see you outside there at eleven minutes past one.' Williams paused. 'Tim, think what Emma Bagg and Polecat had in common – they both knew Primakov's real name and they're both dead. Take care.'

As Tim emerged from Leicester Square underground, a fair-haired teenage girl in a dufflecoat ran ahead of an older man to sit on a bench. She bent down and, with the utmost concentration, began to pick up small pieces of paper and litter. She folded them neatly and transferred them into a growing pile in her left hand. The older man smiled and took her right hand as they walked on together. Tim

311

found the scene intensely poignant, but did not know why. He was early and slowed down to stroll under an ornate arch of dragons and golden snakes and past telephone boxes disguised as pagodas. Wind-dried ducks hung in the windows and cooks with sharp cleavers chopped and sliced meat and vegetables in clouds of billowing steam. He remembered he'd brought Sally here that first night.

Williams turned the corner from Shaftesbury Avenue at precisely eleven minutes past one.

'Years of practice,' he explained as Tim complimented him. 'The trick is to know exactly how much ground one covers in one of three speeds. Then it's simple.'

Finding a table to Williams's liking was not so simple. He passed up two tables in the middle of the cavernous restaurant, waiting until one against the wall and near the rear came vacant. No one in their right mind would choose to sit facing a blank wall, but no one could point a directional microphone at anyone sitting there, either.

Waitresses in black skirts and white blouses pushed shiny metal trolleys laden with bamboo steamers around the room in an unending, circling wagon-train of food. Soon their table was piled with spare ribs in black bean sauce, steamed rice flour rolls with shrimps, minced pork dumplings and meatballs on large flat mushroom tops.

Williams picked up a prawn in rice paper with his chopsticks and dipped it in hot chilli oil. 'The French say Chinese cuisine is second only to their own. Considering the French ego, that's an admission of defeat.'

Relaxed and friendly, he led the conversation into sport, displaying an unexpected knowledge of cricket and bemoaning the state of Welsh rugby: the smaller the country the more internecine its quarrels. Finally he declared he could not eat another dumpling, leaned forward, one hand shielding his mouth, and began to talk seriously. He spoke so quietly that Tim had to strain to hear.

'Generally, we have an excellent record. The job you and

Mickey did in Afghanistan over Christmas will be regarded as a model of its kind for years. It's going in the training manual. But we're expected to tackle organized crime and its implications for intelligence gathering and here we're starting to come unstuck. We get results against Azeris, Georgians, Chechens, mobs from Ekaterinburg, but never Moscow. We never score against a Moscow organized crime syndicate.'

Tim was beginning to get an uncomfortable feeling about the conversation. Was Williams obliquely coming around to accusing him? His eyes darted around the restaurant for the men in dark suits who would be on hand.

'Why are you telling me this?' He tried to keep the tremor out of his voice. 'Three of my operations have failed. Are you saying that . . .'

'You're not the sort to sabotage his own operations.' Williams gave his best reassuring smile. It reminded Tim of a crocodile. 'It has been known, but three's pushing the bounds of credibility. No. Either you're the most plausible double agent I've ever met or you're a conscientious young army officer with his heart on his sleeve. With all respect, Tim, I think you're the latter and I'm very glad you are. I need an ally.'

'Yes, sir.' A heavy weight was lifted from Tim's chest and he found he could breathe again.

Williams had enjoyed a busy but productive time after Tim had identified Linnikov. Computers could be helpful in research, but more useful was Derek – the almost blind archivist researcher. To see Derek at work was painful. His spectacle lenses were as thick as magnifying glasses. He held files and pictures so close they touched the large nose on his pale, uneven face. And he could be a crotchety old woman, too busy to help when he chose not to. But Williams had cultivated him, made sure he stayed on his right side. Canteen ladies and librarians were the most important people in the building, he preached. Stay in with them and you'll never want.

Because Derek found it so hard to flip through files, he remembered them. Remembered tiny scraps and obscure facts.

Williams had gone to see Derek in the cubby hole he had fashioned out of bookshelves and desks in the open plan office and listened while he fulminated against computers. After a while he trickled in the questions. Derek fell silent, as was his way, giving tiny negative shakes of his head. Finally he ran his hand, a gravedigger's hand, through sparse oiled hair, swept straight back, and remembered.

'Don't know if this'll help . . .' he began slowly and Williams felt a thrill, knowing it would. 'Eighteen, no seventeen years ago, a low-grade KGB hood in Sofia made an approach. He was an errand boy; one of the foot soldiers. He'd tried to inflate his worth, but old Ronnie Marshall saw through him. Strung him along nicely, though. We had a good laugh about it afterwards. You saw the guys in the field then. Not like now. Now everyone's got these bloody data retrieval systems.'

'I've got one,' said Williams. 'But I'd rather be down here, talking to you.'

Derek took the compliment lightly. 'You're old, you see. That's why.'

'Ronnie was a good hand.' Williams steered him back to his story.

'Indeed he was. Ronnie is dismissive of the Joe and the harder the Joe tries, the more Ronnie tells him he has nothing to sell. Finally he's so keen to impress he shows Ronnie a picture of the KGB's May Day dinner. Can you believe it! The whole Sofia team. Legals and illegals posing as though they were in a school photo. In uniform. With medals. The Resident was in the centre sitting down. On his right hand side was a young bull of a man. He was new to Ronnie and the fact that he was on the right hand of God had to make him an archangel at least. You know how hierarchical the Russians are. But Ronnie won't show he's interested. "You're showing us nothing we don't already know." The Joe is put out. "I bet you don't know this one," he said, pointing to the very mystery man Ronnie wants to know about. "He only arrived two weeks ago, running agents in the Bulgarian party and General Staff." Ronnie's got his ears pricked by now.'

'I bet,' said Williams.

'It gets better. "He calls himself Kolchak but that's just a cover name." Would you believe this Kolchak left Moscow without paying a florist's bill – maybe for some woman, I don't know – and Moscow sent it after him in his real name. Our Joe had to sort the mail and he had a hell of a time trying to find the culprit.'

'And Kolchak's real name?' Williams knew by now, of course, but he had to give Derek his moment.

'Linnikov.'

'And the Joe?'

'Didn't make a treff two days later. Never seen again. No great loss.'

Williams made fulsome noises of gratitude and prepared to leave. He was halfway through the room full of hushed operators bent over humming screens when Derek called.

'Don't you want to see the picture?'

Williams now cleared a space on the cluttered table and pulled out the picture the size of a large postcard. He placed it between the dirty plates.

'Anyone there you recognize, Tim?'

Tim's eye skimmed over the beaming faces under large officers' caps to settle on a man with a chest like a barrel. He pointed and Williams gave a contented nod of approval.

'Linnikov is a case officer, an agent runner.'

Tim frowned. 'Then why's he in London as a crime liaison officer?'

'Because in our service we have a traitor, an informant, a mole, as modern jargon has it. Though it's hard to consider a tiny blind rodent as being any threat. Our Cossack friend has come here to run him, or her.'

315

Someone split the atom inside Tim's forehead. He was lost for words.

'It's all so beautifully symmetrical. He turns us inside out. He's supposed to be feeding us. In fact we treat him to an epicure's table.' He picked up the photograph and put it carefully away. 'All illicit information has to be passed through someone. It has to be got back. How elegant if that person is the official KGB liaison man. There would be nothing untoward being seen with him. Indeed it would be expected, encouraged.'

'Hell!'

Williams smiled at Tim's fierce reaction. 'Parts of the KGB and the Russian Mafiya are two heads of the same hydra. And so closely joined, they frequently share the same brain. It goes back to document 174033 signed by Vladimir Kryuchkov. Lovely man, but does like his vodka. On 5 January 1991 the KGB's Third Main Directorate, responsible for military counter-intelligence, sent a message to Soviet army and naval bases instructing them to set up private firms to sell military technology overseas. The new companies were to act as cover for the KGB if the domestic situation deteriorated, provide money for the leadership if a new regime wanted to disband the organization and create foreign and domestic networks during a period of increasing instability. From there it was only a small step into total illegality and the decision to syphon funds for the good of oneself rather than the state.'

'So that's why you were so keen for me to ask Valentine about Primakov?'

'I thought it strange he was using a work name. It's possible that the idea of you helping the Americans in Vietnam was to make sure you didn't meet Primakov in London – just in case you'd seen him around Rostov. Of course, whoever it was didn't know of our hidden agenda.' Williams contemplated a passing chariot of food but somehow his appetite had been soured. 'Soon I shall ask for your help and possibly your protection. In the meantime say nothing of this conversation to anyone. And I mean anyone. That includes Mickey and Sally.'

Tim was unnaturally quiet that afternoon, trying to work through all the implications of Williams's news. Alison called in around four o'clock to say she was going early and was there anything he wanted in the post? Yes. The awkward letter of sympathy and condolence he had composed to Mr and Mrs Bagg. It had really needed a woman's touch, but Alison was preoccupied and he didn't feel he could ask Livy Hull. So he had struggled through on his own and hoped his genuine feelings emerged through the clumsy, contrived sentences.

Sally phoned soon afterwards to announce she was in his flat and God, it was a tip.

'How did you get in?'

'Finishing school . . . Has this place ever been cleaned?'

'I've been meaning to get around to it.'

'I've got your fire on because it's so cold. If anyone could see me now they'd think I was mad.' She giggled.

'Why?'

'I don't wear anything when I'm cleaning. It saves getting my clothes grubby.'

Tim conjured an erotic picture of a naked Sally stretching up with a feather duster.

'Stay like that. I'll be home soon.'

When the phone next rang it was Felicity Plumridge, short-tempered, short of breath and at her most imperious.

'I want you to get a message to my husband,' she began.

Tim wondered why Plumridge could not take his own calls. 'Yes, of course,' he said politely.

'Tell him to call me immediately. His mobile seems to be switched off. It really is most annoying. I know he's at that security conference in Aldergrove but you must have ways of reaching him.'

Tim hadn't known there was a security conference at Aldergrove. 'I'll do my best.'

317

'It really is most trying. Phaedre has come a cropper on Daisy. She's probably broken her collar bone and I've got to take Tabitha to the show in Reigate tomorrow. He's going to have to get back as soon as he can. Got that?'

'Um.' Tim hadn't been concentrating. He wished he'd taken notes. 'Daisy's fallen off Phaedre . . .'

'No. No. No,' barked Mrs Plumridge. 'Do listen. Phaedre is our daughter. Daisy is the pony. God, is there anyone there with a shred of intelligence?'

Tim's hackles rose. He was not prepared to be insulted by this braying woman who, after all, was asking a favour of him. 'I'll see if it's possible to get a message to Plumridge,' he said briskly.

Then he was stumped. Ultimately he asked Williams about getting a message to the conference. Williams regarded him over his glasses before saying, 'Leave it to me, boy. But write it down so I don't confuse the girl and her blasted pony.'

There had been an undertaker's in that part of Warminster for as long as anyone could remember. In the last century the buildings had been used by a corn merchant and across the small courtyard at the back the old grain store had been turned into a chapel of rest. It was there Emma's mother and father spent the afternoon, talking quietly and stroking the white pine coffin. Once such a coffin would have been of lead, explained the funeral director. Now it was made of wood and plastic. He did not mention the corpse was wrapped inside a body bag. Banks and drifts of daffodils and narcissi filled the chapel. Emma's favourite flowers, said her mother.

There was also the sweet scent of lilies, which was the first thing Tari smelled as he silently let himself in. At first he thought the room was in pitch blackness, but as his eyes became accustomed to the darkness he made out the night sky through a small fanlight. The muted sounds of the occasional car came from Silver Street. He locked the door behind him and turned on his pencil torch. There was just one coffin, the brass plate bearing the name EMMA BAGG.

The large-headed castle screws had been put in by hand and not too deeply. The first one came out easily. He put it carefully to one side and paused, the stillness of his surroundings making him nervous. He told himself harshly not to be so childish. The dead girl could not harm him. Only the living did harm. The last screw was obstinate. Tari was concerned not to damage the screw head in case it was spotted next morning. He finally persuaded it to turn with a large hand screwdriver held in a wrench. With difficulty he lifted off the lid. The stench of formaldehyde sent him reeling back, gasping for air. He wiped his eyes to see a Russian military body bag. He'd seen many of those in his time.

Why are you so frightened? It's only a dead body. No big deal. Tari muttered to himself as he clenched the bag in his left hand and unzipped it with his right. As he did so the moon freed itself from behind fleeting clouds to cast a pall of silver light on the coffin, the window frame forming a cross on Emma's pale, bloodless breast.

Tari whimpered. No one had bothered to tie up her jaw so it sagged open. Her head had been almost totally severed. Tari felt his bile rise and swallowed quickly. Sweating with fear he leaned over the cadaver. His eyes streamed from the formaldehyde fumes rising off the wood chippings around the torso. The stomach was tinged with green from the onsetting putrefaction. Tari recoiled. He tried again, slid his arm under her buttocks and lifted. He was muttering all the time; words of apology, begging forgiveness, curses, imprecations. Words of hate, words of love. Her legs were glued together, set stiff in death. Tari sobbed a prayer he would not have to tear her muscles. With a creak like a rusty hinge her legs came apart and Tari withdrew what looked like a dull metal cigar tube. With shaking hands, he unscrewed it. Inside, wrapped in cotton wool, was a small glass phial, no bigger than his little finger. He held it up to the moonlight in both hands so that in the argent light the liquid appeared pale and translucent.

Emma's unseeing eyes had opened. She was watching him worship the phial. From her hollow mouth Tari imagined he heard her laughter mock him. He clenched his jaw so tight that his facial muscles twitched and spasmed. He mopped his sweating forehead on his sleeve and gingerly put the phial back in the cigar tube.

In an act of obeisance, he closed Emma's eyes, weighted them and straightened her body, arranging her hands across her breasts.

'Go with God.' Tari zipped up the body bag.

Positioning the lid was difficult for one person. He stopped himself hurrying in case he left marks on the pale wood. Finally the last screw was back in place. He carefully wiped the coffin and let himself out to drink deeply of the cold night air, leaning against the wall feeling as limp as a dishcloth. His legs were trembling, but after a while he made himself walk out of the alley on to the lighted street. The pungent smells of an Indian takeaway restaurant assailed him and he knew he was going to be sick. He made it around the corner where he crouched on his haunches above a drain and vomited until sweat ran into his eyes and blinded him.

Thursday 2 April

Tim and Sally sat in the line of cars waiting to crawl down the hill into Winterbourne Stoke and knew they were going to be late for the funeral. A quarter of a mile away opposite the Bell Inn a breakdown truck pulled the wreckage of a saloon car away from a dented milk tanker. An ambulance had just taken off, blue light flashing, and firemen were hosing down the road. Traffic was backed up in both directions. With the stoicism born of years of waiting in the Army, Tim squeezed Sally's hand and turned off the engine.

He had hurried home the previous night to find Sally still naked, apart from a pair of knickers, finishing off the cleaning. He was not to know that Sally had finished the cleaning some time before and dressed because it was so cold. She had kept a lookout for him and as soon as he turned into the road, stripped off again. They had got up mid-evening to make omelettes and drink wine, but mostly they had drunk of each other.

The traffic began to inch forward. A mile further on the A303 opened out into a dual carriageway and Tim put his foot down. They turned up the Wylye Valley and finally saw the squat Norman tower of the old grey church on a knoll between them and the river. The lanes were full of parked cars, including a Mercedes with a chauffeur in a uniform and peaked cap. They hurried under the lychgate, turned the corner of the church and saw a semi-circle of mourners around the graveside. It was too late to join them. A wind was rising, exposing the grey underside of the leaves of the willows lining the river bank and carrying away the vicar's words. Sally thought how peaceful the scene was. The escarpment sloped down to water meadows and the narrow river. Ahead Stockton Down rose above a patchwork of green fields and hedgerows and to the west a heron flapped lazily upstream.

Sally fumbled for a tissue, dropped it and watched helplessly as it blew towards the grave. The chauffeur had left his car and was observing the burial from a stile in the low stone wall on the far side of the churchyard. Finally the coffin was lowered into the waiting earth. The mourners began to disperse and became individuals; a lank-haired, red-faced girl with a mewing baby on her hip, sobbing uncontrollably; older women in black coats and headscarves, younger men in high street anoraks lighting cigarettes as soon as they were away from the graveside.

The wreaths were dominated by a huge display in red and yellows. The card said, 'From your friend Igor.'

Mr Bagg sought them out and introduced his wife, who insisted that they come back to the house. The small red brick bungalow nuzzled next to cowsheds and a high Dutch barn. In the kitchen local matrons organized pots of tea and sliced and buttered bread. On the sideboard under a large framed photograph of Emma and between the cards of condolence sat a Wiltshire ham, chicken drumsticks, pork pies and mountains of sandwiches. Emma's friends from Bath stood in a self-conscious group, wondering how soon they could leave politely. Tim and Sally found themselves objects of curiosity, Tim because people had heard he was making a film on a mass murderer while Sally stood out for her looks and London clothes. Tim was the last person to have seen Emma.

'She was fine,' he lied to Kath Bagg. 'But I think she was looking forward to coming home.'

'That she was,' smiled Mrs Bagg. 'A home girl was our Emma. That's why we were surprised she went off all that way. Thank you again for what you did.'

Tim tried to discover which of the mourners had a chauffeur but no one seemed to know what he was talking about.

He and Sally had a cup of tea and a ham sandwich and left, feeling they were outsiders in a kind couple's grief.

'Give us ring to let us know you're down safely.'

'I'll be all right.'

'Remember you're going to have to start sitting your written exams. You're not far off your GFT and you'll find it'll all come in a rush.'

Tari had no intention of getting involved in the CAA examinations. He wouldn't be around by then. In his pocket was his club membership form, taken from the office a few minutes ago when Cheryl was away. He was cutting his links with Biggin Hill.

'Yes, Eddie. I promise.' He was eager to get away in his new plane. He had racked up his hours, paying Eddie to instruct him privately so that he had already completed his qualifying cross-country flights. He felt comfortable in the aircraft and he knew the south-east corner of England.

'You've a good bargain here.' Eddie patted the fuselage of the ST150.

And you did well out of the commission. Tari lifted off from runway 21 with a sense of relief that at last he could stop play-acting. No more inane grins, no more false bonhomie. He climbed out over the valley and the chalk escarpment until he saw the M25 and turned to port. No point in instruments or navigational computers for this flight. Where the M26 joined the M20 he turned south until he saw the arrow-straight railway line. He followed it to the east, picked out the station at Marden and began looking for the two oast houses and the small lake. He cruised along at 2,000 feet, thinking that for once Ilse had done well. Four acres reached by a grass track off a small lane, lying along the prevailing winds with an open-fronted shed to hangar Romeo Romeo. The farmer had been only too happy to let the field, already committed to set-aside, and the nearest habitation was the farmhouse over a mile away. Tari had not had time to set up a windsock. Today

323

he had arranged with Ilse to park the car with its bonnet into the wind to indicate the direction to land.

The field came into view and he concentrated on judging height and distance. He made a pass to the south of the field at two hundred feet and frowned. The Mercedes was pointing to the north-eastern corner. He'd taken off from Biggin Hill in a south-westerly direction. The wind couldn't have changed that much in twenty minutes. Tari climbed again until he could see the smoke from the farmhouse chimney. As he thought. The wind was coming from the west. That stupid cow! He flew a circuit at 800 feet, turning too early on to finals so he had to sideslip off his height and kick the aircraft straight at the last minute. He flared too high, dropped the last twenty feet in a bone-jarring crash and bounced. The second landing was better. He taxied slowly over the uneven ground up to the shed.

'Which way is the wind coming from?' Tari demanded once he and Ilse pushed the craft backwards into the shed.

She brushed a strand of blonde hair off her face and grinned. It was obvious she had no idea. 'The wind. It is all around us.'

Tari resisted the temptation to strike her. Instead he took her right index finger, slid it into her open mouth and held up her hand. 'Which side feels coldest? Right. So that's the side the wind comes from. I must always, always land into the wind or I will crash.'

Ilse looked as if she might burst into tears so he smiled to show it was really a joke and she smiled too, the vacant smile of someone who was elsewhere. He kissed her lightly, thinking that one day soon he was going to have to kill her.

'Promise me you will not smoke dope or do drugs when I am flying. Please.'

'Okay. I promise.'

The rear seat of the plane came out easily. He placed the container in the back and measured the distance to a spot under the elevators where he intended to drill a small hole. Everything was almost ready to go.

He remembered to phone Eddie.

'Yeh. Brilliant. No probs. Wow. My own plane and my own field. Next the world. Magic.'

Taking Tari's role-playing for the real thing, Ilse began stroking his groin in invitation. Tari took away her hand, still smiling so the tone of his phone voice would not alter. He would have to kill her sooner rather than later.

Friday 3 April

'Iraq, Iran, Israel, Libya, Syria, China, North Korea, Taiwan.' Dotty Di took another breath. 'Russia, Belarus, Egypt, Pakistan, South Africa, Ukraine. Possibly Algeria, Cuba, Jordan and Kazakhstan. And a few I've forgotten, all have undisclosed offensive biological weapons programmes. It's the cheapest way to acquire weapons of mass destruction. And much harder to detect. It's relatively easy to tell if a state is developing nuclear weapons – satellites pick up the building work – but distilleries, dairies, even breweries can be used to culture micro-organisms.'

'*Armis bella non venenis geri*,' murmured Williams. 'War is waged with weapons not poisons.'

'Oh, aren't you a clever old thing.' Dotty Di wobbled her chins approvingly. 'A load of bollocks, of course. How do you think the three-year siege of Caffa was broken in 1346? By the Tartars slinging the bodies of plague victims over the wall into the city, that's how.'

'But this is different,' insisted Plumridge. 'This is state-sponsored terrorism.'

'The CIA project that rogue nations, terrorists, religious zealots, even individuals with a grudge will launch a biological or chemical attack within the next ten years. It's not a question of if but when.'

'Americans project for everything,' scoffed Plumridge. 'But what damage can one madman do with an aerosol spray? Really!'

Diana was beginning to scowl. 'He can bring Britain to its knees in a dozen ways. For example, in Moscow in 1960 one person with smallpox infected forty-three others, three of whom died . . .'

'So?'

'The authorities mobilized 5,500 vaccination teams who jabbed more than six million people within a week. They placed 9,000 people under medical supervision and 662 in hospital. It paralysed the whole of Moscow region's health care. Think what would happen in Britain. The hospital system would break down. It could not cope.'

'Psswah!' Plumridge made a dismissive noise. Diana regarded him as though he was a stain on a silk blouse.

'You don't understand, do you? You really don't. Biological weapons are a thousand times worse than nuclear ones. The panic is greater because the uncertainty is greater. You can see a nuclear explosion. You can see the damage. But you don't know where a biological attack is happening or when. How do you know the person you're fleeing with is not infecting you? Where is safe to run? Who will welcome you or receive you?'

'And what are the intended victims supposed to do?' interrupted Livy Hull, who was hosting the meeting in Six's spanking new headquarters in Vauxhall Cross. Each service took it in turn to host monthly meetings to foster inter-service cooperation and understanding – went the notion. In practice it provided ammunition for mutual sneers and envy, especially at SIS's £200 million pleasure dome.

'Take shelter in homes or offices. Masks are useful, although we don't have gas masks for civilians.'

'I suppose you have one, do you?' demanded Plumridge.

'Oh, yes. Rather,' smiled Diana. 'I don't think you do though, do you?'

'And where can I get masks for myself and my family?'

'Any hardware store. Simple oro-nasal masks like the ones to protect workers in dusty jobs will help.'

'What will the Army be doing?' asked Livy.

'Turning back the millions who will try to flee London. Public transport systems will fail inside hours, of course. Stop looting. There will be riots, pitched battles, civil war. Society will tear itself apart . . .'

'Bloody charming,' complained Plumridge. 'And we're no nearer finding the Marburg.'

'We're doing our best,' protested the deputy chief constable of Kent, folding his arms across his chest defensively.

'If it's there to be found,' reminded Livy Hull.

'We have to assume it's out there,' said Williams, deciding the open-ended discussion was getting nowhere – as usual.

'We've uncovered two Iraqi front companies, Al Insha'at and Al-Nandusia, run by the Iraqi Directorate of General Intelligence,' announced Livy Hull. 'They were masterminding the exchange of oil for Russian mobile radar installations, operating on behalf of Iraq's Military Industrialization Commission. Saddam will not be best pleased that little scam has been blocked.'

Williams thought this glorious building was wasted on Six. From the conference room he had a excellent view over the Oval cricket ground. Shame most of SIS's senior officers were members of the MCC. They should have built their headquarters overlooking Lord's.

Ooops!

'Put an armed guard around that balloon,' snapped Williams.

They all turned to look towards the Oval. A huge helium balloon was tethered on a patch of green this side of the cricket ground, waiting to load visitors seeking high-level views over London. Williams remembered watching it rise and sink all day during the last Test Match at the Oval. If Barbel got into that, with a westerly wind behind him, the spray would cover most of central London. It made him think.

'It'd be wrong to assume Saddam will go for the big bang, so let's find out what large population gatherings, including sports events, there'll be in the next, say, fortnight and check on high-rise buildings around those venues. Let's have the long-term weather forecast. Are we checking private aircraft, deputy chief constable?'

'Yes, sir. We began yesterday.'

'If we've all finished, I suggest we have a drink on the terrace.' Livy glanced at her watch. Everyone shuffled their papers in a general mood of acquiescence. Six were very proud of their river terrace. You'd pay a fortune for such a view, they chorused, aware that Five's Thames House headquarters had no comparable facility.

Tim's mobile phone rang as soon as he switched it on. 'I've just had Mr Bagg on,' said Alison. 'He wants to know if you're okay.'

'Yes, of course,' replied Tim, walking behind Williams. 'Why shouldn't I be?'

'I don't know,' snapped Alison. 'A lot of people at the funeral have gone down with stomach upsets. He wanted to know how you were. Speak to him.'

'Problems?' inquired Williams at the door to the terrace.

Tim recounted the conversation.

'But you're all right? And Sally?'

'As far as I know, sir.' She had been when they got up this morning, but he did not say that.

'This is the famous view,' announced Livy Hull with a sweep of her hand. Tim took in the broad river and the heavy traffic churning over Vauxhall Bridge. A motorcyclist in leathers and a crash helmet had broken down in the northbound lane. He was bending over his machine, removing something from a pannier.

'Stomach upset,' repeated Williams almost to himself. 'Diana. Would early symptoms of a biological attack, say from Marburg, be vomiting and diarrhoea?'

'Almost inevitably,' boomed Diana, looking like a stately man of war. 'It's the body's way of getting rid of something nasty.'

Williams turned towards Tim. 'Apart from the container, what else do we know that's come out of Rostov recently?'

'Emma's coffin,' replied Tim. The motorcyclist was still

329

crouching behind his bike. He seemed to be assembling something.

'Exactly.' Tiredness, almost pain, swept over Williams's face.

'They wouldn't.' The sheer audacity overwhelmed Tim. 'But . . . but in that case, the flask must have leaked.' Tim paused and picked his words carefully. 'Are you saying the people at the funeral were exposed to Marburg?'

'If they were, why haven't you gone down with the symptoms?'

'Because we arrived late. We stood apart from the other mourners. *And we stood upwind.*' The motorcyclist had pushed up the visor of his helmet. He was balancing something across the saddle. Christ! 'Get down.'

The shot rang out as he crashed into Williams. Tim felt the wind of the bullet and heard the thud as it hit home. Then he was lying on top of Williams and blood was running over the marble paving.

Cold cobalt rays pulsed into the clear night sky. From behind the blunt stone tower of the lonely church an orange glow spread over the old gravestones.

'Creepy.' Sally clutched Tim's arm.

A shadow detached itself from the blackness. Sally gasped as she made out a soldier in full combat gear, his face blacked up with camouflage cream, SA 80 in his hand. Tim flapped open his ID and the soldier melted back into the trees.

As they crunched over the gravel path they made out the shapes of spacemen in bulky suits and helmets moving in and out of a large tent erected over the grave.

'Don't get too close,' muttered Sally.

One of the spacemen began waving its arms and another larger one appeared. They gesticulated together and the bulkier one stomped towards them.

'Come to see the fun?' boomed Diana, her voice muffled by her helmet.

'Anything?'

'Not yet. We've just got the coffin open. How are the parents?'

'They're fine.' Tim's breath billowed out on the frosty air.

Inside her helmet Diana frowned. She had expected they would be the first to go down, having spent longest at the coffin side.

'They're worried it might have been the fish paste. Neither ate anything because they were too upset.'

The local health authority was treating the outbreak as suspected food poisoning. Environmental health officers had already taken away leftovers from the funeral gathering and vacuumed the Baggs' bungalow, collecting samples of dust.

'How many so far?'

'Twenty-eight in hospital. Two are in a serious condition. They've opened two wards in the old local hospital in Warminster as an isolation unit. There's a few who aren't happy at being banged up, but they're being reminded that people actually died of food poisoning in Scotland recently. Most are grateful they're being so well cared for – although they're a bit confused by the army nurses in masks and protective clothing.'

Diana chortled. 'This couldn't have happened in a better place. Just up the road from Porton Down and just down the road from the army's NBC school.'

'What's NBC?' whispered Sally, digging her hands deeper into her coat pockets.

'Nuclear, biological and chemical. It's part of the School of Infantry at Warminster,' explained Tim.

'We're trying out our new wizardry – a portable IBDS, Integrated Biological Detection System,' enthused Diana. 'It's never been used in the field before.'

'What actually are you doing?' inquired Sally.

'We're seeking to identify airborne agents by examining their behaviour in a beam of light. We're analysing 10,000

331

particles a second in the one to ten micron range. One instrument collects the particles, then another determines whether biological material is present. The agent's finally identified by determining which antibodies they react with.'

'Oh,' said Sally, wishing she hadn't asked.

'Well, I must get back to the fray. We'll take the body back to Porton and sanitize the area.' She turned to go. 'There was one thing that was strange.'

'Yes?'

'There were ten-pence pieces over her eyes.'

Saturday 4 April

Williams was sitting up in bed, glasses on the end of his nose, reading a report. He looked remarkably healthy apart from a bandaged right shoulder and a large plaster on his ear. He scowled suspiciously at the bunch of grapes Sally was arranging in his fruit bowl.

'I don't like them if they've got pips in.'

'You're an old curmudgeon,' she declared, giving him a peck on his cheek in a gesture which surprised Tim by its intimacy.

'I've brought the medicine you requested,' said Tim, pulling out a bottle of claret from the poacher's pocket of his Barbour.

'Excellent. I need a glass of wine to take away the taste of that vile lunch. Sally, find us three glasses, there's a good girl. Ask one of the SP men. All they do is chat up the nurses so they should know where to find a glass.' Williams waited until Sally was in conversation with one of the guards outside his room to beckon Tim closer. 'If I told you Mickey had been in Moscow the last few days, what would you say?'

Tim was at a loss. 'I'd say Mickey came back from Holland on Tuesday. He had a day's leave and then he's been in Poole on an equipment evaluation . . . But I could be mistaken.'

'Who knows he's been in Poole?'

'The SBS guys there.'

'No one on our floor?'

'No.'

Williams looked Tim directly in the eye. 'Mickey's been in Moscow.'

'Okay.' Tim got the message. 'Mickey's been in Moscow.'

Sally poured three glasses, admiring the view out of the window across to the Houses of Parliament. A staff nurse came in and picked up the chart on the bottom of the bed. She tutted when she saw the bottle of wine.

'Not a word, woman,' said Williams. 'Or I'll have you sent back to the bogs.'

'If he gives you a hard time just bang him on his shoulder,' smiled Sally.

'Him. Och, he's a lamb. Aren't you so and all? A complete lamb.'

Tim had heard Williams called many things but never a lamb.

'Bah,' he exclaimed.

'He's a baa lamb.' Sally's giggle was so infectious Williams was forced to smile.

'Isn't laughter the best medicine,' said the nurse, making a note on the chart. 'And isn't he a lucky man, to be sure?'

'I've a feeling I owe my life more to Tim than to luck,' admitted Williams when the nurse left.

'Do you think the shot was meant for you?' asked Sally.

Williams pulled a face. 'Logically, how can I? How did the gunman know I'd be on the terrace at that time? He could have been a wild cannon; a terrorist with a grudge who fired on the first group to offer itself. He chose the oldest person believing him to be the senior.'

'But?' probed Sally.

'It's too . . . random for my liking. Few killings are completely motiveless. There's usually a connection between killer and victim, a cause and effect.'

'So you believe this wasn't a chance hit. You were the target.'

'Yes, I was the target.'

Tim, glancing at Sally's sceptical face, saw that she found

334

it as difficult to believe as he did. Perhaps being shot had made the old boy paranoid.

'Is it possible he was aiming at someone else?' asked Sally. 'Tim was on one side of you. Perhaps he was the target.'

Tim answered. 'No. The gunman was firing from approximately two hundred and fifty yards. You have to believe he was a professional to try to make the hit. At that distance, with a telescopic sight, it's like shooting fish in a barrel.'

'It's a shame there's nothing to go on,' said Sally. 'No bullets or anything.'

'He had the presence of mind to take the cartridge case with him and the round itself seemed to have a mind of its own,' said Williams, fingering his bandaged ear.

'Have they pieced together what actually happened?' she asked.

'The SOCOs estimate that if Tim hadn't pushed me aside, the bullet would have gone though my heart. As it was, it went clean through my shoulder, out the other side, hit the back wall, ricocheted and took off my ear lobe before disappearing into the Thames for ever.'

'So we don't know the make of rifle?'

'No,' said Tim regretfully. 'Something with a folding stock. Could be a Barrett Light.'

'You're going to have a full house,' exclaimed Sally as their colleagues arrived in a noisy chatter.

'We found a Suzuki 750cc with pannier thirty minutes ago in a mews off Buckingham Palace Road,' announced Plumridge. 'It fits the CCTV pictures the Met got of the hitman driving away. He vanishes off their screens near Victoria, so the location makes sense. Of course the press blackout means we can't appeal to the public.'

'Here's some black grapes,' said Livy Hull. 'They're organic.'

'Thank you. Put them next to the inorganic green ones.'

'The forensic boys are looking forward to seeing what's in the tyre treads and the air filter,' continued Plumridge.

'I've brought you the *Economist, New Statesman*, the *Foreign Policy Review* and *GQ*,' said Commander Penn.

'The latest Terry Pratchett,' offered Bill Jones. 'Can I borrow it after you've finished?'

Alison was already plumping up Williams's pillows and slipping packets of cigarettes and a lighter into his bedside locker. 'Here's a Walkman with some tapes of Boccherini, Vivaldi, Albinoni and Debbie Harry.'

Only Plumridge came empty-handed.

'What's the latest from Wiltshire?'

'It seems to be a genuine outbreak of food poisoning,' said Tim. 'Diana's team has drawn a blank, much to her chagrin. The chicken drumsticks are the prime suspects at the moment. Most of the victims are on the mend.'

'As some of us knew they would,' said Plumridge pompously.

'How do you explain the ten-penny pieces on the eyes?' demanded Livy.

'She could have had them in Russia and whoever laid her out put them in with her. No one is going to open the coffin just to put ten-pence pieces over her eyes.'

'Porton Down believes the coffin has been opened.' Tim was keeping the best news for last. 'Under a microscope you can see the screw heads have been tightened more than once.'

'So! The Russians use second-hand screws.' Plumridge airily dismissed the findings. Tim was reminded just how much he disliked him.

The door flew open, knocking Alison sideways.

'Oops. Sorry, luv.' Mickey New, wearing a smart suit, stood in the doorway. 'I didn't see you there.'

'Clumsy oaf.' Alison rubbed her elbow.

'Well?' inquired Williams, raising an expectant eye-brow.

'Sorted, guv. He's on his way but, blimey, what a two and eight.'

'Have you been drinking, sergeant?' Livy Hull glowered

through her spectacles in her most schoolmarmish way.

'I had a couple on the flight,' admitted Mickey.

'And quite right too. Good reason to celebrate,' said Williams, quickly. 'Mickey's been away arranging for the delivery of Valentine's entrance fee. A gift from beyond the grave, so to speak. One for Mickey to get his teeth into.'

'Don't talk about teeth. You should see the hampsteads on the mutt.'

'I should explain . . .' Williams wriggled to sit more upright and Alison was instantly at his side rearranging the pillows. 'Mickey has been organizing the liberation and transportation of Valentine's girlfriend's dog. You remember the one which was not to be quarantined. Now we know why. It was – or rather is – carrying his insurance . . .'

'Not that it did him any good,' interjected Plumridge.

Williams ignored him. 'The dog has a microchip implanted in his neck containing, we believe, copies of files from the Moscow Narco Group and featuring our new friend Colonel Primakov. His real name's Linnikov, by the way.'

'How do you know?' demanded Plumridge.

'Valentine left certain proofs behind.' Williams smiled at the collective incomprehension on the faces of his visitors.

'You never told us this, Haydn,' objected Livy.

'It's recent information and until we'd established that the dog has the microchip, completely unsubstantiated. Valentine was a careful man – or rather a vengeful one. He wanted to make sure if he went, others would go with him.' Williams took a sip of wine and enjoyed the attention. 'You know I couldn't understand why a legal such as Primakov would have a work name. Valentine hints he's here to act as a case officer for an agent in place. The microchip should tell us who. When's the mutt arriving, Mickey?'

'Early next week, if it hasn't eaten its way out of its cage and killed the guards.'

'Does it have a name?'

'I've called it Rasputin. God, you should see it. Like a

cross between a bad-tempered Hound of the Baskervilles and Godzilla with toothache.'

'And you're certain the microchip is there?' demanded Livy Hull.

'Oh, yes. It's only in the surface skin, if you understand. You can feel it. You could prise it out easily with the point of a penknife. Only you'd have to sedate the beast first. He'd eat you alive otherwise.'

'How's he getting here?' asked Livy.

Mickey glanced at Williams for guidance and shook his head. 'Sorry.'

'Are you going to keep the dog at home the night he arrives, Mickey?'

'How can I, guv?' Mickey held out his hands in a gesture of helplessness. 'I've got my nipper. I wouldn't trust the dog near her. Rasputin can stay in kennels. I'll arrange for a dog van to bring us in next morning and an army vet to be on standby.'

'How does Valentine's girlfriend feel about you borrowing the brute?' asked Bill Jones.

'She doesn't know,' replied Mickey.

'I don't want to stay in bed. I want to get up and play.'

'Soraya is on the mend. She feels well enough to wish to have fun with her sister Leila and her dolls but doctors insist she continues to rest to build up her strength. Dr Aziz.'

'There's always a danger in letting the patient decide the rate of his or her recovery, especially when the patient is an active little girl,' said the authoritative brown voice. *'In Soraya's case the spirit is strong but the flesh is still weak. She must be restrained from over-exerting herself and retarding her recovery. We can take her liveliness as an indication that she is getting better but she must stay in bed for a day or two yet.'*

In the background Tari could hear the sisters' chatter, punctuated by giggles.

The narrator was speaking again. *'The girls are excited because here in Ramath-lehi a brightly coloured humming-bird* is hovering, attracted by the pollen in a hibiscus flower outside the window.'

Tari went cold.

'Soraya can see the humming-bird from her sickbed. She is entranced at the delicate way it drinks from the hibiscus flower. But it is time for Soraya to rest. We close the shutters on the humming-bird and the sunshine and soon Soraya will be asleep, her little body strengthening every day from her illness. Will Soraya soon be well enough to go out and play with Leila in Ramath-lehi? Listen again and learn how our great leader Saddam Hussein cares for and protects his children – the people of Iraq.'

Tari pulled back the long curtains and regarded the night through the french windows. He was a maelstrom of emotions. Soraya's recovery cheered and fortified him. It was timely. The operation was about to begin. Ramath-lehi. He had hoped the Iraqis would not take that route. He understood but it smacked of weakness – and it made him vulnerable. He knew from newspaper accounts that the US and Britain were about to block an attempt to lift sanctions against Iraq, claiming Saddam had not destroyed his weapons of mass destruction.

What right had they in Iraq! The western effrontery made Tari's hackles rise.

The Iraqis had opted for a warning demonstration. Tari thought they misjudged the resolve of the British. Such an act would bring reprisals. Reprisals against Baghdad – and his daughters were in Baghdad.

Ultimately it was up to his masters. It was their train set. He was just the driver. He went to get ready.

'How could you? How could you?' Fatima, tears streaking her worn face, beat her fists against Dr Aziz's chest. 'You hypocrite. Everyone will know you are a liar. Soraya isn't any better. You know she's not. You've cheated us.'

Leila crouched in the corner, the whites of her frightened eyes visible in the gloom.

The sick room was heavy with the cloying sweetness of incense. The permanent twilight, the smoke and the heady richness made Fatima claustrophobic. She wanted to open the window, let in the night air and shout out: They are all liars. They cheat.

But they would kill her, and who would look after the little girls then?

Dr Aziz caught her pummelling fists and held her away. He was not a bad man. Just one who wanted to carry on living. So he did what he was told and hoped none of his family or acquaintances fell foul of Uday or his clique.

'Soraya is holding her own.'

The little girl should be in hospital, he knew, but they refused to let her leave the villa. He had done what he could; set up a drip and a basic monitoring machine above her bed. He was concerned about the build-up of fluid in her lungs. In hospital he could have drained it off and reflated the lung but here . . .

Diphtheria killed in two ways. It grew a membrane across the throat so the patient suffocated. He could correct that by a simple tracheotomy to open the windpipe. But the infection generated poisons which sometimes concentrated in the heart. If that happened to Soraya, there was little he could do.

Fatima slipped to the floor alongside the bed where Soraya gazed up at the ceiling with dull, lifeless eyes. Her glossy raven black hair was lank and greasy, her forehead damp with perspiration. Leila joined Fatima on the floor and they gently stroked Soraya's face and hair. There was nothing else for them to do.

Tari's breath rasped through the filter at the side of his helmet. It was hotter in the NBC suit than he had anticipated. He made his way across the lawns to the paddock in an ungainly swagger and stepped through the gap in the hedge. The murmur of traffic from the dual carriageway rose up from the cutting. The night was dark, both a blessing and a curse. He stumbled through gorse and bramble, stunted white thorn and holly trees until he came to the ditch. Ahead was a wide flat field and to his right the cattle bridge over the road. Gingerly he hoisted the garden spray up on to the track. Strange to think that the contents of this plastic container, decorated with green and blue flowers, had the power to kill a whole city.

He crept out to the middle of the bridge and dropped flat. The wind was perfect. A steady breeze from behind blew straight into the oncoming traffic as it climbed the hill. He extended the hose to the edge and began pumping the handle to build up pressure. It reminded Tari of the time he had lain on his stomach and pressed the plunger of the detonator to send Israeli Jeeps somersaulting into the air. When he felt firm resistance he locked the handle in place.

Almost eight o'clock and the traffic was flowing in a stream of bright lights towards him. Tari pressed the lever on the nozzle. The fine spray drifted slowly away. Tari, clumsy in his two pairs of rubber gloves, adjusted the nozzle to make the droplets heavier and prevent the virus drifting over the nearby countryside. A cluster of victims on his doorstep would be a giveaway. The pale mist rolled out into the blackness and over the edge on to the rush of cars twenty feet below. Most would have their windows closed. But it would only need one or two with an open window or a driver with ventilation controls set to draw in air from outside.

Tari did not have any idea how many he would infect. Two or two hundred. As long as the authorities got the message. This was just a demonstration.

An articulated lorry thundered below, the driver's window half open; a school minibus and then a small coach of old people. Tari examined his conscience. Those infected would die a horrible and prolonged death, but he had seen his comrades, his countrymen, die such deaths. Jemal, his best friend and his blood brother, lying in the desert, his guts coiled on his chest, taking all of a hot day to die and Tari helpless and weeping beside him. The two strong men tortured by the Syrians and released as a message to the others. They had lasted a year, each long day an agony and remembrance of their suffering. And the old people, dispossessed and homeless. They died painful lives yearning for their homeland. The true Palestine.

Instead of guilt, Tari felt rage boil up inside him like a seething cauldron. The English carried their grief like a pocket handkerchief – to be paraded to blow their noses when they felt misty-eyed.

It was right that these fat, indolent, privileged people driving in their cars should know what suffering was. They had never felt anything deeper than an emotional graze. He recalled the collective hysteria when that princess had been killed. The British had nothing to grieve over so they filled their shallow lives with vicarious mourning. Such an empty people. They could not hate, they did not love. Tari despised them. The spray was petering out. Tari began pumping furiously to restore the pressure.

He stopped as a car indicated it was pulling on to the hard shoulder. The interior light was on and he saw a man and a woman in the front and two small children in the back. It stopped under the bridge. The woman got out of the passenger side and held on to a little boy's hand.

'You should have gone before you left grannie's.'

'I did, mummy. Honest.'

He stood between the rear of the car and the bank.

No. No. This was wrong. The child was a little older than Leila. Don't stand there. Not there.

'You all right there, Jason? Hurry up or the ducks'll have it.' The man's voice, patient and humorous.

'No, they won't,' Jason giggled as the spray fell in his hair.

Sunday 5 April

'Anyone seen Alison this morning?' demanded Livy Hull, marching into Tim's office where he and Mickey were trying to balance a spoon and a fork on the rim of a pint beer glass with a matchstick. 'She wasn't going to church or anything like that was she?'

'Not that I know of,' said Mickey.

'The bloody girl's taking advantage of Williams's absence. Where's bloody Plumridge?'

'One of his daughters . . .' began Mickey.

'Harrumph.' Livy took off her glasses and began twirling them like an aggressive stripper. 'Nothing trivial, I trust. What are you two wasting your time doing?'

Livy was not in the best of moods and she made no attempt to hide it, although she would never admit the cause. The exhibition had closed last night with the vast majority of works unsold, so now she was facing a steep underwriting bill. The money hurt, but not as much as Peter's arrogance. She had mentioned that his vanity show-case was going to cost her a packet and all he had done was to sneer at morons who did not recognize art. She was thinking seriously about chucking him. She had few illusions. She knew he was using her and such knowledge was never comfortable. He could be a wonderful, passion-ate, caring lover. He could also be a selfish, trampling louse. If she threw him out he could really suffer for his art. And it might actually simplify her life. It was easy to get laid in London and perhaps Peter's absence would free her for a more committed relationship. Now that would be a thing! After all, her biological clock was ticking away, as her mother reminded her weekly. But she was ahead of herself. First work out what to do about that ungrateful bastard Peter. No, first find Alison.

'Has anyone phoned Alison's home? Switch will give you the number.' She frowned at the cutlery apparently defying gravity. 'That's very clever. Why don't they fall down?'

'It's mechanics. It's all to do with forces acting on a point,' explained Tim. 'But you have to get the balance absolutely spot on.'

'There's no reply,' said Mickey. 'Perhaps she went to the hospital. I'll try there.'

Williams hadn't seen Alison. It was ten-thirty and the thought police – as internal security were known – would have to be told soon. Williams had the same idea. He called back two minutes later. Livy, deeply engrossed in balancing the cutlery, swore.

'Hello, Haydn. Yes, all right. Someone will go round.' Livy wrote down Alison's address half a mile away in Kennington and handed it to Tim with a smile.

'I'll take the keys just in case,' said Mickey, pulling out the skeletons he illegally kept in his desk. As they left Livy had locked spoon and fork together and was sliding a match through the prong in another attempt, her tongue protruding from the corner of her mouth as she concentrated.

Alison lived in a small terraced house within sight of the Oval's gasometers. There were lace curtains over the downstairs window and a stripped pine front door which opened directly on to the pavement. They made out an impeccably tidy front room with cushions on the sofa which appeared never to have been sat on. Peering through the letter box, Tim saw a Sunday newspaper on the hall floor. The house had an unoccupied feel. They tried the neighbours on either side and across the street but no one had seen Alison. They weren't sure if they had seen her yesterday either, so that wasn't much help.

'What now?'

'You're the officer. You tell me,' retorted Mickey.

'Break in,' ordered Tim.

The Yale opened easily. There was a security chain still on.

'Shit.'

Mickey took a step back and kicked the door under the chain. The door frame splintered. Another kick and Tim shouldered the bolts loose. Passers-by crossed to the opposite side of the street.

They found Alison lying on a single bed in the back room wearing a white, heavy cotton nightdress. Like a shroud, thought Tim. She had closed the door. There was an empty pill bottle and an almost empty pint glass of water on the floor.

'Fuck.'

'She's still breathing.'

Alison opened her eyes, heavy as lead. 'I'm sorry to be so much trouble,' she murmured.

'I always wanted to fly,' smiled PC Ian Watson, not realizing that the next few minutes would blight what had been a promising career.

'It's surprising how many people do,' Cheryl smiled back. 'We've a milkman, a bus driver, doctors, teachers, a builder, a journalist. No policemen, though. I suppose you've got your own club. Would you like a cup of tea?'

It was no good, she admitted to herself. She liked a man in uniform, whether flying instructors or handsome young policemen.

'Thanks. The Met might have, Kent police hasn't.'

While her kettle boiled – none of that machine muck – she slid open the three drawers of the filing cabinet and explained. 'These are the current membership forms. I went through them about six months ago. These are the aircraft documents, insurance, licences, that sort of thing. And on the bottom there's old exam papers, rotas and past membership details. I must have a good clear-out one day.'

'It's only the current membership we're interested in. I'll need to take away the forms to photocopy. I'll bring them back this afternoon.'

'You can copy them here. I'll give you a hand.' He really had a lovely smile. 'Milk and sugar?'

'Thanks.' After a while he remembered to ask if the flying club had any foreign members.

'There's Dr Patel, flies every Sunday morning, weather permitting. And an Irishman, not seen him for a while. And of course, there's Ali. Right character he is. Bought us all champagne when he first went solo. Dripping in money. He's from the Gulf somewhere.' Cheryl loaded the next batch in the photocopier. 'Why do you want these details?'

'I honestly don't know. We're just the foot soldiers. Do you fly?'

'No. I've never got round to it.' Cheryl tugged at a long strand of blonde hair. 'But you should try it.'

Her eyes suggested that he should try something else as well. PC Watson left fifteen minutes later with the copied membership forms and a date for next evening. He handed over the forms to the collator and thought nothing more about it until the bloody post mortem the following week into how Barbel had slipped through their Biggin Hill inquiries.

Williams sat up in bed determinedly compartmentalizing his problems. Alison was in intensive care under a police guard. Mac and his thought police were searching her house. There was nothing further to be done in that direction at the moment. Address the problem in hand.

Tim, calling to report, had been surprised to meet Sally, who was hospital visiting. Williams invited them both to stay to hear the new development. Bill Jones and Commander Penn sat on the far side of the bed.

'The latest transcript of the saga of Soraya – with a twist,' announced Williams.

'How is she?' inquired Tim.

'Why is everyone more concerned about this little girl than they are about me?' exclaimed Williams, passing a transcript to Tim and Sally.

'Where's Ramath-lehi?' demanded Sally within seconds.

'Good girl.' Williams proudly regarded his protégée. 'Fortunately our biblical scholar knows the answer.'

Commander Penn cleared his throat. 'It's where Samson slew the thousand Philistines.'

'Is that a code word to let off the virus?'

'It's possible, but Samson went on to do greater things.' Williams held up a small thick Bible. 'This was given to my mother by her father in 1920. I've not opened it in years. Everyone must read the story of Samson in Judges in the Old Testament so they know the references. Commander Penn, will you give the heathens among us a run-down on Samson's activities? Not a nice chap, was he?'

'No. Bit of a wide boy really. He begins to show his true form when he demands to marry a Philistine woman from Timnath, despite his parents' objections. At that time the Philistines were rulers over the tribes of Israel and it wasn't the done thing. Just before the wedding Samson picks on a young lion roaring nearby and throttles it with his bare hands. He goes away and when he returns he finds bees are making honey in the carcass. His bride has brought thirty male companions to the wedding feast. Samson sets them a riddle and bets them a change of raiment each that they can't solve it within the seven days of the feast. This is not too long, is it?'

'No. Not at all,' replied Williams. 'Please carry on.'

'Thanks. Samson cheats with the riddle. "Out of the eater came forth meat and out of the strong came forth sweetness." No one had a clue what he was on about. On the seventh day the companions threatened to burn down the bride's house if she didn't tell them the answer. She wheedled it out of Samson with no problem. Samson was

347

so angry he'd lost that he went and slew thirty men and took their clothes to settle the bet.'

'Charming,' commented Sally.

'You can already see that the young fool can't keep a secret or resist a woman's charms. He stomps off and by the time he returns, her father has given his bride away to another man. He offers Samson the younger, fairer daughter but he doesn't want her. Instead he catches three hundred foxes, ties firebrands to their tails and lets them loose in the Philistines' cornfields. Not surprisingly the Philistines blame the father and burn him, his daughter and their house. Samson took revenge and smote them hip and thigh with great slaughter.'

'So this is Ramath-lehi?' asked Tim.

'Ah, no. Actually, I'm coming to that.'

'Sorry.'

'Once he's smote hip and thigh, three thousand men of Judah came to him and basically said, "What do you think you're doing attacking our masters? We're going to have to hand you over." Samson allowed himself to be bound until the Philistines started shouting at him. He didn't like this so he snapped his bonds, picked up the jawbone of an ass and slew one thousand men forthwith. He called the place of slaughter Ramath-lehi.'

'Oh,' breathed Sally. 'But what about Delilah?'

'Samson fell for Delilah, a woman of the valley of Sorek. The Philistine lords each promised her eleven hundred pieces of silver if she could make him reveal the secret of his strength. The first time she asked him, he told her to bind him with seven green withes. When he slept Philistines crept into his tent. She shouted, *"'The Philistines be upon thee, Samson.' And he brake the withes as a thread of tow is broken when it toucheth the fire."*'

'What's a withe?' demanded Sally.

'What's a tow?' demanded Bill Jones.

'A withe or a withy is a thin flexible branch or osier. A tow is a coarse strand of flax or hemp used in spinning.'

348

'Thank you.'

'Delilah tried three more times. Samson told her unused ropes would sap his strength, so she tied him with those. He said if seven locks of his hair were woven into a web, he'd lose his strength. She wove away and still the silly boy didn't learn. Finally he told her the secret of his strength lay in his long hair – presto. "Eyeless in Gaza, at the mill with slaves".'

'But if Ramath-lehi's not the code word to trigger the Option, then what is it?' asked Bill Jones.

'It could be a milestone on the path,' hazarded Williams. 'We don't know. That's the problem. We just don't know.'

General Jakob Grib took little pleasure in his food. He would have denied he was an aesthete, attributing that description to effeminate western society, but he despised those who found such wholesale pleasure in eating as did the Cossack Umar Linnikov. Grib fastidiously wiped the last crumbs of choux pastry off his plate with his little finger and scarcely concealed his impatience as the barrel of a man crammed yet another éclair into his mouth. The coffee shop of the Radisson Slavyanskaya Hotel was impossibly busy. They would have to speak outside but first the pig had to finish eating. He would not have much appetite by the time Grib had finished.

Finally Grib's patience, as scant as his frame, cracked. 'Come.'

Reluctantly Linnikov rose to his feet. Outside Grib wrapped his scarf tightly around his throat against the Moscow afternoon; the Cossack made a point of leaving his coat open. Grib nodded in the direction of the river.

'The Polecat Igor Botkin has left a strange legacy,' he began softly. 'It appears he was moonlighting for a Palestinian working for the Iraqis. He stole a flask containing a biological weapon from the depository near Rostov. Your last post.'

Linnikov stayed silent.

'Those involved have made a grave error of judgement.'
Grib paused. 'That can be forgiven if the damage can be undone.'

They walked past the Kievska Metro station. Thirty yards behind, two men kept pace with them. Linnikov found he was holding his breath.

'I don't think Tatum's killer will ever be caught, do you?'

'No, General.'

Paul Tatum had been a flamboyant American partner in the Slavyanskaya Hotel. For the last eight months of his life he seldom left his room, convinced there was a contract on his life. One day he made a rare foray to a meeting. As Tatum walked down the steps to Kievska station, a gunman leaned over the parapet and stitched eleven rounds from an AK 47 from his groin to his throat.

It was rumoured he had been cheating his partners. Linnikov understood the allusion.

'No,' repeated Grib. They reached the kerb. An alert militiaman stopped the traffic for them to cross to the riverside. 'Botkin's operation has reached the ears of the Directorate. They are fucking furious. And they are right to be.'

Linnikov felt a chill of fear speed through him like ice cracking. 'Why?'

'Hell, Linnikov, have you gone mad? Think what would happen if Russia was found to be involved in releasing biological weapons in London. Such an attack is akin to an act of war. We would be political pariahs and more importantly, economic pariahs. The West doesn't need to threaten us with nuclear weapons. They can cripple us financially by freezing economic credits, refuse to keep our banking system afloat. If they withdraw international cooperation Russia will be ruined. Secondly, consider the implications on an international level. If the attack succeeded the West would act against Saddam. If they were to go nuclear on Baghdad it would be catastrophic. How would we react? Could we contain our own nuclear triggers? Our fail-safe systems are so antiquated it would only take one hothead. And then what? This time the West will not stop until Saddam is dead. We need a strong man in Iraq – maniac or no. Now do you start to understand where a small man's greed can lead?'

Linnikov bowed humbly. 'Yes, General.'

But Grib had not finished. 'If we were caught it would be the end of the KGB. The West would demand our emasculation and yours would be the first balls in the wringer.'

They leant on the parapet staring at the chill grey waters. Linnikov shivered.

'The Palestinian must fail. I am telling you this as your superior officer and a friend. Others will reinforce my words. Wars stop trade, any sort of trade. *Understand?*'

'Yes sir.' It was as though the big man had been deflated; his skin, like his personality, had become too large for him.

'Errors of judgement are not fatal if they can be corrected. What do you know about this Palestinian?'

'He calls himself Tari. I don't know if it's his real name. He works alone. We assume he'll be triggered by a message from the Amn al Khas. An operation like this would be overseen by Saddam's son Uday. Saddam wouldn't trust anyone else.'

'We must find and terminate this Tari. Preferably without the Iraqis knowing.' For a moment Grib almost allowed himself to smile. 'It would be sweet if the Iraqis thought the British were responsible, but whatever: he must be killed and the biological weapon returned to Russia.'

'There is a safe house in London,' confessed Linnikov.

'Good.' It was not clear whether Grib was complimenting the Cossack on the fact or his honesty.

'It's a fall-back in case of emergency, but it's the only lead we have.'

'Make sure the house is under constant surveillance. Call

on the London residency for manpower. Find this man before he plunges our world in chaos. If he succeeds . . .' The small man shook his head sorrowfully and raised his arm in a languid gesture. A government Zils limousine drew up at the kerb side.

The Cossack watched Grib drive off into the gathering gloom. Despite the cold, Linnikov found that his shirt was sticking to his broad back. It passed through his mind that he could have picked up Grib and snapped him like a twig – but then he would not live to see nightfall.

Melanie Whittle frowned anxiously down at her six-year-old son Jason lying on the sofa. He wasn't getting any better. The doctor had been once already today. She felt guilty about calling him out again on Sunday, but her mother's instinct said there was something wrong, something seriously wrong. Jason had woken her at seven o'clock that morning complaining he had a headache and felt sick. The sheets on his bunk bed were sodden with sweat. Melanie's first fear was meningitis. She read the information leaflet. *Early symptoms vary and can be difficult to detect. There may be a rash of red/purple spots or bruises which does not fade when a glass is pressed on it. If the rash is present the disease is in an advanced stage and medical help must be sought immediately.* There was no rash but Melanie ran into the kitchen for a glass and pressed the cold rim against Jason's flesh. The imprint disappeared.

Her husband set off at eight for his job as a manager in the DIY superstore, now open seven days a week. He promised to phone later. Three-year-old Jonathan wailed that he also felt ill, but Melanie suspected it was a bid for attention. By ten o'clock Jason was crying with a pain behind his eyes. She carried him into the living room and called Dr Gear. He arrived an hour later, young, earnest and diligent. He came as Jason was showing an improvement. No, he hadn't actually been sick, just complaining of nausea. No, no diarrhoea. Just a pain in his forehead. Dr Gear noted there was no pallor, cyanosis, or jaundice. Jason's temperature was 38.1°C with a relative bradycardia. He was alert and apart from an abdominal tenderness there were no abnormal findings. The doctor reassured Melanie that he did not mind being called out, agreed that it was better to be safe than sorry and confessed he did not really know what was wrong with Jason. Dr Gear recommended junior aspirin and Calpol and advised Jason should be kept warm with lots of fluids. If there was any change, let him know.

The child dozed much of the day, not even showing any interest in his favourite videos. Melanie was about to prepare dinner when he screamed that his eyes hurt and his muscles were aching. He began to retch. This time Dr Gear found a very sick little boy. Jason was glistening with sweat even though his mother was mopping him with a cold flannel. His temperature had soared to 39.6°C and his pulse was 100/minute. Dr Gear found he had an inflamed throat and the lymph glands were palpable in the neck and axillae. He asked if the family had returned from anywhere exotic where Jason might have contracted a tropical disease. No further than Sandwich to visit her mother yesterday, said Melanie. Jason began shivering violently. That decided Dr Gear. PUO – pyrexia of unknown origin, Gear told admissions at Hemel Hempstead General Hospital. By a small miracle there was a room available.

In Dagenham in Essex, two pensioners, Martha Bowen and Mary Miller, who had been on a shopping trip to Calais the previous day, were also developing pains behind their eyes and nausea. In Preston, Lancashire, lorry driver Gerry Brathwaite cursed: he was going down with flu.

Monday 6 April

Tim had never been more comfortable. He was neither awake nor asleep but floating luxuriously between the two. And everything was snugly right. The pillow had moulded to his head, the sheets were cool. He was possessed by a wonderfully drowsy feeling of absolute bliss. He slowly opened his eyes and found crinkled green ones watching him from a foot away.

'Good morning.'

A warm wave of remembrance eased over him. 'Good morning.'

'You sleep well,' smiled Sally. 'My fingers have been strolling up and down your back for five minutes. I thought highly trained men like you would be instantly alert and ready for action.'

Tim licked her nose.

They smiled at each other. Tim stretched luxuriantly. 'D'you know what I'd really like to make my life complete?'

'Hmmm. I think I can guess.'

'A cup of tea.'

'Bastard. I'm not going to be your handmaiden.'

Tim pretended to frown. 'You couldn't be a maiden.'

Sally smiled at him with soft welcoming eyes.

'Witch.'

'Part of you has woken up, anyway.'

'Why can't we stay here, suspended in our half dreams for ever.' He pulled the sheet over their heads and they delved back into their own world, two as one, away from the cold, grey morning. Away from the realities that awaited.

*   *   *

'I hate hospitals,' moaned Tim two hours later. 'The smells make me go weak at the knees.'

'Why are men always so squeamish?' chided Sally. 'Lord knows how you'd cope with something like childbirth.'

'Being at the conception's bad enough. All those squelchy noises. Ouch.' He rubbed his stomach where Sally hit him. 'You're a vicious little beastie on the quiet, aren't you.'

'Carry on like that and you'll find out.'

They showed their passes to a guard on Williams's corridor and again to another one sitting outside his room. From the bulge in his suit jacket, Tim knew the guard favoured a right-handed cross-draw from a low shoulder holster – yet he held his newspaper with his right hand as the pair approached him. Sloppy.

'I'll be in soon.' Tim crouched down beside the guard. He spoke quietly so no one else could hear, but the guard went crimson. For a second the man bristled as if he was about to strike out, but he ended by nodding in agreement and when Tim stood up the guard stood with him and gave a shamefaced smile of apology. Tim went into Williams's room leaving the guard thinking what a decent fellow he was. Other SAS hotshots would have reported him to his boss and that would have been him back on traffic.

Williams greeted Tim and Sally thinking they made a handsome couple. He did not normally approve of relationships in the office, but Sally was doing Tim the world of good. He'd lightened up; become more cheerful and confident. Williams hoped it wouldn't end in tears.

'How's Alison?' inquired Sally.

'The doctors say she'll be well enough to be interviewed this evening. I can't hold off the thought police any longer.'

Doctors had pumped out her stomach and she lay weak and exhausted under armed guard in a private room on the floor below. Williams found the idea that Alison was the traitor distasteful. He had regarded her as a surrogate daughter as well as a colleague. She'd had plenty of opportunities for betrayal, but he found it hard to divine her motive. He'd been meaning to ask Plumridge to positively vet her, but he'd been so busy and now with his injury . . .

'Do you want us to have a friendly chat with her?' suggested Tim.

Williams appeared to hesitate. 'It would have to be totally off the record. Mac would go potty if he knew someone had been in ahead of him and muddied the waters.'

'Was it a serious suicide attempt or a cri de coeur?' asked Sally.

'Serious,' replied Williams and Tim nodded. 'There was a chain on the front door. If you want to be found, you don't want those who find you to wreck your house. Poor girl. What can she have been thinking of?'

'Haydn. *Bore da*. And how are you today?'

'You haven't met my wife, Bethan.'

'Hello. No, I never get to meet anyone from Haydn's office. I think he's ashamed of me.'

Tim found himself smiling at a friendly woman with a perfectly oval face and a lilting Welsh accent.

'Rubbish. You know you get bored. Bethan's a music teacher. She believes all civil servants are pompous, grey dullards. I tend to agree with her.'

'Look at those flowers. Already wilting. I've brought your post. There's a letter from Greenwich Council. Remember your blood pressure when you open it. I'll put these new daffodils in water.' Bethan bustled off.

Williams, face set in the manner of one expecting a hefty tax bill, ripped open the envelope. They held their breath. His scowl lifted until you couldn't get the smile off his face with a scrubbing brush. He waved a sheet of paper at Sally and Tim.

'Greenwich Council's backed down. Thrown in the towel. Bottled it, as Mickey would say. They're not going to contest the case. They claim they don't have the resources to fight. Right. Now it's my turn. I want to know what sort of petty bureaucrat can write such an illiterate rejection of my appeal and then be so arrogant and dismissive as not to sign it. And this comes from a borough which professes to put people and services first. Pah!'

'You're getting yourself worked up,' warned Sally.

'We'll visit Alison,' said Tim, thinking it was time to go.

'Bethan's a nice lady,' said Sally as they emerged on the floor below. 'Someone you warm to.'

'Yes,' agreed Tim, remembering the tiny smile lines around her eyes. 'You never think of Williams having a home life. He's sort of married to the office. Don't doctors look young?'

They stepped aside for a porter pushing a patient in a wheelchair, his plastered leg sticking out before him like a battering ram.

'I thought that was supposed to be policemen.'

'At my age, commissionaires are beginning to look young,' replied Tim.

They were approaching a reception desk for directions when Sally suddenly stopped and frowned after a doctor with a stethoscope hanging out of the pocket of his white coat striding into a corridor on their left. 'I know him from somewhere.'

'You've probably seen him on Williams's floor.'

'No.' Sally furrowed her brow in concentration. She could picture the man – tall, cropped sandy hair, jug handle ears. She could visualize him laughing, or was it eating? Where? 'I've seen him in a totally different context but I can't place him. Oh, it's so annoying. It's like presque vu where you almost glimpse the secret of the universe but then it slips away like a dream in the night.'

'I've never had that,' said Tim. 'I reckon I suffer from jamais vu. Don't have a clue.'

The receptionist indicated down the same corridor where Sally's mystery doctor had disappeared.

'What are we going to say to Alison? Hi. How are you? Why did you try to top yourself?'

'Don't be so callous. We'll say we hope you're feeling better and we're all thinking of you.'

'Two to one she'll want to know if Mickey's been at her chocolate biscuits.'

'Of course!' Sally slapped her palm to her forehead. 'That's where I saw him. At the races. He popped briefly into the box. He grabbed a handful of sandwiches, crammed them into his mouth and disappeared. You must have seen him.'

Tim, who had spent most of the time at the front of the box, shook his head.

The plain clothes policeman outside Alison's room rose as they approached. 'I wouldn't go in, sir. There's a doctor with her.'

'Short hair, big ears?' guessed Sally.

'That's the one, miss.'

Tim opened the door. Alison was lying flat and the doctor was standing by her bed, holding her bare left arm in his left hand.

'Please wait outside.' He did not turn around.

Tim thought the doctor was about to take her pulse until he caught a glimpse of a syringe.

'What are you doing?' he demanded.

'Giving an injection.' There was a definite accent. 'Please wait outside. I shall only be a moment.'

'It's him,' whispered Sally fiercely. 'Do something.'

The doctor stretched out Alison's limp white arm and tapped inside her elbow with the back of his hand to bring up a vein.

'Put down that syringe,' commanded Tim and stepped forward. Alison lifted her head. The doctor ignored him.

'Guard,' yelled Sally. Tim went for the doctor's arm. In a flash he swung around and stabbed the syringe at Tim's face. Tim ducked, threw up a protective hand and tripped backwards over Sally's feet.

'Get him.'

The guard reached for his gun. The bogus doctor squirted the syringe in his eyes and made a break for the door. The officer fell screaming. Sally lunged at the assassin, but he hurled her away and fled into the corridor.

'My eyes. My eyes.'

Tim, torn between pursuit and tending the policeman, hit Alison's panic button, plunged his handkerchief in her water jug and pressed it to the officer's eyes. By the time he ran outside, the bogus doctor had vanished. Back in Alison's room he sent an alert and a description on the officer's radio and sprinted to the lift. He was in the foyer when the first squad car squealed to a halt. Within minutes the hospital was sealed off. Tim knew it was already too late. He returned to Williams's room to bring him abreast of developments.

'That's twice you've saved her life,' commented Williams.

'This was down to Sally. But why would the Mafiya want to kill Alison?'

'For her silence,' replied Williams. 'If she's unstable enough to try to commit suicide then she can be broken. She'll tell us what she knows.'

'She's the traitor?'

'It looks like it,' said Williams, sadly. 'Don't bother to talk to her now. Leave it to Mac.'

'We have to say something after what's just happened,' protested Tim.

'I suppose so, but keep it brief. By the way, Bethan wants to invite you both to dinner. One day next week? If you'd like to, that is?' he added in a bout of uncharacteristic nervousness.

'Of course, we'd be honoured.'

Tim found Sally outside Alison's room. The guard's eyes were being treated while the hospital laboratory was already analysing what had been in the syringe. It couldn't have happened in a better place, Tim pointed out.

'And Bethan Williams wants us to go to dinner at their place next week.'

'Darling, our first social engagement,' breathed Sally, opening her eyes in pretended wonder. 'We've arrived.'

Two uniformed officers with pistols in their holsters stood guard before Alison's door. An intense floor by floor search of the hospital had drawn a blank, but mysteriously the killer had not shown up on the closed circuit TV at the main entrance.

'Where better to hide a doctor than in a hospital,' said Tim. 'Everyone in a white coat and a stethoscope is assumed to be a doctor.'

'Yes, Sherlock,' said Sally. 'Now be nice to Alison.'

The room, Sally now had time to notice, was bare of get well cards, flowers or fruit. Alison was sitting up, her skin grey and clouded.

'Hi.' She managed a crooked grin.

'How are you feeling?' Sally sat on a stool by the bed while Tim stood behind her.

'Like a steamroller ran over my stomach. I suppose I should thank you. God, that sounds ungracious. It wasn't meant like that.'

'Don't worry.' Tim gave an encouraging smile. 'As long as you're all right. And promise you won't try it again.'

Alison's eyes cleared. 'I couldn't do that again. I'm not that brave. It was all I could do to muster the courage the first time. There won't be a repeat performance.'

Sally took her hand. 'Good.'

'Has he said anything?' Alison inquired in a small voice. She wore no make-up and Tim saw that she was older than he had thought. Certainly in her mid-thirties. He'd put her down as the same age as himself.

'Who? Williams? He's concerned about you and he wants to know why you did it.'

'No, not Williams.' Alison gave a small shake of her head. 'Maurice. He's not been. Are they stopping him?'

'I don't know,' replied Tim, at a loss. 'I don't think so. Why?'

Alison's face crumpled like damp tissue paper. She began

sobbing, her fists pressed into her eye sockets. Sally pulled her gently into her shoulder.

'Did he promise to leave her?' she asked softly. There was a strange smile on her face.

Tim had to listen hard to hear the faintest murmur of agreement. 'Yes.'

'He told you he loved you?'

'Yes. He said he couldn't stand her any longer . . . She made his life a hell . . . his daughters . . .' Alison stifled another sob. She was speaking and sniffling at the same time. 'I even decorated my bedroom . . .' She descended into a shuddering wail.

Tim was slower on the uptake. He pointed at Alison, face buried in Sally's shoulder and mouthed 'Plumridge?'

Sally nodded.

'Jesus! Listen to me, Alison. Are you saying you tried to commit suicide because you've been having an affair with Plumridge and he went back on his word to leave his wife for you?'

Alison wailed even louder.

Williams burst out laughing and kept on laughing.

'Priceless. Absolutely bloody priceless.' He wiped away tears. '*Duw*, boy. It's time I gave up all this and started making cheese or growing tulips. Under my very nose and I didn't see it.'

Williams could be very Welsh at times, noticed Tim.

'She'll still have to be vetted, mind, and her story checked and double checked. Mac can start on that straight away. Bloody Plumridge. He and that cow of a wife deserve each other.'

'But why were the Russians trying to kill Alison?' asked Tim.

'She's put herself firmly in the frame. We think she's tried to commit suicide because of her guilt. They finish it off and we're convinced. Case closed. The real villain stalks away quietly – and continues. And I almost fell for

361

it. I owe Alison a very large apology and an even larger dinner.' Williams shook his head in disgust with himself. 'And I'd bet a pound to a penny they've planted collateral in her house.'

'Is that what happened to me?' inquired Tim.

'Something like that,' replied Williams, but he did not volunteer to elaborate.

PC Simon Richards was conscientious. He had diligently studied to pass his sergeant's exams and he had steadfastly worked through his week's leave decorating their new home outside Maidstone. Against all superstitious parental advice, they had even painted the nursery blue once the scan had shown Jayne was expecting a boy. Don't tempt providence, their parents had said. Don't be silly, they'd replied.

Simon knew his superior officers regarded him as one of the most thorough coppers on the force. Which was why his interview with the German woman Ilse Schmidt, the day before he'd gone on leave, left him feeling dissatisfied. He had not seen the Turkish chauffeur, yet the black Mercedes had been in the drive. Maybe they had two cars – that was the logical explanation – but he should have asked. Police work was made up of small painstaking inquiries. An investigation was like the Yellow Brick Road. Miss out on one small brick and you'd never get to the end. He knew he was going to have to go back, even though he'd now transferred to Maidstone headquarters. Tomorrow he would make the time to see Frau Schmidt again. This time he'd take a colleague in case she tried anything on.

It was almost the end of his shift. He should have been back at the nick by now, but he'd lingered over a break-in at a timber yard and then gone out of his way to call in on an old lady who'd been burgled the week before. Simon had nothing to tell her but he knew she enjoyed the company. It was the side of policing he enjoyed. Let others catch Mr Big – he'd look after the little people.

A light aircraft glided down through the upper corner of his windscreen, the last thing he expected to see on this quiet Kent road. It disappeared over the trees to the right. Simon thought he'd better investigate in case the pilot was making an emergency landing.

A lane turned off to the right and on the spur of the moment, Simon Richards followed it. He found a grass track and bounced slowly along until it opened out into a large field. The aircraft, a low wing monoplane with a tricycle undercarriage, was at the far end, taxiing towards him. There was a black Mercedes by an open-sided barn and Simon parked next to it. It was the same model as the one in the Old Rectory. And it had a German numberplate.

The same car?

Simon climbed out of the police car and adjusted his equipment belt complete with side baton, CS spray, handcuffs and first aid kit. His lapel radio was ominously quiet. For a relatively flat county Kent had so many black spots. The car radio still crackled and hissed. The plane with red and blue trim was closer now. Through the shimmering propeller arc he made out the pilot. Ten yards away the engine died. In the silence Simon heard birds singing. The pilot slid back the canopy and climbed onto the wing. He wore a grey windcheater which accentuated his foreign looks and a blank expression.

The expression made Simon uneasy. He began to sense he might have stumbled upon something. He decided to play it light and friendly.

'Sorry to trouble you, sir. I saw the plane come down and I wondered if everything was all right.' Simon walked around to see G-BDRR on the side of the fuselage.

'Everything's fine. I rent this field as a private strip.'

'No problem. Is that your car, sir?'

Tari calculated quickly. A British car numberplate could

be checked in seconds, European ones in minutes. 'No. It belongs to my employer, Frau Schmidt. I am her driver.'

'Ah, yes. I called at the Rectory. You are Turkish, I remember.' Simon didn't think he looked Turkish. Too smooth somehow. 'And the plane?'

He was getting an increasingly funny feeling about this set-up.

'Frau Schmidt bought it as a surprise for her husband. I am the mechanic. They are rich.' Tari rubbed his thumb and index finger together. 'Very rich.'

Simon smiled to show he understood. 'Do you have any documentation?'

'In the cockpit. I will fetch it.' A few paces away, he halted. 'Do you fly? Have you ever seen inside a cockpit?'

'No.' Suddenly Simon knew he must not go near the plane.

He did not know he was already dead.

Tari pushed back the canopy and stretched down to reach the net pocket at the back of the pilot's seat. As he did so his windcheater rode up. Simon saw the outline of the pistol stuffed down his waistband.

That was enough for him. He had to get out of here and call for assistance. His lapel radio was useless. He must get back to the car.

The sun emerged and for some reason Simon shivered. The pilot was advancing with the papers. Simon scanned them.

'That's fine. I'm sorry to have troubled you.' He was already turning to walk away in a measured tread.

He could not help but look back. The man had the gun in his hand. Simon began running.

The first round hit him in the back, but he was young and strong and had a determination to live. He pressed the useless button on his lapel radio and gasped for help. Another shot and a sledgehammer thumped him in the left shoulder, sending his flat cap flying off.

He staggered, down on one knee, up again, rasping

364

blood. Five yards to the police car. He heard the chatter of the police radio, heard his safe haven. He lunged despairingly and rolled over. The man stood between him and the sun.

Tuesday 7 April

Williams, right arm in a sling, emerged from the lift and fumbled for his pass. The Ministry of Defence police sergeant wrote down his name and time of entry. Quaintly old-fashioned, thought Tim, seeing himself on a timed monitor camera. Williams signed him in.

'It's a long way down, isn't it?'

'You're well below Roman London here. Most Whitehall civil servants don't know this place exists. COBRA ran the Iranian embassy siege from here, and one or two crises the public never heard of.'

'It's like our briefing room, only bigger,' remarked Tim, entering the stark rectangular room with its pale plastered walls. Same large central table cluttered with different-coloured telephones. Moulded plastic chairs against the wall, translator's booth in the corner. The quiet hum of the air conditioning and the smell of paper and warm dust from the computers. Well-groomed young women were tapping away at keyboards while others laid out nameplates and writing pads for the Home Secretary, Foreign Secretary, Secretary of State for Health, DGSS, 'C', Director Special Forces, DIS . . . The big guns. Tim was impressed.

'Ours was modelled on this one.'

An impatient Plumridge emerged from a side door with an earnest bespectacled man he introduced as Russell Foot, Department of Health liaison. Obviously Plumridge had decided to brazen out the episode with Alison.

'There's been a cock-up,' he announced briskly.

'A six-year-old boy named Jason Whittle was admitted to Hemel Hempstead hospital the night before last with an unidentified fever,' said Foot. 'Last night the hospital asked the London School of Hygiene and Tropical Medicine for help. That was the first we heard about it.'

'How did he slip through the net?' demanded Williams.

Foot swallowed. 'When we alerted local health authorities' consultants in communicable diseases it wasn't made clear that they should monitor hospitals. Sorry. It has been corrected.'

'There's more,' said Plumridge, enjoying Foot's discomfort.

'The first sample of Jason Whittle's blood was contaminated. We should hear about the second sample very shortly.'

'Where's Jason now?'

'On his way to Coppetts Wood isolation hospital together with his brother and parents who all have fevers.' Foot cleared his throat and prepared to fight back. 'On the plus side the system is beginning to show up an abnormal number of cases of PUO – pyrexia of unknown origin. Not all may be related, of course, but Coppetts Wood is preparing to clear a wing and if necessary evacuate all current patients.'

A secretary, telephone tucked under her chin, raised an arm to attract Foot's attention. 'Here's the latest list of suspected victims, sir. They're being kept in isolation at their local hospitals. There's more reports coming in and they'll update you in an hour.'

Williams scanned the list. Apart from the Whittle family, there were two pensioners in Dagenham, three members of a family in Carlisle, a Preston lorry driver, a young couple in Rochester, a twelve-month-old baby in Reigate, another one in Devon and a teacher in Barking.

'The Surveillance Centre for Communicable Diseases will monitor the outbreak and coordinate local health inspectors' investigations,' said Foot, eager to make amends.

'Dr Philpotts on the telephone, sir.'

'Put it on the speaker.'

'Haydn, you lovely man.' Dotty Di's voice boomed around the room. 'The boy Whittle is positive.'

'How can you tell so quickly?'

'We used mass spectrometry to unravel the basic chemical structure. It's Marburg all right, but it's like nothing we've seen before. Some of the viruses appear to have shepherds' crooks which are more representative of Ebola. It's fascinating, Haydn. Absolutely fascinating. Can't wait to get it under an electron microscope.'

'Thanks, Diana.'

'Gosh! This is exciting.'

Williams shook his head in despair at her madness. He looked at the clock.

'The Prime Minister's due to finish his meeting with Dr Mowlem in five minutes or so,' he told the Number Ten liaison. 'I must see him then. Absolute priority.'

'Yes, sir.'

Williams pulled Tim to one side. 'Between you and me, they're hoping for an agreement on the Irish peace talks by Good Friday – three days' time.'

'Is that good or bad?'

'Both,' replied Williams. 'It's good because newspapers and TV will concentrate on the talks; bad because the politicians can only think about Ireland and there may be some unpleasant decisions to be made. But we'll press on. Go back over what we have on Russian Mafiya connections in London. We must be missing something. Let's try to take an overview. Go through Kent police reports on aliens again. Everything points there. I still can't get the feeling out of my water that Barbel's close to where he made that second phone call. SB say Colonel Primakov came into the country yesterday. Maybe he can help in his official role – after all that's what he's supposed to be here for.'

'Prime Minister's ready to see you, Dr Williams.'

'Doctor?' repeated Tim.

'They tend to use the proper form here,' explained

Williams, looking sheepish. 'I'm not a medical doctor, just a PhD.'

The tenth floor was largely deserted. Even Mickey was away arranging for the arrival of Rasputin the dog. Tim dialled Primakov's direct line, but there was no reply. He frowned at the idea of wading through photostats of Kent police inquiries and remembered the undercover videos of Russian Mafiya and KGB connections. Sally was in the sound booth monitoring lunchtime Baghdad Radio. Tim gave her a silly wave of his fingers and she replied with a wicked wink. He showed Maisie, now standing in for Alison, where Williams's spare office key was hidden in her desk.

He settled down to concentrate on the tapes. He didn't expect Barbel to be on them but . . . you never knew. There had been bigger and more obvious misses before. Never assume, Williams had drummed into him. He could understand that. It was akin to the ethic in the Regiment. Check, check and check again. And then when you know your equipment works, check it again. If he'd done that the Brigand would be alive today . . .

Tim stared at the surveillance shots with their date and the time imprinted on the top right-hand corner. They were dreary in their ordinariness. Men walking along the pavement, others getting in and out of cars, entering or leaving buildings. All vital fragments of some grand mosaic, but bloody boring if you didn't know who was doing what or why. On the third video, Tim recognized scenes Williams had showed him. Men gathering outside a restaurant; two smaller Hispanic men joining them and the party entering the restaurant together. They crowded around the bar, blurred shapes of women in the background. A series of stills, featuring the long-faced man Tim had identified as being at the races.

The man who was Valentine, although he was never to know it.

A new scene. A bedroom. A high camera pointing down onto a double bed. The same man sat on the edge with his shirt unbuttoned to the waist.

A woman's arm came into view.

She knelt on the bed.

She was naked.

She started undressing the Russian.

She was Sally.

Someone dropped an anvil on Tim's stomach. Icy sweat erupted on his face. The picture swam before his eyes. When he looked again Sally was totally naked and she was undressing the Russian while he fondled her. She pulled off his trousers and buried her head in his groin. Tim felt the bile rise in his throat, but he could not take his eyes off the screen. She laid the Russian on the bed and lowered herself onto him, smiling as she did so. The same smile Tim had seen that morning when she had done exactly the same thing to him.

He became aware someone else was in the room. He turned. Sally was looking at the TV set, her face a perfect blank. Her eyes flickered towards him in a pitiful silent cry of pain, a plea for forgiveness. She moved and Tim thought she was going to touch him. He recoiled and the pain in her eyes redoubled.

'Don't think too badly of me. It doesn't matter now, but I meant every word I said.'

Then she was gone. Tim turned off the TV and stood immobile, staring out of the window at the Thames and the pleasure boats below. Down there couples were enjoying themselves but he was hurting. Hurt such as he'd never known. And he was alone.

Dotty Di thought she would swoon with gratification. She had quite simply never seen anything like it. It was spellbinding. Majestic. Unbelievably beautiful. Marburg viruses squirmed, writhed and coiled in a three-dimensional mosaic of death. Never in her life had she ever come across so many threads packed into a droplet of fluid. A pulsing spaghetti ball of hell.

Diana's face glowed green as she squinted through the electron microscope. Golly. This stuff was hot. Hot as hell. The cellscape was alive with worms. Here and there the filovirus had formed complete loops – Marburg's unique signature. There were threads shaped like shepherds' crooks – or eyebolts, as they were known in the States. To her eye they rather resembled croziers or even a Celtic Cross. Those shapes were more often found in Marburg's evil sister Ebola. The threads were longer than usual. Whatever those Russians had done to poor Nikolai Ustinov's legacy, they'd created something the like of which she'd never even dreamt of.

She focused on one cell which was packed solid with building bricks – inclusion bodies, broods of viruses getting ready to hatch. The bricks first appeared in the centre of the cell. As the virus grew, they moved outwards towards the cell wall. When they touched the inner surface they split into hundreds of tiny elvers which pushed through the wall forcing the cell to bulge, pregnant with death, before it exploded. Then the threads swam on in the bloodstream searching for the next cell to call home.

It was glorious. Gorgeous. Life at its most primitive. Almost as old as the planet.

Those Russian scientists had done brilliantly well. These viruses were hungry, replicating faster than any she'd known.

They had to replicate to survive, but in doing so they killed. Like fire, they destroyed to keep alive. They did not mean to destroy their benefactor. They had one simple dynamic. Survival.

Anatoly Storozhov, KGB Resident in London, was furious. Linnikov, or Primakov as he was calling himself this year, had marched into his office and peremptorily demanded two teams of watchers. Storozhov was too much of a survivor to show his anger; he merely stared woodenly at the Cossack and demanded his authority.

With a sly grin Linnikov produced a single sheet of paper from his inside pocket and laid it on the other's desk.

The order signed by General Jakob Grib gave Linnikov carte blanche. The resources of the London KGB station were to be placed at his disposal.

'The General is waiting by the phone,' insisted Linnikov, glancing at the clock on the mantelpiece of the fine old room at the back of the embassy in Kensington Palace Gardens. The bosses did themselves proud. They should get out in the field once in a while. Discover the real world.

Storozhov did not trust the phone link to Moscow even though his experts assured him it was impossible for the British to listen in on the secure scrambled line. But this wasn't his operation. He was smarting at being treated in such a cavalier fashion. He wasn't even allowed to know why Linnikov wanted his watchers – although he'd make damned sure his men told him. What did he care if the operation failed?

'I will do as you ask,' Storozhov conceded.

He picked up the direct line to KGB headquarters and said clearly, 'General Jakob Nikolaivich Grib. Extension 2329.'

'Yes?'

'Storozhov in London, sir.'

'You recognize my voice?'

'*Da.*' Who could fail to recognize the reedy pipe of the small man?

'You are ordered to give every assistance to the man with you. You will accord him every facility. This takes priority over all short-term operations. Understand?'

'But . . .'

'There are no buts. If you wish to question your orders, you can do so back in Moscow.'

'Yes, Jakob Nikolaivich.'

The Cossack Linnikov was looking out of the window at

the trees in their first buds of spring. Even with his back turned, Storozhov detected the smirk of triumph. Russians had a saying – he thought the English had a similar phrase – he who laughs last, laughs longest. They would see.

'I'm surprised you've got the gall to show your face,' snapped Livy Hull. 'Treating the poor girl like that. Disgraceful.'

'With respect, it's nothing to do with you or anyone else,' replied Plumridge with icy hauteur.

'Oooh, ah.' Livy was deep in her Dorset burr, purring like a cat while she sharpened her claws. 'Respect is it? What respect did you have for Alison? God, you're a bastard.'

'Those in glass houses shouldn't throw stones,' sneered Plumridge.

'At least I don't have a husband to cheat on. What does Felicity think about this – or doesn't she know?'

Plumridge lifted his right forefinger, his lips drawing back into a warning snarl. 'It's nothing to do with you . . .'

'Poor Alison cannot come back here. What's she going to do?'

'Don't ask me.' Plumridge shrugged dismissively and for a second Williams thought Livy was going to slap him. He almost hoped she would.

The others filed into the conference room. Tim looked sullen. Sally was nowhere to be seen.

'There's still no news of the missing Kent policeman,' began Plumridge, keeping his head down over his notes. Livy was still glowering furiously. 'He and his car have vanished. He was last seen driving away from a timber yard about five yesterday afternoon in the Paddock Wood area. It was his first day at Maidstone, though no one knows if that's relevant.'

'Why did he transfer?'

'Newly married and bought a house in Maidstone.'

'How far is Paddock Wood from Faversham?'

'About twenty miles as the crow flies. You think this is connected with Barbel?'

'Don't you?' Williams sighed heavily.

'Kent police are moving heaven and earth. They don't like to lose one of their bobbies.'

'Newly married,' murmured Williams almost to himself. 'I wonder what he stumbled across. What's the latest on the victims?'

'Six confirmed and another nine possible. Jason Whittle's in a critical condition,' replied Plumridge. 'Coppetts Wood's been cleared and newspaper and TV editors are being called in for a confidential briefing.'

'It's up to the Prime Minister to convince them that the danger to the public is minimal while any leak about a state-sponsored terrorist on the loose with a deadly virus will cause untold harm. It's a question of balancing the public good,' explained Williams. 'He's also canny enough to spell out the position to the opposition leaders. Not only will that elevate the issue into one of state but then they can hardly complain if there's fall out about vital facts being withheld from the public.'

'There is a common denominator emerging among the confirmed cases,' announced Plumridge. 'They all travelled along the A2 and M2 on Saturday night. It's possible Barbel drove along the route spraying the Marburg. The Whittle family were coming back from her mother in Sandwich, the Dagenham pensioners had been to Calais, the lorry driver was on his way back from Spain, the Rochester couple were returning from the French Alps and the parents of the twelve-month-old baby had been to see friends in Canterbury.'

'It was the night Radio Baghdad mentioned Ramath-lehi,' said Commander Penn quickly.

'So Barbel received orders to give us a whiff of gunpowder,' mused Livy. 'A warning but not the Samson Option.'

'It appears so,' agreed Williams. 'But there's a growing

danger of the Samson Option becoming a self-fulfilling prophecy. The Kurds have got wind of it.'

'I don't understand,' said Livy.

'Once the Kurds know that Saddam's threatening to bring down the temple then it's in their interest to foment all the trouble they can to force Saddam to trigger the Samson Option. If he does, the West will respond. Whatever happens the Kurds will benefit.'

'What about the innocent people who'll die in Britain?'

'With the Kurds' history of suffering and genocide a few hundred thousand dead is neither here nor there. They'll try to destabilize the region for all they're worth.'

'By the way, the Russians are up to something,' said Plumridge.

'Yes?'

'Our special liaison friend Primakov was seen entering the Russian embassy and minutes later Storozhov was on the phone to Grib in Moscow complaining he'd been ordered to give unconditional help to the person with him. We assume that was Primakov. Grib gave him very short shrift.'

'And we all know Grib is the linchpin between senior serving KGB and the Moscow Narco Group,' said Livy.

'Linnikov and eight KGB hoods were clocked going into the Moscow Kiev bank in Cheapside within the hour. They entered separately but no one stayed less than thirty minutes.'

'A possible briefing?' Williams thought aloud. 'Perhaps Rasputin will be able to help us. Change of plan, Mickey. I think I'd rather the dog was brought here.'

'What! Tonight?'

'He'll be safer here.'

'Okay, guv. I'll tell his handlers to come directly here,' said Mickey. 'I'll organize food and water for the mutt, give him a good walk and leave him in our office.'

'You can't leave a dog in here overnight,' complained Plumridge.

'Why not? He's house-trained. More than you are,' shot back Livy Hull.

Tim knew what he would find before he opened the door. Sally had removed every trace of her presence. The flat again seemed empty and incomplete. It was silly, but he had become used to the second toothbrush in the mug in the bathroom, her make-up bag on the old chair and the sight of her wandering around at breakfast time in one of his shirts. He opened the wardrobe. Her few clothes had gone.

The day had passed with an empty ache in his stomach. He had controlled his anger and pain and repressed all emotions as he had done for so long – until he had fallen in love with Sally. He was tempted to have a drink but he had to work later. Hell to it! Why was he always so responsible. He poured himself a whisky and added ice. Sally had remembered to refill the ice tray. He never did. There were salmon cutlets and a good bottle of New Zealand Chardonnay in the fridge. That was to have been their supper.

God! He picked his women, didn't he. First Linda and now Sally. What had he done to deserve those two? He tried to crush the glass in his hand until he told himself not to be so stupid. That was his trouble. He was too sane. Tim stood in the window measuring his sips, staying sober while London fell dark. Pigeons homed on to the chimneys opposite, lights came on, curtains drew, even the whine of evening jets into Heathrow finally petered out. He felt hollow and sad. There were so many questions, but he wasn't sure he wanted the answers. Sally had met that man at the races. And slept with him the next day. The day she told Tim she was busy. Sally had been keen to join those awful people. Perhaps she had been going to meet them all the time and Tim's suggestion had upset her arrangements. But she shouldn't have been consorting with Russian hoods. Not in her job. It didn't make sense.

And Williams had known. He must have seen the video of Sally doing things to that Russian. That left a particularly nasty taste in Tim's mouth. But who had filmed her and why? Did she know she was being filmed? Why hadn't Williams steered Tim away from her? Why had he let him fall head over bloody heels in love with a whore? Tim finished his whisky in one angry swallow, changed into dark clothes and left for work.

The massive black and tan dog rose slowly on its great haunches and planted paws the size of boxing gloves firmly on Mickey's shoulders. Mickey got hold of handfuls of fur on the dog's ruff and shook. The dog growled affectionately and began licking his face.

'Get off, you great slobbering fool.'

'Where'd you find him?' laughed Tim.

'He's Cautious Kenny's. Cautious wanted a guard dog and ended up with this mutt. Daft as a brush, aren't you, Brutus? Never get on the floor with him. He loves nothing better than flopping across your chest. And he weighs over fourteen stones.'

'What is he?'

'A cross between a St Bernard and a Rottweiler. My nipper rides on his back and he doesn't mind. He didn't even complain when the vet put the microchip in. You can feel it – somewhere.'

Tim felt among the dog's thick coat. 'You reckon you can get that out with a penknife?'

The phone on Tim's desk rang once.

'Yeh, easily. Good boy. Stay here.'

He and Tim locked the door and crossed the corridor into Williams's office which they also locked behind them. They did not turn on the light.

'I hope Brutus'll be all right. I'll never forgive myself if anything happens to that dog.'

'Nothing'll happen to him.' Tim repeated Williams's argument. 'If the dog's found dead, then we'll *know* it's been tampered with. The chip has to be removed without it appearing that anyone's been near the dog.'

'So what do you reckon they'll do?'

Tim didn't think he had ever seen Mickey so nervous. 'Sedate him with knock-out drops. You shouldn't have said Rasputin was so fierce.'

'Yeh, got a bit carried away there,' agreed Mickey. 'He's taking his time.'

'Checking the book to make sure there's no one on the floor.'

They heard the lift arrive and lay flat behind the sofa. The doorknob began to turn in the moonlight. Tim found he was holding his breath. There was a creak as someone tried the door then silence while Tim listened to his heart beat. From across the corridor came the faintest of scratches as a key felt for a lock. The rustling of paper. A door being opened and quickly closed.

Someone had just thrown something into their office. He grinned at Mickey's look of anguish and slid back the mechanism on the 9mm Browning he had drawn from the armoury earlier that evening. He felt foolish carrying a gun, but Williams had insisted.

'You don't know what will happen.'

'But Mickey and I can handle any trouble.'

'Carry it.'

Strange to think there was a person the other side of the wall, waiting, as they were waiting, in the quiet of the deserted building. Tim forced himself to breathe regularly. What was the person doing out there? Just standing, as taut as they were, nerve endings screeching at the stillness. Finally there was the snick of their office door opening again. Tim nodded to Mickey. A thumping bass proclaimed a disco boat going up the Thames towards Kew. At the door, Tim carefully inserted a fisheye fibre optic probe into the keyhole. The corridor was in darkness. The intruder had gone into their room and closed the door. With infinite patience Tim put the key into the lock. Mickey had spent twenty minutes oiling and manipulating it earlier so the key turned without a sound. Mickey strapped night vision goggles over his head and they stepped into the corridor. Tim pressed the button on his comms set twice.

He held his fist in front of Mickey's face and began the countdown. One finger, two fingers . . . like a referee in a boxing match. Three. He turned the handle. The intruder had locked the door from the inside. They had anticipated this. Tim rocked back at the same time Mickey gave a flying kick under the lock. The door exploded inwards. Tim's left hand brushed the light switch in a movement he'd practised fifty times. In his right hand he held the Browning.

Livy Hull was bending over the unconscious dog. For a second no one spoke. She rose slowly.

'Hello, my dear.' She put on a broad Dorset accent as if she was talking for someone else. 'Just thought I'd pop in.'

She had a penknife in her right hand. She closed the blade and went to reach for her handbag on a nearby chair.

'Please keep your hands where I can see them,' said Tim, self-consciously aiming the pistol at the ground ahead of Livy. Mickey removed his goggles, stepped forward and took away the handbag.

'Silly boy,' she said in a scolding tone. She put her hand up to Mickey's cheek in part slap, part caress.

That was how Williams found them as he entered the room with Mac behind him. Livy Hull in slacks and coat, her palm on Mickey's cheek, and a strange brightness in her eye.

'Please come with me, miss,' said Mac.

She gave a resigned half-smile. 'At least Peter will have to stand on his own two feet. Rather saves me the emotional turmoil of giving him the elbow.'

Livy went to take her handbag.

'No,' said Williams.

Straight-backed, she walked out of the door and turned right to the lift.

Tim found he could at last exhale.

Mickey was on the floor cradling the dog's massive head and lifting an eyelid.

For Tim the next hour or so possessed a dream-like quality. Two stern scenes of crime colleagues of Mac's came and put the knife in a plastic bag. A second microchip was found in a film container in the handbag. She would have been unable to implant it, said Williams, so she'd place it in his fur so they'd believe it had worked lose. A vet examined Brutus and pronounced him well but heavily sedated. Mickey volunteered to sleep in the office with the dog. Tim returned the gun to the armoury and he and Mickey gave signed statements. There was a newly arrived fax from the Cousins in Livy Hull's office which would have been her excuse for being in the building so late. It transpired later she had been instrumental in having the fax sent.

It was most unlikely Livy Hull would be formally charged, Williams told Tim. We tend not to do things that way. Too public and messy. If they could turn her quickly she might be of use. They'd probably find it all came down to money, although knowing Livy's sexual appetites it was likely she and Linnikov were lovers. Williams still referred to her by her Christian name and he seemed to hold no animosity towards her. Tim had not explored his own feelings – if he had any to spare.

It was past midnight when he let himself into his cold and empty rooms. He left the curtains open and watched the moon travel past his window. He wished he was on it.

Wednesday 8 April

The night sky was crystal clear. Golden and silver stars twinkled in the infinite blackness. In the warmth of the Land Cruiser Shane Cosker felt like cheering.

'Maybe there is a God, after all.'

'So far he's been an Iraqi God,' said Tennessee Joe Bradley, sourly.

'Yeh, but that's all about to change, sport.'

Cosker could not help his elation. After months of procrastination, obstruction, sneers, hostility and downright lies, they were on the verge of the biggest breakthrough in UNSCOM's history. The discovery that would prove incontrovertibly that Saddam and his cronies were liars and terrorists. After this no Iraqi foreigner minister could ever stand up in the United Nations and again swear with hand on heart that his country had destroyed all weapons of mass destruction – and be believed.

Cosker hoped they were about to find eight warheads containing biological weapons. The ones made to fit the Al-Hussein rockets, which Saddam's ministers had sworn had been destroyed after the Gulf War. Only they weren't.

Amazingly it was the little clerk who had been so uncomfortable when he had been forced to lie about the fire in the filing cabinet who had come forward. Men like him astonished Cosker. The clerk, now codenamed Bobtail, had risked his life, and the lives of his extended family. He had sought out the UN inspectors and showed them documents to prove the warheads were hidden inside small concrete tunnels set in the side of a wadi at a desert training camp.

The Toyota's rear wheels slid sideways over sand which

had drifted over the arrow-straight road. Cosker took his foot off the accelerator. They were already running more than thirty minutes late because of a puncture to the second cruiser and they couldn't afford another mishap in this bleak and barren moonscape of bedrock and shale interspersed with lakes of hard sand. There was little traffic, the odd heavy truck chugging in a cloud of blue smoke, water bowsers and the occasional Land Cruiser. The highest things for miles were the pylons running by the roadside.

'I reckon this is the one,' decided Tennessee Joe, looking up from the map as the sun came up in a deep red ball of fire. They turned on to a hard track bounded by thorn bushes. A desolate herd of scrawny goats watched them incuriously. Cosker, chewing gum hard, took in the tense faces of his three companions and knew he must look the same.

So far so good. The inspectors had slipped their watchers by leaving at two in the morning. Their visit to the camp would come as a complete surprise. By the time the local ragheads got through to Baghdad, Cosker meant to have smashed through the concrete caps and exposed at least one of the warheads. Just one was all he needed. Then despite the weasel words of the UN Secretary General they would have won. Saddam would have been exposed exactly for what he was. The Gulf War coalition would close ranks against him and he'd have to open up the country for humiliating inspections or face new and indefinite sanctions.

After five kilometres, Cosker spotted a cloud of dust behind them.

'Someone's coming at a hell of a lick. Reckon it could be our old friends from the Second Battalion?'

The driver of the second vehicle came on the radio to report they were being followed by six or seven vehicles racing abreast over the hard desert.

'Fuck. Step on it.'

In wild spirits, Tennessee Joe wound down the window and waved his baseball cap to urge on their second cruiser. He gave out a spine-tingling whoop.

'Christ! What's that?'

'That is what Johnny Reb gave as he went into battle. Scared the shit out of those goddam Yankees. That is the Confederate rebel yell.'

'You silly bastard,' cried Cosker. 'Do it again.'

The cruiser rounded a shallow ridge and the camp lay a quarter of a mile ahead of them. They could make out the barbed wire perimeter fence, the water tower, barrack blocks and half a dozen trucks in the central parade ground. On the right, exactly as Bobtail had described, was the wadi opening out at two o'clock.

'What the fuck?'

Soldiers were crowding around the front gate. As they roared up, the mob parted to reveal a man, hands tied behind his back, dangling on the end of a rope, strung up from the centre bar of the wooden gate. For a second he squirmed and twisted before, with one convulsive jerk, he hung motionless, his head at a crazy angle.

Bobtail.

'Bastards,' spat Cosker. The Iraqi Land Cruisers were almost up with them, angry soldiers waving their guns out of the windows.

Cosker had had a belly full. He began barking orders.

'What?'

'Just fucking do it.'

'We're with you, man.'

They drove hell for leather towards the open gate where the corpse of their informant turned slowly in the early morning sun.

'Sheee – eeeet.'

Cosker winced as the Toyota's roof struck the corpse, sending it flying to one side like a mad pendulum. The second cruiser skidded in a shower of stones and dust to block the entrance.

A 20-kilowatt generator coughed and fired into life in the rear of Cosker's vehicle.

'There. There, between these huts. The concrete caps. Take the left-hand one. Go.'

The cruiser screeched to a halt in front of the wadi. Wheels spinning, it reversed furiously up to one concrete cap. The rear door flew open.

'Fucking mental, man.' Tennessee Joe was already attacking the concrete with a shoulder-held Kango pneumatic drill. Cracks appeared in seconds.

Tennessee Joe let out a whooping rebel yell as the first shots rang out.

Tim believed he could always tell what sort of day it was going to be by how long he had to wait for the bus. It was going to be a bad day. Fifteen minutes of huddling against the squalls blowing in from the west before a bus arrived. Then three turned up at the same time, close together like a timid herd.

The office was deserted apart from Maisie, who told him Williams had phoned from the Cabinet Office. Livy Hull's name had been removed from her door. She had ceased to exist. Tim signed for copies of Kent police files on aliens in the county, made himself a cup of tea and watched the trains come and go until he made himself sit and concentrate. It was not easy. He found he was reappraising old value systems, calling into question everything he believed in. He was not even sure he wanted to be in the Army any more. The lure of comradeship, a large part of army life, had been a compensation for a loveless home, he recognized. But the job he was currently doing did not involve comradeship, apart from Mickey, and he had the odd feeling that he had grown out of the need. Those in the intelligence game were clever people who would sneer at a soldier's belief in my country right or wrong. They lived by different moral precepts. Williams hadn't shown any anger at Livy Hull when her treachery had been revealed, even though she had been behind the attempt on his life when she feared he was getting too close. If that had happened in the Army, the bastard would have been beaten to pulp before reaching the door. Here treachery wasn't a personal betrayal. Intellectually it could be managed, emotionally it could be ignored.

Tim read the reports in a half-hearted manner. If the police hadn't found anything, what chance did he have? His mind moved between Livy Hull and Sally and slowly he found their betrayal was not the same. It surprised him that he was arguing in Sally's favour. It was her life, her morality to do as she wished. They had not been in any sort of relationship when they had gone to the races. What had it to do with him who she slept with? He forced himself to read.

What were all these foreigners doing in Kent? An Austrian countess, a French shopkeeper, a Dutch nurseryman. He was wrong to have judged Sally. A German wife of an industrialist and her chauffeur. There had been no declarations of love and fidelity. Except he knew he loved her and believed, as much as he dared, that she loved him. He came to a batch of students at the University of Kent. Canadians, Ghanaians, Nigerians, Egyptians, Arabs. He read the Arab file again and moved on. If he saw Sally again what would he say? Ask for an explanation. He had no right. Something was trying to nudge him in his mental ribs, whispering, 'Oi. Look this way, mate.'

Presque vu, almost seen. Where had they talked about that? In the hospital when Sally had clocked that bogus doctor. What had he skipped over? He frowned with the effort of concentrating. If only he wasn't so tired. The chauffeur. Someone had a chauffeur. He flicked back. Frau Ilse Schmidt of the Old Rectory, Boughton, had a Turkish chauffeur, Kasir Mahmeti. Tim looked in the Ordnance Survey map book for Boughton and felt a tingle at the back of his neck. Not only was the village near Faversham, fitting in with Williams's hunch that Barbel had made the second phone call from close to his base, but all the Marburg victims had travelled along the A2/M2 on Saturday night. And Boughton was next to the A2.

There'd been that chauffeur at Emma's funeral. Poor Emma. The only decent one and she was dead. God Almighty! He recoiled from his uncharitable jibe. The Irish poet Yeats had said something like, out of quarrels with others we make rhetoric, out of quarrels with ourselves we make poetry. Tim made cheap cracks. What was happening to him? The chauffeur had been sitting behind the wheel of a Mercedes when they'd arrived at the church. Then he'd watched the burial some distance away from the stile. He'd worn a cap and dark glasses. Afterwards Tim had asked about the chauffeur but no one had known anything about him.

It was still possible the virus had entered Britain in the coffin.

What the hell! Rather than just sitting here, he'd go and explore. Shame he'd given his gun back. He scribbled an explanatory note to Mickey, due back soon from taking Brutus home. Maisie had disappeared so he left the note in a prominent place on her desk, remembered to pick up his mobile phone and went to requisition a pool car.

Two minutes after Tim had driven away, Sally, feeling a cloud of butterflies clog dance in her stomach, entered the building and took the lift to the tenth floor.

Angry? Yes. Bitter? Yes. Vengeful? You bloody well bet. He could have come to see her. It was the very least he could have done. And after what she'd had to put up with the last few months. The double life, the lies, the whispered phone calls. And now blanked. Williams had been to see her. So had the others including Sally and Tim. He was sweet. If things had been different . . . but he was going out with Sally, according to rumours. Not that he had ever given her any encouragement. Tim had been afraid to say boo to a goose in case the goose booed back. Not like Mickey. Cheeky git! He'd spent an hour telling her an endless string of dirty jokes and risqué stories which had made her laugh when she thought she'd never laugh again. She couldn't remember laughing with her lover. She just listened to him proclaim and remembered to nod in the right places. So why the hell . . . ? Because in his own way he had made her feel special. Mickey and the guys in transport treated her like one of the lads, Williams treated her like a young friend of the family. She saw the signpost for Brockham and turned off. Bill Jones had called twice yesterday. Soft, understanding, non-judgemental, with egg stains on his shirt and a frayed collar. Someone who needed a woman to look after him. She'd seen herself as a fiery mistress; perhaps she was more cut out to be a mother figure. Would anyone give her a second glance after the fool she'd made of herself?

She kept returning to the fact that he had not even contacted the hospital to see if she was alive or dead. She could almost tolerate the fact that he'd lied to her, cheated her, used her. But his callous indifference was just too much. The last thread of scorn which whipped up the hell of her fury. A sign by the road announced she was entering the village of Brockham. It was as she'd suspected. Full of mock Georgian boxes pretending to be country houses. Why did he ever promise to leave his wife and kids; give this up to live in a two up two down in the shadow of the Oval gasometers.

She recognized his house. His Christmas cards had shown his daughters on their ponies flanked by preening parents in front of the white porticoed mansion. She felt amazingly calm as she turned into the gravelled semicircular drive and stopped by the front door.

No servants' entrance for the mistress.

She knew Felicity Plumridge to be a first-class bitch. Today she'd meet her match. She leant back and picked up the Harrods plastic bag – deliberately chosen – on the back seat. It contained two pairs of his underpants, shirts and socks, razor and toothbrush he had kept at her place. Feeling stronger than she had done for days, Alison rang the doorbell.

The first incumbent had clearly believed in living on top of his job – or maybe he was lazy. When the church had been built in the 1850s, the rectory had been erected a toss of a prayer book away. Tim crawled through the daffodils up to a straggling yew hedge dividing the house, an unfortunate cross between heavy Gothic and elaborate Victorian, from the now redundant church. A black Mercedes, similar to the one at the funeral, was parked by the front door. Tim inched into the rough grass between fruit trees. Lawns led to a small swimming pool and changing hut and on to a paddock. A glass extension grafted on to the side of the house served as a scullery. The front door opened and a man emerged carrying a garden spray and tubing. Tim's heart gave a leap. The picture of the Palestinian was seven years old but there was no doubt. He had found Barbel.

Barbel leisurely placed the items in the car boot, looked around, checked the front door was locked and drove off. Tim fought down the temptation to see the numberplate. Instead he rolled on his back and pulled out his mobile phone. He switched it on. Nothing happened. It remained dead and lifeless. Hell, bells and damnation. The battery was flat. Like an idiot he had failed to check it before leaving the office. Once before he had failed to check equipment . . .

If he was sensible he should pull back and call up the cavalry. But Tim was fed up with being sensible – and when had the SAS ever needed the cavalry? He crawled towards the house.

The early morning squalls had died away leaving blue skies and high clouds. It was still windy, but Tari intended to rig up the equipment inside the plane and conduct an airborne test. He had decided to dispense with the electric pump as an over-complication. Keep it as simple as possible. He needed to ensure he could pump up enough pressure while flying to push the liquid through the nozzle. He felt the time for the order for an all-out attack was close. The Kurds and the Shi'ites were challenging Saddam's regime, America and Britain had blocked moves to lift sanctions at the United Nations despite Saddam's warning of the consequences and UNSCOM inspectors were daily being thwarted and insulted. A confrontation was inevitable. He prayed his girls would be safe when the Americans started bombing Baghdad. As soon as he had played his part he would fetch them out and cherish them. He hadn't known he would miss them so much.

The missing policeman dominated the local news. At the moment the search was being concentrated miles away from the airfield, but it was only a matter of time before they spread outwards and found the plane. He had not wanted to kill the policeman – but he had no option.

Tari suddenly feared he had forgotten the awl he was going to need to lead the nozzle through the rubber washer. At the foot of the hill he pulled in at the Woodman's pub and inspected his tool kit. No, there it was. Tari drove on.

Tim was flat against the wall of the house, his hand pressed against the sliding glass door of the scullery. It gave a fraction. Tim was suspicious that it was almost too easy – not knowing that Ilse had forgotten to lock it the previous night. He slipped in. Facing him was an upright fridge freezer. Both compartments were empty. He peered under a stack of cardboard boxes and moved a pile of plywood trays and a rolled-up carpet under an old table.

He let himself into a long galley kitchen in pale blue wood. A mug, plate and spoon lay on the wooden draining board, evidence of one person's breakfast.

The virus would probably be in a freezer, said Dotty Di. He couldn't immediately see one – though he didn't believe any sane person would store the Marburg alongside food, never mind how well it was secured.

Tim opened the far door an inch at a time. He found himself in the hall with a broad staircase climbing the wall to his right and ending in a gallery which looked down at the front door. Tim gingerly tested the first stair and, keeping close to the wall so the old wood did not creak, ran lightly up to the gallery. A short corridor on the right led to bedrooms and a bathroom.

A door opened and a naked blonde woman drifted towards the open bathroom door. Tim froze. There was nowhere to hide; nowhere to run. The woman gave him a dreamy smile and murmured deep in her throat. She swayed towards him, draped her hands around his neck and began gyrating her pelvis against him. Her eyes closed and she held up her lips to be kissed. At a loss, Tim removed her arms and turned her so she could see the bathroom. She shuffled away and closed the door. Her bedroom was heavy with marijuana smoke. Piles of clothes lay scattered around the floor and a syringe sat in a saucer on the bedside table. The next two bedrooms were empty but then he came to Barbel's. He must have lived in a barracks to keep his room this tidy. Tim began searching in cupboards and pulling open drawers, even looking under the bed, recalling Dotty Di's words that an industrial freezer just fifteen inches high could comfortably hold a Dewar flask. All he found of interest was a pilot's headset.

Tari waited patiently to pull around the bakery van outside the village shop and despaired of Ilse. He could have done with her help this morning to pull the aircraft out of the shed and help position the tubing. He would have liked her on the airfield while he made a low pass spraying water to check on its spread and density. She had become a security risk. She had to be dealt with. Tari acknowledged a wave from the last motorist in the oncoming stream and pulled out. He could not send her back to Germany. She knew too much. He couldn't turn her loose and he was unsure how long she would remain in her drugged, semi-conscious state. She might take it into her head to go walkabout at any time. He would have to kill her and dump her body, as he had done with that interfering policeman. He accepted the impending killing as a matter of fact and concentrated on the operation. He planned to cross the Thames and practise low flying over the Essex marshes. He'd need to talk to Southend air traffic. He had the frequency in the cockpit but he did not have his headset. He'd left it in his bedroom. Stupid. At the roundabout leading to the A2 he made a complete circle and headed back to the Old Rectory.

Tim drew a blank in the bedrooms. When Ilse wandered back, seemingly oblivious to his presence, he checked the bathroom. Back downstairs he searched the large living room and moved back to the kitchen. Behind the matching cupboard doors he discovered a dishwasher and a well-stocked fridge freezer. The last door on the right revealed a deep saucepan drawer. There, humming away, was a compact freezer sealed with broad sticky tape.

A breath of cold air made Tim turn. Barbel stood at the doorway, a gun in his right hand.

Tim was surprised how slight the Palestinian was close to. All those vast efforts being poured into his capture – and he turned out to be disappointing in the flesh. A slender man in a white shirt and grey windcheater over black trousers. Rather like a policeman coming off duty.

But his eyes did not blink and the hand holding the gun was steady as a rock.

'Put your hands up and move away. Here into the hall.'

Professional, noted Tim. More room in the hall, harder for Tim to jump him.

'Ilse. Ilse,' he called.

'She's not in there,' said Tim, thinking the Palestinian did not look like a fanatic. Then he found himself wondering for a microsecond what a fanatic looked like.

391

Barbel regarded him coldly. 'Reach up against the wall. Spread.'

He expertly ran his left hand over Tim's body, searching for a weapon.

'Turn around. Who are you?'

Tim considered which reply would keep him alive the longest. British Intelligence? Police?

'The first of many,' he said.

'How did you find me?'

Tim shook his head.

'Tell me or I will shoot your kneecap off.'

'Mmmm.' Ilse stood on the landing above them, swaying as she held on to the banister. Tari's eyes flicked up to her. Tim leapt. He knew it was going to be close once he was in the air. His balance was wrong and he could have done with being two feet nearer. His flailing hand smacked down over Barbel's right wrist, knocking his gun towards the floor, but he was at the limit of his reach. Barbel fell back. Tim made to lunge again but already the gun was coming up.

Tari knew he had won. He locked both fists around the butt, his arms outstretched. He took up the first pressure on the trigger.

'Stop!' A sharp command in Arabic.

A woman appeared from the kitchen and stepped between the two men.

Sally!

Tari's gun did not waver. 'Get out of the way.'

'You owe me his life.'

They were speaking Arabic in quick-fire bursts. Tim did not understand, yet he caught no supplication in Sally's voice. She was demanding, not begging.

'No.'

'He could have killed you in Russia as you ran from the ambulance. I came between you then. I am doing the same now.'

'I owe you no favours.'

Sally faced him, proud and upright and so sure of her

392

strength that she kept her hands in the pockets of her jacket. 'Oh, you do. You know you do.'

Tari thought quickly. First the man, now Salilah. Who next? He had to get out immediately. The witch was regarding him as she would a chess opponent when she was one move from mate. Yet he had the gun. Damn her. Almost as if she read his mind, she took a pace towards him.

'No,' he said.

Simon Richards's body was washed up on the lonely fore-shore at Shoeburyness by the noon tide. A nature warden walking his golden Labrador saw a shape, a bundle of rags in the muddy shallows. In the local pub last night two fishermen had sworn they had seen an aircraft performing aerobatics over the Thames estuary. At the top of a loop something had fallen out of the cockpit. They thought it was the pilot but the plane righted itself and flew on. They had been well and truly mocked. But now there was the shape in the mud two hundred yards out. The warden put on chest waders and struggled out.

He found a rag doll in a policeman's uniform. By the way the body lay like an empty sack, every bone had been broken. Then the warden realized that would be the effect of falling out of a plane. Hitting water from height was like hitting concrete. He used his mobile phone to call the local police.

It was pitch black in the cellar.

'All right?' Tim asked softly.

'Yes, and you?'

Overhead they heard Tari dragging something heavy in front of the outward opening door in the corner of the kitchen which led, like a narrow entrance to a cave, down to this large cellar. Tim stood absolutely still and allowed his eyes to become accustomed to the darkness. Sally began to retch. He put out a hand and touched her hair. Softly he pulled her to him until her head rested against his chest.

Sally had made Tim go down the steep ladder to the cellar first, keeping herself between him and the gun, while she tried to reason with Tari.

'Why are you doing this? So many innocent people will die.'

'So that many innocent people may live,' Tari shot back.

She knew this mood of stubborn dogmatism. When Tari was like this he would swear the sky was pink and believe it. Still, she tried again. 'Helping a madman like Saddam can have no part in the struggle.'

He had not replied. He slammed the door and locked it.

The dragging noise stopped.

'Thank you.' Tim didn't know what else to say. He could feel her body quake as she sobbed silently. 'Why . . . ?'

'Why what?'

In spite of their predicament, Tim gave a stifled laugh. Why what, indeed. So many questions. Start with the present.

'Why didn't he kill us?'

'Oh, Tim.' She nuzzled into his chest as if seeking shelter there. 'You're wet.'

'Comes with crawling through grass. Tell me.'

'He owed. Tim, there's so much you don't know.'

'Then explain,' he implored, speaking as gently as he would to a child. 'Please.'

'You were going to shoot Tari in the forest. I came between you. I reminded him of it. We are quits. If we meet again there will be no favours.'

Still it did not make sense. 'But how do you know him?'

'I was his wife.'

It was only afterwards, when Tim endlessly re-ran the conversation in his mind, that he realized it was a very Arab way of putting things. Not, he was my husband. I was his wife.

'His wife!'

Sally sighed. The darkness made it easier for her. She didn't think she could have stood Tim staring at her while she confessed.

'I was seventeen when I married. We were . . . separated when I was twenty. I went my own way.'

'You're not still married?'

'No. He divorced me Arab style. I did not have to be there.'

Every answer of Sally's generated a dozen more questions. It was hopeless. Tim gave up. There were more pressing things to do – like getting out of here.

'Okay. Promise me you'll tell me more later.'

'Later?'

'Over dinner.'

'Oh Tim.' She flung her arms around him and cried hot tears. 'Maybe when you've heard everything you'll not want to stay for the sweet course.' She spoke artfully, hoping against hope that he would.

'I promise I will.'

'No. Don't promise. You don't know.'

Tim kissed her forehead and climbed the ladder to the door. He opened out the bottle opener on his keyring penknife and felt for a screw head. Five minutes later he was still trying to achieve a purchase when Sally put a hand on his arm.

'Shush.'

There were footsteps in the kitchen. A heavier, more measured tread than Barbel's.

'Shall we call for help?' she whispered.

'What have we got to lose? *Help . . . Help!*'

'That you boss? Where the hell are you? It sounds as though you're coming out of the wall.'

'Mickey.'

A minute later they were climbing through the splintered door.

'How did you get here?'

'I found your note. Maisie said Sally had set off after you,

395

so I thought I'd better do the same. Williams is doing his nut he's not heard from you.'

The freezer had gone. Tim used Mickey's phone to bring Williams up to date and to start the hunt for the black Mercedes. He heard Williams relaying orders to Kent police as they spoke. Sally gave a shrill cry from upstairs. Still clutching the phone, Tim ran up to her.

Ilse lay still and naked on the bed. A crumpled pillow suggested she had been suffocated. Tim told Williams to call an ambulance and rang off. He failed to find a pulse and was about to give up when Sally took a mirror from the dressing table and held it against Ilse's mouth. Very gradually, it misted.

'She's breathing but only just. Put her on her side. Make sure her airways are clear. Mickey, get an air ambulance here soonest.'

Ilse opened her eyes. They looked far away. Her lips twitched and her mouth opened and closed like a fish out of water.

'She's trying to say something,' exclaimed Sally.

Ilse's voice came in aspirate whispers, so faint it sounded like the faraway rustling of leaves on a summer breeze. Sally held her ear next to her mouth, frowning as she strove to catch the syllables.

'Lun S. I think she's saying Lun S. Does that mean anything to you?'

Tim shook his head. Ilse's eyes were deepening with the effort of communicating.

'Lun S. Rife.'

Ilse gave the tiniest shake of her head and puckered her face in exasperation. Her chest filled as she prepared for a final effort.

'Lun S. Rife. Flug . . .'

'Flug,' repeated Tim, who had caught the word. 'Isn't that plane in German?'

'Yes,' agreed Sally. She smacked her forehead as realization hit her like a jack-hammer. 'She's speaking German.

What did she say? Lun S. Rife. Of course! Landestreifen is a landing field. An airstrip. Yes?'

Ilse was making feeble movements towards her handbag on the bedside table. She gave a half-smile and closed her eyes as Sally picked it up and emptied out the contents. Folded neatly at the back of the purse was a receipt from a farmer for the hire of four acres known as Barn Field near Milebush, Marden.

'Thank God for Teutonic thoroughness,' exclaimed Tim. 'Even in her state she kept a record.'

The first police car arrived. The driver knew Marden. It was about twenty miles away.

They were doing seventy down the hill with Mickey still attaching the blue light to the Land Rover's roof.

'Tooled up?'

'Sorry, boss. Didn't think.'

'Nor did I. We'll work something out.'

Sally, being tossed around in the back, held herself upright long enough to tap Tim on the shoulder. He turned to see her offering a small automatic pistol.

'Why didn't you . . . ?' He stopped as Mickey let out a flood of oaths at a blind woman in an old Morris Minor who had pulled on to the road ahead of them. It was just one more question to ask that night.

Dr Aziz shook his head over Soraya's small still body. As he had foretold, the toxins had spread to her heart. Help had come too little, too late. In a hospital, he may have saved her. But here . . . Soraya would be buried at first light. Fatima and Leila wept uncontrollably, kneeling by her bedside, the darkened room heavy with myrrh and smouldering rosemary.

Dr Aziz felt uncomfortable about losing a patient and angry that he had not been called earlier. That oaf Al-Sayeed was responsible but he dared not criticize him, related as he was to the ruling clique.

He had grown fond of Soraya, fonder than a doctor

should be of a patient. Soraya had fought. How she had fought! Soraya's body contained the heart of a lion, but tragically her strength was that of a little girl.

'My sister. My sister,' wailed Leila, sobbing her little heart out.

Fatima tried to comfort her. 'God needed Soraya more than we did.'

The trite things we say to try to excuse death, thought Dr Aziz.

'No, he didn't. He never played with her. I did.'

Fatima pulled Leila to her and held her tight.

'I want to go home. Please Fatima, can we go home? I want to see my daddy. Please, Fatima.'

Fatima shed her own tears of helpless grief. And felt the guilt that the little girl she loved more than herself had died in her care.

'Soon, little one, soon. Be brave. Be brave for me and for daddy.'

It had taken Tari all his self-control not to speed, but he knew he must not draw attention to himself. Every minute expanded into an hour and with each minute his anger grew until he reached the field furious with himself for allowing sentimentality to overcome his operational judgement. He should have killed the pair of them as he had killed that drugged-up German bitch.

How had they found him? He should have interrogated them. If he'd made a mistake he needed to know. He untied the ropes which held down the aircraft's wings, unlocked the canopy and kicked off the brakes. Grasping the propeller, he hauled the ST150 out into the open. He parked the Mercedes in its place and piled bales of straw in front of it.

Tari was overcome by an immense desire to fly, to rise up from the problems and dramas of the ground, to be by himself up in the clear air – a huge and perfect hiding place. He transferred the NBC suit, hose and sprayer to the

398

cockpit. He was finally stowing the virus when he paused. A police siren wailed in the distance. There was no reason why it should be connected with him. As he stood listening, an irrational fear grasped him. Within seconds, with the instinct bred of years as a fugitive, Tari knew he must flee or be trapped.

He had to take off. He needed the plane to spray the Marburg over London. No time for pre-flight checks. He jumped into the left-hand seat, pushed the throttle in twice to prime the carburettor and set the mixture control. The engine turned, spluttered and died. Swearing, Tari enriched the mixture and tried again. As soon as he smelled petrol he knew he had flooded the carburettor. It would take a minute to drain.

The siren had stopped now. Perhaps, Tari tried to tell himself, it had not been connected with him. But he knew it was.

A Land Rover slewed around the track into the field and charged towards him. Tari turned the key again. The propeller turned once, there was an explosion of acrid smoke, Tari reamed back the throttle and thinned the mixture. The engine caught. No time for pre-flight checks. No time to let the engine warm up. No time for anything. The Land Rover was closing by the second. A short field take-off.

Tari increased the revs until the airframe juddered and shook. He released the brakes and put in a hefty boot full of rudder to keep the plane straight. The blustery wind meant he had to take off towards the Land Rover. He began rolling forward, gathering speed. He let down one-third flap. The distance was closing. He picked a mental point where he and the Land Rover would collide and let down full flap. It was going to be a close thing. It was up to the will of Allah.

'Get down, Sally.'

'Jesus. It's going to make a right mess of the car,' said Mickey, staring at the whirling propeller drawing nearer and nearer.

And of us, winced Sally.

Mickey's knuckles were white as he gripped the wheel. He had his foot to the floor, screaming along in third gear.

A collision was inevitable. At the last second, when they were less than ten yards apart, the aircraft went up like a lift.

There was an almighty crash, the screech of tearing metal and the windscreen frosted into a million stars. Mickey skidded blindly to a halt. They leapt out to see the plane lumbering into the sky, like a stricken bird dragging a damaged leg. The port undercarriage waved loosely in the wind and petrol was already spewing from the torn wing. Yawing drunkenly from side to side, the plane disappeared over the trees to the west.

The blow had ripped out their aerial so they could not get on the radio net. Mickey's mobile phone showed no reception. Swearing, he jogged off to the main road to flag down the first car.

In the barn Tim found the black Mercedes and in the corner, under a tarpaulin, a police car.

The plane was wallowing like a drunken hippo. She was constantly trying to spin to port. Tari needed both hands on the stick to keep her straight and level. The electronic gauges had ceased to work. He had only compass, altimeter and artificial horizon. Over his shoulder he could see petrol streaming from the fractured fuel line. He hoped the wing was not structurally damaged. If it was, it would fold in on itself and he would die. The ST150 was known as the Steel Umbrella for its strength and stability, but no one had tried to fly one with the undercarriage ripped off.

He was heading west – into the heart of the search area for the policeman. He gingerly turned south, watching the wing for telltale cracks. The Marburg was stowed securely behind his seat. Tari had no clear plan. He knew he had to buy himself time and distance and start afresh. He was flying around eight hundred feet between two minor roads. There were occasional villages, small woods and oast houses with roofs like nuns' cowls. Ahead a large reservoir grew on the horizon. The engine coughed and died. The propeller stopped in the vertical position. It was eerily quiet, the wind whistling around the broken struts. Tari switched fuel tanks, checked the pump was on and turned the key. The engine fired. He decided to land while he had power to make a controlled descent. He chose a large grass field on top of a lonely ridge.

The flaps refused to come down on the port wing. He was 100 feet up when the engine stopped again. Tari was committed now. He allowed a little starboard flap to help him keep the other wing off the ground as long as possible. He switched everything off to cut down risk of fire. The absence of flaps meant a long glide slope and a faster approach. He struck, bounced. Tari fought to hold the stick well back and to the right. He was rolling too quickly. Tari braced himself for the inevitable.

The port wing was dropping, dropping. Bang. Suddenly it hit the earth. The undercarriage collapsed. The plane slewed violently around, pitching Tari against his harness. Stillness.

He pushed back the canopy and smelled the petrol. He was out with the Marburg, running towards the nearby hedge. He stashed the virus and made himself return to the crippled aircraft. He was bending over the cockpit retrieving the rest of his equipment when an old blue van turned hesitantly into the field.

'The plane was totally destroyed by the fire. The investigation team believes there's a body in there, but they've been pulled back until the Porton Down people give the area the all clear,' reported Plumridge.

'So far my people have found no evidence of a biological agent, but we're still checking,' said Dotty Di.

'Is it possible the intense heat of the explosion destroyed the virus?' demanded Williams.

'Possible, dear heart,' Di conceded grudgingly. 'Possible but unlikely. We found a basic isolator cabinet at the Old Rectory which confirms our theory that the Marburg's held in a phial of blood serum. You'd think some of the virus would have got into the atmosphere in the initial explosion.'

'But you've not found any.' Williams rose to look out of the window at a small oil tanker beating its way up river.

'The blustery wind isn't helping. The agent could be quickly carried some distance and then when the wind falls, it'll linger and concentrate in one spot. We're expanding our search area all the time.'

'So Barbel just mixed a little of the serum with water and sprayed it along the road on Saturday night,' said Williams.

'Quite. The isolator cabinet is primitive. It'd give the Americans the vapours to see it, but I did warn against applying western standards to these things, didn't I, dear heart?'

'For the moment we have to assume Barbel is still alive.'

'Who else's body could it be in the aircraft?' demanded Plumridge.

'Who knows,' replied Williams shortly. 'But it's too tidy for my liking. I'll want a positive identity before we call off the hunt. Let's find out if there's anyone missing in the area.' He was surprised to see a red, white and green canal narrow boat surging downstream on the tide, a man in yellow oilskins at the tiller. He assumed the boat was heading for the Grand Union lock at Limehouse. 'We didn't find Barbel's passport or money at the Rectory, so we know he has cash and alternative identities. All ports and airports are on full alert. Police leave has been cancelled. It's clear that he intended to spray the virus from an aircraft.'

'Is that why he killed the policeman?' asked Mickey.

'It appears that he blundered on to the airstrip. He was shot twice in the back and finished off with a close-range shot to the head.' Williams stole a glance at Sally. She was wooden-faced. 'Flying clubs and private aircraft owners are being ordered to immobilize their planes. We're posting armed guards at every airfield.'

'Barbel would have been ours if someone hadn't blundered into his hideout unarmed. Stupid half-baked thing to have done,' carped Plumridge.

'Most of us are grateful for Tim for finding him,' pointed out Williams.

'Yeh, right,' muttered Mickey. If looks could kill Plumridge would be half a pound of minced beef on a butcher's slab.

Tim stared at the carpet. When he risked a glance up towards Sally he was rewarded by an encouraging smile. She had spent twenty minutes closeted with Williams as soon as they'd returned. Tim had no idea what she had told him about her ex-husband, but nothing was ever what it seemed in this hall of mirrors and the fact that she was still here must mean that all was well.

'What do you feel, Sally?' asked Williams, abruptly. Time for her to show her colours in public. 'Is that Barbel in the wreckage?'

'I feel he's alive,' she replied in a small voice.

'So do I. He's out there somewhere with a small freezer which needs to be plugged into the mains and a test tube of the most dangerous virus in the world. Where will he hide? Where will he run? Does the German woman know anything?'

'She's not properly conscious or cogent,' replied Plumridge. 'She was impersonating her elder sister who's genuinely in Britain house-hunting. She's one of those committed middle-class revolutionaries following in the steps of Baader Meinhof. BND reckon she was recruited by the Palestinians and left to sleep for years. They're reopening old files to see how many more like her there are out there.'

There was a sharp tap at the door and Commander Penn hurried in. 'Sorry for being late, but I was trying to put together the latest on the UNSCOM guys.'

'Eight UN inspectors took off in the early hours to try to verify a secret location for those biological warheads Commander Penn briefed us on,' explained Williams, standing in front of the window.

'They managed to get out a short Satcomm message giving their position and what they were after. They were drilling into a concrete cap when the phone went dead,' reported Penn. 'There are unconfirmed reports that they've been murdered. It doesn't look good.'

'Even Saddam couldn't murder eight UN personnel,' cried Dotty Di in horror.

'Signal traffic between the area and Baghdad has gone potty,' said Penn grimly. 'There was a garbled report that they were executed on the spot by the Republican Guards who had followed them. The Americans have gone on full alert.'

'This time they will not stop until Saddam's been overthrown,' forecast Williams. 'If the UN men have been killed, it'll reunite the anti-Saddam coalition behind the United Nations flag. There are already accounts of riots in the north, in Mosul and Kirkuk, and unconfirmed reports that units of the Republican Guard were fired on in Sinjar, near the Syrian border. It's coming to a head.'

'All the more reason to have apprehended Barbel,' sniffed Plumridge.

The phone rang. Williams listened and his face creased in sadness. When he replaced the receiver he said sombrely, 'Jason Whittle died twenty minutes ago. His parents and his brother are in intensive care. They are not expected to live. There are now twenty-two confirmed and another ten suspected cases. Coppetts Wood's at full stretch. God knows what'll happen if there's an all-out attack.'

'What about precautions? What's being done to inoculate people like ourselves against this thing?' demanded Plumridge.

He's become more pompous since the Alison affair, thought Williams. Perhaps it was his way of coping in the face of disapproval, but it made him even more insufferable. Mickey especially was looking at him as if he was a dog turd. But Mickey had a young wife and child – living right in the line of likely fall-out. Williams made a mental note to tell Mickey to move them out of London immediately. He realized with a start he must tell Bethan to do the same.

'During the Gulf War build-up we worked twenty-four hours a day for weeks preparing anthrax and plague vaccines for just fifty thousand troops. It would take years to supply the population of London.' Diana decided to come clean. 'We've started producing a vaccine against Marburg U for troops and emergency workers. That's all we can do.'

'Can't this be mass produced?' inquired Williams.

'Only if we involve commercial chemical companies in a large way and at the moment our political masters aren't willing to do that.'

'The civilian population is on its own,' summed up Commander Penn.

'I'm afraid so,' admitted Diana. 'We've prepared advice, of course. Stay off the streets. Stay at home or in your workplace. Wear a mask if possible. Mere bromides, I'm sorry to say.'

Sally broke the silence. 'But that's terrible.'

'Soraya's sparkling,' cried Fatima. *'I can't believe the change in her. She's come back from the dead.'*

Tari, sitting in the old blue van, blinked in relief as he heard the voices of his daughters, chattering like jackdaws and occasionally bursting into snatches of song which ended in giggles and laughter. His resentment that they were being held hostage to his deeds grew daily. When he'd made the agreement with the Iraqis, there had been no mention of his daughters. The sooner he finished this operation and got them out of that stinking country the better.

'*How do you feel, Soraya?*' asked the narrator. Tari rotated the short wave radio to improve the signal.

'*Fine, thank you,*' she piped up.

'*You are feeling better?*'

'*Yes, thank you.*' A pause. '*Can I go and play?*'

'*Of course. Leila, are you happy your sister's recovered from her illness?*'

'*Oh yes, it's much more fun with her to play with. But she wasn't ill long . . .*'

It seemed to Tari listening intently that Leila had been going to say something else.

'*Time rushes past when you are a child,*' continued the narrator. '*Dr Aziz, you are satisfied?*'

'*Soraya has made a full recovery. But without the antibiotics she would have died.*'

Tari winced.

The narrator again. '*Soraya owes her life to the glorious Ba'ath party and our heroic leader . . .*'

Tari mentally switched off from the repetitious paean of praise. The musty loose straw in the back of the van tickled his throat but he could not help smiling. His girls were safe. The sun was beginning to sink towards the western skyline. From his vantage point outside Greenwich Observatory London spread out before him. He knew all the tall buildings in the capital. Opposite was the blunt needle of Canary Wharf, to his left along the Thames, St Paul's Cathedral loomed over Tower Bridge. The NatWest building soared above the City and further away he made out the Telecom Tower in the West End.

The patriotic drivel ended and he began listening again. A new voice he had not heard before said, '*Tomorrow Soraya will go and see her new friend Dagon . . .*'

Tari stiffened. Something expanded to fill his very being

and then contracted leaving him hollow and empty. He felt very calm. It had been a long road, but at last he was near its end. They had found his base and his aircraft, but he had the virus and a safe house to fall back on. He'd find another way of spraying the Marburg over this city and her people. He'd got rid of that liability of a German cow, the nosey copper and the farm labourer. Now there was just him and the virus. Him and his daughters Soraya and Leila against the world. He set off for north London.

The direct line to GCHQ rang softly in the corner. Bill Jones murmured his apologies and answered it. He began writing immediately.

'We're deploying BRACIS to give us some warning,' mumbled Diana apologetically, the ebullience drained out of her.

The lower jaw of the body in the burned aircraft had survived intact. The dental work was British. Police were now checking for missing persons in the area.

Barbel was alive.

'BRACIS?' echoed Williams.

There was a cold chill settling over the room. It had been easy to discuss the possibility of a biological attack on London and wryly despair at Diana's mad enthusiasms, but now the theoretical was about to happen it wasn't exciting any more. It was bloody terrifying.

'Biological, radiological and chemical information system,' explained Diana. 'It's a portable computer which predicts the path of the virus and where it'll form its heaviest concentrations. In the Gulf War it was estimated that an anthrax warhead on a Scud would reduce the effectiveness of forces downwind by ninety per cent if they had no warning but only twenty per cent if they knew it was coming. In our case it'll give us time to evacuate certain personages.'

'You mean people,' said Tim.

'No, sorry, old thing. We wouldn't even try to evacuate

the population of London. They'd block the roads, panic and cause absolute chaos. In fact troops will be brought in to make sure the civilian population stays in place and to handle riot control. Personages means senior politicians, vital civil servants, royalty, of course.'

'Of course,' growled Mickey.

'Do we get to know where the danger areas are?' insisted Plumridge.

Williams knew the answer, but he was not going to put Plumridge out of his misery. Let the worm squirm. In fact Di did the job for him.

'You will if I'm with you, dear,' she chuckled.

'And if you're not?'

'I don't know if you're on the list, do I?' She gave Plumridge a sickly grin.

'This is preposterous.' Plumridge was growing red in the face. 'As a member of the Security Service I expect . . .'

'Courtesy of Mickey.' Williams cut short the outburst. He produced a box from under the table. 'Respirators, Special Forces for the use of.'

'You can even drink with one on,' said Mickey. 'I'll talk you through them later. Get one thing in your heads. The key to survival lies in speed. In the event of an attack you have just nine seconds to get your mask on. Be in time, mask in nine.'

Sally turned the rubber mask over in her hands and felt panic rising. She didn't think she'd be able to cope with putting one on. Her claustrophobia would not let her.

The red phone made them start. 'Priority one for Mr Plumridge,' announced Maisie.

Plumridge, bloated with importance, took the receiver. As he listened the colour drained out of his face. Sally feared the worst. This was it. We're all going to die. Instinctively she wanted to reach out to Tim. She wanted to touch him, more than she had ever wanted anything in her life. To touch him and hold him. To be one with him – before it was all too late.

Plumridge was trying to speak. 'Please don't . . . I can't
. . . don't be hasty . . . I can explain . . . with you now! . . .
I . . . Felicity . . . I –'

He slowly replaced the receiver and stared at the wall.

'Everything all right, old boy?' enquired Commander
Penn.

'Felicity says she never ever wants to see me again,'
Plumridge said in a strangled tone. 'She's talking to a
solicitor within the hour.'

'Hard luck, old boy. If you're pressed you can stay at my
club,' volunteered Commander Penn. Sally didn't know
whether to laugh or cry.

Bill Jones came off the phone scrutinizing his notes.

'There's been another Soraya broadcast. She's completely well, but there's a reference to a new character
called Dagon. Soraya's going to play with him tomorrow.
Apparently it's the name of an ancient God.'

'Dagon was the god of the Philistines.' Commander Penn
was sitting bolt upright. He began quoting, '*Then the lords of
the Philistines gathered them together for to offer a great sacrifice
unto Dagon their god, and to rejoice: for they said, Our god hath
delivered Samson our enemy into our hand.*'

In the silence which followed Tim felt ice form over
his heart.

'The Philistine lords were worshipping Dagon when
Samson brought down the temple.'

They leant on the cold stone parapet, side by side, close but
not touching, and looked out over the black waters of the
Thames at the string of lights along the Embankment. Sally
was confused and afraid. She was at the centre of a massive
drama, but for the moment she cared only for Tim. She felt
they were in a tiny rowing boat, just the two of them, being
tossed about on mountainous green seas. The boat was out
of control. They had only themselves and each other and
they should cling to each other.

She knew that against all her intentions she had fallen

in love with Tim – and that's where it became difficult. She wished to assuage his anger, to explain her motives; but her need to tell the truth, knowing the hurt it would bring, fought against the easier option of little white lies and omissions. Sally did not know whether to risk all, tell Tim everything and chance losing him, or tell him just enough to be satisfied and risk him finding out later – when he would feel infinitely more cheated.

They turned towards each other at the same time, as if hearing an unspoken signal. The overhead lights gave Tim hollow eyes and sharp cheekbones. She wanted to kiss his parted lips.

'I owe you an explanation,' Sally faltered.

Tim put his arms around her waist. She draped hers over his shoulders. They smiled precariously at each other.

'No, you don't.'

'I do.' Don't stop me now. I've almost decided to come clean, almost clean.

'Sally, what you did before we met is nothing to do with me.'

He kissed the tip of her broken nose.

'I want you to listen.' She gave a little frown. 'I want to tell you.'

'Why?'

'Because if we're . . . if we're going to . . .' She wanted to say, if we make a go of it, then you need to know about me.

'If we're going to what?'

'Don't tease me.' Sally put on a show of petulance. 'You wouldn't want to live with someone with a beard until you knew what they looked like clean shaven, would you?'

'But I'm not going to live with someone with a beard. I want to live with you.'

'Fool. You know what I mean.' She felt a breeze on her cheek. The wind getting up from the west.

'Sally. I love you.' God! He had said it! Those words.

'Good. But . . .'

'No. Not a word. I don't want to know about where you come from, what you did, your husband, anything. Let's start now, eh? Wipe the slate clean.'

She regarded him for what seemed an eternity. He was conscious she had not responded to his declaration of love.

'Oh.' She tried hard to keep the smile off her face. 'But you said in the cellar you had so many questions.'

'I was wrong. Sally, now's not the time. If . . .' Tim hesitated, wondering what to call her ex-husband. His code name seemed the most impersonal. 'If Barbel lets off the Marburg, God only knows what'll happen. Let's get this over first. Okay?'

She nodded, eyes cast down.

'Yes. But you do love me?' She said it in such a pathetic little voice that Tim placed a hand under her chin and lifted her face so their eyes met.

'Very very much, if you want me to.'

'Oh, yes,' she whispered. 'I want you to.'

'Where now?'

'Home?'

'Whose?'

'What have you got to eat?'

Tim considered. 'Corned beef and brown sauce.'

'Come home with me.'

Her flat in Highgate was warm, soft, comfortable with a welcoming air – all qualities Tim's garret lacked. Sally slid open the glass door and they stood on the sixth-floor balcony and held hands, looking out across the lights of London.

'What an incredible view!' Tim was enthralled. He had not realized London was in a basin until he looked down and across to the gently swelling heights across the river. And between there were millions of people – but you couldn't see a single one.

'I think it's nicer at night. You can see only the lights, so you make up the rest yourself.'

Sally opened the fridge and giggled. It was empty apart from two bottles of wine and a jar of olives.

'Microwave pizza all right?'

'Fine, but we could go out to eat.'

'If you want,' said Sally. 'But I thought you'd like to see the rest of the flat.'

'Is there much more?' Tim was puzzled.

'Well, there's the bedroom.'

The blue van drove slowly past the darkened house and Linnikov nudged the man standing next to him. The same van or an identical one had cruised down the quiet residential street only a few minutes ago. The curtains twitched in a third-floor bedroom window opposite.

'Get away from the window, you arsehole,' Linnikov barked into the two-way radio. 'I'll tell you when.'

When the Palestinian had demanded a safe house, Linnikov had provided one in north London which the group had bought in money laundering operations. The house opposite had fallen vacant at the same time and they had bought that too. From the point of view of an ambush it was perfect. Once Tari closed the door of the safe house behind him he was caught like a rat in a trap. Two men were already hiding upstairs and another in the shed in the back garden. Linnikov and three others were concealed across the road. They merely had to be patient.

Five minutes later the same van crawled back up the road as if someone was searching for a house number. The Palestinian was being very careful and very suspicious. Linnikov swore as a police car, blue light flashing, sped past. Softly, softly. All the Palestinian had to do was put his head in the trap and they would cut it off.

Tari pulled over to allow the police car to pass. Everything seemed in order. The curtains in the first-floor bedroom were drawn on the left side to show the house had been checked and it was safe for him to enter. Once a week someone put a long-life milk in the fridge and made sure there was a store of tinned and frozen food.

He had made the mistake of driving through the City on the way from south London. He'd seen the CCTVs on each corner monitoring traffic and cursed his carelessness. The van was safe for the moment, but then he had believed the Rectory was safe. And how had they found the aircraft so quickly? He didn't know and it worried him. Maybe the German had given herself away, but she did not know about the safe house. No one knew except the Russians.

He needed to get off the streets, to lie up while he took stock and worked out how to deliver the Marburg.

Tari parked a few doors away from the house and picked up his soft bag. In his pocket he carried two passports, £5,000 in sterling and another £5,000 in Deutschmarks. But the bag was more precious. It contained the flask with the phial of Marburg, a respirator and one or two small pieces of equipment. He left everything else in the van to collect when he knew all was well. The virus never left him. The lights were on in the houses on either side. He could smell onions frying. Tari remembered he had not eaten since breakfast.

'Stand by. Stand by. He is approaching the house.' Linnikov caught himself whispering.

'I have a clear shot,' reported the sniper in the bedroom above him.

'No,' snapped Linnikov. 'Do not fire in the direction of the container. Take it off him first and then kill him. How many more times must I tell you?'

Tari hesitated for a split second at the garden gate before striding confidently up to the front door, key in his right hand. It turned easily. He closed the door behind him and stood in a long gloomy hall. The house had a dusty feeling of disuse and a hushed stillness which made him want to walk on tiptoe. For a moment he experienced a wonderful sense of elation that he was safe; off the streets and away from watchful eyes.

But ... but ... something was not right. His senses tingled. He was aware of the lingering smell of cigarette smoke. The other smells were old and musty but this was new and pungent. Someone had been smoking recently. It could have been the person who serviced the house. It did not necessarily signify trouble. But ...

He took two paces into the hall. Upstairs a floorboard creaked. The old house settling? Or someone moving stealthily?

Tari turned his head to listen. Out of the corner of his eye he could see through the clear glass fanlight above the door to the upstairs window of the house opposite. The sash was open – unusual in this weather. There was a solid shadow behind the window. A dull gleam caught the street light. The barrel of a rifle.

Tari stood stock still and pulled out his pistol. At the end of the hall was a door, the top half in coloured glass. He guessed this led to the kitchen and through to the garden. There was another creak above his head.

Someone was coming down the stairs.

It was darker in the kitchen. He made out a table in the middle, an old-fashioned square sink under the window and, next to it, the garden door.

A shape sprang at him. Tari dodged behind the table and fired. The explosion was deafening in the enclosed space. The man crumpled to the floor. In his ringing ears, Tari heard the heavy thump of someone leaping down the stairs. The front door crashed open. There were hoarse shouts. Russians. Tari dashed across the kitchen, holding the bag up high so it did not knock against the furniture. He was two paces from the door when it flew open. Someone behind him switched on a powerful torch. In its beam Tari could see the crinkles in the other man's leather jacket. They fired at the same time.

The man reeled away, blood spurting from his throat. Tari grunted as a red hot poker seared into his left shoulder. He gritted his teeth and fought to prevent himself dropping the bag. With his gun hand, he grasped the screaming man, reeling like a drunk, and hurled him back into the kitchen. The window exploded into a thousand shards.

'Niet. Niet.'

Tari slammed the door, turned the key and threw it away. He ran across the garden, hearing the door creak and splinter, tensing for the inevitable blow as the bullets struck into his back. There was an apple tree in the middle of a small lawn, a shed, some shrubs and a low, battered wooden fence. It occurred to Tari they were not firing at him. They must be worried about hitting the Marburg virus. He clambered over the fence into another garden and stopped to fire back at the shapes on the lawn. A dog began barking. Tari reeled down a drive, his feet crunching on the gravel. A side door opened and a woman's voice called, 'Who's there?'

She caught sight of Tari and screamed. Across the road a narrow footpath climbed uphill between two houses. He followed it, slicing diagonally through the neat estate. He heard the siren of a police car and then another. A quarter of a mile away, the path opened out into a small green with a bench under a thick gnarled oak.

Tari sank down out of breath. Bastard Russians. His safe house had been a death trap. There was an Arab saying, Never trust a Russian – especially when he smiles. Bastards.

Tari found his eyes closing and he made himself rise unsteadily to his feet. His shoulder throbbed and an almighty tiredness drew him down. His options were diminishing all the time. He would have to abandon the freezer and the sprayer in the van. But he still had the Marburg. And he had money and passports. He was not finished yet. He would act swiftly and then fly the country. He would not commit suicide. He had no fear of death; he admired the suicide bombers – but he had his daughters to live for.

His head swam and his left shoulder was stiffening. He

could still flex his fingers so it was probably only a flesh wound, but it would take its toll if it was not treated. He made himself concentrate.

Could he steal a plane? Not easily. He would have to steal a car to get to an airport. And airports would certainly be guarded.

If he sprayed it from a car? How far would he get before he was spotted and gunned down like a mad dog? He had to survive to bring his hostage children out of Iraq.

If he sprayed it on the underground he would need to wear the respirator. Instantly noticeable. On top of a bus? The river?

He could see the lights of the office towers of the City in the distance. Could he get to the top of one of those?

His body felt heavy, so heavy. It would be the easiest thing in the world to sit down again. He pushed himself upright with his good arm. Willpower. Strength.

Tari felt blood trickling down his arm and over his wrist. He needed to clean himself up and get off the streets before the manhunt proper began. His luck was running out. It had turned sour after he had been soft with Salilah. He believed fortune favoured the bold, not the weak. You worked for your luck, grasped it, wrestled it and then hoarded it – not squandered it in quixotic gestures. Since he had spared Salilah every man's hand had turned against him.

Salilah. Of course. She lived near here. In that flat on top of the hill. He'd seen her road on the same page of the *A–Z* as he had navigated his way up here. He mentally pictured the map. Her road was in the top left-hand corner. He needed to head north-west. His knowledge of London was scant, but he made out faint stars. He glimpsed Ursa Major, drew a line from the last two stars and found Polaris. The Pole Star. Always in the north. He set off to tack in her direction. If he missed he knew he would come to the main road. After that it would be easy.

The wind was in his face. It was coming from the

416

north-west. It would carry the spray from the hill over huge swathes of London. Not as good as if he'd flown but . . .

A cacophony of sirens was converging from all directions. He would hide up at Salilah's until dawn, whether she was there or not. He'd dress his wound and rest. If the man was with her Tari would kill him – and regain his luck. In the morning, in what they called rush hour, he would mix the Marburg and spray it from the topmost window so the mist would blow gently over teeming London.

Thursday 9 April

Tim's phone rang at two minutes past midnight. For a moment he lay in the darkness wondering where he was, then Sally sleepily murmured, 'Answer the bloody thing.'

It took him a while to find the light and locate the phone in the pocket of his jacket on the floor by the curtains. Sally sat up in bed and giggled at the sight of Tim, standing naked with a mobile phone to his ear.

'On my way.'

Sally whimpered. 'You're leaving me.'

'It's Williams. There's been a shooting incident involving Russians. Not far from here.'

'Do you want me to come with you?' she asked as Tim began to dress.

'Wouldn't that be rather a giveaway?'

Sally gave a dirty laugh. 'I hadn't thought of that. Lots of Russians from the embassy live in Highgate. It's a sort of diplomatic ghetto.'

'Williams thinks these are connected with Linnikov.' Half a mile away he could see faintly pulsing blue lights.

'I'll give you my key. I must get another cut. Where's my handbag?' With a sigh Sally climbed out of bed. 'You can take my car or there's loads of taxis. It's civilized up here.'

'What d'you mean, civilized? You don't get dead Russians in Battersea.'

'Only because they can't find the place.' Sally fumbled in her handbag. There was her gun, but no house keys. 'You'll have to take a taxi. I don't know where my keys are. It's your fault for sweeping me off my feet. I don't know whether I'm coming or going.'

'Coming in your case.'

Again Sally gave her dirty laugh.

'Press the buzzer on the main door when you get back and I'll let you in from here.'

The police had cordoned off the street with white tape. A small cluster of TV cameramen and late-night reporters gathered around a Scotland Yard duty press officer. Williams took Tim's arm and led him to one side.

'One dead and one seriously injured. Both KGB hoods briefed by Linnikov on Tuesday. I'm assuming this was part of the special operation. It might involve Barbel.'

'It went pear-shaped,' observed Tim.

'Quite. First reports suggest there was a shot inside the house and then three or four men ran across the road from the house opposite. Both houses have been unoccupied for some time. There were further shots. A man escaped over the back fence. We know he was wounded because there's a trail of blood. Every hospital in the country's been alerted.'

'Did the Russians fall out among themselves?' suggested Tim. 'You said the KGB London chief was none too happy about having his men taken away.'

'It's possible,' conceded Williams. 'We don't know whether these goons were working for the KGB or moonlighting for the Mafiya. I had a brief word with Storozhov who claims the shooting was news to him. I think I believe him but I had the distinct impression that he was quietly delighted. Linnikov has gone off radar.' They moved aside to allow local residents to identify their parked cars. No one was claiming a battered blue van. 'As a precaution we've turned out Di and one of her BRACIS teams. She's loving it. She's like a vastly overgrown girl guide.'

'Is there any news about the UNSCOM men?'

'No.' Williams rubbed the side of his face with his hand in a gesture of tiredness. 'It looks as if they have been killed. The Americans are beginning bombing operations

419

tomorrow night. Privately they are canvassing support for an all-out attack. They will not stop until Saddam's dead.'

Police officers were taking an interest in the van. One opened the back with a set of keys and held out what appeared to be a shiny pair of overalls.

'Put it back,' shouted Tim. 'Get away.'

The startled policeman did what he was told.

'It's an NBC suit, sir,' Tim told Williams. 'This must be Barbel's van.'

'Find its owner and you've found the identity of the body in the plane,' said Williams.

The street was evacuated and the tapes moved back around the corner. When they were sure no one could see up the road, a spaceman emerged from one of the houses and waddled towards the van. Tim started fidgeting. As the scientist reached the van doors, Tim could contain himself no longer.

'I hope you don't mind me saying this, sir.'

'What?' Williams could not take his eyes off the van, lit by brilliant halogen lamps.

'We're standing downwind.'

'Ah, yes. Good point. Good point.'

Williams strolled around the other side of the van, accompanied by Tim. The spaceman opened both back doors wide and then did the same with the driver and passenger doors. He inspected the back and behind the seats. Finally he disappeared inside the van. He emerged to wave his hands in a scrub out sign.

'Too much to hope, I suppose,' sighed Williams. 'The question is: Who's got the Marburg? The Russians or Barbel?'

Forensic officers began erecting a tent over the van as the officer in charge approached them.

'It's a little puzzling, sir. We've found a sizeable stock of frozen and canned food at the scene of the crime.'

'Has any been eaten? Any empty packets or tins?' Williams perked up.

'No, sir. Nothing's been touched. There's a pile of cigarette butts upstairs suggesting at least two people spent some time there,' replied the detective. 'From the left-overs and wrappers in the house opposite it looks as if someone's been camping out. Why consume food in one house and not the other?'

'Thank you.' Williams waited until the detective had walked away. 'There's no mystery, Tim. The special operation was to ambush Barbel at his safe house. It looks as if Barbel escaped although he's wounded.'

Plumridge arrived, bleary-eyed and smelling of sour whisky, and went into conference with Special Branch senior officers.

'You are armed, aren't you, Tim?'

'Yes, sir. Both Mickey and I drew firearms.'

Tim's phone rang.

'Hello.' He stiffened. 'Yes . . . He's here alongside me . . . I'll pass you over.' Tim cleared his throat. 'Mr Storozhov, sir.'

'Nikita . . . Sorry, must be switched off.'

Tim discreetly walked a few paces to be out of earshot, still trying to get over the shock of the head of the KGB in London calling him on his mobile phone – and addressing him by name.

'I'll never get used to these damn things,' said Williams, handing Tim back his phone. 'It was an official operation to regain the Marburg and they failed. Barbel's on the run. He's friendless; he's running out of hiding places and he's running out of options. But he's still got the virus.'

'How did Storozhov know my number?'

'Ah, Tim.' Williams put his hand on Tim's arm. 'You've lots to learn.'

'Coooeee. Coooeee.' Down the street four policemen appeared to be wrestling with a flapping black tent. 'Tell these heathens to let go or, so help me, I'll bite one of them.'

Williams waved to let a dishevelled Diana through and

brought her up to date with developments. 'Any forecast from BRACIS?'

'From the top of one of those blocks up on that rise and with this breeze, allowing for population density over the next mile and then reducing the toxic effect geometrically, we estimate somewhere between ten and twenty.'

Tim breathed a sigh of relief.

'Thousands.' Williams was sure Di had done that deliberately. 'It's two miles to Camden Town and another mile to Kings Cross and Euston. If it reaches that far, double it. The figure will also be substantially higher if the wind backs, as it's forecast, because the virus will cover a whole swathe of more densely populated areas around Stoke Newington and Dalston.'

'Twenty thousand people,' whispered Williams.

'Those are guaranteed fatalities. Add a factor of four for the infected who may or may not survive. Say, one hundred thousand as a very conservative round figure.'

'One hundred thousand.'

'Oh, yes. Absolutely.'

Williams aged before Tim's eyes. A wave of exhaustion pulled his face down into a long mask of hopeless defeat.

'Walk, Tim,' he commanded. 'Give me your arm.'

'Will you tell Downing Street, sir?'

'I'll have to. Our masters are burning the midnight oil trying to thrash out the Irish agreement. Apparently the PM likes the idea of calling it the Good Friday Agreement. I just hope this Good Friday is not remembered for a different reason.' Williams sighed. 'Isn't Gehenna a beautiful word? Elegant and cool. It was the valley of Hinnom, near Jerusalem where the Israelites sacrificed their children to Moloch. Later they burned the rubbish of the city there. A place of torment.'

'Um, yes, sir.' Oh, Christ, the old boy's cracked.

The weight of one hundred thousand lives would crack anyone.

'Did you know Calvary and Golgotha both mean the

422

place of the skull? Don't they sound different? Calvary, Calvary. Clean and noble from the Latin *calvaria*. Golgotha from the bottom of the mouth and the back of the throat. *Gulgôleth* in Hebrew. The site of the crucifixion.'

'Yes, sir. Shall I . . .' What a bloody time for Williams to start barking.

'Barbel can't be far, can he? Is he going to run or press the button? He's been given the go signal, he has to press the button.' Williams was discussing the case as if he had never digressed. Perhaps he didn't know he had. They turned and slowly strolled back, still arm in arm.

'Where did you set up your gear, Di?' asked Williams.

'On that hill behind us. It's one of the highest points in London. Perfect setting if you have to be stationary.'

'Sally lives up there,' blurted out Tim.

'I wondered how you arrived so quickly,' smiled Williams. Then the implications cut in. 'Get her away from there. Mickey's on his way with the respirators, but get Sally away.'

'Coming.' Sally leapt out of bed as the buzzer sounded. She had been sleeping lightly, worrying that she wouldn't hear Tim when he returned. Slipping on a tee shirt she ran to the entryphone in the hall. She spoke into the grille and pressed the button to open the street door at the same time. 'It's open.'

Sally took her time in the bathroom. She cleaned her teeth and sluiced water over her face and body to freshen up. She didn't intend to go back to sleep straight away. She walked into the living room.

Tari stood there.

He had taken off his jacket and was examining his shirt soaked with blood over his left shoulder and down his left arm. At his feet was a holdall like a plumber's bag.

'You.'

Her eyes flicked to the door.

'It's locked,' he said. 'Don't run away. I need you.'

His eyes were boring into her. The eyes of her hero, her leader, her husband.

'No.' Sally wrenched herself away from their magnetic hold. 'No.'

'I'm wounded. Help me.'

Despite herself she went to his aid, unbuttoning his shirt and gently easing it over his damaged shoulder. She remembered his body well. Thin and hard, flat planes and taut sinews. He had not changed.

'I will tend your wound.' It was strange how easily she slipped into Arabic. 'But I must stop you killing.'

She led him into the bathroom and with her own face flannel wiped away his blood from his chest and arm. There was an exit hole under his scapula. It was a clean wound, but he had lost a lot of blood and he was in shock.

Only his willpower held him together. Only his fanaticism carried him forward. Sally dabbed around the wound with cotton wool soaked in TCP, watching his face as it stung and smarted. His cheek muscles contracted once but he did not move his arm an inch.

He ignored her words. His face was grey, as though someone had rubbed wood ash into his skin. Only his eyes burned alive.

'Do you hear me? I will help you escape but you must leave that terrible virus here. What you are doing will not help our people. You will kill innocent children. What good will that do? How will that regain the land?'

'You are not part of the struggle,' he replied coldly. 'I have a task.'

'No.'

'They have my children, my daughters.' Tari spoke robotically, staring into the distance. His lack of contact with his immediate surroundings unnerved Sally. 'The Zionists killed their mother. They mistook her for me. They killed her and they took you.'

'It wasn't like that,' protested Sally. Maybe it was, but now I look back and it's all so different. How can I tell him

424

that I despised him for killing the old man. And I despised myself more for allowing him to use me. It was right to stop. But he wants to kill again and he wants me to help him. I cannot. I will not. No sane person would do this.

And, chillingly, she glimpsed the truth: he had slipped over the rim of fanaticism into pale-eyed lunacy, sliding beyond passion, where belief rested upon reason, into a world of absolutism.

'You're mad,' she whispered. If he heard her he made no sign.

Sally bandaged the wound as best she could. As he put on his blood-soaked shirt, she tried one last time.

'Please go, Mahmoud,' she said, addressing him by his name from the camps. Mahmoud. Mahmoud the Martyr. 'Take my car, but leave the Marburg here. For your salvation.'

He gave her a queer look; one of wonder at her temerity in questioning the integrity of his soul mingled with one of pity, though whether for himself or for her she could not say.

The buzzer sounded. It woke him from his living sleep to glare accusingly at Sally.

'Of course. You are expecting someone. That's why you let me in. Get rid of them.'

'I can't. He's expecting to come in.'

'Still playing the whore, Salilah.'

She stepped forward and slapped his face.

He refused to touch his stinging cheek. 'Don't answer.'

'He'll see the light.'

A spasm of anger ricocheted across his face.

'Who is he to call so late?'

'A friend. He was here earlier but he had to go out.'

The buzzer sounded again. Tari suddenly guessed. 'It is the man from the security forces. You pleaded for his life.'

'I offered you a life for a life. I would have shot you had you refused.'

425

Tari decided. He reached in his jacket for his gun. 'Tell him to come up.'

'No.'

'Tell him.'

He grasped her arm, but Sally broke loose and ran into the bedroom. She snatched up her handbag and turned. Tari followed her in. He swept the bag from her hand and the small gun clattered across the pine floorboards. He picked it up.

Silly girl, thought Tim. She's fallen asleep. I knew she would. He buzzed again and wondered if there was a way he could break in. The street door was opened by an electronic signal to withdraw a bolt. You needed a special gadget set at the correct frequency and then it was easy. Mickey might have one in his bag of tricks. Tim wished he had not sent away the police driver. He could have nipped back to the scene to see if Mickey had arrived.

Tim walked back on to the street and looked up at the lights on in a top-floor flat. He was sure it was Sally's. If the lights were on, why didn't she answer? He returned to the door. He was about to try the buzzer one more time when he saw the dark splash on the path. There was another beneath the entryphone. Tim knelt and touched the blot with the tip of his index finger.

Blood. Fresh blood.

'He's gone,' said Sally when the buzzer had been silent for more than a minute. 'He knows you are here. Your only hope is to leave now, instantly. Save yourself.'

The thinnest crack of uncertainty opened in his face. She saw the idea was beginning to appeal.

'You've done your best. No one could have done more. Think of your daughters.'

For a moment hope flickered behind his determined scowl. A longing, a liberation, freedom from the burden,

426

the weight of the temple lifting off him. Almost. Almost. But Tari was too committed. Whatever the outcome he could not allow himself to turn away so close to the end of the operation.

Perhaps he was too stubborn, fixed and lacking the imagination to change. Perhaps he had slipped over the edge into madness, as Sally divined. Perhaps it was pride, a desire to join his brothers who had died gloriously for their cause; each one a Samson causing more deaths by their own end than they had taken lives in life.

Ignoring Sally, he transferred the gun to his left hand, picked up his bag and walked over to the balcony. Tari slid open the door and stepped out, nodding in a satisfied way at London spread beneath him. He looked around and saw, tucked in the corner of the balcony next to the potted plants, a green plastic watering can. He carried the watering can and the bag into the kitchen and allowed himself a smile of triumph.

He knew he had to act now. He could not afford to wait until morning. He would vaporize gallons of the virus and let the wind do the rest. He could spray more than he could have from the air. The sheer volume would make up for being in one place. From the bag he pulled out a curled length of tubing and a plastic head designed to fit on the spout of a watering can. Water from the tap ran through the hose to the spray head while a thin tube sucked up small amounts of concentrated liquid from the reservoir in the can. It was absolutely perfect.

Sally, tears streaming down her face, watched from the doorway.

'Please go,' she pleaded. 'Go while you can.'

'No,' he replied. 'It is you who should go. Travel north. This is my parting gift to you.'

'I am staying,' she sobbed.

'If you interfere, I shall kill you. You understand.'

They were like sparring partners, shadow boxers. He could not ignore her presence. Nor did he trust her, but to tie her up would be an admission that he was not in control. So he let her stand by helplessly.

The telephone rang on the wall. Sally snatched it up.

'Sally. It's me.' Tim spoke rapidly. 'Is he in there?'

'Yes.'

'Near you?'

'Yes.'

'I'm two floors below. Keep him away from the balcony.'

Tari ripped out the phone wire.

'Who is it?' he demanded.

'You are surrounded,' lied Sally, defiantly. 'Surrender before they kill you.'

Tari continued as if he had not heard. From the bag he produced gloves and a respirator. Finally he brought out a silver metal flask like a cocktail shaker. Sally's heart missed a beat.

'Go, Salilah. Go while you still live.'

Growing inside Tari was the chilled realization that he would not live through the night; that he would never see his daughters again. So be it. It was as though a page turned inside him and in an instant he became reconciled to the idea. The nobility of his sacrifice strengthened him. Again he would become Mahmoud. Mahmoud the Martyr.

Tim clung to the drainpipe. It was four feet to the corner of Sally's balcony and sixty feet to the ground. Now or never. He pushed away from the pipe, heard it crack and flung himself across the void. One hand brushed a metal railing, missed, slid down and finally closed over it. The base of the balcony jarred his wrist. A red hot pain shot up his arm. Still he clung on, his body revolving slowly from the one precarious hold. Then he stretched up to the rim and held on by the tips of his fingers, dangling over the void. Panting with exertion, he heaved himself up to see over the balcony. Barbel had his back to him, filling something from the kitchen tap. Sally was to one side, distraught and tearful.

The sound of running water would cover his arrival. Hand over hand, Tim hauled himself up, his muscles screaming in protest. With a final effort he grabbed at the top rail with one hand. Now both. He was almost there.

Tari turned round.

Tim straddled the top rail.

The first shot missed. The second took Tim in the lower back. For a second he balanced, poised to fall back into the darkness.

Sally screamed, dashed forward, grabbed his clothing and pulled him on to the balcony.

Tim flopped like a rag doll. He could not move. His left leg twitched uncontrollably.

Tari stirred Tim's body with his foot. He lifted his pistol. Sally was the other side of her man, all eyes and teeth and claws. Ready to spring. A wild animal prepared to fight with her life for her loved one. Tari lowered the gun. He strode back to the sink to continue filling the can. The shots would attract attention. Time was running out.

From his worm's eye view in the corner of the balcony Tim watched the events unfold.

Sally seemed to be saying something. He could not hear. He was seeing through bottle bottoms into an unreal world, conscious but helpless. All he could feel was a burning core in the middle of the numbness in his lower back. He saw his leg kicking as though it belonged to someone else. It came to him that the bullet might have damaged the spinal nerve. That scared him and he closed his eyes.

Tari carried the full watering can to the centre of the balcony, positioning the jet so it would fly out into the night where the breeze would pick up the lethal droplets and carry them away over London. Back in the kitchen, he struggled to attach one end of the hose to the tap.

Something disturbed Tim's rest. A pain. In his fingers. Pins and needles like he'd never known. God! The pain was excruciating. He could feel. He was not totally paralysed. He clenched his teeth to stop himself crying out as the nerves in his arms came alive in a series of massive electric shocks. He rolled his head to look in the room. Tari had a respirator on his head, ready to pull over his face. He was peeling back the wide brown sticky tape from around the neck of the Dewar flask.

From the flask Tari extracts a slender phial of pale red liquid. Sally is mesmerized, amazed how delicate the glass, how pastel the shade. How can something so small be so deadly? It is inconceivable that this can kill every man, woman and child in London. This rare destroyer no bigger than her slim wedding finger.

Tim began to drag his useless body into the room on his elbows. More feeling was returning all the time. Soon he would be able to hold his gun but for the moment all he could do was crawl.

Sally saw him move. She started.

Tari's eyes followed hers. He transferred the phial to his left hand and reached for his gun.

'No.' Sally screamed. 'No.'

She snatched the virus from Tari's fingers and darted to the other side of the kitchen table.

'Give it to me.' He would make her buckle to his will. Force her to do what he wanted – just as he had when they were married. Just as he had always done.

'No.' She met his eyes, ran towards the balcony. Towards Tim. Halfway across the room she stopped and looked beseechingly around. Tari understood.

'There's nothing you can do with it. Give it back.' He held out his hand.

Sally was sobbing. The phial grasped in her right fist, her left hand closed over her right, her two hands close to her chest.

Tari was right. What could she do with it?

She couldn't hide it. She couldn't throw it out of the window, stamp on it or break it. She couldn't pour it down the sink or flush it away. Whatever she did would kill others.

She tossed her head from side to side, seeking desperately about her. Tari sensed victory. He came closer to collect his prize. Hidden in her hands she picked away at the protecting tape, inched out the closely fitting cork.

He was just one pace away. With a piteous look on her crazed face, Sally lifted the phial to her lips. She drank.

'*Noooooo.*' Tari's scream of revulsion rent the air. They stared at each other, immobile and wide-eyed, breathing heavily in horror.

Tari collected himself first. The mad woman was dead, but there would still be enough of the virus on the sides of the phial.

Sally had thought of that too. As he sprang, she rammed the glass into her mouth, bit, crunched, bit again and chewed on the thin glass.

He reached to prise open her teeth.

Sally spat in his face.

Tari raised his gun. He was trembling, but from there he could not miss. He aimed at her heart.

There was a shot. Tari opened his mouth in surprise. Tim, striving to hold the pistol steady in his shaking hands, fired again. The round entered Tari's left eye.

Sally swayed, tried hard not to be sick. Under her white tee shirt, cold sweat was sluicing down her body. Blood was trickling out of her nose and from the corners of her mouth.

'Sally. Sally.' Somehow Tim found his voice. He crawled towards her.

'Please, no. No, Tim.' She held out a hand to fend him off.

She bent down, scooped up something and ran into the bedroom. She locked the door.

'Come out. Please, Sally. I want to hold you.'

'You can't hold me, Tim. Not ever. Just in your thoughts. Yes?' Sally sounded very calm.

'Always, Sally.' Tim was at a loss.

He heard her catch her breath. 'Oh, Tim. It's not safe in

there. Get out quickly, my love. Lock the door. Let no one in. Remember, I love you. I love you to death.'

'Sally . . .'

Behind the door, Sally, tears streaking her pale face, tasted the bile, the poison of millions, and lifted the muzzle of the pistol to her mouth.

The Drumbeat of Jimmy Sands

Murray Davies

Duggie Fife and Paddy O'Keefe. Two sides of the same coin. Both soldiers, both brought up on the meanest streets, one in Glasgow, one in Belfast.

They are bound together by more than friendship when O'Keefe saves Fife's life on a behind-the-lines operation in the Falklands War.

But later, serving in Northern Ireland, tragic fate will separate them on to different sides, and then it can only be a fight to the death.

A story of hunter and hunted, *The Drumbeat of Jimmy Sands* is one of the most relentlessly powerful and suspenseful novels of this or any other year.

'A seriously arresting thriller, at once convincing and compelling'   *Scotsman*

'Clever, poignant, expertly-crafted piece of story-telling, which robbed me of a night's sleep'   *Mirror*

ISBN 0 00 651155 4

Tomorrow Belongs to Us

Larry Collins

How the international drugs trade fuels the new nuclear arms race

An explosive thriller packed with authentic detail, *Tomorrow Belongs to Us* tells the story behind the headlines as it exposes the terrifying link between religious fundamentalism, the world drugs trade and Iran's nuclear programme.

Former CIA agent Jim Duffy, a Near East expert, is urgently recalled from retirement to investigate reports that the Iranians have got hold of three nuclear warheads. With heroin flooding western markets, the CIA believes that the Iranians are financing their pursuit of nuclear capability with vast sums of money from drug trafficking.

Meanwhile, in Europe, the 'Professor', a senior member of a secret Iranian terrorist organization, is shopping for high-tech equipment. His job is to obtain the hardware required for Operation Khalid, a devastating plan to blow up Tel Aviv and take back Palestine for Islam.

When Duffy brings Washington confirmation of Iran's possession of nuclear devices, the Americans must confront their worst nightmare. It can only be a matter of time before the Iranians are capable of inflicting maximum destruction. Can Duffy track down the warheads before it is too late and prevent the nightmare from becoming reality?

ISBN 0 00 649835 3

Fatal Terrain

Dale Brown

Dale Brown's spectacular new international bestseller – packed with high-action entertainment, cutting-edge technology and breathtaking scenes of aerial combat – looks forward to a near future where Taiwan's declaration of independence from mainland China brings a very real threat of major conflict to the Pacific.

As China prepares its military response, the US president attempts to avert an international crisis by calling on his own tried and trusted secret strike force. But soon it becomes horribly apparent that with China and the USA moving ever closer to a nuclear showdown, it could be a mission too far for Patrick McLanahan, Brad Elliott, Jon Masters and their high-tech EB-52 Megafortress – the 'Old Dog' itself.

'Like the thrillers of Tom Clancy, Stephen Coonts and Larry Bond, the novels of Dale Brown brim with action, sophisticated weaponry and political intrigue . . . first-rate.' *San Francisco Chronicle*

'You have to hug the seat when reading Dale Brown. The one-time US Air Force captain navigates his way at such a fearsome pace it is impossible to take your eyes off the page in case you miss something.' *Oxford Times*

'Dale Brown is a master at mixing technology and action. He puts readers right into the middle of the inferno.'

LARRY BOND

'The best military adventure writer in the country.'

CLIVE CUSSLER

ISBN 0 00 649847 7

Night Trap

Gordon Kent

This exhilarating tale of modern espionage and breathtaking flying action introduces a major new thriller-writing talent. With its striking authenticity and remarkable psychological depth, *Night Trap* is sure to appeal to the many fans of Tom Clancy, Stephen Coonts and Dale Brown.

Night Trap follows the career of Alan Craik, a young Intelligence officer in the US Navy, whose relentless investigation into the unexpected death of his own father, a legendary naval pilot, sets him on the trail of a father-and-son team of spies within his own ranks – serving members of the US Navy who have been betraying their country for years, and will risk everything not to be discovered.

'Flying, spying and dying – *Night Trap* is the real straight Navy stuff. Better strap yourself to the chair for this one. I loved it.'   STEPHEN COONTS, author of *Fortunes of War*

'Here's a thriller that really flies. Gordon Kent knows his subject at first hand and the expertise shows on the page: high stakes, pounding tension and the best dogfights put on paper. A lot of thrillers these days, you come away feeling like you've been in a simulator. In *Night Trap*, Gordon Kent straps you into the real thing. Enjoy the ride!'

IAN RANKIN, author of *Dead Souls*

'*Night Trap* roars along like an F-14 in afterburner, taking the reader on a wild ride of suspense, intrigue, and gripping action. Plug in your G-Suit and get ready for the best military thriller in years.'   PATRICK DAVIS, author of *The General*

ISBN 0 00 651009 4